PRAISE FOR *IN THE CARDS*

"Infused with . . . fresh detail. Between the sweetness of the relationship and the summery beach setting, romance fans will find this a warming winter read."

—*Publishers Weekly*

"Fans will love the frank honesty of her characters. [Beck's] scenery is richly detailed and the story engaging."

—*RT Book Reviews*

"[A] realistic and heartwarming story of redemption and love . . . Beck's understanding of interpersonal relationships and her flawless prose make for a believable romance and an entertaining read."

—*Booklist*

PRAISE FOR *WORTH THE WAIT*

"[A] poignant and heartwarming story of young love and redemption and will literally make your heart ache . . . Jamie Beck has a real talent for making the reader feel the sorrow, regret, and yearning of this young character."

—*Fresh Fiction*

PRAISE FOR *WORTH THE TROUBLE*

"Beck takes readers on a journey of self-reinvention and risky investments, in love and in life . . . With strong family ties, loyalty, playful banter, and sexual tension, Beck has crafted a beautiful second-chances story."

—Starred review, *Publishers Weekly*

PRAISE FOR *SECRETLY HERS*

"[I]n Beck's ambitious, uplifting second Sterling Canyon contemporary . . . Conflicting views and family drama lay the foundation for emotional development in this strong Colorado-set contemporary."

—*Publishers Weekly*

"Witty banter and the deepening of the characters and their relationship, along with some unexpected plot twists and a lovable supporting cast . . . will keep the reader hooked . . . A smart, fun, sexy, and very contemporary romance."

—*Kirkus Reviews*

PRAISE FOR *WORTH THE RISK*

"An emotional read that will leave you reeling at times and hopeful at others."

—*Books and Boys Book Blog*

PRAISE FOR *UNEXPECTEDLY HERS*

"Character-driven, sweet, and chock-full of interesting secondary characters."

—*Kirkus Reviews*

PRAISE FOR *BEFORE I KNEW*

"A tender romance rises from the tragedy of two families—a must read!"

—Robyn Carr, #1 *New York Times* bestselling author

"Jamie Beck's deeply felt novel hits all the right notes, celebrating the power of forgiveness, the sweetness of second chances, and the heady joy of reaching for a dream. Don't miss this one!"

—Susan Wiggs, #1 *New York Times* bestselling author

"*Before I Knew* kept me totally enthralled as two compassionate, relatable characters, each in search of forgiveness and fulfillment, turn a recipe for heartache into a story of love, hope, and some really good menus!"

—Shelley Noble, *New York Times* bestselling author of *Whisper Beach*

PRAISE FOR *ALL WE KNEW*

"[A] moving story about the flux of life and the steadfastness of family."

—*Publishers Weekly*

"[A]n impressively crafted and deftly entertaining read from first page to last."

—*Midwest Book Review*

"*All We Knew* is compelling, heartbreaking, and emotional."

—*Harlequin Junkie*

PRAISE FOR *JOYFULLY HIS*

"A quick and sweet read that is perfect for the holidays."

—*Harlequin Junkie*

PRAISE FOR *THE MEMORY OF YOU*

"[Beck] deepens a typical story about first loves reuniting by exploring the aftermath of a violent act. Readers will root for an ending that repairs this couple's past hurt."

—Booklist

"Beck's portrayals of divorce and trauma are keen . . . Readers will be caught up in their journey toward healing and romance."

—Publishers Weekly

The Promise of Us

ALSO BY JAMIE BECK

In the Cards

The St. James Novels

Worth the Wait
Worth the Trouble
Worth the Risk

The Sterling Canyon Novels

Accidentally Hers
Secretly Hers
Unexpectedly Hers
Joyfully His

The Cabot Novels

Before I Knew
All We Knew
When You Knew

The Sanctuary Sound Novels

The Memory of You

The Promise of Us

A Sanctuary Sound Novel

JAMIE BECK

Montlake
Romance

Published by Montlake Romance, Seattle

www.apub.com

Amazon, the Amazon logo, and Montlake Romance are trademarks of Amazon.com, Inc., or its affiliates.

ISBN-13: 9781503905245
ISBN-10: 1503905241

Cover design by Emily Mahon

Photography by Regina Wamba of MaelDesign.com

Printed in the United States of America

For my agent, Jill, who saw something she liked in my writing and has worked tirelessly to help me navigate the highs and lows of publishing. Thank you for everything you do to keep me on track. I know it isn't an easy job!

Chapter One

Claire would rather stand naked in the middle of Sanctuary Sound's town green to expose her scars than start this conversation with Steffi. She'd dismissed her father's warnings about going into business with a friend, certain that she and Steffi could weather any dispute. After all, they'd managed a workable solution to the Peyton problem when Claire couldn't have imagined anything more difficult. Apparently, her imagination hadn't worked hard enough. This current mess, Steffi's beloved 1940s bungalow that had exacerbated their remodeling company's financial troubles, proved that a personal bond was exactly what made partnership conflicts so sticky.

Before taking her seat, she leaned Rosie—her worn rosewood-and-ivory cane—against a chair at the dining table. Overhead she heard Steffi's boyfriend, Ryan—his heavy footfall on the bathroom tile, followed by the sound of the waterfall showerhead at full blast.

While Steffi poured them each a mug of hot chocolate, Claire inventoried the recently renovated interior for the millionth time. They'd tested six blends of "Espresso" and "Jacobean" stain before settling on the darkest one for all the floors. A gray glass-tile backsplash and white quartzite counters had been splurges. The assortment of modern lines and rustic, antique finishes might inspire a *Town & Country* feature, but that didn't make the project any less fiscally irresponsible.

"Did you highlight your hair this morning?" Steffi grabbed a can of whipped cream from the refrigerator. "Strawberry blonde's *tres chic.*"

"Thanks." Claire threaded her fingers through the front of her hair self-consciously. The impulsive decision had more to do with Peyton's impending return than with a desire to be stylish.

Peyton Prescott, the other part of the childhood triumvirate Steffi had named the Lilac Lane League. *Peyton*. For the past eighteen months, any mention of her name had nicked another piece of Claire's heart. Bad enough that she'd swept through town and bewitched Claire's then-boyfriend, Todd. Worse that Todd then ran off with Peyton on her travel-writing adventures. Betrayal by a man sucked. Betrayal by a man *and* a former bestie—although Peyton obviously hadn't been a true friend—was excruciating.

In truth, Claire could admit Peyton wasn't the only woman more venturesome than she. The lame hip and chronic pain from the bullet wound had put Claire's high-adventure days in the rearview mirror since before she learned to drive. No more tennis. No hiking. No heels. Even dancing could be iffy, especially on dank nights. Her cane had become her most reliable companion, which was why she'd given it a name. And travel? Claire had put the worst of her PTSD behind her, but hypervigilance remained a family credo. No city or vacation destination was worth the risk of another life-altering event.

So be it. She was alive, which beat the alternative despite her limitations. But moving on didn't mean rolling over, so Claire had declared good riddance to both Peyton and Todd, thankful she wouldn't have to face them again.

She'd never dreamed Peyton would come home to live, even if only temporarily. Claire wasn't dating anyone now, which meant the only thing left for Peyton to steal was her pride. Given Claire's state of mind, it could happen. At the very least, Peyton's return would stir up dust and make Claire the subject of more gossip. Unlike when she used to compete in the USTA New England's district tournaments, Claire now hated being the center of attention almost as much as she hated brussels sprouts.

Peyton's return would also bring her brother, Logan—the star of Claire's teenage fantasies (and only real rival to her girlhood crush on then up-and-coming junior tennis champ Andy Roddick)—to town. He'd been different from other teen boys—more clever and creative. The last time she'd seen him, this past fall, she'd stammered and scampered away. That recollection made her hot—in a bad way.

She'd sworn to herself that the next time she saw either Prescott, she'd be prepared.

Determined to be on equal footing with her golden-haired rival, Claire had lightened her hair. Silly? Sure. But in the heat of the moment, it had made perfect sense. Then she'd remembered Peyton's ongoing battle with breast cancer—and her probable lack of *any* hair—and prayed for forgiveness for such petty thoughts.

Claire smoothed one hand across the waxed surface of Steffi's farmhouse table, her fingers tracing the ridge between two planks of wood. This bargain find—a benefit of having lived her entire adult life within a ten-mile radius of home and knowing every local craftsman— had been a coup. Claire smiled to herself, picturing Steffi, Ryan, and his daughter, Emmy, carving the holiday roast and blowing out birthday candles at this table.

Steffi carried a round metal tray with the oversize mugs and whipped cream into the dining room and set it on the table, then handed a mug to Claire. "Here you go."

"Thanks." She inhaled a whiff of milk chocolate, then gently blew into the cup to cool the beverage. "Looks like you're almost finished unpacking."

"Can't believe how long it's taking, but I won't complain." Steffi sat, slung her dark hair into a low ponytail, and rolled back the sleeves of one of Ryan's faded "BC Law" sweatshirts. "Sometimes I wake up and need to pinch myself. I never dreamed I could be in love again and living out my teenage dreams."

Claire reached across the table and squeezed Steffi's hand. "I couldn't be happier for you."

She couldn't. Mostly.

Steffi and Ryan had worked through a lot of mistakes and Steffi's violent assault to get to this place. They'd earned their happiness, which was why Claire had agreed to take on this project and let them buy the house at practically no profit. Maybe her dad hadn't been wrong about the complications of mixing friendship with business, but she could hardly regret *this* choice.

"Thanks." Steffi's gaze strayed from Claire's open laptop to Rosie and back to Claire's face. She patted Claire's hand. "I want you to be happy, too. Ryan has a cute colleague . . ."

"I *am* happy." Claire withdrew her hand. Totally true, although that didn't mean a little pang didn't squeeze her heart now and then from the way her own love life had fizzled. Fizzled? No. Exploded—imploded?— or, more accurately, absconded.

But she'd moved on—really, she had. She no longer pictured Todd with horns and green eyes. She stifled a smile at the thought of that favorite pastime. She'd done it so often that she'd sort of forgotten what he actually looked like.

Now, most nights she collapsed into bed, eager to read a good book after a long, productive day. Only the occasional unexpected moment unlocked that bleak, frosty spot in her chest that ached as much as her hip, like when she watched diaper commercials or decorated a nursery or watched *The Notebook*.

Steffi offered a smile, then cracked her knuckles.

Enough about Peyton and Todd and my nonexistent love life.

"I'll be happi*er* once we sort out our financial problems." Claire snatched the whipped cream and shook it hard before layering three full rotations of foamy, chilled sweetness atop her cocoa. Simple pleasures nourished the soul, and enough of them strung together made up for the inevitable disappointments and devastations everyone faced. "All the time spent on this project kept us from finding new ones. At the moment, my small decorating jobs can't keep us both employed and pay our bills."

"Bigger reno work will start up soon. People generally try to avoid construction projects during the winter." Steffi cast a glance through the French doors to the snowy backyard, where young Emmy was building an igloo.

Claire rarely recalled the time before her injury, when she'd been carefree, dragging her toboggan up Nob Hill, battling in neighborhood snowball fights, and snuggling up in the window seat near the hearth of her parents' home to watch giant flakes swirl to the ground. Now the pleasant memories spread bittersweet warmth through her chest.

Steffi sighed. "I know the business took one on the chin so Ryan and I could afford this house. I swear, I'll make it up to you."

"I did it with love, so you don't need to 'make it up' to me. But we veered from our original business plan in order to do this project, and to take on a small crew. We need to be more strategic. Let's go back to our plan to rent retail space to help drive business." Her former job at Ethan Allen had taught her the value of having a space where potential customers could easily walk in, ask questions, and see samples. She'd already planned out their retail space on paper—gigantic plateglass window, white-and-cottage-blue interior, round worktables, and assorted fanciful light fixtures—and couldn't wait to see it come to fruition. "To do that, we need more money ASAP. I'm not complaining, but we need new leads and more traction with our website and social media presence." Claire closed her eyes and massaged her temples. Neither of these things eased her stress the way a good junk-food binge could, but Steffi hadn't put cookies out, so this was her best option.

When she heard Steffi add more whipped cream to her mug, she opened her eyes and peered across the table. Steffi had fallen silent while sipping her cocoa, but her constipated expression snagged Claire's attention.

"What are you thinking?" Claire dropped her hands to the table.

Steffi shook her head, waving one hand. "Nothing."

"Don't lie. Is there another problem I'm not aware of?"

"No." Steffi inhaled, held her breath, then exhaled slowly. "I know of one project that would make a sweet profit and let you really stretch your talent. 'Sky's the limit' kind of budget."

Excitement lifted Claire's spirit, straightening her spine. Anything that accelerated plans to open a retail outlet merited her attention. "Sounds amazing. What's the catch?"

Steffi hesitated.

"Never mind. You won't take it, so let's move on." Steffi spooned whipped cream into her mouth. "Oh! Molly says that Mrs. Brewster is thinking of remodeling her master bath."

Mrs. Brewster's late husband had left her comfortably well off, but you'd never know it. She clipped every coupon available to humanity—Claire had been behind her at the grocery store more than once. She put only two dollars in the collection basket at church each week, despite having enough money to leave more. And she gave out bite-size candy at Halloween. Bite-size!

"We can't rely on Ryan's mom as our major source of leads, and Mrs. Brewster spending big bucks on a remodel sounds improbable. Betcha she pretended to be interested so she could get the inside scoop about our business from Molly." Claire leaned forward, elbows on the table. "Don't make me beg. If you have a solution, I won't dismiss it out of hand, I promise. I'm not an idiot. We need income. I'll do whatever it takes to keep the doors open."

Steffi went still, her chin just above the mug held midair. "Whatever it takes?"

Claire's hair stood on end, but she motioned "Let's have it" with both hands.

Steffi hesitated. "How would you like to redecorate a high-end condo in Chelsea?"

"In the city?" Her entire body prickled painfully at the thought of putting herself in the midst of that chaos and danger. She'd already been one madman's random victim. Manhattan teemed with crazy people, not the least of whom were the ones who drove their cars like heat-seeking missiles. "Who'd hire *us* instead of any of the premier designers there?"

Steffi met Claire's gaze. "Logan."

Claire's tongue seemed to swell and turn sticky. *Work with Logan . . .* Her blood thickened like warm syrup. Tingles and terror all at once—a sensation she both loved and loathed. Her own brand of crazy. Maybe she *did* belong in New York, after all. "No."

"You just said you'd do whatever it takes."

"Not that. *Never* that." Claire didn't need to look into a mirror to know that her fair, lightly freckled cheeks now looked like someone had smeared them with ripe strawberries.

"As I suspected." Steffi shrugged nonchalantly, as if she hadn't just pulled the pin from a grenade and dropped it on the table. "So that leaves us a little tight until something else comes up. In terms of our social media presence, I just read an article . . ."

Claire heard Steffi talking, but the words ran together like white noise because Claire's brain was still stuck on the idea of working with—no—*for* Logan Prescott. His obvious ploy made her want to laugh. Did he really think he could buy her forgiveness for his sister? Well, Claire would never, ever forgive Peyton. Not even if he paid her a million dollars to renovate his condo.

The very condo Peyton had moved into while undergoing chemo because Todd had dumped her when she got sick. Given how Todd had treated Claire, his leaving Peyton shouldn't have shocked her. Either way, it served Peyton right for breaking a cardinal rule of friendship.

Eyes closed, Claire pressed her palm to her hot cheek, silently asking for forgiveness for yet another bitter thought.

"Claire? Did you hear anything I said?" Steffi turned her hands out in question.

"Sorry." She rubbed the scowl from her forehead. "I'll find another way to turn up new leads. Working with Logan is a hard no."

"Too bad. You'd have so much fun decorating his place. I'm sure he'd let you do whatever you wanted. Anything would be better than how it looks now. Guess he never cared before, since he was rarely around to enjoy it."

Only a Prescott would own a million-dollar property that sat vacant as often as it was occupied.

Their family's legacy stemmed from their great-grandfather's famed body of literature. The Prescott mystique—and coastal home here in town—was like something out of *The Great Gatsby*. Logan, like his sister, had chosen a career that let him jet-set around the world. Former fashion photographer turned documentary photographer. Cool jobs. Suited to his enchanting mix of charmer, adventurer, activist, and artist. Not that she paid *too* much attention to his comings and goings.

"I'm not an idiot."

"Did I call you one?" Steffi had the gall to look stunned.

"This has Peyton's paw prints all over it. I'd bet my last penny that she put him up to it. I don't know what I hate more—that she did it, that you took the bait, or that she knows we're desperate for money."

"It's not a conspiracy. I mentioned that I felt bad about putting you in this situation because of this home. Logan tossed out the idea on the spot."

"I can't deal with the strings that would come with his offer." Except now Claire couldn't focus on anything else because thinking about Logan took up all the space in her head. If Peyton hadn't stolen Todd, Claire might've pounced on a chance to work closely with Logan. Of course, then she wouldn't have been free to act on her desire. Not that she had ever acted on it before Todd, either. The hawkish way Logan could stare at her turned her to jelly around him and—oh, just no. "I thought you finally understood that."

"I do. That's why I wasn't going to say anything." Steffi crossed her arms. "You forced me to tell you."

True enough. Logan's image flickered through Claire's mind again, poking at the tender spot of her pointless longing, like always.

She'd memorized his face so long ago, during the countless hours she'd hung out at his house with Peyton and Steffi. Sandy-blond hair, worn in lengths ranging from shaggy to shoulder-length, which had the added bonus of annoying his father. Piercing green eyes that glowed like phosphorous in the dark. A patrician profile that befitted his family's prominence. All that and a surprisingly generous smile. *Logan Alder Prescott.* Even the sound of his name belonged on a lighted marquee.

From their very first meeting, when she'd barely been thirteen years old, she'd concocted adolescent fantasies about him professing his secret love for her. He *had* fulfilled her wish for him to be her first kiss. He hadn't known that wish part—at least she hoped he hadn't. She'd been fifteen, but he'd kissed her only because he felt sorry for her after her surgeries. Just thinking of his gentle lips made her pelvic area throb as if the bullet were striking anew.

She shook her head, dislodging all thoughts of Logan. "I'll catch up with Mrs. Brewster and pitch a proposal for her bathroom. But we also have to scrape together funds to advertise and update the website, and you need to scare up reno work pronto. Promise me we'll earmark new revenue toward retail space—"

A knock at the door interrupted her monologue.

Ryan called downstairs, "Steffi, can you get that? I'm not finished dressing."

"Sure." Steffi held up her index finger, silently begging for Claire's patience, before she rose from the table and disappeared around the corner.

Claire added another dollop of whipped cream to her last bit of cocoa plus a spray to the tip of her finger, grateful for her superhuman metabolism. From the other room, she heard Steffi's surprised voice say, "Oh, we didn't expect you so early."

"Hope that's not a problem," replied Logan, in his unmistakable baritone.

Claire choked, spewing bits of whipped cream and cocoa across the table. She grabbed at paper napkins to start cleaning up, which was impossible while her vision blurred.

Logan noticed Steffi's jaw twitch. She remained still in the doorway except for a quick glance over her shoulder. He couldn't stop a stupid grin from forming when he realized he might've just cock blocked his buddy Ryan. "Am I *interrupting?*"

She batted his shoulder while rolling her eyes, although he noted tension tightening her smile. "No . . . Ryan's upstairs dressing."

Uh-huh. As he'd suspected. He guessed those two had a lot of catching up to do. They'd been gaga for each other back in high school, but he never would've believed Ryan could forgive her for ghosting him in college. If Ryan could forgive Steffi, then Logan could hope that, one day, Claire might forgive Peyton.

In his ragtag circles, loyalty was a rather flexible concept . . . as was friendship. What his sister had done to Claire, however, had shocked him, given the history of the Lilac Lane League. But he loved his sister, and she regretted her actions, missed her friend, and wanted to atone. Seeing her suffer so much these past months—contemplating her mortality and begging to make amends in case she died—made him desperate to help her earn Claire's forgiveness.

"Can I come in, or should I freeze my ass off out here on your porch?" he joked, shoving his hands in his coat pockets.

"Sorry!" Steffi smiled and backed up. "Come in. I, uh, I—"

A noise from the left caught his attention, but the living room was empty. And inviting.

Logan whistled, his eye noting the shadowy crisscross pattern cast by the French door mullions. The hot spot of honey-colored light glinting off the oval mirror on the corner elevation. The contrast of coarse and soft textures of the fabrics. "Picture-perfect, Steffi."

A massive river rock fireplace anchored the room, but its refinished beams drew his eyes up. The L-shaped navy sofa absorbed most of the floor space. Coral-colored mix-and-match pillows filled the sofa's corners—but his attention fixed on the needlepoint one displaying Ryan's, Steffi's, and Emmy's names written in the shape of a heart.

"I assume Claire designed all this?" The room practically glowed with warmth and love—two things noticeably absent from his condo. Not that he needed those. Life lived in the moment couldn't thrive inside the picket-fence trappings of the suburbs. Spending a single afternoon with his parents proved that fact of life.

"She did." Steffi's expression changed as she cleared her throat. "She's great with personal touches, like that handmade pillow."

"Not a surprise." He recalled that Claire had always been thoughtful and attentive to details, like with the gift she'd given him for his sixteenth birthday—Lee Child's *Persuader*. She'd wrapped the book in a desk blotter–size monthly calendar page, circled his birthdate in red marker, and tied the package in a red ribbon, leaving it for him on his bed. Her short note had revealed that she'd spied him reading Jack Reacher novels at the library, presumably because his parents sneered at anything other than literary fiction.

It'd been disquieting to be so unaware of being watched, yet somehow sweet at the same time. Most of the women he'd known in his life never knew him—or even attempted to know him. They'd been more interested in his face, his money, and his name. Claire had always been different from most women.

He strode into the cozy space—a sort of foreign concept to him, given the formal places he'd called home. He fingered the chenille sofa, then went to the fireplace to inspect the framed photographs on display, which were sure to be the sort of uninspired candid snapshots taken with smartphones. It perturbed him when people didn't bother to capture interesting images. He didn't get a chance to let his critical eye go to work because motion to his right drew his attention . . . to Claire.

He gripped the mantel.

She'd always been cute with that shy smile, but something had changed. Gold highlights. A longer, angled bob that brushed her shoulders. Its lighter color didn't suit her skin tone as well as her natural shade, although it didn't look bad. Her eyes remained the same, thank God.

Most would call her irises blue. He would not. Setting aside the enlarged jet-black pupils, Claire's irises were an ever-changing medley of arctic blue, turquoise, and cobalt—with occasional streaks of white to make them glitter—rimmed in navy. A quick assessment proved them as round and kind as ever, but not as trusting.

She remained stiffly seated beside Rosie, the souvenir of a psychopath. That old cane had been a talisman of strength and survival after an unfortunate mass shooting at the Yankee Crossing Outlets killed her promising tennis career. Better the death of that dream than a literal one, though.

Having one of its own become a victim of random violence had shaken their small town, which had then rallied around the McKennas. Although Claire had been fifteen at the time, he'd never once caught her feeling sorry for herself despite being forced to walk away from a top tennis ranking in her division. Never seen her break down or give up while relearning to walk. In her quiet way, she'd shown more mettle than he'd ever been required to muster.

Her bravery had moved him in ways his sixteen-year-old self hadn't fully understood. To this day, that uneasy awe remained with him, affecting the rhythm of his heart.

"Claire." He nodded, oddly tongue-tied. He'd hoped to run into her soon, but on his terms, not hers. Not unprepared. He had a plan, after all. One that required careful plotting. He wouldn't let Peyton down. And if spending time getting reacquainted with Claire was part of the process, well, that would be no hardship.

"Logan." Claire's voice squeaked. It did that often when she spoke to him. Sometimes she'd sputter, too. Endearing, frankly. He'd secretly liked her little crush on him. It'd been so authentic—another thing he was unaccustomed to with most.

"Didn't mean to interrupt." He gestured around the space. "But since you're here, let me extend my compliments. You did a beautiful job. I can only imagine what it looked like when old Mrs. Weber lived here."

"Thank you." She fidgeted with her hair, which was a couple of inches longer than his. "Steffi and I have similar taste, so it was easy."

"It's comfortable, unlike my museum in the city." He purposely avoided meeting the stony gaze he felt coming from Steffi. "Maybe you could transform my place to better reflect me?"

"But a museum is perfect for you," came Claire's brittle reply. "You can display all your photographs to impress all your girlfriends."

He flinched. When he'd last seen her a few months ago, she'd been harried in her attempt to dodge him. Of all the reasons he'd imagined for her running from him that afternoon, he'd never considered that her feelings toward *him* had changed because of Peyton.

The loss of her affection deflated him.

Surely she couldn't disapprove of him supporting his sister. Then again, maybe Peyton had nothing to do with Claire's change of heart. Throughout the years, he'd enjoyed a different date on his arm for each social event that his family expected him to attend. After Claire's experience with Todd, she'd probably lost all patience for that kind of thing.

Nonetheless, her prickliness provoked him. "I'm getting older. Who knows, maybe one of these days I'll follow in Ryan's footsteps and start a family of my own?"

She snorted a laugh, then covered her nose and mouth with one hand, mumbling, "Sorry."

"Apology accepted." He smiled because she'd unwittingly given him an opening regarding his sister. With a happy sigh, he said, "Gee, that felt good."

"What did?" Her brows gathered.

"Letting you off the hook." He tucked his hair behind his ears and nodded at Steffi before returning his gaze to Claire. "Forgiveness is such a win-win, don't you think?"

Claire's expression turned as icy as the sidewalks outside. She pushed herself out of her chair, shoved her laptop into its case, and grabbed Rosie. "Steffi, we'll finish our discussion later. In the meantime, I'll find a way to tempt Mrs. Brewster."

Claire limped across the room to the coatrack by the front door, each uneven step leaving an imprint on his gut as if she'd trampled right over him. Needling Claire had been a shitty move—a knee-jerk reaction to her cold shoulder, and in poor form. "Hang on. Let me help you to your car."

"I can manage." She rose onto her toes to reach her jacket at the top of the coatrack.

He dashed across the room and reached for her bag. "I insist."

She yanked her arm away, but he'd clutched her elbow too tightly for her to escape. "Claire, it's slick out there."

"And yet I got inside on my own." Her gaze flitted around the entry like a butterfly looking for a safe place to land.

He tipped up her chin, hungry for her eye contact, which somehow simultaneously calmed and excited him. "But you weren't upset when you first arrived."

She stared back at him. A flicker of something—sorrow, regret, surrender—rippled through those azure pools.

Ryan came trotting down the stairs, oblivious to the tension in his entry. "Where are you going?"

Logan slapped Ryan's shoulder, sparing his old friend a brief smile. "Just helping Claire to her car. I'll be right back."

"Maybe we should salt again," Steffi said to Ryan, although her gaze remained fixed on Claire.

"I'll take care of it." Ryan grabbed his coat from the rack and dashed ahead of them, kissing Claire on the cheek on his way out the door. "See you later, Claire."

Logan followed Claire onto the porch. Ryan's footprints wound around the house toward the detached garage. His disappearance left Logan alone with Claire for a few minutes. All around them, snow blanketed every shrub, lawn, and branch like a thick coat of icing. He kept hold of her elbow, allowing her to set the pace, somewhat distracted by the play of light and glitter on the snow. If he'd had his camera with him, he'd have caught some intriguing images.

Once they crossed the porch and descended its two steps, she turned. "Logan, I'm fine. Please, let me go."

He stopped and held her in place on the walkway, softening his voice. "I didn't plan on bumping into you today, you know."

Claire glanced at an orange VW Beetle at the curb before raising one brow. "You didn't see my car?"

"I didn't know that was yours." He covered a smile because he could picture her tooling around town in the miniature car. Bright and preppy like her, in her turtleneck, corduroys, and fuchsia crewneck. "I figured it belonged to someone on the street."

Her cheeks flushed bright scarlet. He'd always liked that trait because it made her easy to read. Today was different. She didn't smile or fidget with her hair. She didn't stutter. She held her arms stiffly at her sides.

"Claire, what's with the hostility? Come back inside and let's catch up. Steffi's told me about your business, but I'd love to hear how you're liking it."

She narrowed her eyes. "Don't play dumb. I know you're exploiting our financial situation as a way to buy my forgiveness for your sister. Well, listen up. I'd rather lose my business than forgive Peyton."

Logan crossed his arms, the chill in his body having nothing to do with the single-digit temperature. "You've changed."

She huffed. "I've wised up. I'm no longer too shy to speak my mind or willing to take a back seat simply to make everyone else happy even when it makes me miserable."

Her words settled between them like a barbwire fence. He said nothing, hoping she'd take them back. When her gaze didn't waver, he said, "I always thought you were naturally generous and kind, which was so appealing. Pity to learn it was all an act."

Her nostrils flared, and those bright eyes darkened with a mix of pain and something else he couldn't identify. "Just like your sister's friendship, I guess."

He hated that Claire's tongue was now as sharp as a scalpel, although maybe he shouldn't judge her for it when Peyton's behavior might well have been the whetstone.

She turned from him and took two quick steps. The next few things happened in slow motion: Rosie skidding on a patch of ice and Claire's feet going out from under her. She landed with a dull thud, faceup, in a snowdrift.

"Claire!" Logan lurched forward to help her up. "Are you hurt?"

She waved him off, but not before he saw tears shining in her eyes. "Just leave me alone, Logan. Please. Go inside."

He hesitated, jaw clenched, arms lowering as fists formed at his sides. Every ounce of breeding he'd ever had pushed him to assist her, but her flinty attitude held him at bay. "Fine."

He turned his back on her and strode to the porch just as Ryan came around the side of the house, carrying an open bag of salt. Ryan took in the scene, scowled at him, and then dropped the salt bag and jogged toward Claire.

Logan watched Claire take Ryan's hand as he helped her stand. She never once glanced over her shoulder at Logan, but she must've known he was waiting on the porch while watching them. Ryan loaded Claire's bag into her back seat, then closed her door and waved her off.

She pulled from the curb and crept down the residential lane, where kids were building snowmen.

"What the hell, Logan?" Ryan scoffed as he retrieved the discarded salt bag.

"She ordered me to leave her alone." His lungs now had frostbite from Claire's chilly new attitude.

Ryan scooped some salt and tossed it across the walkway. "What did you say to upset her?"

"Nothing. I complimented her work. She threw the first barb, and the second. Even then, I tried to help her to her car, but she broke free." He crossed his arms, newly affronted. "If anyone has the right to feel pissed off, it's me."

"Get your head out of your ass." Ryan hoisted the bag onto his hip. "You know you're the second-to-last person on the planet she wants to see. She didn't expect to face you this morning. Give her a break. She and Steffi are under a lot of pressure now, and you're a life-size reminder of something else that's painful."

Logan resented being persona non grata because of what his sister had done. "Well, she'd better get used to seeing Peyton and me around town. Despite what my sister did, she has as much claim on this town as anyone, maybe more."

Their great-grandfather, William Herbert Prescott, or Duck as Logan had named him because of the way he'd often spoken to kids in a Donald Duck voice, practically founded the town. A Prescott had lived on Lilac Lane for ninety years. Logan should know. In less than two months, he'd be required to attend an annual fund-raiser to celebrate that fact and raise money for the local library's literacy program.

Ryan narrowed his eyes. "Don't pull the Prescott card, buddy. It doesn't suit you."

In some ways, it didn't. He'd rather be admired for his own talent than the long shadow of his family name. While he'd had moderate success, he'd yet to produce a truly noteworthy project. This morning, however, Claire's dismissal had thrown him out of sorts, although he couldn't honestly say why it hurt him so much.

It wasn't like he saw her often. She'd simply been part of his life here, like the rambling mansion his mother and father still called home, and Donna, the aging waitress at the diner who knew to bring him black coffee and coconut cream pie when he sat down, and the sense of peace he knew when kayaking on the Sound during the golden hours. "Sorry. Maybe I should go. Steffi's likely to chew my head off, too."

Ryan rolled his eyes. "Shut up and get inside. Her bark is worse than her bite. Besides, she planned a whole lunch thing."

"She cooked?" Steffi Lockwood was not someone anyone would deem domestic.

"Takeout." Ryan smiled and raised his index finger to his lips, forcing a chuckle from Logan. "Lasagna from Lucia's."

"Thank God coming home can still yield a few good surprises." Logan smiled and headed for the door, noticing for the second time its canary-yellow appeal. A nice contrast to the Wedgwood-blue clapboard trimmed in cloud white.

It'd been a long time since he'd spent more than a few hours in Sanctuary Sound. When his sister first announced her wish to come home for her double mastectomy after the final round of chemo, he'd been skeptical. Her relationship with their parents was only slightly better than his own, and Peyton had burned some serious bridges last year. The sleepy town also wouldn't offer much entertainment.

But a growing part of him had looked forward to catching up with old friends. He'd assumed that list included Claire, but apparently his last name had cost him that privilege. That left him with two choices: pursue his original plan or let her go.

The past six months had been a grueling challenge with Peyton, so how hard could one more battle be?

Chapter Two

Claire frowned, muttering to herself throughout the drive to her mother's house. She jabbed the seat-heater button, but the lukewarm cushion scarcely melted her frozen behind. The humiliation of landing on her butt in front of Logan had stung a whole lot less than the crestfallen look in his eyes when he'd said, *"Pity to learn it was all an act."*

She hated disappointing anyone, including him. The fact that she'd done so with false bravado, well . . . karma had swooped right in to make her pay.

Dicey roads and slippery thoughts made the drive treacherous enough without the added distraction of her phone pinging text messages. Steffi? Logan? A potential client? She couldn't check while steering, but each ding sparked along a new nerve ending until she shook with frustration.

As soon as she parked in her parents' driveway, she scrolled through Steffi's messages.

10:42 a.m.: Sorry! Logan showed up an hour early.

10:43 a.m.: Are you okay? Text me so I know you're all right. I promise finding new work will be my number one priority this week.

10:46 a.m.: What happened outside with Logan? He's kinda sullen, and you and I both know that rarely happens.

10:50 a.m.: Logan asked if he should call you to apologize. Since I know you don't want to deal with him, I said I'd pass along the message and you'd call if you wanted to talk to him. Here's his number, in case you don't have it: 203-555-9753.

Claire's derisive snicker echoed off the windows of her car. As if she didn't know Logan's number. She didn't even need to check her contacts. She'd memorized those digits when he'd been showing her his first iPhone back in 2008.

Sighing, she typed back:

It's fine. I'm at my mom's. Tell Logan

She hesitated and then deleted those last two words. Tell him what? She had nothing more to say. As much as she wished things hadn't ended on a horrid note, she couldn't pretend that they could pick up as friends now. Not when he'd take Peyton's side of everything.

She hit "Send" before hauling herself out of the car, which smelled like damp laundry that had been sitting in a warm dryer too long. She peeled the seat of her wet pants away from her bottom. *Nice.*

"Hello!" Claire called out as she entered her folks' house. She leaned on Rosie while shucking out of her snow boots.

"Claire?" Her mom appeared from the vicinity of the kitchen, wearing a warm smile and a pink flannel robe. Saturdays at the McKenna home usually involved lazy mornings of crossword puzzles, breakfast strata, and gossip. "I didn't know you were stopping by."

Within three seconds, Claire found herself in the middle of her mom's reassuring bear hug. Ruth McKenna was a champion hugger. When Claire was young, the overt affection had been a bit suffocating and uncool, especially in front of her friends. With time, she'd come to appreciate the comfort.

Her parents had suffered two miscarriages before they had Claire, and one after, which explained why they'd always treated her like she was made of spun glass. Things got worse after the shooting. Those surgeries. The recovery. Back then, Claire could hardly blink without her mom taking her temperature and calling the doctor. If her folks could've locked her in the house forever, they might have. She might've let them, too.

That was back in the days of frequent nightmares and panic attacks, when any unexpected sound or semblance of a crowd had made Claire nauseated, sweaty, and weak.

Bit by bit, she'd assimilated back into the familiar setting of her hometown, uninterested in venturing out into the nasty world where the news rarely made anyone smile. After all, life-changing danger had visited her just thirty miles up the highway. At least her previous years spent in tennis training and competition had given her a taste of big cities like Boston and the rural beauty of Vermont. Now, her simple, safe life seemed like the smartest choice, and not only because it helped keep the nightmares and panic attacks at bay.

"I just left Steffi's house." She yanked her scarf off and tossed it over the back of a wingback chair, then shrugged out of her coat and threw it over the scarf. "Can I borrow some PJ bottoms and toss my pants in the dryer while I'm here?"

Her mother's brows drew together in that familiar pattern of concern. She had one of those pretty heart-shaped faces. Short, curly auburn hair fringed her forehead, framing bright-blue eyes so disproportionately large she looked like a Bratz doll. "What happened to you?"

Claire placed both hands on Rosie's ivory handle. "An unfortunate run-in with a gnarly patch of ice."

Her mom clapped her hands to her cheeks. "Are you hurt? How's your hip?"

"A snowdrift cushioned the fall. I'd be completely fine if it hadn't happened in front of Logan." She started toward the kitchen. "As you might guess, I need chocolate. And maybe some Cheetos."

To date, her unfortunate stress-eating habit hadn't been a problem because most days she remained fairly calm, and so far, her body still melted calories like butter in a frying pan. Peyton's impending arrival, however, might take Claire from a size two to a four.

"Let me go find you some bottoms," her mom said as she went toward the stairs.

Claire rounded the corner to the kitchen, intending to beeline for the junk-food drawer, and nearly smacked into her dad as he stirred sugar into what she presumed, at this hour, was his third cup of coffee.

"Claire Bear!" He kissed her cheek. "What a nice surprise. Are you having lunch with us?"

She opened the cabinet below the silverware drawer and rummaged around. Oreos, Twizzlers, kettle corn . . . aha! She grabbed two bright-orange bags and tossed them on the counter. "If Reese's and Cheetos count as lunch, then sure."

"Uh-oh." He chortled, taking a seat at the table, where his glasses rested on the open newspaper alongside a pencil. He pushed his glasses back into place and smiled. He wasn't a handsome man—sort of average looking, with thinning brown hair, smaller brown eyes, and a dimpled chin—but his face radiated the kind of sincerity that instantly put you at ease and made you spill all your secrets. "What happened today, sweetie?"

How lucky to have two parents who not only loved her to pieces but knew her so well. Some adult children might complain about the daily reporting and general nosiness, but Claire didn't. Her parents' involvement gave her the deep sense of belonging that kept her grounded. "Logan."

"I thought you liked Logan?" He scratched his head.

"I did." She *really* did, which was part of the problem. She unwrapped three mini Reese's and popped them into her mouth in quick succession. *Milk.* She needed ice-cold milk. "But now he's Peyton's emissary."

"Oh." He nodded, frowning with a slight nod. "Well, he's in a tough spot."

"Really, Dad?" she asked, her mouth still pasty from the peanut butter. She poured herself a tumbler of milk and guzzled a bit before speaking. "My relationship with his sister is none of his business. He should just butt out."

"Who should butt out of what?" her mom asked, dangling pink-and-gray polka-dot drawstring pajama pants in one hand while gesturing with the other. "Give me your wet pants."

"Logan," Claire muttered, popping another Reese's. "And my relationship with Peyton."

"Oooh." Her mom grimaced in agreement.

Her dad covered his eyes while Claire wiggled out of her damp corduroys. Her fingers brushed the scars from the bullet wound and her surgeries, which were partly visible despite her undies.

The shot from the high-velocity rifle had punctured the front of her left hip and blown out the back, shattering her acetabulum, the fragments of which caused additional trauma requiring multiple surgeries, leaving her with lifelong damage and sciatic nerve pain. Few people had ever seen the scars, though. She'd had little dating experience prior to Todd—a side effect of having lived at home with her parents for too long. She'd rushed headfirst into that relationship, although it had taken her a while to let him see her naked. The first and only man she'd trusted enough. What a waste . . . and a lesson.

She handed her pants to her mom and slipped on the pj's. "You can look now, Dad."

"Pass me some of those." He gestured to the Reese's with one hand.

Claire took her milk and the bag of candy to the kitchen table and sat down.

Her mom returned from the laundry room within a minute. She must've decided that anything would be a better topic of conversation than Logan, as she suggested, "If you're not too busy today, we should get a manicure. That always makes me feel better."

Her mom wasn't wrong, and a manicure sounded like a little bit of heaven. A bit Claire couldn't afford at the moment. "Thanks, but I need to conserve every penny so we can afford decent retail space."

"Why pay rent when you can work from your home office?" Her mom poured herself another small cup of coffee.

"Right now we're only reaching customers by word of mouth and our website. If I had a storefront, people would drop in, and I could sell services. It'd give us more legitimacy, I think. If I could find something supercheap, I might even dip into my rainy-day fund to make it happen."

"That's not wise, honey." Her dad scratched his chin.

"Tom, why can't we give the girls a little business loan?" Her mom rubbed his shoulders and kissed the balding spot on his head. Claire had watched her mom maneuver him with this soft touch a thousand times.

"I wasn't a fan of her going into business with a friend because of the risks. Now you want us to get involved, too?" He patted his wife's hand before looking at Claire. "But if you get into a real bind, come talk to me, and we'll see how we can help."

"Thanks, Dad, but I'll solve my own problems." She hated that the first thing most people thought of when they saw her and Rosie coming was how to make things easier for her. "Needy" and "incapable" weren't words she associated with herself.

She'd been a fierce competitor before the accident. Disciplined. Strong. Ambitious. Those traits didn't disappear just because she'd healed funny, post-traumatic arthritis sliced through her hip like a hot knife, and nerve damage sent a jolt of lightning through her back and leg every now and then.

She'd survived the bullet, blood loss, and surgeries. She'd learned to walk again, graduated high school on schedule despite missing many classes during rehab, and gone on to have a satisfying career. The only battles she'd lost were some mental ones—missing what had been, and fearing what else could happen. But she'd hidden those blues from most everyone, so why did people still treat her as less than?

Her dad smiled. "Just because you can take care of yourself doesn't mean you can't lean on others sometimes, too."

"True. And on that note, Mom, have you spoken with Mrs. Brewster lately?"

"No, honey. Why?" Her mom slid onto an empty chair and sipped from her coffee cup.

"Rumor has it that she might be looking to remodel her master bathroom. I haven't seen her in a few weeks, so I wondered if you'd heard anything."

Her mom shook her head. "Sorry."

"No worries." Claire's book group—an odd assortment of local women spanning a few decades—met in a week. They might know something. "She still works at Earth Garden, doesn't she?"

"I think so."

"Maybe it's time to spruce up my porch with a new plant." Claire downed her sixth Reese's with a long swallow of milk before rising and setting the glass in the dishwasher. She always felt better after chocolate, and now she had a goal. Goals were good. Goals kept her moving forward so her mind didn't dwell on things that couldn't be changed. "See you later!"

"Um, honey," her dad said. "You might want to change your pants first."

Oh yeah.

"I'll go dress in the laundry room." Claire meandered around the bend to the back hall. Few things felt better than sliding into a pair of warm pants. It would've been pure bliss if not for the unpleasant memories of why they'd gotten wet in the first place.

Hopefully she wouldn't run into Logan—or Peyton—anytime soon.

—⁓—

Gravel ground beneath the tires of Logan's Wrangler as he drove along the winding driveway that led to Arcadia House, Duck's rambling summer retreat. Originally occupying a fifty-acre pie-shaped lot along Connecticut's shoreline, it'd been that man's place of peace, where he'd continued writing best sellers after the success of his most famous work, *A Shadow on Sand.* Sixteen million copies later, that book's royalties still helped pad the Prescott coffers, despite Logan's grandfather's profligate lifestyle nearly stripping them bare at one point. Logan's dad had saved the estate in the midnineties by subdividing forty-five acres for a residential development.

That deal had resulted in the dedication of Lilac Lane as a public road, which, along with the creation of a few other streets, turned the former estate into a neighborhood.

Logan didn't mind the new neighbors. In fact, thanks to his father's transaction, families like the Lockwoods and McKennas had given Peyton and him nearby friends. Yet a part of Logan mourned for the earliest days of his childhood, when the entire acreage—wooded areas, grassy fields, and one thousand feet of private beach—had led to hours of discovery. He'd caught turtles and snails, climbed trees for hours, and made art from broken shells and sand and the occasional piece of trash that would wash ashore.

Duck had always told Logan that creativity came alive when the body and soul were at peace. He'd never been much interested in the fame or money that his work derived, except for how they enabled him to keep doing what he loved. Logan's dad, on the other hand, cared very much for the wealth and societal position, and very little for creativity. Thus, the bastardized version of the onetime refuge of a great writer.

Now Logan parked beneath a gleaming white portico at the far right side of the antique-gray shingle-style home. From there, he could see down the sloped lawn to the remaining four-hundred-foot-wide private shoreline on Long Island Sound. His father's carbon-gray GranTurismo was parked in front of the newly constructed detached four-car garage.

Dealing with his dad always involved a risk of nausea, which could be a bad thing given how much lasagna he'd gobbled at Ryan's today. Logan drew a deep breath before grabbing his computer and camera bags from his back seat.

Arcadia House's interior maintained its vintage style. Any remodeling done throughout the years had preserved the home's heritage. His mother, in particular, insisted on refinishing and recovering older furniture rather than replacing it with more comfortable, modern pieces. One of his favorite bathrooms still retained the original turquoise-and-black tile work.

Maybe his folks thought this tactic would also maintain the family name's prominence. Maybe they were right. But the hypocrisy of it all troubled Logan. His parents publicly supported the arts to further the Prescott name, but privately they'd never supported or praised *his* career choices. *Whatever.*

He strolled through the side door and pantry into the kitchen. Peyton was heating a can of soup at the stove. Sunlight slanted through the windows, casting a ghostly aura around her thickening frame. Her skin had lost its pretty peach hue months ago, giving way to a ruddy complexion courtesy of her TCHP cocktail of docetaxel, carboplatin, and trastuzumab plus pertuzumab. Weight gain had been another unwelcome side effect of those drugs.

She adjusted her head scarf when he entered the room. "Hi."

He dropped his bags on the counter, irritated that neither of his parents was tending to her. She'd just been released from the hospital a week ago following her double mastectomy. She was still bound in dressings and on Vicodin, and a visiting nurse stopped by daily to check on her. In two days, they had an appointment at the hospital and hoped the bandages and drains would be removed. "Sit. Let me take care of that for you."

He took the spoon from her hand and guided her to a stool, then kissed her head and returned to the stove.

"How are Ryan and Steffi?" she asked.

"Great. Steffi asked when you'd be up for visitors." He risked a glimpse of her reaction. She winced, as he expected.

"Not yet."

Logan reached for a deep bowl and ladled some soup. He set it in front of her with a spoon, then took a seat beside her. "You can't hide forever."

Peyton reflexively tugged her robe across her flattened chest before sipping from her spoon. She wouldn't undergo reconstructive surgery until she'd finished the rest of her treatment protocol, which would be at least another few months from now. Even that would require uncomfortable expanders and other things he'd rather not think about.

He looked away, knowing how self-conscious she'd become about her loss of hair and breasts, her skin texture, brittle nails, and a host of other side effects she'd suffered.

She might mourn the temporary loss of her beauty, but what he'd always loved best and now missed most was her spirit. She'd glowed with a spark born of daring and humor. More than anything else, he wanted to see her old smile return and, with it, the gleam in her eye when she had a wonderful, terrible idea for the two of them.

"I'm not ready."

He covered her free hand. "Sis, it's time. *You* wanted to return to this small town, so you can't keep tucked away in this house."

She strained to reach up and grab a handful of his hair, pulling it into a short ponytail at the base of his neck, then let it fall. "Easy for you to say."

Heat rose up his neck and cheeks. He couldn't be sure he'd face his own mortality as well as she had. She'd fought bravely. Continued working to the best of her ability, on the days when she could drag herself from bed or away from the toilet. She'd been determined to survive. The hardest part should be behind her—in his mind anyway—but it seemed that facing the world without the armor of her beauty was as big a challenge as battling the cancer itself.

"Did you see anyone else while you were out?" she asked.

He thought of Claire's bitter words, and then of her falling into the drift and showering herself with a puff of snow.

Peyton raised a barely there eyebrow. "What's with that look?"

He shook his head. "Nothing."

"Liar." She pushed the half-eaten bowl aside.

"Eat more." He set the bowl back in front of her. "You need your strength."

She sighed and picked up the spoon as if it weighed twenty pounds. "Tell me what made you frown."

Well, there'd be no hiding from Claire McKenna in Sanctuary Sound. Everyone here knew and loved her. Peyton and he were bound to keep running into her as long as they remained in town.

"Claire was at Ryan's house when I arrived." He settled his chin on his fist. "She's . . . not the Claire I remember."

Peyton idly stirred her spoon in the bowl. "I hate that I hurt her, and that my behavior changed her."

Logan covered her hand again, because the sound of the spoon against the bowl frayed his nerves. "You've made mistakes, but Claire is *choosing* to hang on to hate and anger. That's on her."

She laid her head on his shoulder. "You're a good brother."

"Thanks." He slung his arm around her shoulders. "I'm here for you, whatever you need."

She met his gaze, then hers flicked to his hair, and she wound a hank around one finger. "Wish you could give me all of this."

"My hair really gets to you?"

She shrugged. "You've always had better hair than me, but now . . ."

Their father strode into the kitchen, a newspaper tucked under his arm, interrupting the private moment. If Logan hadn't been so absorbed by his concern for Peyton, he surely would have recognized the tingles climbing up his neck as the warning sign of his dad's approach. Honestly, it was hard to miss.

At six feet two, his father looked like a Nordic god. Broad shoulders, carved cheekbones, and a glacial expression in those eyes that was colder than their iceberg-blue color. Although his blond hair had started to turn silver in spots, relentless exercise kept him trim at sixty-two. Relentless—a descriptor that could be ascribed to many of his father's attributes.

"Logan." His father stopped upon the sight of him. "When did you get here?"

"A few minutes ago." His shoulders tightened, preparing for the inevitable sparring.

His father raised his brows before frowning. "How long will you be staying with us?"

"Not sure." Logan interlocked his hands atop the kitchen island, squeezing them together.

His father huffed. "Must be nice."

"What's that mean?" Logan watched him pour himself two fingers of Michter's.

"Most of us have schedules to keep—a job that requires us to show up." His dad knocked back half the glass. It wasn't the first time he'd whipped Logan with that kind of remark, nor would it be the last.

"Lucky for me I've got autonomy." He forced a smile, even as he fought the urge to knock that drink from his dad's hand.

His dad's gaze went straight to Logan's long hair, collarless shirt, and discarded camera bags. "Yes. Like my father."

In many families, that might sound like a compliment, but Logan knew his father had nothing but disdain for the "feckless" man who'd nearly bankrupted the Prescott family with his expensive hobbies and contempt for work. How many times had he heard his parents deride Grandpa for "farting around" with paints and charcoal in France, Italy, and Sedona?

"No, Dad. Like my *great*-grandfather." He unclenched his hands and spread them on the marble counter. Peyton set her hand on his thigh, silently asking him to stand down.

"Dad, please," Peyton implored, touching her head scarf. "Can't our family enjoy a relaxed afternoon?"

Their dad finished his drink, set the glass in the sink, and crossed to kiss Peyton's forehead. "Sorry, sweetheart. I've got a call in ten minutes."

"But it's Saturday."

"Development work never ends, and I'm this close to signing a deal for a string of boutique inns." He held his thumb and forefinger about an inch apart. "They need work, but the property and bones are stellar, and I'm going to get them for a song."

"Really?" Peyton sat up straighter. "Where are they located? Maybe once I'm a bit stronger I can visit them and put together a great write-up."

It would be good for her to get back to her travel-writing work. She had always loved exploring new places and had built up quite a healthy social media following as a result of her witty accounts of interesting adventures. Still, Logan bristled at the thought of her helping their dad.

His dad shot Logan a derisive glance, as if saying, "Now there's a working Prescott." He then smiled at Peyton just before gesturing around the room. "Thank you for taking an interest in what I do to keep all this over our heads. The inns are strategically located along the Atlantic coast, from Maine down through Maryland."

"Sounds idyllic." She grasped Logan's hand. "Maybe Logan can come with me and take photographs for brochures and promotional materials."

Logan flinched. "I don't take *architectural* photographs."

"Of course not." His father scoffed. "Why take a paying gig when you can fart around with artistic development?"

There it was—the gassy comparison.

"Daddy!" Peyton admonished her father, and he quickly tucked his chin and frowned.

"I'll leave you two to your lunch while I make my call." He started to leave but then stopped at the kitchen door and turned to Logan. "Your mother wanted me to run to town to pick up some things. How about you make yourself useful and run those errands for me? List is on the fridge."

He tapped the woodwork twice and exited without awaiting a response.

Logan inhaled slowly and blew out a loud breath.

"I know he's hard on you, but please try to see it from his side." Peyton swiveled to face him. "His sense of security was shaken by Grandpa's spendthrift ways. I think he truly worries about your future, and is hurt that you never show any interest in what he does."

Perhaps she had a point. That didn't make his father less of a dick, though. Any man who could withhold affection as a way of manipulating his kids and their choices should not be a father. Logan had no idea if *he* would be a decent father, but he doubted he'd find out. He wasn't made for staying put, and the example of his parents' marriage hadn't provided much in the way of motivation, either.

Like Duck, Logan was a storyteller, and storytellers seek freedom and adventure. He expressed himself through images instead of words. Duck hadn't written *A Shadow on Sand* until he hit his thirties. This would be Logan's decade, too. He just needed the right story. The right project.

He rose from the stool and carried Peyton's bowl and spoon to the dishwasher for her. "Go rest. I'll run these errands, and then, when I return, maybe we can work a bit on the memoir."

He'd convinced his sister to document her journey from diagnosis through remission with a journal and weekly photographs. She'd even gone so far as to allow him to take raw pictures in the hospital and at home. Neither knew exactly how the project would ultimately come together, but it had given them a vehicle for so many emotions throughout the trying experience. Beneath his tears, hugs, and occasional sarcasm had lain a bone-deep terror of losing the person he most adored in life. His only confidante. In a twisted way, he was almost grateful for all of it, though, because he'd never felt closer to her than he did now.

Peyton sighed. "Fine."

She wasn't, but coddling never helped her move forward. Logan nodded and snatched the list from the fridge. "See you later."

—⁓—

He had no idea why his mother needed Krazy Glue, an X-Acto knife, and carpet cleaner today, but his role was not to question. Logan walked into Lockwood Hardware, a place he'd loitered in as a kid. The two-story shop hadn't changed much at all since his childhood.

Same dusty aisles he'd roamed every summer as a kid with Ben and Ryan, each of them investigating every doodad on the shelves. Just as often, Mr. Lockwood would empty the change from the gumball machine and let them take it to buy ice cream or get bait from the local tackle shop.

Logan was crouching to reach the Krazy Glue when he heard Ben Lockwood speaking to another customer at the cash register.

A genuine smile formed from someplace deep in his chest. Ben and Ryan were two of the reasons Logan had looked forward to helping Peyton recover here in Sanctuary Sound. It'd been years since he and his old buddies had been in the same place at the same time.

A reunion might help him reconnect to a part of himself that had gotten lost in the last decade. The part that might have something genuine and interesting to say.

He strode down the aisle, noting the similarities between Ben and his sister, Steffi. Tall, athletic builds. Hair in shades from caramel to umber. A warm skin tone and golden-brown eyes.

"Benny Boy," Logan teased as he laid his mother's booty on the counter and stuck out his hand. "How the hell are you?"

It took a second for Logan to register the tension tugging at the corners of Ben's smile. "Logan. You look good."

"Thanks, so do you. I just saw Steffi and Ryan earlier today. How about *that* reunion?" He folded his arms across his chest, widening his smile as if that might jostle Ben out of his unusually stiff manner.

"It's been good to have my sister home and see her happy."

Logan nodded. "I hope I can say the same thing in the coming months."

"I hope Peyton's feeling better soon." Ben's gaze drifted away. He didn't elaborate, ask questions, or offer to send a message to her, all of which Logan found odd. Offensive, even.

"So do I." Logan pushed his items forward and Ben rang them up. "Maybe you could swing by the house and visit. Come with Steffi. It'd be good for Peyton to see old friends."

Ben flashed a sad kind of smile and scratched the back of his neck. "Maybe . . ."

He ran Logan's card, bagged up the goods, and tossed the receipt in the bag without another word. Just that weak smile pasted on his face.

"Before I jump to conclusions, let me ask—do we have some problem, or are you just having an off day?"

"Sorry?" Ben stapled the paper bag shut and set it aside.

Logan tugged the bag closer. "You don't seem happy to see me, and given the magnitude of my sister's health issues, your lack of interest in her is glaring."

"We've got no problem, Logan. And I wish Peyton well with her recovery, but things are complicated."

"How so?"

Ben crossed his arms and looked Logan dead in the eye. "Honestly? I'm team Claire."

The fluorescent lights buzzing overhead disrupted Logan's thoughts.

"Are we back in middle school?" He couldn't keep the scorn from his voice.

Ben cracked his knuckles, then pulled Logan aside and spoke in a quiet but firm voice. "Understand something, Logan. Claire and I have lived in town together for the last decade while all of you ran away to live bigger, better lives. I hung out with Claire and Todd, and was there to pick up the pieces when he left. She's like a sister to me, and I won't hurt her by hanging out with Peyton until Claire is okay with that."

Logan should respect the loyalty, but they'd *all* been friends for years. He was counting on friends to help him smooth the way with Claire, not to support her decision to freeze Peyton out. "Don't you think Claire's being a bit unreasonable now? My God, it's been more than a year. Todd was a jerk, anyway. They're *both* better off without him."

"You don't know jack shit." Ben propped himself up against a shelf. "I know Peyton's been through a lot these past six months, and she's still got a tough road ahead, but eventually she'll likely go back to traveling the world, charming the pants off folks, and living the high life.

"Claire will still be here with me, living with pain that never really goes away, self-conscious about her limp and limitations. I have no love lost for Todd, but she loved that guy, and when Peyton took him away, it broke Claire almost worse than that bullet. So don't come back here now and act like it's up to Claire to move on and get over her pain. She's entitled to her anger, and she's entitled to choose not to trust or forgive your sister. That's *Peyton's* fault, not Claire's. And I'm not going to hurt a friend who's been here with me all along just to make things easier for you or your sister. Sorry."

Logan's blood boiled like a steaming teakettle. This day had not gone according to plan. Not one bit. Claire had snubbed him, and now Ben was drawing his own line in the sand. "Well, I appreciate your honesty. Glad your sister doesn't feel the same way. Guess this means we won't be hanging out while I'm home."

He spun on his heel and strode out of the store, but even in the midst of his righteous indignation, he couldn't quite block out Ben's words. *"She loved that guy, and when Peyton took him away, it broke Claire almost worse than that bullet."*

It sucked to be stuck in the middle when someone he loved had done something so wrong. He didn't always know what to do with his own feelings of disappointment and shame about Peyton's choice. Still, he loved her. He had to help her atone, for all of their sakes.

When he reached his car, he glanced back at the store, letting the acid in his stomach settle. Two petty arguments with old friends in one day. A new record and another thing he'd have to fix.

Holding on to resentment wasn't good for anyone. He didn't have to look any further than his own hostility toward his dad to know that much.

Chapter Three

Connecticut Muffin's blue-and-white-striped awning beckoned from the opposite side of the street. Claire told herself to walk past the shop, even as she found her feet ambling across the crosswalk. No chocolate croissant, no matter how flaky and sweet, would solve her problems. Those delicious five hundred calories would not convince Mrs. Brewster to change her mind and renovate her bathroom soon. Nor would the burst of pleasure soothe her stomach, which had been doing somersaults every day since that run-in with Logan.

Her eyes ached from the strain of searching for him and Peyton everywhere she went. This anxiety was exactly why she hadn't wanted Peyton coming back to town to recuperate.

No amount of junk food or reality TV had driven away Logan's disappointed words—worse, the disillusionment in his eyes when he'd said them. She'd scarcely slept for the way she replayed that conversation over and over, each time coming up with a better, classier, stronger means to have handled the unexpected run-in.

Next time she'd be prepared.

As she traversed a small opening in the plowed snow and neared the store, two women in yoga pants and Bean Boots walked out, carrying steaming to-go cups while chatting. In their wake, the aroma of fresh-baked goods warmed the cold air as it wafted out to the sidewalk, curled around Claire, and dragged her inside. *Heaven.*

She shouldn't waste five dollars on anything these days, let alone pastries. But, oh, how she wanted one. *Needed* one.

The small storefront's scuffed wood floors creaked beneath her and Rosie. She circumnavigated three small café tables to get to the display case, which was filled with muffins, cookies, and a variety of bread. Warm, buttery delights made more golden by the soft light coming through the shaded plateglass window.

Betsy Gamble, a forty-year-old divorced mother of two and member of Claire's book group, was working the counter. "Hey, Claire. Croissant and Earl Grey?"

"Am I so predictable?" Claire snickered while loosening the scarf around her neck and removing her mittens so she could fish for her wallet. *Weak, weak, weak!*

"You'll be glad today because these puppies are still warm." Betsy used the tongs to nab the fattest croissant and slip it into the thin paper bag. While she turned to fill a to-go cup with hot water, she asked, "Did you finish *The Great Alone* yet? Meeting's coming up."

"Almost." Thank God for books. Her safe way to explore other places and time periods. *No one* gets hurt from reading a book.

Betsy pushed the bag and cup of hot tea in front of her, then took her cash. "I tell you this much, I could never, ever live in the wilds of Homer, Alaska."

Frankly, right now that almost sounded easier than living in Sanctuary Sound with the Prescott siblings circling.

Claire tapped Rosie. "I certainly couldn't hack it in those conditions, nor would I put up with Ernt!"

Betsy handed Claire her change. "Should be a good discussion."

Claire had just snapped her wallet shut and picked up the croissant bag when the bell above the door rang. She looked over her shoulder to find Logan and Peyton standing just inside the glass door. Her body electrified as if she'd been plugged into a high-voltage power line. The room even seemed to brighten during the second that Claire's breath hitched. Her grip on Rosie could well snap the ivory handle if she didn't loosen her fingers.

Betsy's obvious interest in this unexpected run-in caused Claire's hair to tingle. Everyone in town knew the story. Everyone pitied her—poor gimpy Claire, who'd lost her man to the glamorous Peyton Prescott. And now, everyone would gossip about any encounter between the two ex-friends.

She couldn't even blame Betsy for her curiosity. Juicy scandals didn't come along all that often around here. And Claire couldn't lie to herself. Rumors and gossip were kind of fun when they weren't about you, which explained the popularity of reality TV. Fortunately there were no cameras in the bakeshop. Being the next viral sensation would *not* be a good way to build her professional reputation.

Claire felt Logan's presence, but her gaze had locked with Peyton's. The blue head scarf didn't flatter Peyton's new scarlet skin rashes, and her eyes no longer sparkled with life and wit. Her coat and clothing fit more snugly than normal thanks to chemo weight gain, which Claire was sure Peyton hated as well.

Memories bombarded Claire, starting with the first time she'd met Peyton, when Steffi had invited them both for a sleepover, and Peyton had arrived looking like Britney Spears in a Juicy Couture velour tracksuit, like the coolest girl on the planet would. And when they all celebrated their high school graduation with a spa day at the Norwich Inn.

Hopeful, happy times filled with sisterhood and support. But then Claire remembered Todd breaking up with her. His deceptively kind face, glistening with the sheen of nervous perspiration, as he handed her a box of the things that she'd kept at his apartment. Even now, she went numb with the same dismay and pain as when she realized the reason behind his sudden change of heart. At least today there wouldn't be a days-long crying jag that followed. Or the whispers and consolations of well-intentioned neighbors and friends. Or the shame. Oh, the shame.

The details of Peyton's current appearance turned blurry as tears coated Claire's eyes. She squeezed them closed to stave off crying. When she opened them, she saw Peyton whisper something to Logan before she turned and left the store.

Breathe.

Her lungs burned—a feeling she'd once loved after an intense tennis match, but not one she welcomed now. Her muscles were tight. Honestly, she couldn't believe that Peyton didn't force a conversation. That woman never backed down from anything in her life before today.

"Claire." Logan started toward her. Only then did she notice that he'd shorn his hair. All that gorgeous hair, gone!

She dropped the croissant bag. *Shoot.* She'd just promised herself she'd be prepared when she saw him next. He'd better not say one word about his sister. She wasn't ready to defend herself, especially not after seeing Peyton look so sick and defeated.

Crouching hurt Claire's hip, but she needed that croissant more than ever.

Logan leaned forward just as she bent over to pick up the bag, so they bumped into each other. His strong hands gripped her shoulders to steady her, then he handed her the croissant. "Here you go."

"Thanks," she mumbled, eyes downcast, gripping the bag so tightly the chocolate had probably squirted out of the pastry. She'd have to lick the paper, or smear the chocolate over the top of the crust. She peeked up at Logan again. Short hair only emphasized his refined bone structure and those penetrating green eyes. Who knew he could be even better looking? She didn't want him so close. "You cut your hair."

The right side of his mouth turned up as he ran his hand over his shorn head. "You noticed."

Impossible not to. Many of her fantasies about him had involved her hands playing with all that hair. Now she'd never get the chance. Not that she would've been offered the chance anyway. Or wanted it anymore, darn it. She was an independent woman Logan Prescott could not hold sway over anymore.

"Trying to keep the peace at home?" She knew his father disliked Logan's artsy side, and she knew Logan both loved and hated that fact. But if he wanted to help Peyton transition and rest, he probably needed to appease his father while they were all living beneath one roof.

Logan tipped his head, his eyes searching hers, almost smiling. "This wasn't for my dad. I did it for Peyton."

"What do you mean?" Claire's palm itched to feel the tickle of his short hair.

He shrugged one shoulder, his voice wistful. "Solidarity."

Oh.

They'd all envied Logan's hair for years, but now that Peyton had lost hers . . . Claire's heart swelled with respect and awe for the depth of love and commitment he had for his sister. Having a big brother must be such a comfort. Then again, given the unfamilial feelings she harbored for Logan, she thanked God he wasn't *her* brother.

Her thoughts continued to ping-pong, proving she'd lost her mind this morning. First, the disappointing news from Mrs. Brewster, then this run-in with Logan and Peyton.

Peyton, who left because she couldn't face Claire . . . or didn't think Claire could face her. That thought was rather lowering.

She noticed Betsy wiping down the counter, pretending not to be taking copious mental notes. This was all too much. She had to get outside so she could breathe. Nothing like cold, salty air to stimulate the senses. Of course, Peyton might be waiting for her on the sidewalk.

"Where'd your sister go?" Her words spilled out fast and hard.

He sighed. "To wait in the car."

"Why?"

"We planned to have a coffee before going to her post-op appointment, but she didn't want to upset you. She asked me to get the coffee to go." Logan's expression gave no hint of his feelings about that, which made her squirm. Maybe that's what he wanted. He nodded at Betsy and raised two fingers. "One caffeine-free mocha latte and one red eye to go, please."

Claire didn't want to think about the fact that Peyton just lost both of her breasts last week. The scars. The pain. The sorrow. Absently, she rubbed her left hip.

"I'm leaving, so Peyton can come inside and you two can relax here with coffee and whatever." She sidestepped him and started for the door, then paused. A few yards away, Peyton sat alone in a cold car. A small kindness that, even with Claire's vault full of anger, she couldn't dismiss. "I appreciate that she didn't force me to talk to her today and hope the appointment goes well."

"Thank you. I'll pass it along, but you *could* thank her yourself," he suggested.

Behind him, Claire noticed Betsy's eyes bug for a second while she made the mocha latte.

Claire met Logan's assessing gaze and, despite the sympathy for Peyton's medical situation, found her voice. "Sorry, Logan, but it'll be a long time—if ever—before I thank Peyton for anything."

Logan didn't care what Claire said. He heard a hint of a softening. *Long time. If ever.* Equivocal words. Proof that she wasn't as hard and cynical as she'd led him to believe just before she'd landed on her ass in the snow.

The friend he'd known still existed somewhere beneath the distant gaze and layers of clothes—at the moment she was dressed like Nanook of the North. He couldn't deny admiring—enjoying, even—her candor. But just now she'd given him an opening, however narrow. Logan never let any opening go. "Don't suppose you've given more thought to decorating my apartment? I could also introduce you to other people in the city with bare walls and money to burn."

She hesitated. *Good.* The opening kept widening.

"I don't see how it would work, Logan. Putting aside the whole Peyton situation, I'm not inclined to go to the city."

"Seven fifty, Logan," Betsy interjected.

"Keep the change," he said, tossing her a ten-dollar bill. He returned his attention to Claire. "You have a thing against Manhattan?"

"I have a thing against danger." She tipped her head toward Rosie.

She'd remained a hometown girl, but he hadn't realized she avoided *all* urban areas. At first blush, it made sense, but her logic was flawed. Yankee Crossing wasn't, in and of itself, a dangerous or even urban locale, and yet she'd been shot there.

"I've lived in New York for years without injury." At least not physical injury. Wounds to the soul were an issue open to debate. "It's not that dangerous."

"Any place with crowds can be dangerous." She stared at him, calm and assured, leaving no opening whatsoever.

He could work with that, though. He didn't need her to go to New York. Hell, he didn't even need to have his apartment redone. He just needed to spend time with her. Wear her down, little by little, until she had enough sympathy for Peyton to be willing to extend some forgiveness. "Well, what about floor plans and photographs? If you had dimensions and images, could you work with that?"

A responding spark flickered in her eyes, like sunlight hitting a sapphire. Curiosity. Suspicion. Even a dash of excitement. Her response ignited a little unexpected curiosity in him, too.

But her white-knuckle grip on Rosie also spoke volumes. "It's not ideal. I couldn't get a true feel for the space without physically seeing it."

He understood that, of course. Space, light, the feel of the area— these things all mattered in any good design or photo. But a perfect apartment wasn't his ultimate goal. "But it *is* possible."

She crossed her arms now, the little paper bag dangling from her fingers. "You could easily hire someone in the city instead of playing games with me."

"Games? Why can't I help an old friend keep her new business going? We are old friends, aren't we?" He'd known her since before her braces had been removed. Played volleyball in the side yard of Arcadia with her and others on warm summer nights in middle school. Even traveled with a group of friends to Yale to watch her win a sectional championship mere months before the shooting that changed everything.

"Exactly. Old friends, which means I know you, so I know what you're really about."

He couldn't help but smile. She did know him. He'd always liked that best about her. He wouldn't sully their past by denying it now.

Instead, he tore a page from her playbook of avoidance. "I've got a budget of fifty grand to spend on new living room, dining room, and bedroom furniture and whatnot. That should provide a nice fee. I don't care what the split is, as long as the place looks and feels like me when you're finished. And of all the designers out there, I doubt any know me as well as you—as you've pointed out."

Few, if any, women had ever paid as much quiet attention to him as Claire used to.

"Fifty . . . I . . . that's . . ." She clamped her mouth shut. He doubted she noticed her toe tapping at this point.

"I won't push, but I hope you say yes. It'd be nice to pool our creative forces on a project, wouldn't it?" He meant that despite his ulterior motives.

Her eyes clouded with spinning thoughts, and he found himself holding his breath, waiting for her response. "Thank you. I'll think about it."

Yes. She might not know it yet, but he'd just won the first battle in the war for forgiveness. He didn't even feel bad about it. Claire would be better off when he was done. Her business would be intact, and she'd be unburdened by the resentment that weighed her down. A bonus would be if he could get her to come to the city, just once. An adventure to break her free from her self-imposed prison.

He'd enjoy seeing the city through her eyes.

"You know where to find me." He hoped that sounded nonchalant.

"I doubt I'll have to go looking. Seems certain I'll be bumping into you wherever I go."

He grinned. "Lucky me."

She opened her mouth but then closed it again. He found himself wishing to know what she'd almost said. Funny, because he often found himself bored with what most people said. "Bye, Logan."

Between her parka, her cane, her purse, and her bag, she barely fit through the narrow door.

When he turned to grab his and Peyton's coffees, he noticed Claire's tea. "Thanks," he mumbled to Betsy as he balanced the third cup in his hands and took off after Claire.

Fortunately the patchy sidewalks had slowed her down. "Claire, you forgot your tea."

"Oh." She lumbered back to him, her furtive gaze roving for bystanders. "Thanks."

"No problem." He smiled. "Have a nice day."

She nodded and hobbled off, disappearing around the corner.

He stood for a moment, noticing the symmetry of the frame in front of him—a rainbow of awnings, and coal-black street lanterns with empty hanging baskets acting like buckets for the snow. If he returned during the blue hour, maybe he could capture some great Americana photos as long as some stores remained lit with incandescent light. A picture-perfect view that likely obscured some imperfect interactions taking place inside, like the one that had just unfolded in Connecticut Muffin.

How often *did* pretty outsides hide unseemly truths?

He crossed the street to his car. Peyton had turned it on, so it was toasty warm when he got in and handed her the coffee.

She didn't ask him why it had taken so long or whether Claire had said anything about her. He started the engine and backed out of the parking spot, pointing the car toward Yale New Haven Hospital.

"I think us being here together will be good for everyone." He squirted washer fluid on the windshield to clean the grime.

Peyton slid him a glance, her eyes filled with doubt. "Why's that?"

"It's peaceful, which you need now. And everywhere you look, we have memories. Mostly good ones, too. Ones other people share. Seeing you—us—here will force them to remember those good times, and that will make it harder to hold on to the bad ones." He patted her thigh. "You're going to get a chance to talk to Claire. Maybe not this week or next, but soon. I feel it."

"What did she say?" Peyton stared ahead. His sister's distinctive profile, with the slight upturn of her nose and the strong, square line of her jaw, always made him want to reach for a camera.

"Nothing specific." He thought about that some more and decided to share the catalyst of his hope. "She appreciated that you didn't confront her. Good move."

"It wasn't calculated, Logan." Peyton threw him a disappointed look. "It was simply the right thing to do."

"Even better." He scratched his head. Was his sister really less calculating than he was, and did that matter? It was a useful trait as long as you weren't a selfish prick about it.

"Logan, don't get involved. I tried putting Steffi in the middle, and that was wrong. It's my mess to clean up. I'll handle it." She sipped her coffee and let her head drop back against the seat.

Surely, she knew him well enough to know that he wouldn't stop being involved until she was happier. He'd cut his hair for her, for God's sake. Meddling with Claire would be so much easier, and more pleasant.

A little hum rattled in his chest at the thought of Claire's fiery eyes. The other day he'd been hurt, but today squaring off had been fun. She *had* found her voice, and *he* liked it. He looked forward to her call, which he knew would come. She'd never been stupid, and his offer had been too good to ignore.

Chapter Four

Claire eagerly entered Pat Waltham's house with her book tucked under her arm. Her fine-tuned olfactory system immediately sniffed out something sweet—berries and baked goods. Few things were better than book group discussions, but pairing them with homemade goodies did top the list. "Smells wonderful, Pat. What did you make?"

"A strawberry galette with basil-infused cream." Pat helped Claire out of her coat, with a smile. She was seventy-five but more vibrant than most despite the wiry gray curls springing from her head. Typically clad in turtlenecks and khakis, she'd sometimes wear a chunky necklace for oomph. She liked her brandy and loved to travel, so she often shared the best stories.

"Is it too soon to ask for seconds?" Claire teased while following Pat into the living room, where Betsy was seated beside Naomi Tinio, the local librarian. At sixty, Naomi was something of a hipster, a rarity in their conservative New England town. Claire's mom might call Naomi groovy, with her jet-black hair with bright-purple swaths, bucket hat, oversize glasses, and wacky T-shirts, like the green-and-white "If you don't eat tacos, I'm nacho type" one she was wearing tonight.

"I'll cut you an extra-large slice," Pat promised. "Let me finish bringing everything into the living room. Then we'll get started."

Pat had just left the room when Betsy patted the cushion of the chair to the right of the sofa. "Sit here."

Claire rested Rosie against the sofa arm and plopped onto the comfortable recliner. She set the massive orange hardcover book on her lap. "I'm so interested in hearing what everyone thought of this book. I have some pretty strong opinions about Cora."

"And *I'm* so interested in knowing whether you've run into Peyton or Logan since my shop." Betsy's eyes glittered with interest. "I thought you handled yourself beautifully, except for when you dropped the croissant . . . and left behind your tea."

Well, thanks for the reminders. Claire slid a brief glance at Naomi, whose gorgeous, warm Filipino skin tone filled Claire with envy, but she seemed more interested in her tumbler of Armagnac than gossip about the Prescott siblings.

"I haven't seen them since then, but if or when I do, there won't be anything to gossip about. Live and let live. The past is done, and I'm focused solely on building my business and opening a retail shop. There won't be any hair-pulling or name-calling."

"Peyton's lucky she crossed you and not me. I'm not above a little name-calling," Betsy snickered. Her divorce had been a nasty cliché. When her husband left her for his secretary, Betsy had made things as difficult for him as possible, which didn't help lessen the sting or make raising her two young kids any easier. "Of course, it's hard to pick on someone who's so sick. She looked dreadful, didn't she?"

"Chemo isn't a spa treatment, for chrissakes." Naomi scowled while knocking on wood. "Be careful how you talk about her illness, or karma will kick your ass."

"Karma or not, I'm not discussing Peyton. Not tonight. Not ever." Peyton had vilified herself without needing Claire to pile on. Besides, she still hadn't shaken off that troubling image of Peyton from the bakeshop.

Hearing about her breast cancer last fall and understanding its severity had not motivated Claire to show mercy. But seeing the distorted version of Peyton . . . well, that had chipped away at her resolve.

Peyton's sickly eyes and quiet shame had revisited Claire for three days, forcing her to draw a few conclusions. First, a person can't truly hate someone he or she didn't once love. Sure, mass murderers, crooked politicians, and other things are hateful, but a person won't feel that intense blistering of acid in her gut when thinking about those folks the way she will when betrayed by a trusted friend. Second, hatred can burn like a hundred suns for an infinite time if stoked with self-pity. Third, even when hate burns the remnants of friendship to the ground, fond childhood memories are sowed so deep in the soul that it takes very little to till that fallow soil.

No, Claire wasn't willing to talk to Peyton or befriend her again. But she couldn't deny that the grace Peyton had exhibited by leaving the bakery had shifted the scales the tiniest bit away from hatred. That, and Logan. No matter how hard she resisted, he'd always be her weakness. His love for his sister and his wish to see her forgiven were hard for Claire to ignore.

"Well," Betsy huffed, slouching back onto the sofa, "that's . . . mature of you."

Pat strode in and set the galette on the coffee table, alongside dessert plates and silverware that she'd placed there earlier. Claire's mouth watered at the first hint of those glistening strawberries.

"Help yourselves," Pat said. "Claire, would you like some Armagnac?"

Pass! One whiff of that stuff singed her nostrils. "No, thanks. Don't want to dull the taste buds."

She helped herself to a large slice and cut into it with her fork, grateful for the sugar rush and book discussion that should sweep the Prescott siblings from her thoughts for a while.

"What did I miss when I went to the kitchen?" Pat settled her well-padded behind on the wingback chair.

"Not much." Betsy licked her finger after using it to push some of the dessert onto her plate. "Claire isn't in a sharing mood, even though I heard Logan offer her a job. One she turned down. Call me crazy, but if I had a chance to spend time with that fine-looking man, I'd take it. He wouldn't even need to pay me." She cackled, and Pat and Naomi sniggered along with her.

"If I were a few decades younger, I'd fight you for him." Pat added a dollop of the cream to her plate, then turned to Claire. "Honey, please tell me you aren't passing on a job opportunity because of Peyton."

"It's not just that . . . ," Claire replied through a mouthful of berries and crust. Deep down she knew she should take that job. The commission would go a long way to fixing the company's financial trouble, and the job itself would give her a kind of creative challenge and freedom she'd rarely get around here. "The job's not practical. It's in New York—almost two hours each way. And we all know he's trying to buy my forgiveness for his sister. I won't be manipulated by another Prescott."

Betsy elbowed Naomi. "I'd let him manipulate me, if you get my drift."

"We all get your drift, Betsy," Naomi muttered. "Claire, I respect your integrity."

"Thank you, Naomi." One supporter was better than none, she supposed.

"Listen up," Pat instructed. "I'm the oldest, which makes me the wisest. Who cares about *his* agenda? Think about *your* goals, and do whatever is needed to keep your business going. Tell him straight up there won't be a quid pro quo where his sister's concerned, but take the job. Refusing it because of Peyton isn't integrity, it's fear. And, honestly, you're better off without a weak, faithless man like Todd, so maybe you should be thanking her instead of holding a grudge."

"Thank her?" Claire choked before she dropped her gaze to the bottle of Armagnac, which she might actually be willing to toss back now. Might need, even, to get through the night.

"I heard Todd skedaddled as soon as she got sick. He left you, he left her . . ." Pat fluttered her hand in the air. "Who knows how much time you would've wasted on that guy had Peyton not been the one that got him to show his true colors? Now you're free to find a good guy."

"It's not much fun being free in a town where there aren't many available men," Betsy moaned. "Ben Lockwood's cute, though. Why don't you date him?"

"He's like my brother," Claire said.

"Logan's available." Naomi shrugged. "Never heard a mean word about him, and he's got that sexy artistic thing going for him."

"Logan Prescott goes through women faster than I inhale a sleeve of Oreos." Claire set her empty plate on the table for emphasis. It'd taken months for the ache of losing Todd to go away. If she ever let herself get close to Logan, she'd never recover when he left her. And it *would* be when, not *if*. Logan didn't settle down. Not for anyone. "Let's please change the subject and talk about the book."

"Fair enough," Pat conceded. "I don't know about all of you, but the descriptions riveted me. It might sound crazy, but I think we should take an Alaskan cruise."

The others began to chatter excitedly about that fantasy, while Claire spent the next few moments talking herself down. Pat had a fair point about taking the job. Logan couldn't force Claire to talk to Peyton, and she'd been clear that she wouldn't be pressured.

If he wanted to take the gamble and pay her, why shouldn't she profit off his misguided loyalty? Claire could avoid the transit and work off architectural drawings and photographs. Visions of racks of Scalamandré fabric and shelves of trendy home accessories danced before her.

And, after years of wondering about where Logan lived, she'd finally learn every nook and cranny. She could make it a true home for him. Pick the fabrics, the styles, his bedding . . .

Therein lay the only real danger—the risk to her heart. Rationally, she knew she had no future with Logan, but working closely with him could make that hard to forget. Make her miss him anew when he and Peyton finally took off again, like when they'd all left home after college.

"Claire, are you even listening?" Betsy snapped her fingers right in front of Claire's nose.

"Sorry." Claire puckered her lips.

"If we're seriously going to plan a trip together, let's choose a book set in Italy or Greece or some other warm Mediterranean location. Why spend a week of summer vacation being cold in Alaska?" Betsy shook her head.

"Didn't this book strike a chord with your sense of adventure? I kept picturing the vastness of Alaska. It seemed so freeing." Pat drummed her fingers on the book cover. "I really want to visit."

"I'd go," Naomi said. "Assuming we could get a reasonable cruise package."

"Well, I *have* read that men outnumber women by a lot in Alaska. Maybe it'd be worth a visit," Betsy conceded.

Everyone looked at Claire, who'd remained silent. "Sorry. I can't go."

"Why not?" Pat asked.

"I need every spare penny for my business this year."

"Unless you take that job with Logan." Pat shot her a pointed look.

"Even if I do"—Claire couldn't believe she was even contemplating that—"I can't take that kind of trip. Hiking? No. Even being on a ship . . . I wouldn't feel safe." She slid a glance at Rosie.

"Honey, life isn't about being safe." Pat filled her plate with a second slice of the galette and more cream. "One of these days I really hope you spread your wings again. Don't you miss taking flight?"

"That's what books are for. I got to know Alaska well enough. I walked in Leni's shoes and experienced her courage." She opened the book to her first tabbed page. "And I think we should read Tara

Westover's memoir, *Educated*, next. We'll get to 'visit' Idaho in that one."

"When do we get to go to the Mediterranean?" Betsy whined.

Logan paced the living room floor while Peyton sifted through the batch of photographs he'd taken of her after the doctor removed her bandages. She'd looked right into the camera, but he could see the wall she'd put between herself and the lens. He couldn't blame her. She'd shown remarkable bravery and vulnerability by even letting him shoot the pictures. Still, he'd wanted her to drop her guard.

Now she'd spread them out on the Aubusson rug, beneath the rows she'd created from the best of his earlier work. All around them lay pictorial evidence of her battle, from the first appointments through the most recent. The past six months had been a blur, yet these photos forced him to recall particular moments in excruciating detail.

Light flooded the spacious room through its oversize windows and reflected off the shiny surfaces of the polished wood and mirrors. The brightness imbued the images with a sort of starkness that made him restless and uncomfortable. Apt, since nothing in the living room was comfortable. Antique, fussy furnishings with hard, tufted cushions. The opposite of welcoming . . . or of "living."

He missed the sweet, smoky scent of Duck's cigar and the sound of his rumbly voice reading aloud. Missed the way his aging eyes lit with delight whenever Logan had shown him something he'd built or drawn or written. Once he died, this house had become a war zone between Logan's father and Grandpa, with his dad emerging as the victor.

Logan shook his head and refocused on his sister, whose gaze lingered longer on certain photos than on others. Her mouth remained slightly downturned, her eyes distant and muddied.

"What are you thinking?" He crouched beside her.

She covered her face with her trembling hands. "I'm not sure I can do this."

He laid a hand on her back. "Why not?"

"Look!" She gestured across the floor. "If we publish this memoir, I'll be showing these to the world. Hideous images. Images of me, weak and ill, I'll never escape or forget, and neither will anyone else."

He held her shoulders and kissed the top of her head. "When I look at these pictures, I see a *beautiful* fighter. A woman who's brave enough to share her truth to help others."

"You need glasses." She elbowed his hip. Her head scarf started to fall back, so she tightened it.

She didn't meet his eyes. He didn't quite know what else to say to her. Having never faced his own mortality, he had no experience to draw on. No real words of wisdom. Only love.

"You're feeling stronger lately. We'll keep taking new photographs to add as you improve and your hair grows back, so that you and everyone else will see exactly what I already see. The passages you've written so far are moving. Think of the women who might find strength in that. Think of the money we could donate to research from the proceeds."

When they'd started the project, they'd discussed making it a memoir and donating 50 percent of any income to the National Breast Cancer Foundation. He'd been saving parking tickets and prescriptions and other memorabilia, thinking they might juxtapose those things with the photos and narrative. He might even contribute from his own journal, as a family member and caretaker.

"You seem to forget that I'm basically a self-centered, vain person, not someone who's ever been out to inspire or save others," she muttered. "Ask anyone."

"Stop it. Most of us are self-centered and vain now and then. You aren't unique. And maybe you never tried to inspire or save people before, but now you have an opportunity to do just that. To turn this suffering into something good." Logan paused, his thoughts shifting to a particular redhead who'd been on his mind for days. She hadn't called to take him up on his offer. He could hardly believe it. "Look at Claire. She overcame her setbacks and went through recovery like a champ. People admire her for it, and they'll admire you, too."

"I think it's pretty well established that I'm not, and have never been, Claire." Peyton's pale eyes flickered.

"How do you know? You've never been tested until now. You can be like her." He hugged her. "You've already inspired me."

"You're too kind." She reached up and rubbed his head. "I can't wait for the wig made from your gorgeous hair."

"It feels weird to shampoo now." He raked his hands over his bristly hair, missing the silky length of it. "And I hate that Dad likes it."

Peyton smiled for the first time all morning. "Unintended consequences."

Didn't he know it. How unfortunate that doing something for a good reason could result in a negative consequence. He closed his eyes, hoping to purge the image of his father's approving expression. *"Did hell freeze over?"* the man had muttered at dinner that night. Logan had bitten his tongue so hard he couldn't eat.

"Okay, enough stalling. Pick a few and let's move on." He sat on the edge of the coffee table, but then his phone vibrated. He tugged it free from his pocket. *Claire.* A zing traveled through his chest. He looked at Peyton. "Excuse me, I'll be back in a few."

She raised an eyebrow. "Must be a woman. Karina, perhaps?"

He frowned. "I've told you, I *work* with Karina. We aren't a thing."

"You were a thing."

"For about a second." He waved his sister off as he crossed the room, heading toward the French doors that led to the flagstone patio. "Hello?"

"Logan, it's Claire. McKenna."

As if he didn't know her voice. He opened the doors and stepped outside. A frigid blast of wind swept up the lawn from the Sound, which sparkled with sunlight as if someone had scooped up handfuls of rhinestones and scattered them across the water.

He tucked his free hand beneath his armpit, shivering. He could turn back or be glad the bracing weather would keep him sharp. He'd need to be sharp to reel Claire in. "Good morning, Claire."

He shouldn't tease her. At least, not until he was sure she'd called to accept his offer. Another smile tugged at his mouth as he prepared for matching wits with her again.

"I suppose you know why I'm calling." Her voice tightened as if she were being walked down a plank at knifepoint.

"I hope so." He did, and not just for his sister's sake.

Ever since he'd seen her at Steffi and Ryan's place, he'd thought about how much nicer it would be to come home to someplace with style and warmth. His run-in with Claire since that day had only piqued his interest. Something about her was different now. Her hair, of course. But something else had him pumped up by the mere sound of her voice . . . something he still couldn't identify but wanted to figure out.

"Before I commit, I need to see the layout and some photographs. Just to make sure I can give you what you're looking for."

"Okay." In his twisted mind, her innocent words took on a double meaning. He frowned. Claire wasn't his type. She would demand things. Expect things. Deserve them, too. He didn't have that to give. Hadn't ever been interested in traditional relationships and roles. He had his art to pursue. His story—the one he had yet to figure out—to tell. He couldn't stop seeking it even if he wanted to, which he didn't. And yet . . .

"When can you get those to me?" she asked, interrupting his thoughts.

"Are you sure you don't want to take a trip to the city? I'll even throw in a great lunch." He held his breath. Claire had a well-established sweet tooth. He knew a French bistro in his neighborhood that had amazing desserts.

"No. I can't do that. I understand if that's a problem, and like I said before, there are plenty of fantastic designers in New York." Those blunt words left no wiggle room. He backed away from that fight and tried a different tack, enjoying the tug-of-war, picturing her squaring her shoulders while biting her lip.

"But I want you." He grinned at the effect those words might have on her. He'd bet she was blushing. "You've known me forever, so you're uniquely positioned to transform my place into a home."

"I'm not a magician," came her droll reply. She then cleared her throat. "Kidding."

Nicely played, Claire. "So you *are* a magician?"

He could hear her smile through the phone. That warmed him despite another gust of late-winter wind.

"Pretty close. So when will you be able to get me the pictures and dimensions?"

He'd need to move fast so she couldn't rethink her decision. "How about tonight. Dinner?"

Water splattered beside him as icicles melted from the eaves of the house. He squinted in the sunlight reflecting off the snow. There were no buildings or people as far as the eye could see—a change of pace from his hurried life. Things looked and sounded so different when surrounded by so much quiet space.

"That's not necessary."

"No, but it might be nice. Friendly. We can be friendly, can't we?"

He waited, his eyes taking note of the interesting shapes of blue shadows cast onto the snow-covered lawn by the house behind him. Shadows intrigued him. Always had. Like how they become blurrier the wider the light source.

After a brief sigh, she said, "I suppose."

"Don't overwhelm me with your enthusiasm." He chuckled.

"It's just . . . I don't want to be the subject of gossip, Logan."

"Is this town so dull that us sharing a pizza stirs up gossip?"

"Everyone who knows me will ask what's going on with us and your sister, and . . . I would rather not have to fend off those questions. Can we please keep things professional for now?"

For now. He couldn't deny such an honest plea.

Small-town life seemed such a strange world to him after living in Manhattan for the past decade. A city where he could be anonymous in his own building, let alone neighborhood. Where he could share his pizza naked with a harem and not raise an eyebrow.

"Fine. I'll see you at seven at your house." He hung up before she could refuse the offer, and smiled, knowing he'd probably just pushed a few of her buttons.

He liked playing with Claire. She looked cute when she turned pink and her eyes lit up with challenge. Then again, that call must've been hard for her to make. His offer had put her in a difficult spot, as he'd known it would. She'd done the right thing even though it had to hurt, just like she always did. He admired the hell out of her for that while choosing to ignore what his behavior said about him.

His hands and nose were frozen, so he ducked back inside to find Peyton. If Claire could muster courage over and again, surely his sister could this once, too.

When he returned to the living room, she had stacked some rejects in one pile and was stuffing the keepers into the portfolio they were using to keep organized.

He clapped his hands together. "You've decided?"

"We'll keep going forward. I'll work from my journal today and see how far I can get." She hugged her knees to her chest. "If I were less ambivalent, it would improve the tone of the writing. I haven't found my voice for this project."

He got that. Some projects flowed like a good dream, while others required a lot more plotting, planning, and pep talks to mine the passion. "You will."

She shrugged. "Who called?"

Long ago, he and Peyton had made a pact with each other that included a promise never to lie. Even though he was sure a white lie might be the better call at the moment, he kept his word. "Claire."

Her eyes went wide. "Why?"

"I offered her the chance to redecorate my apartment in Chelsea, and after some thought, she said yes. Not that she had much choice, given the current financial state of her and Steffi's business."

"I'm happy for Steffi's sake, but don't use this job to pressure Claire." Peyton pointed her index finger at him. "Do not fight my battle for me. That'll only make it worse."

He slung an arm around her shoulders. "Don't worry. I've got this under control."

Logan lifted the thick manila envelope off the passenger seat and exited his car. From the sidewalk, he studied Claire's Craftsman-style home, with its wide front porch, complete with a swing. He envisioned it in spring, imagining what flowers would pop up after the snow melted. What types of plants and grasses—in shades from green to yellow to blue—might frame the home? Would a pitcher of lemonade sit beside that swing, with Claire lying there reading a book while jazz played through an open window? The daydream filled him with nostalgia, like the whole world would slow down when you crossed the threshold.

His family's life had always been hectic and big. In his youth, he'd wander the streets of town, hopping from one friend's home to another, aware of the easy vibe and closer spaces within their four walls. Families who played board games while mothers cooked meatloaf. In those hours, he'd get to try on a lifestyle he'd never known, seeking answers the way a young girl dresses up in her mother's pearls to learn how it feels to be a woman.

An unexpected bout of flutters arose as Logan trotted up the porch stairs and knocked on the door. For most of his life, Claire had been an adorable sweetheart of a girl who made him feel good about himself. But she'd changed.

Thinking back, he'd first noticed it when he'd run into her in town this past fall. He'd kept thinking about her after that brusque encounter on the street. Kept looking for her in town and checking his phone for messages, and not only because he wanted to help his sister. His heart had practically come to a standstill when he'd seen her name on his screen earlier.

The door opened. Claire looked prim as ever. Dark jeans. An extra-long powder-blue sweater with two box pockets on its front, pulled over a cream-colored turtleneck. Tasseled suede loafers. A single pearl in each ear. And Rosie in her left hand. That's what everyone else would see, anyway.

He noted the catch in her breath. The curve of her heart-shaped face and the bow of her upper lip. The sprinkling of freckles across her nose and the tops of her cheeks. And those eyes. Always those guileless eyes.

"Punctual. That's a nice surprise." Her cheeks flushed by the time she finished speaking, and her gaze wandered away until it landed near her feet.

Oddly, this aroused him. Good God, would *he* start blushing next?

Chapter Five

Focus, Claire. For Pete's sake, get it together.

But this was new territory. Logan had never been to her home—not as an adult. He'd been to her parents' house back in the days when she and the Lockwoods and Prescotts had all run around together. It didn't help to admit that she hadn't gained much confidence around him since then, or that she couldn't speak at the moment because her mouth felt like she'd just devoured a box of saltines.

Black jeans hugged his thighs, while a purple dress shirt spruced up the gray T-shirt underneath. The thick tread of his funky black ankle boots squeaked against the porch planks as he tried to knock the snow free. He looked exactly how she'd picture him dressed for a date, so he had to have plans after their meeting. A pinprick of jealousy pierced her stomach, spoiling the moment.

This girlish infatuation should fade now that they were both adults and working together. In no time at all, he'd go from being that unattainable boy of her childhood fantasies to a regular guy—one with flaws, like all the rest. "Come on in."

"Thanks." He wedged himself between her and the doorframe, brushing against her on his way inside, then patted her shoulder like she was some preppy elfin bouncer. "Sorry."

"No problem." Miraculously, she hadn't melted into a puddle even though her insides turned to liquid in his presence. The brief contact made her body hum, raising another threat to keeping upright.

She leaned on Rosie and fought the urge to tug at her sweater, which she'd worn to appear nonchalant. It had taken four attempts to find an outfit that complemented her coloring without being an obvious attempt to look pretty.

She held her breath while Logan glanced around her living room, his gaze resting on a pillow, then a frame, and then the potted African violets lining the window. She'd bought them and the oxalis after Steffi moved out so other living things could fill the house.

"Another home run, Claire." When he smiled, she blinked as if looking straight at the sun. She missed the halo of long golden locks that used to frame his face. This edgy new look didn't quite match his personality, especially not the tender reason why he'd cut it. "Now I'm more excited to see how you'll transform my place."

"Thank you for the opportunity." Her gaze fell while she screwed up the courage to apologize for her prior behavior. "I know I wasn't exactly gracious when you offered me this job."

"That's one way to put it." He grinned.

Another bloom of heat filled her face. "It wasn't that I didn't appreciate the compliment. I just . . . well . . . issues."

He waved away her apology. "Believe it or not, I understand. I never meant to be cavalier about what happened with Todd. And if I didn't make it clear, I am very sorry that you got hurt. You certainly didn't deserve that."

He stood still, head tipped, a soft expression on his face. She believed his sincerity, which soothed her raw defenses like aloe.

"Thank you." At least that part was over. She would act normal now, although nothing about this situation came close to *her* normal. Any time spent alone with Logan in the past had mostly been a happy accident. To have him choose to spend time with her—to collaborate on redecorating his home—made her feel like the floor beneath her had fallen away.

He raised a manila envelope into the air. "Shall we get started?"

She shot her hand out, eager for a change of subject, and for a peek at his home. Finally, some detail about an intimate part of his life. A place where he kicked off his shoes, cooked for himself, slept . . .

"Good idea," she stuttered, having mentally tripped over the image of his naked torso entwined with linens and pillows.

"You seem tense." He tilted his head. "How about we open some wine?"

"Oh, uh . . ." *It's not a date, Claire. Not. A. Date.* "I didn't . . . I mean . . . sure, I think I've got a bottle."

"Just one?" he teased.

She made bug-eyes before realizing that he was joking. "Come to the kitchen."

She could feel him slowing his stride behind her to accommodate her much shorter legs and limp, so she sped up, which emphasized her off-kilter gait. Far from the runway strut of the women he hung out with most days.

When they got to the kitchen, he took a seat at the breakfast bar while she uncorked a bottle of cabernet and poured him a glass.

With an impish grin, he tucked his chin and looked at her through his thick lashes. "I don't drink alone."

"Oh, all right." She poured a little for herself, paused, then added more.

"To the beginning of a productive partnership." He raised his glass to clink against hers.

Wine with Logan. Another first. Not quite the romantic dinners she used to pretend they'd share, but an evening alone. No Lockwoods, no Peyton.

No buffers.

When she didn't say anything, he added, "And to getting to know each other again through this endeavor. I usually work with writers, so it'll be a welcome change to work with someone else with a visual artistic bent."

She gulped more than half her glass while reminding herself that, despite the flirtatious twinkle in his eye, he hadn't come here for romance. And, even if, by some miracle, he had *any* interest in her after a lifetime of *not* noticing her, it would be moot. She couldn't be with any man whose beloved sister was her mortal enemy. A tad overstated, but basically the facts. Prescott family dinners were not in her future. Period.

"So let me see what you've brought." She ambled toward the dining table. "Come spread it out here, where I've got my laptop and notebook."

He complied, unfolding a printed copy of his unit's floor plan for her and then arranging the two dozen photographs he'd printed, obviously taken when he'd been entertaining friends. Beautiful and exotic-looking men and women in small clusters, talking, drinking, laughing . . . living. The images monopolized Claire's attention. She sat beside him, leaning forward to study each photograph before moving on to the floor plan.

"There are a lot of windows, but you've taken these all at night with artificial lighting. I can't really tell how the sun hits the space. Do other buildings or balconies block the light?" She turned to face him and hitched a breath when she realized how close their faces were. Close enough to kiss.

She hesitated there, mesmerized. At this short distance, he would see every bit of panic in her eyes.

"Maybe you should come see for yourself." He reached out, then retreated and balled his hand on his thigh.

Claire shifted backward to avoid touching him. "I told you already, I'm not going to New York." Even as she said the words, she suspected he didn't believe her. "And just to be clear, this"—she gestured between them and the photographs—"is separate from whatever I do or don't do with Peyton. So please don't try to inflict guilt."

"Claire, even if I wanted to make you feel guilty—which I don't— how could I? You've never hurt a soul."

She narrowed her eyes. "I know you want me to talk to your sister."

"I'd love that, but I don't want you to feel *guilty*. Feel compassion, maybe. Take the high road. Turn the other cheek. Forgive and forget . . . I don't know." He flashed a melancholy smile. "I'm sure there are a bunch of sayings that fit the bill."

"Look at me, Logan." No matter how blotchy her neck and face had to be right then, she meant for him to understand that she was as serious now as when she'd been determined to walk again. "I'll never, *ever* forget."

They stared at each other in silence until Logan reached for her hand. He kept his eyes on hers as he pressed her knuckles to his cheek. She bit the inside of hers as heat flooded every inch of her body.

"I hear you," he said. "I'll try not to push—not about Peyton, and not about New York."

"Thank you." Claire withdrew her hand and curled it against her chest, focusing on breathing steadily. Their conversation had veered into unprofessional territory. Boundaries needed to be maintained, or she'd lose her head and her heart. She flipped her notebook open and clicked the top of a ballpoint pen. "So let's talk about your tastes."

His brows shot up. "I thought I hired you for *your* taste."

"To a point, yes, but your home has to reflect your personality, not mine." *We're not a couple, after all.*

"I'm curious about your instincts. What do you see for me?"

For an artist, his lack of particularity about his home shocked her. Then again, from what she'd heard throughout the years, he'd spent little time there until Peyton got sick. He'd always been running. Away from his dad? Toward a destiny? Perhaps both? She wasn't sure. She also wasn't sure if he knew that answer.

"I'm not sure." As a teen he'd been fun-loving—an adventurer, a boy with a keen eye for detail and a unique way of seeing things. Everything she knew of him more recently came from the stories she'd hear and from brief encounters whenever he'd visit his parents, which wasn't often. "Your adult life is something I know only from a distance. I've no idea what makes you feel comfortable."

"Hang on." He grimaced and shifted his weight while holding up a finger and tugging his phone out of his pocket. "Hey, Karina, I'm in a meeting. Can this wait until a little later?"

Karina must be the woman he'd dressed up to impress. A new girlfriend, or had they been dating for a while? One of the tall, willowy women in the photos, with long, strong legs and no cane? Claire forced a smile to cover the intense envy that soured her stomach.

"Maybe. We'll discuss it more when we meet up." He nodded with a grin. "Promise."

More silence. Did Karina have a smoky or feminine voice? Whatever the tone, Claire doubted Karina stuttered around Logan like *she* did. She chugged her wine, causing Logan's expression to shift, his wide eyes now resembling jade medallions.

"You too. Bye." He shoved the phone in his back pocket. "Sorry."

Her cheeks prickled as she struggled to recall what they'd been discussing before her mind had wandered.

"So you were asking me what makes me comfortable." He rubbed his chin with a shrug. "I like what you did for Steffi and Ryan, and what you've done here. Something homey."

"But your work is bold and intense, like your clothes." She crossed her arms. Her one big regret about her self-imposed travel ban was that she'd never been to one of his gallery openings. She'd only ever seen his work online or in magazines. She sifted through his apartment photos again. "You chose Chelsea as a home base, not New England. Even these pictures show somewhat industrial interiors and stark furnishings. The modern kitchen and this bit of exposed ductwork bear out my assumptions. Same with the huge plateglass windows."

"I bought this at twenty-three when I was trying to break free of my parents' influence. Fit in with the whole artsy city vibe." He snickered at himself. "That furniture . . . Cassie picked it, and I just never got around to changing it."

"Was Cassie a designer?" She hoped her voice hadn't sounded as skeptical as she felt, but if Cassie *was* a designer, she was mediocre at best.

"No. A . . . friend."

"Like me?"

"No, not like you." His eyes flickered. "A friend with benefits."

Claire suspected she now resembled a tomato. Something low in her core pooled with warmth. "Benefits," he'd said with that soft-as-silk voice. Benefits like touching and kissing and . . .

Lord. If she ended up envying all the women who'd enjoyed Logan's benefits, she'd hate a good portion of the female population. Then again, the names Cassie and Karina indicated a preference for a hard *c* sound. Just like "Claire."

She stifled a snigger, then got back to business, holding out one image that showed black and gray shadows or something on a wall in his bedroom. "What's this?"

He smirked. "Body paint."

"What?"

"An artist friend and I got a little wild one night. She wanted to leave an imprint on my room. See the handprint there . . . the foot . . . I think that there might be a breast mark . . ."

Claire clamped her open mouth shut as she tried to imagine leaving an impression of her breasts on any man's wall. "I assume she's another friend with benefits, yet you kept this here for how long?"

"Two years, maybe. Who remembers? I like it. It was spontaneous and sexy. A vivid memory. Why would I want to paint over it?"

"So this stays—in the new design, I mean?"

"Sure."

She frowned. "Don't other women get offended?"

"Why would they?" He dipped his head, his voice teasing her. "They know I'm not a virgin."

Everyone knew that, because Kelsey Dewitt had announced it after their junior prom. Claire could still feel that sting. "I don't think I'd like sleeping in the shadow of my boyfriend's former lover's body parts."

"Well, you're more conventional than most of the women I know." He stared into his glass, brows pulled together, before polishing it off. "But you have a point. I suppose I could part with it. It's just paint. I still have the memory."

She stared at him, trying to read the lines forming between his brows. "Why do you suddenly want a 'homey' place?"

It took him a few seconds to meet her gaze.

"I'm almost thirty-two, and I've never lived in a real home." Before she could mask her surprise, he held up his hand. "I know—boo-hoo, right? But I grew up in one kind of museum and now live in another. For once, it might be nice to come home and have it feel like a place I want to hang out. A place I can just be."

"Oh." His plea sounded lonesome, and she knew something about that. It's why she talked to her plants all the time. She wanted to hug Logan and commiserate, even though she could hardly imagine someone like him being lonely. He wouldn't lie, though, which made it even more critical that she create a cozy yet trendy home befitting him. "Well, then, I'm sure I can give you what you need."

He tipped his head, wearing an expression she didn't recognize, and covered her hand again. "I'm pretty sure you can, too."

Claire's heart bounded ahead of her brain, thumping like a rabbit's foot. She didn't want to read into those words, or into the way he was staring at her now, almost as if he hadn't seen her for years . . . as if he'd never really seen her before now.

Logan withdrew his hand and poured himself a second glass of wine. The room was too warm, his throat too dry. He didn't know why he'd confessed those things to Claire, but now he was picturing her covered in paint.

Not that she would figure that out. Once she'd started to study the architectural plans, he became as interesting to her as the chair he sat on. She focused on them so intently he could practically hear her thinking. Her sharp, earnest, determined mind at its problem-solving best. But even better yet, the way she leaned in to get that close look let him examine her soft skin, the perfect curve of her skull, and the rounded tip of her chin. He'd never before paid attention to Claire's body—other than noticing her limp, of course. Now he noticed and responded in a way he didn't expect or particularly know how to handle.

His scalp and the back of his neck tingled with hyperawareness. The floral scent of her soap awakened him like smelling salts passed beneath his nose. He held his breath for a second when she tucked her hair behind her ear and traced the lines of his apartment walls with her delicate pointer finger. What would that featherlight touch feel like on his chest or lower on his abdomen?

He blinked, snapping himself back to the business at hand.

"You used to love green. Is that still a favorite, or do you like bolder colors like the purple you're wearing?" Claire opened her laptop and pulled up a bunch of Pinterest boards.

Hundreds of them, all labeled.

Living Rooms—traditional—cream and taupe.

Living Rooms—transitional—cream and taupe.

Living Rooms—modern—cream and taupe.

Living rooms—art deco—cream and taupe.

Living rooms—rustic—cream and taupe.

And that was just the beginning of the cream-and-taupe combos. She repeated those categories with earth tones, jewel tones, European, antique, and on and on.

He couldn't believe it. Then again, she had worked in this business for a decade. "Did you do all of these spaces?"

"If I had, I wouldn't need your money," she teased. "I've collected these images and grouped them together by palette and style so I can get a quick impression of a client's tastes." She pushed the screen closer to him. "Scroll through them and tell me which boards appeal or, conversely, which you hate."

In his work, he hungered for bold color contrast and plays of light and shadow. In his living space, he wasn't sure. He eliminated every board featuring ultramodern furniture. Rustic styles held some appeal, but not for everyday decor. In the end, he kept circling back to the "transitional/wine" board—bold yet warm—and furniture that looked comfortable but simple. Nothing fussy. No tassels or fringes or nailhead trim. "I like this."

"Do you?" She smiled like she knew a secret.

A secret he wanted to know. Worse, he wanted to know *her* secrets. "Why do you suddenly look like I handed you a diamond ring?"

She exited the page, her cheeks glowing as red as a hot kiln. "I do not."

"Yeah, you kinda do. Did I pick a girlie board or something?"

"No." She cleared her throat. "These images are rich without being feminine. The style works for a single person or a couple."

"Good to know my 'someday wife' will approve."

Claire's expression froze, her smile fading a touch.

"She should. It's what I would've picked for you, in any case." She turned away and gathered his photographs and drawings. "Let me play around with these for a bit and come up with a general plan, then we can meet again to go over that. In the interim, feel free to send me images you like. Artwork or lamps or whatever. Sound good?"

"Sure." He took a sip of his wine and relaxed into his seat.

She cocked her head, brows pinched in confusion. "I've got nothing more for you at the moment."

The challenge of holding her attention made him dig in. "Are you kicking me out before we finish the wine?"

"Oh?" She twirled a hank of hair in her finger, reverting to the tongue-tied Claire of their youth. "Don't you have to meet your girlfriend?"

He leaned forward. "Girlfriend?"

"The woman who called earlier." Claire smoothed her hand over the envelope of photographs. "Karina?"

Another former friend with benefits, not that Claire needed to know that. He'd already told her too much about his sex life, and none of it had impressed her. He shook his head. "A—she's a colleague. B—we're meeting later next week."

"I thought you worked alone."

"Not always. Karina's a journalist who wants to team up on a new project." She was passionate about shining a light on people in crisis. She'd dragged him to the Caribbean islands, including her parents' homeland, Puerto Rico, months ago to interview and photograph hurricane victims and tell their stories. It'd been timely but lacked an essential element that would make it a standout piece in a sea of similar reports.

"You sounded excited to catch up."

"Honestly, I've stepped away from big projects these past few months while caring for Peyton and taking her to chemo, so I'm ready to do something for myself again. But the timing isn't perfect . . ." They'd have to agree on an idea and conduct research before he'd know if any project called to him in that important way he needed.

Claire fell quiet. Her jaw looked tight, her body stiff, as if bracing for an attack. He'd momentarily forgotten about her aversion to all things Peyton or he wouldn't have brought her up.

Rosie sat propped up against a chair, serving as a reminder of Ben Lockwood's lecture. Logan had promised not to push her toward forgiveness, but she couldn't expect him to never mention Peyton's name in *any* context. "You're mad that I mentioned my sister."

"No."

"What, then?"

"I was just thinking that she's very lucky to have you." Claire glanced at his hair. "You've sacrificed a lot to help her. I hope she appreciates it."

He ran his hand over his head, which still felt so strange. "Looks weird, huh?"

"Not weird. Different. You haven't had short hair since you were thirteen. Even then, it wasn't this short." She reached out, but drew her hand back. "Sorry."

He tipped his head toward her, wanting to feel her hands on his scalp. "Go ahead. It feels like a brush."

She stroked her palm across his head twice, softly playing with the short strands. Goose bumps raced down his neck and spine. If she were any other woman, he'd grab her wrist and pull her in for a kiss. If she were any other woman, she'd want him to, too.

She teased, "You're right. Thick and bristly. Maybe you should use this to paint another wall in your room."

He scanned her eyes but saw no clear invitation in them. He couldn't afford to make a misstep now, no matter how strongly the sudden sexual impulse struck.

"It'll be a year or more before I look normal again." He smirked. Truthfully, he missed his hair a lot more than he would've anticipated. It had been part of his armor as well as a tool of seduction.

"Eighteen months at least." She smiled. "Of course, your dad must think this is the first time you've looked 'normal' in years."

Logan laughed. "You're right about that."

"How *are* your parents?"

He could never answer that question without feeling a slight twist in his stomach. He supposed his parents were happy together. They didn't argue much. They seemed to value the same kinds of things—appearances, ambition, power. They weren't bad parents; they just weren't warm or nurturing.

They had visited Peyton weekly during chemo but hadn't doted on her as many other parents might've under the circumstances. Even now, with Peyton under the same roof, his parents hadn't rearranged their schedules much to assist her.

"Distant" would be the best word to describe them. He'd never really known them—and probably never would. He didn't care so much at this point, although, in a sense, even that fact made him sad.

"The same," he finally answered her question. "He's buying hotels. Mom's planning the fund-raiser."

"Hotels? I thought your dad's company focused on residential developments and apartments."

"It does, mostly. Not sure why the sudden change. Actually, I take that back. Ego. He couldn't resist sticking the Prescott name on seaside hotels. Now we can profit off people's vacations, too." Logan didn't like the sneer in his voice. He could even admit to the hypocrisy of enjoying his trust fund while deriding the company that contributed to its account. "It's a string of boutique inns. I suspect they're on the shabby side, so he'll need to renovate them."

Claire's eyes lit even as she sighed. "Fun project."

Another potential hook. "You should pitch him for that job. It'd make my fee seem meager."

She shook her head. "I won't be asking your dad for a job in this lifetime."

"Just because he and I don't get along doesn't mean you shouldn't use him to grow your company."

"It's not that, although I've never liked the way he's always tried to change you."

He hid behind another gulp of wine. "It's embarrassing to know that you picked up on that."

She shrugged apologetically. "I'm observant, and Peyton shared stuff with us. Don't forget, we were in your house a lot."

"I remember. Three hellions with ponytails." He recalled a young Claire, fresh from tennis practice, racing in to join Peyton and Steffi in the sunroom for their scrapbooking, or whatever the hell they were doing with that big quilted binder they'd lugged around. "You're probably wise to steer clear of my dad. He's a ballbuster."

She bristled. "I can take whatever he dishes out."

"I know exactly how tough you are. I spent plenty of time at your house while you recovered." Claire's parents had been the opposite of his. Warm, welcoming, full of smiles and affection. Maybe if he'd grown up in that type of environment, he wouldn't have been as eager to escape home.

"Yes, Peyton dragged you over all the time." Claire raised her hand to cover her eyes.

"She never had to drag me. I liked checking in on you." He drew her hand away from her face. "You inspired me."

"Did I?" She looked dumbfounded by the idea.

"Hell yeah. A person no bigger than a minute making such a big comeback, always with a determined expression. I wish I'd taken photographs of you then."

"God, no! I'm at least two heads shorter and way less photogenic than your former subjects." She waved both hands in front of her face while referring to his early days as a fashion photographer.

"You're much prettier than any of them—they're all false eyelashes, egos, and bored expressions. Your face is complex. Your eyes emote before you have a chance to filter your reactions. And the shape from your forehead to the tip of your chin forms a perfect heart." His thumb itched to trace that line.

She blushed furiously. "Well, I'm glad there aren't photos of those days. No need to remember that time in vivid detail."

"I disagree. If I had pictures, you'd see how beautifully single-minded and optimistic you were. How brave." Logan recalled with crystal clarity her stubborn, quick smile . . . even the way she'd mourned tennis had been dignified. She'd donated all her clothing and gear to kids training for the Special Olympics and often gone to the local tennis center to offer younger kids tips from the sidelines. "Frankly, having watched you come through that with such strength, and seeing you take a leap of faith with this new business venture, I'm shocked that you let the Todd thing drag at you. Of all the people on the planet, he's the least worthy of your tears or regrets."

The shooting had killed some of her confidence, and Todd's rejection had killed more. Logan wanted to bring it all back to life now.

"I'm over *Todd*, Logan." Ice encased that vehement tone. She cocked one brow. "Trust me, I'm not wasting tears on him."

"Just Peyton, then."

Claire crossed her arms. "You know I don't want to talk about this."

"I'm only trying to understand you, not defend Peyton."

"It's quite simple. I loved Peyton like a sister. Her betrayal hurt me much more than Todd did. Think about how you'd feel if she betrayed you, and then it should be easy to understand me."

Logan rested his chin on his fist and tried to imagine Peyton screwing him over. "I honestly can't imagine that. But if she ever hurt me, I know I'd find a way to forgive her. That's what family does. That's what love is, isn't it?"

"Is it?" Claire shot him a perturbed look. "Then why can't you get along with your dad? He's been demanding and, at times, demeaning, but he's never *betrayed* you. Still, you hold on to bitterness."

"That's different." He closed his hands around the wineglass, the muscles in his forearms tightening.

"Only to you because you're not ready to make peace. That's how it is for me with Peyton."

They stared at each other for a few seconds before he quickly finished his wine *and* what remained of hers. "You're right. So maybe we both need to take a hard look in the mirror, then, and be willing to turn the page and start fresh."

"I'd never trust her again." Claire's voice didn't even sound angry. Just final. Emotion he could work with, but flatness? Finality? Maybe this battle would be harder than he'd thought.

"You could at least let her apologize. How hard can that be?" He knew he'd made another misstep with his abrupt tone.

Claire blew a long, slow breath through her nose and pushed the envelope in front of him. "As much as I'd *love* to do this project, this conversation is exactly why I originally declined."

Shit. He grabbed her hand. "I'll stop. I swear. I'm done. I want you to do this work. Please."

He kept hold of her hand. Not because he wanted to help his sister, but because he wanted Claire's imprint on his home.

"You already made and then broke that promise." She withdrew her hand.

"Sorry. I mean it. I won't ask again."

The skeptical look in her eyes had him planning out another argument, but eventually she relented. "Okay. I'll call you later this week to talk about my ideas."

"Sounds like you're kicking me out." He pushed his chair back and stood.

She rose with him. "It's been a long day. I want to dig into this while I've still got some energy left."

"Fair enough." He leaned forward to kiss her cheek goodbye, but she moved at the same time, and so their lips met. A quick buss, but it brought back an old memory.

"Well, we haven't done that since you were fifteen, Claire. I think I did a better job back then, though," he teased, his lips warming at the thought of it.

She turned so red her face almost matched the color of his shirt. She gripped Rosie and started toward the front door without meeting his gaze. "I can't remember."

Liar, liar. Now he had another goal, though. That first kiss had been to fulfill the wish of a sad friend. This one, an accident. Next time it would be on purpose. And it would be one she'd never forget.

Chapter Six

"Whatever else happens, you must be happy that Logan's project brings us one step closer to making retail space a reality." Steffi set aside the photos of Logan's apartment that Claire had already memorized. "I'm meeting with building-supply companies this week to get us added to the lists they hand to their customers who are looking for small contractors."

"Good idea." Claire had awakened this morning full of creative energy and confidence. Things would turn around for them now. She could feel success in her grasp, just like the rush she used to get after a great practice. "I'm starving. Let's grab a quick lunch."

"Oh." Steffi screwed up her face before stretching her arms along the tabletop. "Peyton called me this morning. She's feeling a little stronger today and wanted to get out of the house, so I agreed to meet her for lunch. Of course, you're welcome to join us." Her attempt at a smile resembled a wince.

"No thanks." Claire unclenched her jaw. She didn't have the right to demand loyalty, but it stung that Steffi wouldn't take a side—her side.

"I understand, but if you change your mind, we'll be at Thai Basil. I know how much you love its shrimp tom yum soup."

She did love that soup. Hearty and spicy, perfect for a cold March afternoon. But sitting across from Peyton would give her heartburn.

She shook her head. "Just as well. I've decided to take another run at Mrs. Brewster to push her into that master bathroom remodel.

The woman has no vision. She couldn't imagine what I was saying. If I sketch a little something and attach some photos, she might change her mind. It's worth a shot, anyhow."

"I like when you get into bulldog mode. Sounds like a good plan." Steffi rose from her chair.

They hugged goodbye before Steffi strolled out of the house they'd shared for nine months. When she left, Claire slouched against the arm of the sofa. The cozy living room looked like something straight out of *House Beautiful* magazine. Comfortable. Welcoming. The kind of environment Logan claimed to want for himself.

This rental had been a place she'd enjoyed coming home to when Steffi lived here, too. A place filled with warmth and love.

But now she saw through the illusion of her own design and knew a truth that Logan would learn only after she'd redecorated his home. No furnishings, drapes, or artwork could infuse a home with genuine comfort. Only the love inside the four walls could do that for people. Until she—and he—found someone to share their spaces with, their homes might always feel a little bit empty and cold. The choices they were both making lately suggested they'd better keep space heaters handy.

An hour later, she saved her drawings for Mrs. Brewster in a working folder. Her stomach grumbled, prompting her to go to the kitchen and check her refrigerator. As she suspected, her options consisted of condiments, milk, and leftover cheesecake. Nothing hearty and satisfying. Nothing healthy.

She opened the pantry door but could hardly get excited about Ritz Crackers and peanut butter. Not after Steffi had put the idea of that soup in her head. Steffi, who was probably sitting down with Peyton at this moment.

Logan's plea nudged Claire again. What she deemed healthy avoidance, others might view as her cowering from Peyton, and that didn't sit well. Even sweet old Pat had sounded fed up with Claire holding on to her grudge. *"Thank Peyton,"* she'd said about Todd. That idea still made Claire huff. However, facing Peyton in public would put an end to the whispers taking place all around her. And she'd get her soup.

She grabbed her keys and coat and went to her car, pumping herself up for what could devolve into an ugly situation. When she arrived in town, she parked a block from the restaurant. She stared at the window boxes filled with silk ivy and ruby-red geraniums while calling in a takeout order, which would provide her an excuse to leave after ten minutes. Plenty of time for Peyton to apologize, yet not enough time to turn the event into an episode of *The Jerry Springer Show*.

While it might be unfair to spring herself on Peyton, fairness wasn't her concern. After all, Peyton had been less than fair with her.

She heaved a sigh and got out of her car. Heavy, clumsy feet made the two hundred yards to the door seem like a ten-mile hike. Her shortness of breath only made it worse. The anxiety attack annoyed her. This was *her* home turf, after all. She inhaled cold air and held her breath, then blew it out, slow and steady, before throwing back her shoulders and opening the door.

The divine aroma of coconut, seafood, and spice stirred her hunger. Lawana, the owner's daughter, greeted her.

"Your order's not ready yet, Claire." Her rich skin and dark eyes always made Claire feel plain and pale. Logan would probably love to photograph Lawana, with her lush mouth and inky hair. Imagine what her ponytail could paint on his walls!

"That's fine. I'm not in a rush." Claire smiled, remembering why she'd come and wondering if Steffi and Peyton were behind her at a table. If so, had they seen her? Every hair on her body vibrated. "Let's get the bill out of the way."

She signed the credit card receipt, then slowly turned and glanced around the room. She spied Steffi and Peyton in the corner.

Steffi saw her first, her eyes widening in shock. Peyton looked in Claire's direction and set down her chopsticks before wiping her mouth and lowering her hands to her lap.

Claire shuffled toward the table, the heat in her cheeks nearly unbearable. Sweat formed on her back and scalp, but she refused to take off her coat or give the impression she'd be staying. She hadn't thought to check to see if anyone else who knew them was watching. She hoped so, only because then the whispered dialogue would finally shift away from "poor Claire" commentary.

"Hello." She cleared her throat while coming to a stop behind an empty chair. She nodded at Steffi before facing Peyton, wishing she'd prepared a speech. Extemporizing wasn't her strength. "I'm sure you know that I'm working with Logan now. You're lucky to have such a thoughtful brother."

"I know." Peyton's thin, ruddy skin looked dry and raw. She tugged at her head scarf and then at her cardigan. "He's the best."

Peyton's apparent shame and fragility twisted through Claire's indignation, loosening the knots that kept her trussed up in anger.

"He's asked me to let you apologize. While I don't like being pressured, I also can't, in good conscience, accept his money while simultaneously denying him something he wants so badly. So I'm here to listen, if that's what you want, of course."

"It is." Peyton darted a look at Steffi.

"I'm going to the ladies' room." Steffi rose from the table and patted Claire's shoulder before she gave them some privacy.

"Do you want to sit?" Peyton gestured to the empty chair.

"No." Claire remained safely behind the vacant seat. "I'm leaving as soon as my lunch is ready."

"Okay. I understand." Peyton drew a breath. "I told Logan not to interfere, but thank you for giving me the chance to tell you, in person, how very sorry I am. It was horribly wrong to hurt you that way.

"I've gone back through the years, remembering all the ways you were a good friend to me. Like when you went to bat for me when Mrs. Morton blamed me for tromping through her garden. Or how you sat with me, holding my hand for the longest two minutes of my life at twenty, and then celebrated the fact that I wasn't pregnant. How you encouraged me to pursue a writing career in spite of the fact that I knew I could never live up to my great-grandfather's legacy.

"I can't understand, let alone explain, why I did what I did, Claire. I justified it a hundred ways in the beginning. The way I first met Todd at the coffee shop before knowing that he was your Todd. How I then tried to ignore him once I realized the situation, but that only seemed to make us both more crazed. The way he convinced me we . . . well, it doesn't matter. Why I thought I could be happy going forward while knowing what I'd done to you I'll never know." Her voice cracked, so she paused to sip some hot tea. Claire hoped her face hadn't winced each time Todd's name had come up.

Peyton set the small cup down, eyes downcast, and spoke barely louder than a whisper. "Until then, I wouldn't have believed I was capable of hurting someone I loved. The fact that I'd convinced myself that I had a good excuse is not something I'll ever get over. I've hated myself for it, but I can't undo it or escape the truth of how selfish I was . . . I am." She then met Claire's gaze.

Claire struggled to maintain eye contact but wouldn't break away. She had to finish what she'd started and remain strong throughout.

Peyton continued, "I don't expect you to get over it, either. You have the right to all of your feelings. But please believe that I deeply regret what I did. If ever you're willing to let me be some small part of your life again, I would prove how much I value you. I've missed our friendship so much. I swear, I'd never hurt you again, and I'd do anything for the chance to rebuild your trust."

If only pretty words could erase pain and betrayal. If they could undo the damage and turn back time to the way things used to be, Claire would rejoice.

Warm tears swam in her eyes. Her throat grew thick and sore, her chest heavy. She couldn't pretend some part of her didn't miss Peyton—the Peyton from before the Todd debacle. The wild friend who'd always made Claire laugh. But the bigger part simply could not open up her heart to forgiveness. "I accept your apology."

Peyton broke into a teary smile and stood to hug her, but she stepped back.

"I accept the apology, Peyton, but I'm not ready to be friends. I might never be ready." Claire watched Peyton's contrite nod as she took her seat again and readjusted her head scarf. "I know that's not what you want to hear, but when I look at you, I see Judas. I don't know how to let you rebuild the bridge you burned. But I won't hate you, and I'm glad that you're recovering. I hope, when all is said and done, that you never have to go through another health scare."

"Claire!" called Lawana.

"You should get your food while it's hot." Peyton refolded her napkin across her lap. "Thanks for hearing me out."

"You're welcome." Claire glanced toward the bathroom. "Tell Steffi I'll speak with her later."

She turned and went to the hostess station to pick up her lunch, then left the restaurant without looking over her shoulder. She gulped for air as adrenaline ebbed. Thank God for Rosie or she might've stumbled all the way to her car. When she got there, she set the takeout bag on the passenger seat and buried her face in her hands.

She'd done it. She'd faced Peyton in public and let her apologize. She'd taken the one step Logan had asked. One that would make Steffi's life a little easier, too. Whether it would improve *hers* was up for debate.

She pulled away from the parking space, her finger pressing the dashboard screen restlessly in search of a decent song and settling for

DJ Mike D's remix of "Let It Go." The hot air blasting her face was suffocating. She blinked a dozen times in a useless effort to clear the image of Peyton's distraught face.

Her pointless attempts at comfort prompted a derisive laugh. No song, temperature, or spicy bowl of soup would restore her balance.

The problem with taking one step was that the momentum then pulled you to take another and another. Maybe one day she'd be able to take steps toward Peyton without feeling like a ginormous hypocrite, but not today.

Her stress level shot well past anything she could manage on her own. With a quick left-hand turn, she soon found herself in her parents' driveway. Hopefully, there'd be some cupcakes on hand for this crisis.

—⁘—

Logan sat in the breakfast room, with its view of the Sound, while selecting photos to go with a section of text Peyton had left for him to read. He took another swig of his midafternoon coffee, when his mother breezed into the kitchen.

Darla Prescott was a beautiful woman by anyone's standard. Elegant, even at sixty. Today, a random Tuesday when she had no plans to meet anyone, she wore her blonde hair in a French twist. Drop pearl-and-sapphire earrings twinkled in the sunlight, as did her gray-blue eyes. The good fortune of porcelain skin enabled her to resort to only the barest beauty treatments—a little Botox now and then—to keep the wrinkles at bay.

Her black slacks and cashmere sweater emphasized her height and slender build. A practiced smile always played at her lips. Still, Logan never knew if his mother was truly happy in her marriage, or if honoring the commitment was simply easier than giving up the trappings of Prescott life. In any case, his parents and many other longtime marrieds convinced him that commitment eventually sapped the excitement from a relationship and from life.

"Would you like some wine, Logan?" She retrieved a bottle of Malbec from the wine refrigerator, swiftly uncorked it, and poured herself a generous glass.

"No, thanks." He smiled at her, thinking, as always, that she would look more at home in a movie or magazine shoot than in a kitchen.

She swirled the wine a few times and took a deep whiff before sipping it. "I could use some help with the gala RSVPs."

God, no.

"Sorry, I'm busy with my own project." Even absent this excuse, he'd prefer torture to delving into the politics that drove the gala seating charts.

"Is what you're working on more important than our annual family fund-raiser?" She peered over his shoulder, setting one of her hands on his back.

All the muscles in his neck and shoulders tightened against the alien invasion. She was queen of the air-kiss, but he couldn't remember the last time his mother had touched him. What kind of son flinches at his own mother's affection? He waged these battles with himself all the time—was it he or she who had the problem?

"I think so," he finally replied. "It's Peyton's memoir."

Although it had started as a productive distraction for him and his sister, the project kept calling to him. It would be a story of the human condition, of suffering, of true beauty and gratitude. Those thoughts swirled around, but he hadn't quite honed the message or hook yet. He wanted to create something distinguished that didn't rely solely on the Prescott name.

His mother reached for one of the photos, her expression morphing from curiosity to displeasure. "Surely Peyton won't be putting *these* in a book."

He snatched it back. "She's planning to."

"For others to see?" she sputtered.

"Of course. We plan to donate fifty percent of the proceeds to cancer research."

Between Peyton's writing experience and the Prescott name, they hoped to secure an agent and, ultimately, a publishing contract. He and his sister both had healthy social media platforms, too, so that should help convince an editorial board that the book would sell.

When his mother scoffed, he frowned at her. "Your attitude surprises me. I'd assume the family would like the idea of a memoir—another literary fund-raiser, if you will."

"You assume wrong." His mom held her hand to her forehead like she was taking her temperature. "Why would she want people to see her like that? If you must be so crass as to air family dirty laundry, please use photos from when she's feeling better."

Dirty laundry. As if cancer were a scandal.

And yet another example of his parents' hypocrisy and feigned interest in literature and art. If they *truly* respected the arts, they'd applaud his career choice and support this memoir. But no. They merely hosted and attended celebrations to perpetuate Duck's legend so that they could bask in the glory of their last name.

"It's not a *Vogue* shoot, Mom. She's being courageous and showing other women struggling through this that they are still beautiful and strong. It's about what's on the *inside*, not about her hair or breasts." He scanned two of the images he'd taken at night in Rembrandt lighting, which had amplified his sister's inner glow despite her barren scalp.

His mother cast him a doubtful look. "Another one of our 'agree to disagree' moments, I suppose." She rubbed his head, tugging at his hair as if she could make it longer by pulling at it. "But I don't fault you for *this* supportive gesture. Your father is thrilled you lost the ponytail."

Peyton came in through the back door, humming, almost as if she'd known when to show up and prevent an argument. She unwrapped the pink wool scarf from her neck, draped it over a chair, then slung her winter coat over it. Her skin still looked ruddy, and her upper-body movement was slow and deliberate, but that should all recede in the coming weeks.

"What's with the powwow?" She looked at the table and rolled her eyes. "Oh, I see. The project."

"These pages are great, Peyton." Logan riffled through some diary entries, but his mother interrupted.

"Honey." She held Peyton by the chin. Touching two of her kids in one day . . . a new record. "You're very sweet to try to be an inspiration, but won't you regret sharing all of these images with the world? Once they're out there, you'll never be able to put this all behind you."

His mother's face lit with maternal concern. She really could have been quite successful onstage if she'd ever had any real interest in the arts.

Peyton tensed. "'All this' will never be behind me, Mom. My future involves many checkups and always wondering if a few mutant cells are attacking some other part of my body. I'll be aware of every little health hiccup for the rest of my life, however long or short that might be. If I can live with *that*, I suppose I can handle strangers I'll never meet seeing me look like a bald, boiled lobster."

Logan reached out to rub his sister's back, knowing she hadn't quite gotten comfortable with this idea. At least he could always count on her to defend his plans in the face of parental disapproval, though. "Attagirl."

"What can I say? I'm feeling optimistic today." She slid onto a seat beside him.

"What brought about this change?" he asked.

Peyton leaned forward with her elbow on the table and rested her chin in her hand. "I spoke with Claire."

"Really?" Their mother took another sip of wine, her concerned expression replaced by one of satisfaction. "How'd you manage that?"

"I didn't." Peyton smiled at him. "Logan did."

The look on his sister's face lifted his heart in a way he hadn't felt in all the months since she'd gotten sick. And yet an unexpected twinge tempered his joy. As much as he welcomed the first hint of light in his sister's eyes, he suspected that conversation had depleted Claire. Not that *she'd* let anyone see behind her stoicism.

"Logan did?" their mom asked. "I don't understand."

"Logan's hired Claire to redecorate his place in Chelsea and asked her to let me apologize. She didn't feel comfortable denying his request while taking his money."

When she put it that way, it sounded awful. A little too much like something his parents might do, frankly. He'd been a tad manipulative, but he'd acted in the best interest of *both* women.

"So it went well?" he asked, distracted by the idea he'd told himself only what he wanted to believe in order to get what he wanted.

Peyton shrugged. "She came to Thai Basil to get takeout and stopped by my table. She accepted my apology, but she's not ready to be friends."

"It's a start." Their mom tapped her fingernail against the wineglass, her mind already churning ahead. "Claire has always been a class act. It's nice that she did it in public. When others see you two speaking, it'll take some of the heat off you. Everyone loves the McKennas. The whole neighborhood defends and protects Claire because of her injury. Your affair with Todd really hurt the family name."

"Mom," Logan grumbled. "Not helpful."

"What? Can't we speak truths in this house?" She waved him away.

Truth. Was there such a thing, or did everyone view situations differently and derive their own truths? This was the kind of debate he'd enjoy with friends, but it would die right here on the kitchen floor if he posed that question to his mom.

She broke the silence. "Since no one wants to help me plan the gala, I'll slink back to my office to work alone while you two do *this*.

Before you shop this project outside these walls, we should have a family meeting and talk about the right kind of PR."

She blew them an air-kiss and strolled away, taking the bottle of wine with her.

Logan shook off the PR remark and turned to his sister. "I'm happy Claire forgave you. That's the first step."

"She didn't forgive me. She accepted my apology. But at least we looked each other in the eye and spoke for the first time in more than a year." She bumped shoulders with him. "Thanks for applying your charming-but-not-too-subtle pressure on her even though I asked you not to. Now I don't have to panic if I see her again. We can be civil, if nothing else."

Peyton might be satisfied, but he wanted more for her, and for Claire. He wanted to mend that relationship so neither of them felt pain anymore. They'd both suffered enough. Slinging his arm around her shoulders, he kissed her temple. "Anything for you."

She squeezed his hand before turning her attention to the pages. "So you think these don't suck? I still feel like I'm not finding the right voice for the project. Look here, how clinical and stiff."

"It's a bit stilted, but there are gems in here when you've let your guard down. When you edit, approach it all through that personal filter. Eliminate the distance. Don't be a narrator. Just be you."

She sighed and let her head fall back. "It's exhausting being me."

"Think about all the fun we'll have horrifying Mom and Dad by putting this out into the world." He smirked, which elicited her laughter.

"You're bad, Logan. Mom tries. She thinks what she's doing helps us, even if you don't agree. And you know I don't wholly disagree with her. It makes me nervous to think about other people seeing these images." She sighed, pulling the photos closer to study them. "Okay, let me see which go best with these pages."

While she sorted the pictures and read through his notes, he sat back and thought about his mom—about his family. He'd never understood why Peyton wasn't more bothered by their parents. Somehow she was able to accept them as they were and be happy enough. Why couldn't he?

If he didn't look so much like the rest of them, he'd swear he was adopted.

The rest of them enjoyed the public role of being a Prescott, while he yearned for something greater. He wanted to make a difference to something or someone before he died, and he wanted to do it on his own talent. It wasn't about money or family prestige; it was about leaving something of real value in his wake.

Then he thought of Claire. A strong yet softhearted woman who, unlike his family, had always remained rooted in things that truly mattered. Who valued courage and integrity over brand and image. Who, because of those values, forced herself to face Peyton for him.

He wanted to do something nice for her as a thank-you. Something selfless to help her reach her own goals and find happiness. He pulled up her website on his phone and scrolled through the gallery, shaking his head. Could he bring himself to do some architectural shoots for her, knowing his peers would frown on him if they found out?

That evening, Logan climbed Claire's porch steps and knocked on her door. If he'd called ahead, she would've put him off with a million excuses. Also, he would've been locked into coming. Until five minutes ago, he wasn't sure the benefit of this move outweighed the potential professional flak. Now he cracked his knuckles and tapped his toes, waiting for her to answer the door.

Within seconds, her eyes and forehead appeared through the windows near the top of the door. She must've risen onto her tiptoes. At the moment of eye contact, she dropped down, disappearing from view.

"Logan!" she croaked through the unopened door. "Why are you here? We didn't have an appointment, did we? I haven't finished the plans for your apartment yet."

He stared at the lemon-yellow door. "I stopped by to thank you."

"Thank me?" A silent pause ensued, broken only by the rumble of the car driving by behind him. "Oh. You spoke to Peyton."

Why was she hiding from him? "Can you open the door before we finish this conversation?"

Two seconds later, she wedged her body into the narrow crack she'd opened, her cheeks blazing like a fiery summer sun before it dips below the horizon. She clutched the neckline of her fuzzy pink robe with one hand, a king-size Snickers bar dangling from the other. Green snowflake slipper socks completed her ensemble. With a resigned shrug, she muttered, "Hi."

Everything about her appearance loosened all his muscles as if he'd just exhaled. If it wouldn't have shocked her, he might've lifted her off the ground and twirled her around. "Is that candy bar your way of dealing with the emotional fallout from Peyton's apology?"

She glanced away, sighing.

"Thank you, Claire. I know speaking with my sister wasn't easy, but I'm grateful. This afternoon is the first time in months that I've seen her look the least bit optimistic."

"Don't get too excited." She peered up at him somberly through her lashes. "I heard her out, but please don't expect more."

"I don't." Not yet, anyway. He clasped his hands behind his back and bowed slightly. "I'm actually here to do something for you."

She released her robe, gripping the edge of the door with her hand. "Why does that make my stomach drop?"

He shrugged. She might not quite know what to make of him, yet her eyes filled with curiosity. The intoxicating combination tempted him to prolong the conversation. "Invite me inside and I'll tell you my idea."

She closed her eyes, her chin dropped to her chest, then she looked up and waved him in. "Why not?"

He breezed past her and shrugged out of his coat, when he noticed the coffee table littered with empty junk-food wrappers and bags. "Jesus. Did you rob a convenience store?"

She crossed her arms, still clutching her half-eaten candy bar. "You said you came to do me a favor, not make fun of me."

"True." He spied some peanut M&M's. "May I have some?"

She hesitated, as if she couldn't spare them, although the amount of chocolate and sugar she'd already consumed would've put him in a coma. "I guess."

"Let's sit." He gestured toward the living room.

She chewed a hunk of the Snickers bar and plopped onto the sofa.

He sat beside her and palmed a few M&M's. When she wedged herself into the corner, he turned his body to face her. Her gaze dropped to his knee, which he'd planted two inches from hers.

"I browsed your website. The colors, fonts, and function work well, but the gallery photos . . . well, those look unprofessional, like you or Steffi used your iPhone and uploaded them."

"We did." She broke another chunk off the shrinking Snickers bar and popped it into her mouth, mumbling, "We're on a budget."

"I know, so let me retake those photos. Better lighting and angles—artfully framed architectural shots—will give your site more polish and reflect your professionalism. No need to announce your meager budget to the world with amateur photography."

That slight smile tugging at the corners of her lush mouth would taste like chocolate and caramel now.

"That's quite an offer, but it'll lead to more strings." She shook her head. "I don't want to feel obligated to deal with Peyton on a regular basis because you've helped me again. You don't owe me anything. I heard Peyton out because you hired me as a favor, so we're even."

She balled up the wrapper and tossed it onto the accumulating pile, then motioned for him to hand her some M&M's.

"I hired you because you're good at your job, not as a favor. Shooting your projects for free is my thank-you . . . no strings. Honestly, it'll give me something to do while I'm hanging out in town." When she seemed skeptical, he added, "I could use an excuse to get out of the house. Otherwise my mom will drag me into all the last-minute gala BS."

"God forbid you help her with that," she teased, popping a green M&M in her mouth.

He shifted his body, edging closer. Fuzzy robes weren't sexy, yet Claire's cozy pajamas lured him nearer, as if proximity would pass on her comfort by osmosis. "You think that sounds like fun?"

"Of course I do. People around here look forward to that party all year. It's a great cause *and* a chance to dress up."

"I suppose I never looked at it that way." The literacy fund-raiser was a snooze fest compared with his typical A-list parties in New York. But maybe there was more value in it than he'd ever wanted to acknowledge.

"You've probably never looked at a lot of things the way the rest of us do. You might have a love-hate relationship with your last name, but most people would kill for the doors it opens."

"You're seeing all the benefits and none of the downside. Trust me, when you've got my name, you're never sure whether people are just using you as a stepping-stone to some other goal."

Instead of mocking him, she regarded him with compassion. "That's sad."

Normally, Logan reflected only what he wanted people to see, but Claire's knowing gaze might as well have been a microscope lens. "It's the way of the world, I suppose. Guess I've become a cynic."

Her responding shallow smile proved she saw his retreat for what it was.

"Don't expect me to feel *too* sorry for you. The name, the money, the looks . . ." She blushed, twining the robe's sash around her fingers.

He watched her fingertips turning white. Still harboring that childhood crush on him? Sweet, but he wanted her to find him attractive for reasons other than his face now.

"And yet none of that has convinced you to take me up on my current offer." He stretched his arm along the back of the sofa, effectively surrounding her from the tip of his fingers to his knees, all of which itched to touch her.

"I don't even know if our clients would let us back into their homes." She hugged her knees to her chest, then popped two more pieces of candy in her mouth.

"Now there's where my name *will* come in handy." He flashed a playful grin. "What Sanctuary Sound resident wouldn't want Logan Prescott taking photographs of his or her home?"

She laughed so hard she almost choked. "You're bad, Logan."

He leaned close enough to smell something other than chocolate and peanuts. Something soft and light, like lilac. "I like you this way, Claire."

"What way?" One of her brows rose.

"This whole 'take no prisoners' attitude seasoned with an occasional wisecrack . . . it's diverting. Keeps me on my toes."

She narrowed her eyes. "Believe it or not, that's not my goal."

"Prove it. Accept my offer." A triumphant smile worked its way through his whole being. "Come on, you can be my assistant. It'll be fun."

"Can you even take those kinds of pictures? I thought you were a street photographer."

He scoffed, easing away. "It's much harder to capture great images in the moment than it is to stage them. Trust me, I can shoot a kitchen or a bathroom."

He wanted to do this with her. *Say yes.* When she pressed herself deeper into the cushions, he added, "Don't underestimate the value of a professional website for grabbing customers' attention and selling services."

Her head bobbed from side to side as if weighing the pros and cons of dealing with him more than she'd already agreed to. "I'll call our clients."

He released his breath in a whoosh. "They'll all say yes."

"All?" Her strawberry-blonde hair shimmered under the lamplight when she shook her head at him. Thick, silky hair that would feel great sliding through his fingers. "Now you're being cocky."

"Maybe." He smirked. "We could make a bet, unless you're a chicken."

She stared at his outstretched hand and bit her lip. When she clasped it, she did so with the healthy caution a snake handler does a python. "What do I get when you lose?"

He gazed into eyes as deep and blue as the Sound on a cloudless day, wanting to dive right in and not come up for air. "Whatever you want."

The flush rose up her neck like mercury in a thermometer. "How do you know I won't take advantage of you?"

"I'm not worried, because I'm sure I'll win." He broadened his grin, still holding on to her hand, wishing she'd use it to pull him into a kiss.

"How do I know you won't take advantage of *me*?" She raised one brow.

He squeezed her hand, refraining from tugging her to his chest. "You don't."

Chapter Seven

"The flowers gave these shots a nice punctuation." Logan placed his camera in its case and began disassembling the tripod. "Good call."

"Thanks." Claire dragged her gaze away from him to glance at the cut-glass vase she'd filled with fragrant white lilies, fuchsia snapdragons, bells of Ireland, and pink peonies. With an unintentional sigh, she said, "I love the romance of fresh-cut flowers."

He paused, flashing her a quick smile. "I meant that the pop of color is a great contrast against all this white tile and marble."

She turned away for a second, closing her eyes as if that would somehow erase the fact that she'd just blabbered about romance while he'd been focused on the work. Maybe she should mention that she'd picked an arrangement that also paired nicely with the "Brittany Blue" cabinets . . . not that he'd care about that.

In any case, the Duvalls' master bedroom and bathroom renovation might be one of Claire's favorite projects to date. Its massive glass shower stall, complete with a built-in bench seat and ledges for soap and shampoo, could easily fit two people. His-and-her vanities flanked opposite walls. And the giant white soaker tub situated in an alcove beneath a large arched window added a romantic old-world touch to the renovated room.

There it was again. Romance on the brain.

Spending the past hour in this intimate space with Logan had produced many fantasies. Heart-pounding, hot flash kinds of daydreams that forced her to fan herself whenever he wasn't looking. Not that she would've traded this afternoon for anything. Time alone with Logan would quickly become addictive if she didn't keep reminding herself that he had his own agenda and, soon enough, he'd be gone. Still, while he was here, she couldn't quite bring herself to push him away.

He snapped the bag shut and started to remove the scrim he'd put in the windows to diffuse the sunlight reflecting off the marble surfaces and mirrors. "Too bad we didn't have real movement in these frames, but without a human element, there wasn't much I could do about that."

The tension of stifled creativity rolled off him.

"Thank you for doing this for us, Logan. I'm grateful." More than grateful. After years of picturing him at work, her now bearing witness to him pacing the floor, considering angles, and setting up shots added new data to her mental dossier. Images she'd be able to revisit once she reached the safe space of her bedroom.

Before today, she'd always envisioned him working with more swagger, his formerly long hair falling across his brow, a half smirk of a smile as he chose his shots, flirty banter with anyone on the set. In reality, he'd focused on the task to the point where she'd felt invisible except for when he'd asked her if she had a preference for what to feature, or if she could move something from one place to another.

He snapped his fingers. "Earth to Claire."

"Oh, sorry!" She jerked to attention. "Just thinking about what to do with these."

She lifted the square vase off the vanity and dashed into the master bedroom, putting much-needed distance between herself and Logan before he caught on to her thoughts. She eyed the long dresser but then set the vase on the mirrored nightstand next to a romance novel. *Perfect.*

"Are you leaving those here?" Logan stood in the doorway between the bedroom and bathroom with his camera bag slung over his shoulder, the tripod case in his other hand, and a gentle smile on his face.

Another rush of warmth flooded her while she stared at him from beside the large bed, with its sumptuous silk bedding and thick down pillows, and tried not to imagine him standing there in nothing but a towel. "It's a little thank-you for letting us invade their home again."

His expression turned cocky. "I told you people would be happy to let me shoot their space." When he winked, she swallowed hard. "Don't think I've forgotten about our bet."

She cleared her throat. "I haven't heard back from the Wagners yet."

"I'm not worried."

"You should be. Mary isn't a big fan of having 'strangers' in her house."

"Still not worried." He strolled into the bedroom. "You can't deny that we make a great team. And seeing this space only makes me happier that I've hired you to redo my place. How 'bout we go grab lunch to reward ourselves for a job well done?"

Yes.

"No, thanks." When he winced, she elaborated. "I'm meeting my mother to make homemade mac and cheese and a cake for my gram. It's her birthday. She's eighty-eight."

"Mac and cheese?" He grinned.

Mac and cheese was no laughing matter in the McKenna house. "With ham and peas. Her favorite."

"Eighty-eight." He whistled. "That's some longevity."

"A by-product of close family ties," Claire blurted, a saying her mom repeated often.

In all the years she'd been friendly with Peyton and Logan, she'd never met their grandparents. The Prescott side had died before she moved to town, and their maternal grandparents had lived in California. "Do you miss your grandparents?"

"We saw my mom's parents only at the holidays, but they never stayed long. And it's no secret that my dad didn't respect his father. They couldn't even get along, so that was always uncomfortable."

"That's a shame, especially when there was so much to be thankful for and enjoy."

"Well, I don't miss what I never had. Prescott parent-child bonds aren't as tight as the McKennas'."

She tipped her head. "If you want to see eighty-eight, maybe try not to repeat that pattern."

He flattened his hand on his chest. "It's not my fault my dad's an ass."

"I bet your dad would say the same about his dad." She tucked her hands in her pockets. "Does it matter whose fault it is when it's your family? Break the cycle so that, someday, your kids will know something better."

Logan blinked at her as if she'd grown another nose. "Let's get rolling. I guess I'll go kayaking this afternoon."

She let the non sequitur pass without comment because panic took over. "It's only March, Logan. There's fresh snow on the ground."

"I know. No one else will be on the Sound. I can clear my head."

"Only because no one else is foolish enough to risk hypothermia. If something happens or you tip over, there won't be anyone there to help."

"It's clear skies and calm seas. I'll be fine skirting the coast." He started for the door.

"Now I'll worry all afternoon." She sighed while following him out of the room and down the stairs. "I wish you wouldn't go."

Before he could reply, Nancy met them at the bottom of the stairwell. Claire preferred tea, but the hazelnut coffee aroma coming from Nancy's cup piqued Claire's appetite.

"How'd it go?" Nancy asked.

"Once we update the website with these shots, you'll be sharing the links with all your friends. Even *Town & Country* will be envious." Logan bestowed her with one of his charming smiles, and Claire watched her preen.

"Claire and Steffi did a beautiful job, didn't they?" Nancy touched Logan's forearm. Claire couldn't blame her. He was a human magnet. "It's my sanctuary."

"Thank you," Claire said.

"Thank *you*," Nancy replied and opened the front door. "Have a wonderful day."

"You too," Logan answered as she ushered them outside.

"Bye!" Claire waved.

Before she knew what was happening, Logan shifted the tripod case to his other hand and took Claire by the arm as they made their way around the patches of ice clumped along the walkway. Typically she resisted being treated like an invalid, but the part of her that had always yearned for Logan's attention couldn't bring the rest of her to fight him off.

When they arrived at her car, he set down the long case and adjusted her knit scarf, his fingers brushing against her neck and sending tingles down her spine. "Enjoy your birthday party."

"Logan." She gripped his arm. "Please don't go kayaking."

"Don't be such a worrywart." A light breeze blew some of her hair across her face, but he brushed it away before she could. "I'll be fine."

"Why are you being so stubborn?" She scowled.

"Honestly?" He shrugged. "I don't want to go home. My mother's itching to drag me into the fund-raiser planning, and my father's working from home. I'm going a little stir-crazy in that house."

"So find something else to do. Something safe."

He grinned. "Like baking a cake."

"Well, no. You'd have to be at home to do that."

He crossed his arms. "Or at your mom's with you."

"Ha ha." Her heart thudded to a stop until she told herself he'd been joking.

"I'm serious."

She paused, resisting the search for candid cameramen waiting to embarrass her. "You do not want to spend your afternoon in my mom's kitchen."

"Why not?" He leaned against her car, staring into her eyes in a way that made her feel overexposed.

"You'd be bored out of your mind." Not a proud admission, but an honest one.

He winked, lowering his voice to a sultry tone. "I'm never bored around women and food, Claire."

The flare of heat in his eyes ignited something daring inside her until she doused it with reality.

"Be serious, please." She opened the driver's door and tossed her purse and Rosie onto the passenger seat.

Logan pushed off her car. "If you won't invite me to join you, then I guess it's back to kayaking."

She narrowed her eyes. "Is this another ploy?"

"Ploy?" He fixed an innocent expression on his face, but she knew that manipulative streak too well to be fooled.

"Yes, all this cozying up to me so you can convince me to befriend Peyton again."

"Do you see hidden agendas in *everything* I do?" He huffed. "Aren't *we* friends? Don't friends do things together?"

"We're friendly, but until recently, we'd never hung out without Peyton." Except that one time, when they'd kissed.

He shrugged, one hand turned outward. "That was then and this is now."

"Only because you want to influence me."

He hesitated, which confirmed her suspicions. "It's no secret that I'd love for you and my sister to mend fences, but it isn't the *only* reason I spend time with you. We're two creative single people in a small town full of seniors and young families. Let's make the most of it. Come on,

I'll only misbehave enough to make you laugh. Your mom won't mind. She's always liked me."

Everybody liked him. That was the problem.

His seeing her as a competent designer—win. Inviting him to her mom's house to bake, where he'd see the mundane details of her life? She suppressed a shudder. "You'll be bored."

"Weren't you listening earlier? I won't be bored." He patted his camera bag. "Maybe I'll even shoot you and your mom in action."

She stared at him, and he didn't look away. The icicles melting off nearby branches reminded her of the icy water she wanted him to avoid. "Fine, but don't say I didn't warn you."

—⁓—

Savory aromas from the ham and cheese blended with the sweet chocolaty scent of the cake in the oven. Arcadia's kitchen never smelled like this. Logan sat at the round oak table, stretching out his legs and observing the mother-daughter duo in action.

Back in the day, all the neighborhood boys had agreed that Mrs. McKenna was a milf. She wasn't sexy, per se, but she'd been chatty, and when she spoke with you, she gave her full attention. She had a gift for making others feel important, one Claire had in a subtler form. He hadn't made that connection until this afternoon.

"You're going to be too sick to eat with your grandmother." Logan watched Claire devour more kettle corn.

"I know my limits." She stuffed another fistful into her mouth. "Just be glad I shared the cake batter."

"Oh, I am." When he licked more off his finger, her gaze homed in on his mouth, making his body warm. His recent responses to Claire intrigued him. Why her? Why now? She had nothing in common with the women of his past. No edge or pretense. No daring clothes or extravagances. Claire didn't even flirt with him. Yet he wanted to engage her. To hear her astute observations. To make her smile.

Mrs. McKenna finished drying a pot and then came to sit at the table beside him. "Logan, I recently read Lynsey Addario's memoir and thought of you."

Lynsey Addario, a Pulitzer Prize–winning photographer from Connecticut and twelve years his senior. Envy niggled. He'd get there, too. Someday.

Mrs. McKenna added, "I saw the *Time* magazine piece you shot in Puerto Rico after Hurricane Maria. That must've been sad and frightening, but you have a gift for capturing people's emotions. Still, I hope whatever you're working on now is less dangerous."

"Well, my mother's wrath might be worse than Maria," he joked, although Hurricane Maria was no joking matter.

Mrs. McKenna chuckled dismissively. "Darla is a dear. I can't imagine her having wrath."

A dear? He'd never heard his mother described as such. Clever, ambitious, even gregarious. But dear?

"What's the project that's upsetting your mom?" Claire set aside the nearly empty bag of junk food and leaned forward.

Both women ceded him the floor, turning their giant blue gazes on him. Saying the *P*-word aloud in the McKenna house might be akin to blasphemy, but it could also give him a chance to cast Peyton in a new light.

"When Peyton got diagnosed, I suggested we document her journey with photos and journal entries. We didn't know if she'd survive, or what the project would turn into, but I thought the process would be cathartic. Once we got started and began discussing a memoir, we also decided to make it philanthropic. If we see it through to publication, we plan to donate a large chunk of any proceeds to cancer research."

Mrs. McKenna cast Claire a hesitant glance before looking at him. "That's a remarkable undertaking. Why would it anger your mother?"

"The photographs of Peyton's experience—the hair loss, mastectomies, and skin discoloration, the pain and terror—are graphic. My mom's uncomfortable with them. She thinks they're unflattering . . . embarrassing, even."

"Peyton let you take them?" Claire held still.

"Reluctantly at times, but she pushed through because she sees the potential value. The question of what makes us beautiful—our faces or our resilience—is compelling and relatable. If we pull this off, something positive will come out of the whole ordeal."

"She's always been very proud of her appearance . . ." Claire set her chin and gazed out the sliding glass door. "The photo shoots must be hard for her."

"I'm sure it's not easy coming to terms with physical changes, but you know that already." He waited for her to face him again, holding his breath.

Mrs. McKenna blew out a quick breath.

"Well, as a mom, I can tell you that nothing was more painful than watching my baby suffer. Darla's probably having a visceral response to seeing Peyton's pain preserved. In time, maybe she'll see the project's value." Mrs. McKenna patted his hand.

"How many photos would be in the memoir?" Claire asked, her voice tinged with dismay.

"Not sure. Honestly, lately I've been getting an itch to use some of the images in a multimedia project. Peyton could record some of the passages, and I'd incorporate other memorabilia like pill bottles and parking stubs and receipts—you know, comparing the emotional 'cost' of medical treatment with the financial cost kind of concept. We lacked focus in the beginning, so we're both struggling to give it the right voice now."

"Peyton could always write well. Her travelogues were vivid. Your combined creative talent should produce something special." Claire clasped her hands together tightly on the table.

"Your support must've been very comforting to Peyton. She's lucky to have you." Mrs. McKenna offered a proud smile. "When this is finished, what are your plans?"

"Not exactly sure, but it needs to be big because I've been out of the game for too long. Politics have been wild lately. I've missed some great opportunities here at home. But I'm craving a trip abroad, too. Been looking at different conflicts, but haven't quite done enough research to find the right one." He thought about Karina's enthusiasm for going to refugee camps in Lesbos to interview the poor migrants hoping for asylum in Europe. "On the other hand, sometimes showing up somewhere and just digging in can produce more spontaneous and genuine work."

"Traveling abroad." Mrs. McKenna's uneasy smile appeared. "That's far from home."

"Have you ever been?" Logan couldn't recall the McKennas traveling outside the United States.

"Oh no." Mrs. McKenna smoothed her hands across the table. "I've heard stories about everything from pickpockets to sex trafficking overseas."

"You just need to follow basic precautions and stick to the safest areas."

Without hesitation, she dismissively shook her head. "I almost lost my daughter once at that crowded outlet mall less than an hour away. I never, ever want to go through another scare like that. We've got a pretty beach right down the road. No need to go halfway around the world, closer to the hub of the terrorists."

She covered Claire's hands and squeezed.

"Don't you ever feel confined in this one small corner of the world?" He frowned. Did getting married and becoming parents lobotomize the part of the brain that craved adventure?

"No." She rose from her seat when the oven timer dinged, took the cake from the oven, and set it on a cooling rack. "Everything I need is here, most importantly the people I love. And on that note, I'd better go change before we go pick up my mom. Excuse me."

After she left the room, Logan looked at Claire. "Do you agree with her?"

She didn't answer quickly.

"Mostly." That one word confirmed what he suspected about her, though. Somewhere in there Claire wanted more. "Sometimes I hear or read about something that I get an itch to see, but then I weigh the risk and can't take it."

"You're giving in to irrational levels of fear."

She twisted a paper napkin around her fingers. "Well, after you've been blindsided and had to fight for your life, then you can judge me."

He drummed his fingers on the table. "Bull."

"Pardon me?" She scowled.

"I would've bought that argument ten or twelve years ago, but not now. You're way tougher than this, Claire. Don't let your parents' fears hem you in."

"In case you haven't noticed, the world has only become more dangerous in the past fifteen years. More mass shootings, bombings. Did you know that one hundred ten thousand are shot annually? That's one person every five minutes, and a third of them die. And that's just gun violence. Cripes, last year that crazy guy drove his car into a crowd in Times Square. And don't get me started on school shootings and political discord ramping up tensions. My fear isn't about weakness or irrationality. It's about reality."

"In reality, the vast majority of people who live in cities and travel extensively never get hurt, robbed, or experience anything other than poor transit service," he shot back. "I can't believe you're actually content to live out all of your days never seeing the colors of the Caribbean, or floating down the canals in Amsterdam, or drinking wine on the banks of the Seine. I *don't* believe it. You're not that unimaginative. It's got to get monotonous and lonely here year after year—same people, same events. And I don't know many men who have *no* desire to venture outside this area, even if only for a vacation." As soon as he said that, he regretted it. No doubt she thought of Todd.

Claire shot out of her chair and grabbed Rosie, her mouth fixed in a harsh line, jaw tight. "Thank you for taking the photographs today, but as pedestrian as it must seem to you, I need to freshen up before we get my gram. I'll call you if I hear from the Wagners. Otherwise, I'll be in touch once I've got design options ready for your place."

She took two steps before he caught her by the arm.

"Claire, I'm sorry. I didn't mean to insult you." He gripped her chin and saw a shimmer in her eyes. "Shit. Call me an ass, but don't cry."

She jerked free, blinking back her tears. "It's a good reminder of why we can't be true friends, Logan. Even if we took Peyton out of the equation, you expect me to see the world as you do—with far-flung adventures and body paints—but I'm content with a quiet, comfortable life near my family. Besides, we don't all have trust funds that enable us to globe-trot."

He might have a black eye from that last quip. "Touché."

"I'm not interested in keeping score of which one of us can say more hurtful things to the other. Relationships aren't a game to me. It's why I invest in mine, like with Ben, who also values family and the familiar. To me, that's more valuable than collecting a bunch of superficial friends, experiences, and lovers around the world. Now, if you'll excuse me, I assume you can find your way out."

She rounded the corner quickly, and he heard a bedroom door close a moment later. He yanked his coat off the back of his chair and took his cup to the sink. Until this moment, he'd always felt a little sorry for Ben Lockwood, who'd, from Logan's perspective, gotten stuck running his dad's business in this tiny town. For the first time, he envied the man for the way Claire clearly respected him.

He dragged himself toward the front door. Clutter littered the living room. Dozens of family photographs taken at holidays and birthdays displayed in mismatched frames. An entire shelf full of school projects. A bookcase filled with books so worn the spines were nearly illegible. A basket with yarn and knitting needles sat beside the sofa, where needlepoint pillows like the one he'd seen at Steffi's were strewn. A stack of *Popular Mechanics* magazines hogged the coffee table.

None of these items came from any exotic locale, yet all of them wove a story of a family life rich with love and happiness. Maybe Claire had a point. Maybe his way of life wasn't so great, after all.

He gave the room one last look before closing the door behind him, zipping up his jacket and trudging through the snow with the uneasy image of Ben and Claire burning a hole in his stomach.

Chapter Eight

Claire barreled into her house and fell back against the front door, desperate to loosen her belt. When she reached her bedroom, she viewed her body in profile in the mirror, smoothing her hand over her distended abdomen.

Thanks to her argument with Logan, she'd eaten at least a full third of Gram's cake, plus a quart of milk to wash down the chocolate, all on top of a lumberjack portion of mac and cheese. She could easily pass for four months pregnant now. Too bad her twenty-month bout of abstinence meant a baby wasn't—and, at this rate, might never be—the cause of her potbelly.

She yanked her belt off and chucked it into the corner before flinging herself backward onto her bed with a great sigh.

Logan's criticisms wouldn't fade, mostly because they might be a little bit true. Had Todd been so intrigued by Peyton's lifestyle because he'd felt stifled by Claire's? Had the shooting and Claire's parents ingrained her with fear for so long that she'd stopped thinking for herself?

Still, her palms grew damp at the thought of putting herself in an epicenter of chaos. The muscles in her shoulders and core clenched as if bracing for another bullet. If she closed her eyes, she could still hear the eerie echo of shots from that rifle, sense the confused panic in the crowd, smell the blood . . .

She rubbed her face with her hands, pushed herself upright, and toed off her shoes. Those recollections helped no one, so she searched for something more pleasant to consider. Her library copy of *Educated* lay on her nightstand.

If her stomach weren't about to explode, she'd make herself a cup of tea and nestle into bed for an hour or two of reading, like always. Until now, with Logan's words ringing in her ears, she'd looked forward to that ritual. Instead, she found herself battling new restlessness about a life that had become a repetitive cycle of overeating, a book on her nightstand, and an empty bed. He was right—it would grow tedious for most others.

The *William Tell Overture* interrupted her pity party. Upon hearing Steffi's ringtone, she fished her phone out of her purse. "Hey, what's up?"

"You never called to tell me about the Duvall photo shoot."

"Oh, sorry. It went fine." She played with the fringe of one of the throw pillows, unable to believe that the photo shoot had happened that morning when it seemed like days ago.

"You sound disappointed. Do you think the reshoots are a waste of time?"

"No, that's not it. I mean, I haven't seen the images, but I'm sure they'll be great. Ignore me. I'm grumpy because my stomach is about to burst."

"Uh-oh. Did Logan do or say something to prompt a binge?"

Claire closed her eyes, frowning. "My mom and I baked a bunch of stuff for Gram's birthday. I might have overindulged . . ."

"Your metabolism is a thing of wonder. If I ate like you, I'd easily be twenty pounds overweight." She paused. "Are you sure nothing else is bothering you?"

"I guess I'd hoped you were calling about a new job."

"No, although I've emailed our former clients and asked them to write a review on our Yelp page and tag us in pictures they post of the work on Facebook and Instagram."

"Good idea." Claire sighed and slid back to rest against the headboard. "I've put together materials to hit up Mrs. Brewster one last time. Maybe we'll get lucky."

"Fingers crossed. Speaking of design plans, how is Logan's condo design coming along?"

"Fine." Kind of a lie. She'd never been so stuck on a project in her entire career. Her crush clouded her judgment, making her doubt herself. He claimed to want something cozy, yet the examples he'd pointed out—Steffi's and her homes—had too much feminine appeal for a bachelor pad.

"I'd expect more enthusiasm given the nice budget you've got. You get a full do-over there, although I did like the rug in the living room. Not that I have your eye, of course."

Claire wouldn't admit that she couldn't get a true sense of that rug and its colors from the photographs.

"I just haven't hit on the perfect design yet." And perfection had never been more important than with this job, which Logan would associate with her for years to come. They might be different as night and day, but part of her wanted him to think of her as his equal. If not in adventure, than at least in talent. "I'm working on it, though. Don't worry."

"I'm not worried, just curious. In other news, Benny is still wasting time with Melanie. I wish he'd find someone his own age and settle down."

"I feel sorry for Melanie. She obviously likes him more than he likes her."

"You should date Ben. Then we could be sisters!"

"Ben is as much my brother as yours." Claire laughed, although it seemed a shame. If only they were attracted to each other, life could be so perfect. "Talk tomorrow, okay? I'm bushed."

"All righty. Good night."

Claire hit "End," then scrolled through her email. Logan's name and the subject line "MY BAD" leaped out at her, prompting a sharp intake of breath.

Claire,

I'm sorry I hurt your feelings today, something I'd never intentionally do. I've no right to judge you for the things that make you happy, but you're wrong to say we can't be friends. We have a lot in common with our history and our creative eye, so I hope you don't really feel that way. As you pointed out, I don't have many real friends and I'd hate to miss the chance to find one in you. Please forgive me and let's start anew.

I'm working on editing the Duvall images tonight, so prepare to be awed.

Good night,
Logan

She reread the note three times, each time the knot in her chest squeezing harder. Closing her eyes, she replayed the look on his face at the Duvalls' when he'd begged to join her and her mom that afternoon, and then his expression later when they'd argued. She thought about the project he'd coaxed Peyton into, the flash of heat that lit his eyes from time to time when teasing her, and the hint of bitterness whenever the conversation involved his father.

Logan had matured into an intense, complicated, sometimes selfish, yet surprisingly tender man. Her weakness for him—an unsettling, reckless attraction—handed him the power to crush her heart to bits at the same time he made it soar.

Risks. Life and happiness always came down to calculated risks. Until now, she hadn't been willing to take any. Where does one start when so out of practice?

Could she be his friend, truly, when she'd always yearn for more? When her heart would twist with jealousy of any other woman in his life?

She hit "Reply" and began tapping out a minimal response so he couldn't read between the lines and learn all the secrets in her heart.

Logan,

I'm sorry for the things I said, too. Let's call it even.
Speak with you soon.

Claire

She went to brush her teeth and change into the red-and-black-plaid pajamas with the elastic waistband. She snapped it against her gut, muttering, "Stupid cake baby."

When she tossed her jeans in the hamper, she heard her phone ping.

Logan, again.

Even-steven works for me. Of course, brace yourself for when I win our bet, because you'll be at my mercy, and I never give up the upper hand.

She gulped as the place between her legs ignited. What was he planning, and what foolish, lonely pieces of her heart hoped that he won?

He won. That panicked refrain replayed in Claire's head even as she returned Mary Wagner's call to schedule a date and time for a photo shoot. It continued—like a distant siren—while she worked her way through page after page of online sites, searching for inspiration for Logan's apartment.

When she couldn't take another minute of quiet, she headed to Stuart's Market for replenishment. Claire parked in the handicap space near the door and grabbed a full-size cart. A dangerous sign that she might not exercise the best control.

She'd been healthy for two days now to make up for the night of Gram's birthday, so she hit the candy aisle first, then palmed a family-size box of Fruity Pebbles. Chicken. Store-made clam chowder. Grapefruit seltzer water. Finally, she forced herself to the produce aisle. Bananas. Pears. She even tossed a bag of fresh spinach in her cart to offset the neon cereal and Twizzlers.

She was eyeing the weird-looking starfruit while pushing her cart when she banged into another cart. She said, "Sorry," just before looking up, straight into Mrs. Prescott's pale-blue eyes. "Oh! Hello, Mrs. Prescott."

Rarely did Darla Prescott do domestic chores. Must be a special occasion.

Mrs. Prescott beamed at her before grabbing Claire's shoulders and pumping out a round of air-kisses. "Claire! What a pleasant surprise. Logan has been singing your praises. And Peyton was very happy to speak with you last week." She clapped her hands to her heart. "You look wonderful, dear. Did you change your hair?"

Claire figured her face matched the shade of the pomegranates in Mrs. Prescott's cart. "I got some highlights."

She smoothed her own golden locks and winked. "We blondes do have more fun."

"We'll see." Claire forced a blithe tone and grin although she could not be less comfortable than if she had a gun to her head. And that was saying something.

"Speaking of fun, I didn't see your RSVP to the fund-raiser. I know why you didn't come last year"—she paused dramatically—"but now that you're working with Logan and some time has passed, I hope you'll join us again. Although it's past the deadline, I'll make an exception for you."

Claire tightened her grip on her cart, wishing she could disappear into another time and place. There'd be no easy way to decline this personal appeal, and she couldn't afford to have Mrs. Prescott turn against her in this small town.

"I don't really have the money to spare this year . . ." Humbling as that confession was, it was easier than showing up to a Prescott event and having to deal with Peyton—and everyone else *watching* her deal with Peyton—for hours.

"Oh, come now. Surely Logan's paying you a nice commission. And the foundation really counts on locals to help promote the cause. Besides, you can network your little butt off, hobnobbing with all the guests. Play your cards right and you'll walk out with a few new projects in your pocket."

Logan must've inherited his talent for manipulation through pointed logic from his mother. Claire couldn't deny the truth in Mrs. Prescott's claims. She and Steffi could work the party for leads. Ben would be there, hopefully without a date. She could impose upon him to run interference with Peyton. And she did always love seeing Logan in a tux. "Good point. Guess I'd better send a check and scare up a cocktail dress."

"Wonderful! I'll make some introductions for you, too. Just interrupt me when you see me. You know how busy I get once the party begins."

"Thank you." Those words chafed her throat on their way out. Another Prescott she'd have to thank when all she'd wanted for the past year or so was to wipe that name from her memory. "Take care."

Claire steered her cart around Mrs. Prescott and dive-bombed the checkout line, grabbing a pack of gum, a small bag of M&M's, and a *People* magazine while waiting to pay her bill. She ripped open the M&M's with her teeth and started guzzling them before she got to the car.

On the drive home, Logan called. *Two Prescotts in ten minutes?* "Hello?"

"Claire, it's Logan. Checking in to see how it's going with my design."

"I'm working on it."

"Where are you now?"

She hesitated, unwilling to get roped into meeting him anywhere. She needed to regroup. "On my way home from the market. I just bumped into your mother, actually. She extended a personal invitation to attend the gala."

"Did she?" He paused. "Well, now I have one reason to look forward to that night."

She almost ran the stop sign, then slammed on the brakes. "Oof."

"What just happened?"

"Nothing. Just . . . nothing." She closed her eyes and slapped her cheek. *Focus!*

"Have you heard from the Wagners yet?" His coy tone made her stomach flutter.

She hung her head and sighed before admitting defeat. "Today, actually. I planned to call you later."

"Why do I think you might've put that off a bit longer?" The little chuckle in his voice caused another quiver in her core.

"Can you meet me there tomorrow morning?"

"No, actually, I need to run to the city tomorrow."

"Oh." The crashing disappointment flashed like a yellow traffic light, warning her that she'd better work harder to kill her feelings where

Logan Prescott was concerned. "Well, send me a few dates that you're available, and I'll set it up."

"I will, but let's circle back a sec. You haven't said much about my design. Are you having trouble?"

"No," she said, realizing too late that her overly bright voice might've given away the truth.

"Liar."

She grimaced. "I'm not lying. I'm just . . . a little stuck. Haven't hit the right note yet."

"Gee, I wonder why." He sniggered.

Did he suspect her crush on him made her unable to do her job? How utterly unprofessional. For once in her life, she wished she were more sophisticated. "Oh? Enlighten me."

"You need to see the space, Claire. Come with me tomorrow. You'll get a better feel for everything when you're there, and I'll have you back before dinner."

"I can't go to Manhattan." Her knuckles turned white on the steering wheel, although part of her did want to visit his home. The two-dimensional images had only whetted her appetite. She wanted to touch the things he touched, hear what he heard, smell what he smelled.

"I could claim this as my prize, you know, but I'd rather not feel like a bully. Please come. I promise I won't leave your side. You'll be perfectly safe."

Thankfully, she arrived at her house and parked her car before accidentally running over some kid on a bike, or Bubba, the neighbors' dog. Her heart raced. She flexed her hands to bring blood to her fingertips.

"Claire? Are you there?"

"Yes." She exhaled slowly.

"I know you're anxious, but I swear the most horrifying thing you'll see is my ugly furniture. In fact, I should rethink the invitation and preserve my mystique."

She laughed. "Hate to break it to you, but your image was blown when you coughed up those photos."

Neither said anything for a moment. It seemed as if he was waiting to see if she'd accept the challenge.

"There's a wonderful bistro near my place that serves the best crème brûlée." His low voice sounded as rich and alluring as that dessert. "It'll be a reward for facing your fear."

When he put it that way, she sounded weak. Her *fear* of going someplace eight million people wandered on a daily basis. She set her forehead to the steering wheel and pictured herself walking down a busy sidewalk.

"I don't know. I . . ." She paused. If she refused, he'd no longer think of her as that brave young woman who'd once inspired him. Worse, though, was the unpleasant acknowledgment that, in some important ways, she no longer was. "I'll try."

All at once, she couldn't catch her breath. Despite the remnants of snow outside, the air inside the car turned as hot and arid as a clay court in Phoenix.

"You have no idea how happy you just made me, Claire. My smile might crack my face. See you in the morning!"

After they hung up, she forced herself to inhale deeply and blow air out slowly until her breathing returned to something approaching normal. *Manhattan.* She hadn't been there in sixteen years. Her heart pumped blood through her veins with such force she swore she felt it sliding through her limbs.

She clutched Rosie as she made her way up the porch steps and into her house. After she dropped her grocery bags to the floor, she looked around her quaint little home, sensing that, after today, nothing would ever be the same.

"Claire, are you going to throw up?" Logan cast a glance at her while pulling his car up to the parking attendant. Had he pushed her too soon?

She dabbed at her pasty cheeks, which were as white as the starched collar of the shirt beneath her sweater. When a car horn blared behind them, she jumped in her seat. "No."

Seeing her visceral reaction to the swarms of pedestrians facing off with cars in the crosswalks drove home for him her deep-rooted fear. "Are you sure?"

"I'm fine." She opened the door and exited his car without meeting his gaze, slinging her computer bag over her shoulder. She stood with her back against the wall, her eyes scanning the entrance and dark gray skies beyond like a palace guard.

Logan sighed and handed his keys to Fred. "I'll be leaving again around three or so."

"Okay, Mr. Prescott."

Logan peeled Claire away from the wall, though she followed with great reluctance. "We have to go out to the street and walk past one building to enter mine."

Again she nodded but said nothing. Late-winter winds whipped down the street, yet perspiration dotted Claire's hairline as she hugged the buildings. Logan walked between her and the street, careful not to outpace her and Rosie. His doorman, Scott, greeted them before Logan escorted her through the small lobby to the elevators.

Once the doors closed, she released an audible sigh. "Sorry."

"Don't apologize. I know this is challenging." He smiled, suspecting that she hadn't quit, puked, or cried because her inner grit refused to give up, especially in front of him. "It won't be as difficult the next time."

She shot him an incredulous look. "Next time?"

"I'm an optimist." He smiled and gestured to the right, once the elevator doors opened. When they reached his unit door, he pulled out his key while saying, "Now, don't say I didn't warn you."

As soon as he closed the door behind them, Claire's shoulders relaxed and the tension around her mouth disappeared. She set her bag on the floor and walked directly to the wall of windows in the living room. She craned her neck and peered down at the street several floors below. "It's so busy. Is it always this noisy?"

He came to stand beside her, wanting to wrap his arms around her for comfort but knowing that would likely insult her or make her less comfortable. "It quiets down in the middle of the night."

She gazed up at him, eyes wide. "How do you get any sleep?"

"You get used to it, like white noise." Of course, it would never be as pleasant as summer nights at Arcadia House with the window open.

"White noise with sirens and horns?" She shook her head and moved from the window, now scanning his furniture. "The light is better than I imagined, even on a gray day like today. Are there any pieces that you want to keep, for comfort or sentimental reasons?"

"Not really. Like I said, I didn't pick most of it anyway."

"I can tell. It doesn't look like you." She pointed at a blank wall. "Why don't you display any of your work?"

"It would depress me to see it here, as if it wasn't worthy of being hung someplace where other people could view it and be moved."

A soft smile played on her lips.

"What are you thinking?" he asked.

"I always wondered why you quit fashion photography so quickly, but maybe I understand better now."

"I liked that job for about three minutes. At twenty-two, being surrounded by 'beautiful' women sounded like heaven." He slouched onto a barstool.

"Don't pretend it was hell, Logan."

"It sorta was. They might've had symmetrical faces and long legs, but nothing about that world felt genuine or interesting. It was impossible to capture any soul." He waved a hand in disgust. "I hated it."

"And you're happier now, traipsing the world in search of heart-wrenching stories?"

"Infinitely."

"Good." She smiled at him like she used to before Peyton hurt her, and like a defibrillator, it kick-started his jaded heart. "Can I go check out the bedroom?"

"Be my guest." He followed her into his room and turned on the light, staying close, allowing a satisfying sexual tension to build.

Her eyes focused on the body-painted wall before she crossed to it as if drawn by a string. She reached out to touch it while licking her lips, but he felt as if she'd touched him. He had a sudden sense of vulnerability as she studied the canvas, such as it was. What did she see, and what did she think it said about him?

"This took some time." She didn't face him when she spoke.

"We weren't in a rush." He looked down, wishing he hadn't deflected with a joke. Not when Claire was always so direct and honest.

Her nostrils flared slightly, but otherwise she remained perfectly still. "How did you get the paint off your bodies?"

"Ever practical, aren't you?" He grinned. "If I thought that way, I'd probably never do half the things I try. As for this, we showered before most of it dried. You'd be surprised how well baby oil and other home remedies work, though."

Her head had tipped to the right as she continued examining the wall. He suspected she was trying to make sense of the choreography, so to speak.

"I almost hate to cover this up, Logan." She finally faced him, then caught her breath when she realized how close he'd come.

"Really?" He inclined toward her as he searched the pools of sapphires and diamonds she called eyes. "I thought you hated it."

She stared back, her expression soft and full of feeling. "It's the only thing in this whole place that is uniquely yours."

Her words seeded a joyful ache in his chest. Once again she saw him—understood and accepted him—as he was. He could kiss her now and she'd let him. He sensed it, and he wasn't often wrong about these things. His insides tightened with his restraint, but if he pushed her too far, she'd become overwhelmed. He'd let this interest stew a bit and enjoy the anticipation. "You make a good point. Let's keep it."

"Okay." She stepped around him and started for the living room again. "I should get started working. I feel fine inside, so go take care of whatever brought you to town while I take measurements and play around with ideas."

He followed behind her, stopping at the kitchen island. "I don't have errands in town. I came to grab my tux for the benefit and get the rejects." He and Peyton had discussed how some of the images she'd previously approved were too whitewashed. The project would be better served by images with more emotional texture.

"Rejects?" Claire frowned in confusion.

"Discarded photographs."

"Can I see?" She lit up.

"Well . . ." He paused. He had almost no latitude when it came to discussing his sister. "They're of Peyton."

"Oh." She hugged herself. "For the project?"

"Yes. She's coming around to using grittier images to make a point."

Claire turned toward the dining area, where the rejects lay scattered across the table he'd dumped them on the last time he'd come home. Before he could warn her off, she'd crossed to the table and picked one up. He studied her reaction from a short distance.

Her body went still except for the way her brows pinched together. Conflict warred in her eyes. She swallowed hard, her gaze fixed on the image of Peyton, in a towel, sitting on the leather bench near the window. Daybreak lit his sister's shoulders and scalp, giving her body a translucent quality except for the red-rimmed eyes staring at the lens.

Moments ticked by until she said, "I can't believe she let you take this."

"She didn't *let* me. I caught her crying." He didn't shy away from Claire's disapproving gaze. "She thought I was still sleeping when she came out here after a shower. I'd heard her moving around and came to check on her, but she was in a zone. I grabbed my camera and zoomed in before she knew what I was doing. She turned once she heard the first clicks, and that's when I got that shot."

"That's so invasive." Claire scowled.

"That's what I do." He pointed at the photo. "See? Genuine, raw emotion. The project won't mean anything if we don't dig deep."

Claire's expression rapidly changed. "Why was she crying?"

He thought about what Peyton had told him that morning. Her story. Her privacy. But he sensed a softening in Claire, and he couldn't pass up a chance to remind her that Peyton was more than the only horrible mistake she'd made. "She came out to get water, then went to the window. She was watching the street below come to life. Apparently it got her thinking about how, whether she lived or died, it would all keep going on, and so few people cared about her or would miss her." His voice cracked a bit, but he covered it with a cough. "Of course, you remember how fond she is of finding silver linings in everything. So she ultimately claimed to be grateful not to be leaving a husband or child behind."

Claire dropped the photo on the table and spun away. Tension tugged at her features. "I shouldn't pry into her pain, or yours. Sorry."

"It's okay. We're not hiding it. That's also the point, right? Our inevitable mortality—the choices and values and relationships we prioritize—all of it creates the life we have and the legacy we leave behind."

Claire blinked at him as if he'd shined a flashlight in her eyes, then crossed to her purse and rummaged for her notebook. "I hope it's successful, because it's so personal to you."

"And to Peyton."

"Yes." Claire opened her notebook without meeting his gaze. He could tell she was having trouble settling her thoughts. "Do what you need to do here. I'll make my notes, then we can go."

While she walked around the living space, measuring all manner of things, looking at all of his furniture, and writing down notes, he went to the table to reorganize the rejects. He then returned to his bedroom to get his tuxedo, dress shoes, and cuff links, pausing on his way out to take another look at the body-painted wall. It *was* the only part of this apartment that reflected anything personal about him. What did it say about him that he could live in such impersonal surroundings for so long and hardly notice?

When he returned to the living area, Claire looked up. "Looks like you've got your party gear all set."

He laid the garment bag flat on the dining table. "How about you? Is your dress pressed and ready to go?"

She shrugged. "I'll pull out a basic black dress. It's not like I've got a date to impress."

Without hesitation, he teased, "If you go as my date, you'll have someone to impress. You look great in blues and greens, by the way."

She blushed like a bed of roses and waved him off. "Stop it."

"I'm serious." He shoved his hands in his pockets. "Be my date and save me from having to flirt with strangers."

"Because flirting is so hard for you?" She rolled her eyes. "I'm not going as your date."

"Why not?" He lifted one arm and sniffed. "Do I stink?"

Claire raised a brow above a sly smile. "Only when you overdo it with cologne."

"Moi? Never." The playful idea took deeper roots. The idea of that third kiss rushed back, tempting him. "Come on, let's go together. It'll be fun. We can go shopping right now for something special. Imagine the shock on people's faces when we show up arm in arm."

Her smile vanished. "I'm not interested in shocking people, being your buffer, or sitting at a table with your sister all night."

"Sorry." He'd screwed up by making his invitation sound like a joke because he'd been afraid of rejection. "I didn't mean it the way it sounded."

She snapped her notebook shut. "Are you hungry? I'm suddenly willing to brave the two-block walk to that bistro you mentioned if the crème brûlée is as good as you promised."

Chapter Nine

Claire greedily dug her spoon into the profiteroles—which she loved even more than crème brûlée—having earned the ice cream–filled pastries drenched in hot fudge and whipped cream today. First she'd lost ten pounds in sweat, thanks to Logan's weaving through high-speed traffic on the drive into the city. Then she'd dealt with the ridiculous fake-date proposition. If that weren't enough, the hectic two-block walk from his apartment to Le Singe forced her to navigate uneven sidewalks through crowds of unfriendly strangers while being assaulted by the sounds of angry drivers and the scent of engine fumes and urban decay. And on top of all that, those photographs of Peyton . . . the depth of sorrow in her eyes . . .

Claire refocused on the sweet, cold vanilla ice cream sliding down her throat.

From her seat in the rear corner booth against the wall, shrouded by warm gold-toned walls with wood paneling and vintage mirrors, which reflected twinkling light from the candlelit tables, she enjoyed a full view of the restaurant. Couples and groups of friends drank and laughed around them, helping her to relax. If she didn't think about where they were, she could almost pretend this was a nice new restaurant in her hometown.

Logan poured her another glass of muscadet, a dry, light French white wine she'd never before tried. When she darted her tongue out to lick a stray bit of whipped cream off her lip, he smiled. "You're enjoying this meal."

The crusty, rich croque madame she'd eaten had topped her family's mac and cheese in the satisfying comfort-food category. And this dessert—there weren't words. "I am."

"If nothing else, *lunch* was worth the trip, right?" He leaned back, long limbed and lazy.

Casual moments like this made it tough to swallow, and not just because the gargantuan bites of pastry and ice cream were lodged in her throat. She felt helpless in the face of her attraction to his nonchalant elegance. If nothing else, being around *him* had made the trip worth it. "Do you eat here often?"

"Not too often. There are so many restaurants in the city I try not to limit myself." He gestured around. "But I do love the lighting here. Plenty of interesting shadows. It'd make for some provocative images."

As usual when he spoke about work, his gaze turned daydreamy. "I'd love to see the world the way you do," she said on a sigh.

"Oh no. I don't think you'd like it inside my head." He chuckled. "It gets a little crazy."

"Crazy good, maybe. I see the world through glass, but you seem to see it through a kaleidoscope. The way you describe colors . . . like that time you told me that grass wasn't green. I thought you'd really lost your mind until you made me study it in the sunlight and see the blades that looked gray because of shade, or the ones that looked white in the sun. The yellow and green and blue blades, too. That was the first peek I ever got into seeing the way an artist does."

"I don't remember that, but, God"—he grimaced in a self-mocking manner—"it sounds so pompous. You should've laughed at me."

"It wasn't pompous. We were on the porch steps at Arcadia on a gorgeous summer day before my injury. You'd come home from somewhere and sat with me for a few minutes while I waited for Peyton. I didn't know what to say, so I talked about the weather—about the clear blue sky. Then you started in on how the 'sky' isn't really blue and how it can be orange and pink and purple at sunset, and then moved on to the grass not being green. It was interesting."

A pleased smile played at his lips. "Sounds like I was trying to impress you."

She snickered. "More likely you were bored and searching for something interesting to talk about."

"You've never bored me, Claire." He stared at her, tapping his thumb on the table. "Who knew a stray comment would make a lasting impression?"

If only he knew how everything he'd done back then had left an imprint. She'd been content to follow him around like a puppy, basking in any bit of interest, lapping up any knowledge he had to share. That hadn't changed much, she supposed. His attitude—even when bordering on obnoxious—still fascinated her. "You must have so many stories from all the places you've gone. The things you've seen. What strikes me most, though, is how, even with the most gut-wrenching, graphic images you've taken, there is hope. It's a true gift."

His previously pleasant smile melted into a solemn expression. "Thank you, Claire. That means a lot coming from you."

She fidgeted under the weight of his gaze as it wandered over her face, intent and searching.

"You're welcome." She swallowed the last bit of pastry. "Have you decided when and where you'll go for work next?"

"Karina and I are still in research mode. We like to focus on a granular perspective, but it's almost impossible to suss out a unique story from here."

"I'd rather not know too many details because I'll worry the whole time you're away. If you're gone a few weeks, I'll empty the grocery aisles from all the stress eating."

"Thanks for caring . . ." He shifted, crossing his feet at the ankles, and tossed back a healthy swallow of wine, his eyes still fixed on her face. A tremor shook her while she waited for him to finish his thought. "Let's assume today is the start of a new trend in which you gradually get more comfortable going farther distances from Sanctuary Sound. What's your dream trip? Where would you go, and why?"

She scraped her dish in a desperate bid to get all the hot fudge off the bottom. "I don't know."

"Come on, you must have some idea." He sipped more wine.

She shook her head. "I don't. I never let myself think about it, I guess. Makes it easier to be happy at home. Where would you suggest I go?"

"Everywhere! A ride down the canals of Venice followed by a private concert by Andrea Bocelli. A trip to Jerusalem to visit the Western Wall and Temple Mount. The bamboo forests of Kyoto. The deltas of Botswana. The lavender fields of France." He leaned forward while her mind drifted along the river of those ideas. "Or perhaps you'd prefer to visit major cities like Copenhagen, London, and Paris on a massive decor shopping spree."

Claire smiled. "Is that a hint? Do you want special pieces from those places for your apartment?"

"Not necessarily. I'm just making an observation." He reached his hand across the table but stopped short of clasping hers. "Although those *are* all great cities. We could take a business trip."

We. When he'd said that word, her heart practically flew out of her chest. But then the words "business trip" knocked it back into its cage behind her ribs.

"You make it all sound very tempting. I just . . ." She shook her head, frustrated with herself for how deeply she'd buried any impulse for adventure.

"Come on, just tell me which appeals most." He studied her closely now.

"All those places sound amazing, but *if* I were to venture far, I'd choose someplace remote, calm, and relaxing, like the Seychelles." Her whole body flared with heat when she pictured herself sunbathing on the sugar-sand beaches in a cove of cerulean water, surrounded by palm trees and lush mountains, sipping a pretty cocktail and holding hands with Logan. She skimmed the last bit of whipped cream from her bowl with her finger and sucked on it hard.

He flashed a sly grin. "A romantic."

Embarrassed, she shook her head. "Just practical. Fewer people, less danger."

"You can't fool me. Remember the flowers at the Duvall shoot?" He cocked one brow. "You picked a honeymoon location because you're a romantic, not because you're afraid."

The waiter set the check on the table, giving her a break from this conversation. Claire grabbed for her purse, but Logan waved her off.

"My treat. I insist."

"Thank you." She kept her purse clutched against her abdomen while thinking of talk of romance and honeymoons. Was she a romantic? Since Todd, she'd seen love only as another enemy that could hurt her.

After Logan signed the receipt, he slipped his credit card back into his wallet and polished off the final drops of muscadet. With a quick glance toward the front door, he turned to her wearing a concerned expression. "You ready?"

She braced for the buzz of traffic and the multitudes of people ambling around in long winter coats that could conceal all kinds of weapons. With Rosie in one hand, she slid out of the booth. "Let's go."

When they reached the front of the restaurant, heavy sleet greeted them.

"We're going to get soaked." Logan looked at Claire, then tugged at the top of her coat, adjusting her scarf to cover her head and hug her neck. "Better."

He raised the collar of his coat and opened the door. "After you."

She stepped into the weather, almost grateful that it had thinned the pedestrian traffic, although cars now sloshed through icy puddles, spraying gritty water onto the sidewalk.

"Any chance you can jog?" Logan asked as he wrapped one protective arm around her shoulders and hunched against the sleet, keeping as close to the buildings as possible, hedging toward any cover the various awnings might offer.

"I can try." Miraculously, the concentration it took to jog with an aching hip and not trip over Rosie kept her mind from dreaming up scary scenarios until they arrived at his apartment again.

The doorman let them in, at which point Logan released her shoulders but then clasped her hand and strode toward the elevator.

She tried not to stumble or make a show of gaping at their hands but—Oh. My. God. He'd intertwined his fingers with hers . . . like a boyfriend. If she hadn't known better, she'd have sworn the sun broke through the clouds behind her. She wiped the stupid grin off her face, but that smile simply burrowed deep inside her chest and hummed.

Logan didn't seem to notice anything until the elevator doors closed. His brows quirked when he realized he had her hand in his, as if he was as surprised as she. He flashed a crooked grin and then, with his free hand, brushed back a bit of her wet bangs. "You look pretty with these wet tendrils and colorful scarf. Can I take some pictures before we go?"

"God no!" She laughed. The elevator doors opened, and she reluctantly withdrew her hand to shake out the wet scarf.

"Why not?"

She wrinkled her nose. "Please, Logan. I'm not photogenic at the best of times, let alone when I look like a drowned kitten."

"You're crazy. Your face has a fantastic shape and curves, and those eyes." He opened the door to his unit, then stopped short and caught her by the arm. He tipped up her chin and stared at her, his voice huskier than normal. "There's such depth and fire in your eyes, Claire. Let me capture that."

She swallowed hard, wishing he wasn't Peyton's brother. That he wasn't a documentary photographer who traveled the world on a whim. That he wouldn't always be chasing his own demons to prove something to himself and the world.

Reluctantly, she shook her head and glanced at the darkened wall of windows now spattered with icy rain. "We don't have time. The roads will get worse if this weather keeps up. Can you grab your tux and those rejects so we can go?"

Logan sighed. "You make me sad."

She let that remark settle on her heart while he gathered his things. In the next room was evidence of the kind of woman who wouldn't deny him much, unlike her, who couldn't even allow him to take her picture. She didn't like how that made her feel about herself, yet she couldn't seem to change.

"I'm sorry . . ." Every muscle in her chest tensed with discomfort.

"About what?"

"Being me. Being"—she motioned around herself with her hands— "so tightly wound. I'm sure you could've made better use of your day without me."

He set his hands on her shoulders. "Stop it. I've enjoyed our day. We're good for each other, Claire. I pull you out of your shell, and you pull me out of mine."

"*You're* in a shell?"

He shrugged. "That of a cynic."

"And how do I help?"

"By showing me that there is at least one genuinely selfless person in the world."

Before she could react to the compliment, he opened his front door so they could leave.

She let that conversation sink in as they made their way back outside, slogging past two buildings and down the ramp to the bowels of Chelsea. While waiting for Logan's car, Claire shivered, partly from wearing wet clothes in near-freezing temperatures, and partly because she'd give anything to teleport to Sanctuary Sound rather than have to drive through Manhattan and on I-95 in this storm.

Visions of eighteen-wheelers careering into them danced through her head.

"Uh-oh. You're turning green again." Logan looked around. "Should I get a bag in case you throw up?"

She blinked rapidly so he wouldn't see her humiliated tears. She wanted to be that strong, brave woman he'd once believed her to be. "I'm good."

He leaned close. "You don't need to lie. I know we're pushing your limits. Next time it will be easier."

Next time. She didn't know if there would be a next time, even though she did enjoy seeing his apartment and dining with him in an authentic French bistro without being bothered by everyone she knew. But her elevated heart rate couldn't be healthy. As memorable as the highlights of this day had been, she couldn't control her anxiety.

As that thought made her frown, Logan wrapped his arms around her, holding her tight. Her cheek pressed against his chest, where the smell of wet wool mingled with his fine cologne. Her breath seemed suspended in this dream state with her as she savored his friendship and understanding. The roar of his car's engine echoed up the ramp before the attendant parked it beside them.

Resigned to the end of their quiet moment, she eased out of his embrace, determined to face the inevitable, terrifying journey home without making a scene. He didn't release her, though. Instead, he lifted her chin. "Claire . . ."

And then he kissed her.

Something about the decided sparkle in her eyes had acted like a match that set to boil the simmering interest he'd been holding inside. Her full, firm lips tasted like sugar and wine and everything decadent and sweet. Desire pulsed through his groin. He could feed on her mouth for days if they weren't in a dirty garage with his car idling beside them while the attendant impatiently awaited a tip.

Logan broke away and stared into her now-dazed expression. As third kisses went, she wouldn't be forgetting *it* anytime soon. He whispered, "We should go."

She nodded, frozen in place, so he directed her to the passenger seat, tipped the attendant, and climbed behind the wheel.

Claire had buckled up, but her fingers weren't in a white-knuckled death grip on the car's arm like they'd been earlier that day. Now she stared into space, biting her lip. This could be a good thing, considering the weather and the ugly two-hour drive ahead. Maybe if he kissed her more often, she'd have better things to think about than her fear.

Yet within five minutes of leaving the parking lot, her fingers began to twist into a knot on her lap.

She needed another distraction, so he plunged right into uncharted territory. "Are you upset that I kissed you?"

He hoped not, because he very much wanted to do so again. Next time without an audience.

"No." She looked down, mumbling, "What's another pity kiss between friends?"

"What?"

"You heard me." She gazed out the passenger window. "It isn't very flattering to know that you're always feeling sorry for me for one reason or another and thinking that your kiss is a magic elixir."

"That's not even close to the truth," he sputtered.

Okay, maybe that first kiss, eons ago, had been somewhat about making a convalescent girl with a crush on him feel a little bit better. But sympathy had nothing to do with his motivation today.

"Forget it, Logan. Really. My anxiety is elevated enough without making this into a big conversation."

He could feel his eyes bulging. "First, I don't want to forget it. In fact, I'll rather enjoy remembering it. I kissed you just now because I *wanted* to. Because we had a nice day and you looked pretty. Because you soldiered on despite your fear. Today reminded me of all the reasons I admire you and made me want to learn more. To have you look at me like you used to, instead of with suspicion. To like me for who I am, nothing more or less."

She turned in her seat to face him. "Forgive me if I find the timing of your interest a bit fishy." Her voice carried a slight edge. "You wouldn't even be in Sanctuary Sound if not for Peyton, nor would you have hired me. We've known each other for half our lives, Logan, yet you never looked my way before."

He stared at the road ahead, turning her words over in his head. He couldn't lie. He hadn't been attracted to her until now. He'd liked her. He'd noted interesting things about her. But he hadn't been *stirred* before this month. Why not?

Hell if he knew, and did that even matter? "I can't say why things have changed, but I promise that kiss had nothing to do with my sister."

"Maybe not, but it doesn't matter. There's no point in exploring whatever feelings might be there. Even if I could see into the future and know that I would, one day, be able to comfortably sit across the table from Peyton, you'd be long gone by then. Our lives have nothing in common, and I have no more ability to traipse the world than you do to stay still." She let out a little sigh and touched her lips as a gratified smile popped into place. "But I won't lie. It was a very nice day . . . and kiss."

He would've smiled back if he weren't now upset by her unilateral dismissal of anything more than a temporary working relationship. "What if you're wrong?"

"About what?"

"About everything."

"Pfft." She rolled her eyes. "Maybe I was a romantic before Todd, but he cured me of any illusions. There's no fairytale ending here, Logan, and we both know that. Let's not ruin our friendship out of curiosity about what can never last."

They drove a mile or two in subdued silence. With each rotation of the tires, he grew more and more frustrated.

"I remember, years ago, you telling me about your first tournament. How, in second grade, you showed up in regular shorts and a single racket and had to play a girl with three Hammer rackets and a matching tennis outfit. She intimidated you and you lost, but you came back fighting and beat her the next time. Where's *that* Claire? Or is giving up your new norm? Does settling for less than you want because it's safe feel good?" He felt the scowl seize his entire face. If she could be frank, he would be, too.

"Those questions assume that I want more than friendship. That's pretty arrogant."

Not arrogant. Honest, based on years of experience with women, and with Claire in particular. "Are you really going to sit there and pretend that you have *no* interest in me?"

She flushed and looked at her hands. "No, I'm not a coward or a liar, just a realist. I'd rather us be friends forever than former lovers who don't speak."

The velvety sound of her voice saying "lovers" ricocheted through him. Unlike her, he couldn't dismiss this interest so easily. He wanted a taste of more, even if it didn't last forever. *Nothing* lasted forever. "Who says it has to be either-or? Life is remarkably fluid if you don't get hung up on labels, or grudges."

"Says the man who's held a grudge against his own father for as long as I can remember." With a little huff, she tugged at her coat and pants, shifting uncomfortably in the seat. "Why are we talking about this, anyway? Let's not spoil our day."

He let the dig about his dad go because the last thing he wanted now—or ever—was to think about that relationship.

"We're talking about this because I want to understand what's changed you into someone who's afraid of taking chances."

"Life!" She shook with frustration now.

"Life?"

She nodded. "Anytime I pour my heart into something—dreaming of it, working toward it, planning for it—I lose it. Tennis. Todd. Not to mention how the bullet that shattered my hip left me with lifelong pain and nerve damage. Maybe I just don't have it in me to throw my heart against a wall again, Logan."

He couldn't argue with her suffering and loss, but her perspective was off.

"Maybe your problem is that you're too focused on an end goal instead of simply enjoying the ride. What if, instead of making tennis or Todd or anything else the focus of your future, you lived in the moment and savored each one, wherever it led? If you'd only let yourself enjoy life as it happened without expectations or judgments, you'd be happier. When you ditch expectations, nothing is a risk. Everything simply becomes another new experience for however long it lasts. That's what life is all about."

She stared at him, wearing the strangest sad expression. "Is it so easy for you to say goodbye to things and people?"

"That's not what I'm saying."

"When you boil it down, that *is* what you're saying. And it's just not who I am."

"You're so sure of yourself. Convinced your way is *the* way. Convinced you can't venture beyond Sanctuary Sound. But, Claire, have you noticed anything about this ride home?"

She frowned. "I don't know what you mean."

"We've already crossed into Connecticut, yet you haven't been gripping your stomach, sweating buckets, or chewing your nails." He glanced at her in time to see the surprise on her face.

"Have we?" Her eyes went wide. "Where are we now?"

"Westport."

"Seriously?" She looked around as if she might recognize something on the highway, which was hilarious considering the fact that she never drove on the damned thing.

"Seriously." Of course, now that he'd called her attention to the road, he noticed her fingers digging into the leather console. Thankfully, the sleet had stopped.

"Well, that's good." She settled a hand on her stomach, her voice flatter than before. "We're more than halfway home."

"That's *not* my point."

"What *is* your point?"

"Yesterday you believed you couldn't leave town safely. Today you did, and you enjoyed it. You got absorbed by what was happening, so anxiety didn't control your behavior. Don't you think, with practice, you could do it again? And the more you practice, the farther you can go? And if you're wrong about those limitations, maybe—just maybe— you're wrong about other things, like me. Like *us*."

Chapter Ten

As Logan pulled up to the curb by Claire's house, her stomach turned over. Not from the drive, per se, but from second-guessing herself and her choices.

She *had* gone to and from the city today without incident. Then that kiss and ensuing conversation had distracted her so much that she hadn't paid attention to the drive home—or most of it, anyway. The painful silence of the past twenty minutes had made her more aware of the cars whizzing past like bullets. But here she was, home again, safe and sound.

Maybe Logan had raised a fair point. But the only thing she knew with certainty was that getting her hopes up where he—a man who'd never kept a girlfriend for long—was concerned would be a one-way ticket to heartache.

She gathered her things before steeling herself to look into those green eyes of his. "Thanks for lunch. Now that I've seen your home, I swear I'll get a plan to you in the next few days."

He reached for her hand as she went to exit his car. "Claire, do me a favor."

"What?" She hated to ask because she didn't feel strong enough to resist.

"Think about painting outside the lines a little with me. Whether for a day, a week, a month, or a year, it could be an extraordinary adventure for both of us."

Painting outside the lines with Logan sounded like heaven, and that was exactly the problem. She swallowed a sigh when her mother knocked on the window, startling them both.

Claire opened the door and got out of the car. "Mom? What're you doing here?"

"Looking for you, honey. I've been calling all day. You never answered, so I got worried, especially when I found your car here but no one home."

Claire couldn't even look at Logan, who was probably thinking her mother insane. "My phone's been in my purse. I didn't check it. Sorry."

"It's okay." Her mom smoothed Claire's hair like she was eight, then leaned down to wave at Logan through the open door. "Hello again. What've you two been up to?"

"I took Claire to see my apartment so she could finish her design plans."

Her mom's eyes practically popped out of her head as she flattened one hand on her chest. "In New York?"

"Yes. Had a great lunch while we were there, too." Logan shot Claire a pointed look.

"Oh," her mom stuttered before flashing a weak smile at Logan. "Well, hopefully you won't have to do that again. Have a good evening, dear."

Her mom shut the car door before Claire had a chance to say goodbye.

Claire bent to wave to Logan through the passenger window before he pulled away from the curb. That little interlude probably made him realize how ridiculous he'd been to think he and Claire could ever be more than friends. Now she wouldn't have to reject the idea, because *he* would.

Instead of bursting with relief, Claire's heart sank to her toes, which, when combined with the ache in her hip from the dank weather, made her climb to the front door hurt all the more.

Her mother followed her inside with her arms crossed, her face a mask of concern. "I'm shocked you went with Logan into the city, especially with that earlier weather. And just last week there was another crazy down there who pushed someone onto the subway tracks. You two didn't go on the subway, did you?"

Claire closed her eyes. "No, Mom. Please relax. We're fine."

"Thank God!" Her mom hugged her. "I don't know what I'd do if anything else ever happened to you, honey."

The burden of that responsibility weighed on Claire's shoulders like an I beam. She understood the worry of a parent. But such suffocating concern might be causing a different, if less visible, kind of harm.

Claire eased out of the embrace.

"Do you want to join Dad and me for dinner?"

"I ate so much today I don't need dinner. Logan took me to this wonderful little bistro." A smile formed the instant she thought of their intimate corner table.

"Mm." Her mom wrinkled her nose. "Well, I'm glad you escaped without any trouble. Manhattan's full of crime, crazies, and traffic."

"I know, Mom. I know." She did know. She'd heard it a billion times. It's why she'd made herself a content life here at home. Yet . . . if she hadn't gone there today, she'd never have been inside Logan's apartment. Or walked streets filled with people from all over the world. Or enjoyed that amazeballs dessert. Most of all, she wouldn't have been kissed by Logan Prescott.

A *real* kiss. One that had resonated throughout her entire body.

Sensations she could reexperience if she were willing to get hurt—again—which no doubt she would. And yet his plea made her wonder if maybe . . . maybe it would be worth trying to be "fluid" and not get hung up on labels for whatever she and Logan felt for each other. Maybe a few extraordinary moments were worth whatever regrets might come later.

"So you really won't join Dad and me for dinner?" her mom asked, breaking Claire's reverie.

"Not tonight. I want to dig into Logan's design plan while my ideas and memory are fresh."

Her mom patted her shoulder. "I'm so proud of how hard you work on this brave new venture, honey." She zipped up her jacket, looking a bit like a navy-blue Michelin Man. "By the way, I'd let myself in before you showed up. I left you a slice of Grammy's cake on the counter."

"Thanks." She'd need more chocolate if she kept thinking about kissing Logan.

"I'll talk to you tomorrow." After a quick kiss on the cheek, her mom took off.

Alone, finally.

After a hot bath to ease her achy hip, Claire pulled on pajamas, grabbed the chocolate cake, and sat at the dining room table with her laptop and notebook.

Whether or not she got out those body paints with Logan, they'd never have a lifelong love affair. But she *would* give him something to remember her by—a home he could return to that offered comfort and a style befitting him.

A few hours later, after she'd narrowed down her search to a few sofa styles, chairs, and carpets, her phone rang. "Hey, Steffi. What's up?"

"Guess who I bumped into today?"

At this point in Claire's day, her brain lacked the capacity to play twenty questions. "No idea."

"Mrs. Brewster. We were both getting gas. When she saw me, she mentioned the pitch materials you left for her to consider.".

"Oh." Claire slapped her forehead. She'd had so much else on her mind she'd forgotten to follow up on that. "Was she upset about being pressured?"

"No. She actually enjoyed looking at it without us staring at her. It gave her time to mull it over. She loved what you worked up and is planning to call you. Congrats, partner. You just got us another project. Pretty soon I'm going to feel like I'm not pulling my weight."

"Oh, you pull your weight. I can't do what you do." Another project put them one step closer to renting retail space.

"Well, I just thought you'd like to know." A happy sigh blew through the line. "Any luck getting unstuck on Logan's design?"

"Actually, yes. I visited his place today, and it cleared the cobwebs." Claire envisioned Steffi's mouth gaping then.

"You went to the city?" Steffi finally asked, her voice high.

"It started off rocky, but I survived." And earned a kiss for the effort, she thought, smiling.

"I'm speechless. Happy, but speechless. Good on Logan."

"Let's not make a big deal of it." Although it had been a big deal in more ways than one.

"Kinda hard not to. I've begged you to do things with me for years, and you always say no. Obviously, Logan has a magic power I don't possess." The saucy sound in Steffi's voice set off alarm bells.

She couldn't allow Steffi to start up rumors. "The magic power of a fat commission check. Very motivating."

"Mm-hmm." Her tone suggested she knew better. "In other news, Ryan's folks are watching Emmy on Saturday. Any interest in joining us on our night out?"

Claire hated being a third wheel. "Would Ben come?"

"Possibly, but maybe you'd rather I invite Logan," she teased.

"Stop it. He's a friend and client." Fresh tingles bloomed from remembering their kiss.

"Fine. I'll check with Benny. Can I count you in?"

Claire shrugged. No reason to be a hermit. "Sure."

"Okay, Lucia's. Seven thirty. Do you want us to pick you up?"

"No. I'll meet you there." They hung up and Claire looked at the ceiling, telling herself she was *not* sorry about spending her Saturday night with Steffi, Ryan, and Ben instead of Logan.

"Where were you all day?" Peyton asked Logan when he strolled in through the back entry.

He hung his tux on the pantry door and set the box of rejects on the kitchen counter. "Ran into the city to grab these things."

Peyton unzipped the garment bag and fingered the black satin lapel. "Last year, Todd and I were the gala pariahs. I don't know if I'm up to going this year."

"I'm never up for the gala, but if I have to go, you do, too." He opened the refrigerator and popped the tab of a seltzer.

"Did you know that Claire's coming? Mom pinned her down." Peyton yawned with a stretch, then winced, presumably because of all the bruising and trauma to her chest and underarms. "I know Mom thinks she's helping me, but after what I did, I don't want anyone bullying Claire into talking to me. That won't fix what's broken between us."

When he'd first returned to Sanctuary Sound, he'd wanted to force Claire to forgive Peyton for his sister's sake. Now he had another motive—his own. Claire would never consider the idea of seeing him as long as she despised his sister. And frankly, Claire's feelings about his sister bothered him.

People could be selfish and ugly at times. Such was the human condition. You learn to roll with the punches, especially if, on the whole, those people have been good to you more often than they've been bad. Peyton genuinely regretted her mistake. Didn't that count for anything?

Claire could be surprisingly obstinate, but he sensed pent-up emotions—a yearning for adventure—bubbling beneath the surface. "I hear you, but maybe Claire needs a little push."

Peyton shook her head. "I can't make demands. I *hurt* her."

"I'm not talking about demands, but maybe there's something else you can do. A favor you can ask. Make yourself vulnerable or indebted to her in some way so she retains the power but you get to talk to her.

I think, deep down, she wants to forgive and move on. She just needs a little nudge."

"That's way too manipulative."

He set the seltzer on the counter and hung his head. "Why do people say that word like it's a bad thing? Everyone manipulates to one degree or another. I manipulated her today to get her into the city. She went kicking and screaming, even got a little green at one point, but by the time we came home, she'd not only had a good day, but I think she's realizing maybe she doesn't need to limit her life so much. If I hadn't 'manipulated' her, she'd still be totally stuck in her fear."

Peyton flattened her hands on the counter. "First of all, I can't believe you did that. Justify it all you want, but that's not cool."

"'Justification' . . . another word people throw around as being awful when, in truth, it's simply the way we make choices. Can I justify spending money on this car? Can I justify taking the day off for this appointment? Can I justify getting divorced? And so on and so on. Bottom line, as long as your intentions are not entirely one-sided, manipulation and justification are not all bad."

Peyton frowned, hesitating before speaking. "I need more time to think about whether or not I agree. Maybe I'm just predisposed to disagree because of the justifications I told myself when I ran off with Todd."

"Well, that was fairly one-sided . . . clearly on the wrong side of the line." He frowned. "Not that I believe in a life controlled by lines."

"Gee, thanks."

"Should I lie? If you ask me, lying is a worse sin than manipulation or justification."

"The point, I think, is not to sin at all, Logan." She sat back, arms crossed. "You know, you sound more like Mom and Dad than you'd ever want to admit. On the other hand, I'm tickled that you got her out of town for the day. Steffi and I were always a little sad that she never psychologically recovered from that shooting. Just don't hurt her, okay?

Not for me. And not for whatever other *justification* you're dreaming up. You don't know her like I do. If you push too far, you'll be sorry."

He knew her better than Peyton realized. "Let's change the subject. We can dig into the rejects, or shop online for a new dress for you. You *are* coming to the gala."

"Karina is coming, I presume, so I can't count on you as my 'date.'"

"Karina's my friend, not my date." He weighed whether to say more. "I actually asked Claire to go with me, but she said no."

Peyton's eyes went as wide as he'd ever seen them. "You did not!"

"I did."

Her eyes narrowed as she shoved her index finger at his chest, poking him as she spoke. "Do *not* toy with her, Logan. You know she always had a thing for you. If you use her feelings in some mission on my behalf, I'll never forgive you."

He batted her hand away. "Jesus, Peyton. Why's it impossible to believe I might have my own interests at heart? I like Claire."

"You like her," she said flatly.

"I *like* her. I'm finding myself . . . intrigued."

"By Claire." Her disbelieving expression said whatever she left unsaid.

"Yes. Claire. Petite. Freckles. Blushes easily. You know her?"

"Stop. Claire is not your type."

He gave a nonchalant shrug. "In case you hadn't noticed, my *type* hasn't been very worthwhile. Maybe it's time for a change."

"I won't argue that, but don't experiment with Claire, Logan. I mean it. She doesn't need her heart broken by you."

"Why is everyone so sure she'd end up hurt? When did I become the bad guy?" He raised his arms out from his sides.

"Who's everyone?" Her brows furrowed. "Other people know about this?"

"Claire. Claire knows. I kissed her today, but she shot me down because she doesn't trust me."

"I . . ." Peyton's jaw dropped so fast he couldn't believe it didn't bounce off the floor. "I think you just handed me a reason to reach out to Claire."

"To help me?" He smiled.

"To warn her off."

"Hey! That's just mean."

"Be serious," she scoffed. "You're the world's best brother. These past six months you've gone above and beyond. But you're not someone who can make Sanctuary Sound his happy home."

"Neither is Claire. Not the real Claire . . . the one from before the shooting. That Claire's adventuresome. Brave. I just need to remind her of the life she loved from before."

"No." Peyton's brows drew close together. "You have to accept her as she is, not try to change her."

"I see who Claire really is. It's all of you who've let her pigeonhole herself. I should've intervened years ago. But now I'm here, and I'm up to the task."

"Why? What do you suddenly see that you missed all these years?"

Everything he'd never had in his life but hadn't known was missing? "I can't put my finger on one thing. It's a feeling of arriving someplace new yet comforting . . . like home, or what most people feel about their home."

"Oh, Logan. That's such a cliché."

Maybe so, but there was a reason clichés existed. He lifted his tux off the knob, refusing to be lectured about dating by his sister. "I'm going to hang this up in my room. When I get back, you let me know if we're shopping for dresses or working on the project."

While he was in his room, Ryan called.

"Hey, buddy. What's up?"

"I need a favor," he replied with a hushed voice.

"Okay. Shoot."

"I've been planning to propose to Steffi this weekend, but she didn't know that and invited her brother and Claire to go out with us on Saturday. I don't want to tell her and ruin the surprise. So Ben volunteered to come up with a last-minute excuse, but that leaves Claire. I'd call her, but I'm not sure I trust her not to accidentally tip Steffi off. Could you invite her to do something under the guise of the work she's doing for you? That way, Steffi wouldn't worry about her and I'd get my girl to myself for the night."

"Congrats, pal. That's a big step." Logan had yet to see a marriage he truly admired or envied, but maybe Ryan's second would be the first. "I'll be glad to run interference. Consider it done."

"Great, thanks. I owe you."

"No problem. Good luck!" Logan hung up and crossed to his window, which looked out over the Sound. The day's cold rain had washed away most of the snow, leaving a windswept tableau of grays, blues, and browns in every direction.

He'd been lucky to grow up in such a beautiful location with all the advantages he'd had. None of them, however, were helping him much where Claire was concerned.

For a few minutes, he considered how to get her to cancel her plans without raising her suspicions. He wanted to take her on another adventure before cold feet and her mom froze her here in town again. He needed an idea that would appeal to her passion for design and beauty. Near enough for her to manage, but far enough to get her out of her comfort zone.

He dialed her number. When she answered, she sounded surprised. "Logan?"

"That's me."

"I know. What's wrong?"

"Nothing. Just calling to say good night and ask a favor."

"Another favor?"

He rested one hand on the window frame overhead while watching a gull fly by. "Do you trust me?"

"I don't think so." She snickered.

"I'm serious. Do you trust me?"

She paused, which bummed him out. "I don't understand what you're asking."

"If I asked you to go someplace with me, would you come without asking questions? Would you trust me that I would keep you safe and you'd enjoy the excursion?"

Another prolonged silence followed. He might have to tell her the truth about Ryan's request if he couldn't coax her into an adventure.

"I guess so."

The shock of it made him break into a smile. "Awesome. I'll pick you up Saturday at noon. Dress comfortably."

"Where are you taking me?"

"You said you'd trust me. Go with the surprise. I promise you won't be sorry."

"Logan . . ."

"Hmm?" He settled his hand against the cold glass and removed it, watching his palm print slowly fade. Here and then gone, like much in life. But if he blew warm air on it, the prints would reappear . . . like a memory.

"If I want to turn around, promise we will."

He closed his eyes. "I promise."

Chapter Eleven

Claire readjusted the lavender-scented eye mask Logan had handed her when she'd gotten into his car an hour ago.

"Keep it on!" He squeezed her hand, which he'd been holding for at least ten minutes, ever since she'd started twisting her fingers together and muttering about how fast she guessed he was driving.

"How much longer?" She continued bouncing her right knee.

"Mmm, less than twenty minutes."

Twenty minutes that could feel like another hour. She tugged at the bottom of the mask. "I'm so disoriented. I don't think I like this."

Logan might be as fluid as water, but clearly she was as immutable as an iceberg.

"Compared with our trip to the city, you haven't clutched your stomach or clenched your jaw. Blocking your vision also let you focus on the guided meditation CD, didn't it?"

She'd take him to task for his self-congratulatory tone, but, truthfully, his tactics *had* kept her from overthinking, until now. "Can you at least tell me where we're headed?"

"And spoil the surprise?"

It would disappoint him, but she'd reached the limit of her ability to surrender all control. "Well . . . yes."

"But I want to see your reaction when we get there." His displeasure rang out. "Just a little longer . . ."

She sighed. "I feel stupid. Imagine what other people who see me are thinking."

"That you're being kidnapped by someone with great taste in blindfolds?"

She'd laugh if the reason she was wearing the blindfold weren't so pathetic.

"Claire, who cares what other people think? We're having our own adventure." He must have glanced over and seen her wrinkle her nose. "How about this? If you can guess where we're headed, you can take off the mask."

"Ooh, a game. I like that." A lifetime of puzzle games with her parents had honed her skills. "Twenty questions?"

"That's too many. Five yes-no questions."

She scrunched her face and thought. "Did we head west?"

"No."

"North?"

"No."

South would've taken them straight into the Sound, so they must've gone east. She wouldn't waste a question to confirm that. East of Sanctuary Sound for ninety minutes might take them into Rhode Island, or possibly the northeastern corner of Connecticut. "Rhode Island?"

"Yes." His tone had shifted from pleased to petulant.

She had two questions remaining. Rhode Island had pretty beaches and Block Island, but late March wasn't the best month to visit either of those options. Block Island was definitely out because they hadn't gotten on a ferry. What would Logan find interesting about Rhode Island? "Are we going to the RISD Museum?"

"No. This trip isn't about me. I planned it with you in mind." He squeezed her hand to emphasize his point. "Shoot, that was more than a yes-no answer."

"Thank you, though, for planning something just for me." She shouldn't hold hands for so long when she'd already told him that she didn't see any point in them being more than friends. Still, she didn't let go.

Back to the puzzle. What tourist attractions in Rhode Island appealed to her? She thought for a moment before it hit her. "The mansions?"

"Okay, smarty-pants." He withdrew his hand, so she lost even though she'd won the game. "Take off the mask."

"I'm sorry, Logan." As soon as she removed the mask, she gasped, regretting her decision. From the peak of the Newport Bridge, sunlight spilled across Narragansett Bay in every direction. Cold fear dampened any thrill of the view from two hundred feet above sea level. The thick feeling in her throat made it hard to swallow.

"What do you think?" He turned to study her. As much as she enjoyed staring at Logan's face, she wished he'd keep his eyes on the road.

"We're up so high." Her breathy voice exposed her rising panic.

"We'll be down in no time. Take a breath." He kept his grip on the steering wheel no matter how hard she wished he'd reach for her hand again. "I thought you'd enjoy The Breakers from a design standpoint. I assume you've never been."

She drew a steadying breath and focused on the conversation instead of the shark-infested water below. "You're right. I've only ever seen photographs."

"Well, as much as I love a good picture, it's never the same as experiencing something firsthand." He winked.

An unexpected admission given his profession. She didn't want to concede the point, because, for so long, she'd convinced herself that books and images were more than enough.

But the moment they passed through the entrance gate to the seventy-room Vanderbilt mansion, she knew she'd lost any argument she might've raised. The home's one-acre footprint provided for four floors of living space inside the limestone castle.

Opulence befitting its Gilded Age construction greeted them the instant they stepped into the great entrance hall, which had six wide doorways leading to other parts of the house. Her gaze bounced from the central marble staircase, carpeted in red, to the ornately carved, gilt-coated ceilings, to the wrought iron railings and figurines and gazillion other details she strained to take in.

Logan was attaching a big lens to his camera. She supposed he might shoot some interesting close-ups of the detail on the high ceilings and other hard-to-see places.

"And you think Arcadia House is fussy," she joked, remembering his endless teen complaints about its touch-me-not decor. To her, the Prescott home had been romantic and nostalgic—a dreamy mansion by the sea. To him, it had seemed like a museum, not a home. Just another point of contention between him and his parents, she supposed.

"Yes. Please don't consider this a hint or use this trip to gain insight into *my* tastes. I only thought you'd find the architecture and design interesting."

"It is. It really is, Logan." She didn't feel threatened in this public space, possibly because someplace so unreal couldn't possibly be dangerous. Or maybe because there weren't many visitors at the moment. "Thank you."

For a while, her gaze remained fixed upward at the art and carvings and ceiling coffers. Between all that and the barrage of statistics dizzying her mind—more than seven hundred fifty doorknobs, twenty bathrooms, forty servants, and more—she practically floated through the palatial home. It was as if she'd stepped into the pages of one of her beloved historical romance novels.

The library's walnut paneling, impressed with gold leaf, made the walls look like a leather-bound book, to say nothing of the room's massive five-hundred-year-old stone fireplace, which had been taken from a sixteenth-century French chateau.

The billiards room, done in the style of ancient Rome, appeared to be carved out of Italian marble. Rose alabaster arches provided pops of color and a frame for the ceiling mural. Assorted semiprecious stones formed mosaics of acorns—the Vanderbilt family emblem. Renaissance-style mahogany furniture lent depth and richness to the room.

Claire had no idea how much time had passed when it finally occurred to her that she'd been so entranced by the self-guided tour, she'd scarcely spoken to Logan. She paused the recording and took off her headset. "You must be bored out of your mind."

"Moi?" He lowered his camera, wearing a playful grin. "I've always been curious about what it'd look like if King Midas threw up everywhere."

She laughed. "So you *have* been bored."

"No." His expression warmed, surprising her with a quick snap of his camera aimed at her. "Watching you respond to it all has been fascinating. Truthfully, I'm rather pleased with my abduction plan."

"Abduction?" She elbowed him gently. "Now who's making your motives sound suspect?"

He leaned close to her ear and said in a low, rich voice, "Well, maybe they are."

A delicious tingle blossomed in her stomach and traveled a little south, but she forced herself to walk without stumbling.

They entered Mrs. Vanderbilt's oval bedroom through one of its multiple doors. "I always find it amusing that spouses kept separate bedrooms. I suppose it could be a good thing if your husband snored or drank too much."

"I'd never put my wife in another bedroom. What's the point of missing the primary benefit of marriage?"

Claire felt herself blush. "I think the primary benefit is companionship, not sex."

"Clearly, you've not yet had the right partner." His hot gaze stirred something in her, even as she gaped at his impudence. The memory of the kiss rushed back, putting questions in her mind.

Rather than give him the satisfaction of admitting he might be right, she gestured to the bookshelves. "This room must've also served as her study. I wonder what all those discreet passageways are for?"

"Probably for ferrying in lovers after her husband banished her to this room." He chuckled, his rich laughter flowing through her like hot caramel. If he kept this up, he'd melt all her ice.

"Har har." She rolled her eyes. "I'm guessing they were for servants to come and go with laundry and such."

"Come now, Claire," he clucked. "Don't spoil my colorful scenarios with harsh reality."

She liked Logan this way—relaxed, teasing, away from their friends. If they lived someplace far from Peyton and the local gossips, maybe she could let go of her misgivings.

"You'd have made a perfect rake back in the nineteenth century." She envisioned him as a debonair earl, seducing women who volunteered as subjects for his experiments with the first photographs.

"I don't know. All those layers of clothing would've been bothersome. My father will be the first to tell you I'm neither that ambitious nor persistent."

Her heart stuttered at the abrupt shift and then ached because his father's criticisms were always just beneath the surface of his thoughts. "Logan."

He held up his hand. "Sorry. Ignore me. I think this place is giving me the willies because my dad would sell his soul to be able to leave something like this behind."

"And you wouldn't?"

"Never. It's wasteful and self-indulgent. I can be both—which can be fun for a while—but never to this degree. When I *do* leave something behind, it will leave the world better off."

She smiled, glancing at the camera in his hand. "I'm sure it will."

"Are you?" He removed the long lens and returned it and the camera to the small case slung over his shoulder.

"Of course. You're talented and passionate. If making a difference is your goal, then you'll succeed."

He grabbed her waist and tugged her close, pressing a kiss to the top of her head. "Thank you, Claire."

Surprise allowed her to submit to his embrace. "You're welcome."

Surrounded by his scent and heat, she worried that she liked being in his arms too much. Her mind raced to piece together what caused him to hold her like she was precious. Could he be that starved for a single word of encouragement?

She closed her eyes to extend the moment in which it didn't seem impossible that he might, after all these years, desire her. A moment in which she could believe her gentle reassurances formed a foundation for lasting love. In which she could commit to memory exactly how it felt to be surrounded by Logan, how he smelled, how his heartbeat pounded in his chest.

So tempting.

Let go before it hurts too much.

With heavy limbs, she forced herself to ease away and face reality. "We should probably get back soon. I'm meeting Steffi and Ryan for dinner."

His jaw ticked. "I actually made reservations for us at Cara, overlooking the water."

That sounded particularly romantic. Thank God for her prior plans, or she'd be hurtling toward certain heartache. "Oh, I'm sorry, Logan, but I can't bail at the last minute."

"I'm sure Ryan and Steffi would love a night on their own."

"But Ben is going, too. If I'm a no-show, he'll end up a third wheel." She watched one of Logan's brows pop up.

He whipped his phone from his pocket. "Wait here."

He wandered a short distance away. She thought she heard him say Ryan's name. He stood with one arm crossed over his chest and a conspiratorial smile on his face. A nod and chuckle, and did she hear the words "good luck" at the end?

Logan returned his phone to his pocket and strolled back to where he'd left her. "Ben's under the weather, so he canceled, which means I'm saving *you* from being the third wheel."

"You're very bossy." She scowled, even as her kamikaze heart leaped at no longer having a good excuse to refuse his invitation.

"But you'll forgive me because we're painting outside the lines today, and I'm treating you to a lovely meal by the sea."

Painting outside the lines. *Ha!* Her pulse fluttered while she groped for another reason to bail. Prolonging this outing was a bad idea on so many levels, not the least of which was that it meant they'd be driving home on the highway in the dark. "You promised we could turn around and go whenever I wanted."

"I did." He clasped his hands behind his back and looked at her, holding very still. "Is that really what you want, Claire?"

———

If Logan had less self-confidence, he'd be quite humiliated. He couldn't remember the last time he'd planned an outing specifically for any woman, let alone one who couldn't wait to get away from him.

"You're making me nervous." She bit her lip.

"I could say the same to you. I've never had so much trouble convincing someone to join me for dinner."

She looked at her feet. "I should text Steffi."

"Ryan will fill her in. Besides, I'm sure she'd rather you be on an adventure with me than at dinner with her and Ryan."

"The adventure part, probably." She tipped her head to one side. "The *you* part . . . I doubt."

He grasped his hips. "Steffi loves me."

"True. But . . . well, I don't want her to get the wrong idea."

"Wrong idea about what?"

"Us." Claire's hands turned upward as if the answer were so obvious it needn't have been stated.

"'Wrong.' 'Nervous.' All these negative words." He affected a pout, tilting toward her. "Let's stay focused on the positive—the possibilities."

"I'm already way outside my comfort zone. I know you mean well, but I also think this is a bit of a game for you. You've turned me into some temporary project."

"That's not true." Maybe it had started that way, but now it was more. Regardless, he admired her for calling him out. Her refreshing authenticity moved him. He didn't need to pretend anything around Claire, which relaxed him in ways he hadn't even known he'd needed. "I wish you'd believe that I'm exactly where I want to be."

"So do I, Logan." She'd said it so softly he almost missed it. Then she turned and started toward the next stop on the tour, headset back in place, leaving him uncertain about whether he should cancel the dinner reservation.

It seemed that the tour no longer held her rapt attention, which meant she was mulling over the pros and cons of his invitation. He trailed behind her, giving her space, trusting that she'd come around if he was patient.

She and Rosie strolled ahead, down the hallway. Given his history, he couldn't blame Claire for her suspicions, he supposed. Even he couldn't quite explain his recent obsession with her.

There was nothing particularly sexy about her Stewart-plaid dress, ivory tights, or oversize ivory cable-knit sweater. The ankle boots and chunky silver necklace gave the ensemble the slightest edge, but nary a hint of cleavage or skin. Yet he found himself curious about what she'd hidden beneath all those layers. Would she be as open and honest in bed as she was out of it? How refreshing might it be to wake up beside a woman he actually enjoyed talking to and with whom he could just be himself?

He'd gotten lost in his musings, so he nearly ran her over when she suddenly stopped and turned on him. "I'll stay for dinner."

"Excellent." He held his arm out for her. She looked at it and smiled before clasping his forearm.

They finished the tour without talking much, but he noticed that she'd started limping. "Does your hip hurt?"

She shrugged. "Sorry if I'm slowing you down."

"You're doing great." A blast of cold air greeted them when he pushed open the door. "In fact, I think you've earned yourself a bottle of good wine, or perhaps you prefer champagne?"

She shook her head as they crossed to the car. "If I drink a bottle of anything, I'll fall asleep at the table."

"I've had worse dates," he teased, opening the car door for her.

"I doubt that." She slid onto the seat with an audible sigh. He closed the door and walked around the car.

"I've never had any woman fall asleep on me, but there have been some who put me to sleep."

She batted his arm. "That's not nice."

"Neither were those women," he teased, starting to drive the mile or so to the restaurant.

"Then why did you ask them out?" Her brows pulled together.

Such a naive question. Or perhaps a straight shooter like Claire wouldn't go out with someone based on sex appeal alone. In any case, best he treated it like a rhetorical question and didn't answer.

After a moment passed in silence, she said, "I have to ask you something, and I'd like you to be honest."

"Okay."

"Throughout the years, I've seen pictures of you with party girls. Ones who will literally paint the walls with you. I'm passably cute at best and probably the most straitlaced girl you know, so what made you kiss me . . . or plan this day and dinner?"

"First of all, you are a beautiful woman, so cut the passably cute crap." Her expression suggested that she didn't believe him. He thought for a moment, searching for the words to describe how she made him feel. "I can be myself with you—the good and the bad. I don't think I realized how rare that was until I spent time alone with you. Now it's as important as oxygen. And when you say you believe in me, I trust you because you aren't expecting anything in return." He shrugged. "You make me feel grounded and free at the same time, if that makes sense."

She stared at him with a soft expression in those wide eyes. "I didn't expect that answer."

He'd reached his limit of intimate conversation, so he shrugged and changed the subject. "Let's see if we can bump up the reservation to an earlier time."

She nodded without pressing him into a deeper discussion about that kiss or his intentions.

Dinner passed in a pleasant ninety minutes once they'd climbed the stairs to the Chanler at Cliff Walk, the boutique hotel in which the restaurant was situated. His father probably hoped to refurbish the soon-to-be-acquired chain of coastal boutique inns in this fashion—romantic, elegant, upscale.

They'd been given a small, round table with a view of the bay. After dining on oysters, lobster, and a tableside flambé, they practically rolled out of the restaurant. He loved her appetite. The soft sway of her hair as she ambled ahead of him made him wonder if she was as voracious when it came to more intimate pleasure.

They strolled out on the back terrace, peering down at the sea below. "I should've brought my camera from the car. The moon and the sea and you—"

"Sometimes a memory is better than a photo. Besides, my lips will turn blue in a matter of minutes. Not a good look."

"I'd keep you warm." He glanced up from the sea to her. "What are the chances I could convince you to extend this walk on the wild side?"

Before she answered, he gathered her in his arms. She was so petite he could lift her without much exertion. She didn't push him away, and even in the dark, he could see her cheeks warming.

"What are you up to now?" she asked.

"Whatever it takes to prolong the night. You're more relaxed here than you are at home." She pushed him away every chance she had when other people were watching and waiting. Here she seemed less inhibited. "Let's run away for a while, or at least take a room for the night."

His hopes soared when she didn't shoot him down right away.

She laid her cheek against his chest. "You're making it very hard for me to keep my head, Logan."

"Good." He held her tighter. "It's past time you led with your heart."

"Except my heart can't be trusted." She peeked up at him. "I don't think I can be 'fluid,' not even for you."

He kissed the tip of her nose, disappointed but not surprised. It had been a long shot. "Then we'll go home. If you change your mind, let me know."

Ninety minutes later, he pulled his car up to the curb in front of her house.

"I'm impressed. You managed the ride home without the mask *and* without turning green. A little pale at points, but not green." He grinned.

She unwound her purse strap from her fingers, then briefly touched his shoulder. "This was a memorable day, Logan. Thank you for planning it."

"You're welcome." He killed the engine. "Can I come inside and see what you've been working on for my place?"

"I'm not finished with the plan." She clutched her purse in front of her like a shield.

"Okay, then just invite me in and we'll see where the night takes us." He opened his door before she could say no.

When he rounded the hood, he met her on the sidewalk.

"Logan, I'm not sure what you have in mind, but I'm not like most girls you know . . ."

He stood face-to-face with her, gently playing with the ends of her hair, watching for a sign. Any sign that would bring him relief from all this suppressed want. "That's exactly what I like about you, Claire."

He brushed his thumb along her forehead and tucked her hair behind her ear, then traced the cup of her ear and along her jaw, coming to rest on her lower lip. She stared at him, short of breath.

"Logan—"

He pressed his finger to her lips. "Don't ruin this moment by reciting all of the reasons you think this is a bad idea. Hold those thoughts. Let's pretend that no one else exists for a while . . ."

He removed his finger, then leaned forward, his lips a hairbreadth from hers. She didn't move except to close her eyes, a move he took as consent. He lifted her chin and kissed her. She tasted like ripe, sugar-sweetened strawberries, and he wanted to devour her right there on the pavement. "Claire, this feels right, doesn't it? There's something here worth exploring."

"Something more than a one-night stand?"

"Invite me inside," he said, his voice roughened by desire. He kissed her again, letting his hands glide down to her waist, squeezing it and tugging her closer.

Her breath quickened, and she emitted a slight groan of pleasure.

"I promise I won't push you anywhere you don't want to go."

"That's the problem. You know I'd probably follow you anywhere, even when I know it's not in my best interest."

"I think it *is* in your best interest. Ditch your preconceived notions and live in the moment. Fling yourself off the proverbial cliff for the thrill of it. You'll survive it. I promise you've survived worse than me."

"That's not very romantic."

"Would you rather I lie and make promises when neither of us knows what the future holds? No one gets guarantees in life, Claire. I only know how I feel right now. Right now, I don't want this night to end."

Her eyes glowed like the blue part of a flame as she whispered, "Neither do I."

He felt his smile spreading as he turned and led her up the porch stairs and waited for her to open the door. He stood behind her, arms wrapped around her waist, and whispered in her ear, "I want you."

She shook her head in disbelief as she opened the door.

"What?" he asked when they got inside.

"From the very first time I saw you—from a spot behind a tree on the shore near the end of Lilac Lane that first summer we moved to town—I wished to hear those words."

"I don't remember meeting you on the beach. I met you at the house, with Peyton."

"I'd seen you before then on my own, when I was exploring the new neighborhood for the first time. I was south of your property, where you were standing by the water. Shirtless and tan, in gym shorts, and the most beautiful boy I'd ever seen. To this day I don't know what you were thinking about, but you were gazing at the horizon for a while before you picked up some stones and skipped them across the shallow water."

"Why didn't you come out from the shadows?"

She set Rosie aside and unbuttoned her coat. "I was shy. It seemed like I'd stumbled onto something private, and I didn't want to intrude."

"Well, don't be shy now." He helped her out of her jacket, letting it fall to the ground as he pulled her close again, nuzzling her neck and nibbling her ear, eager to hear that purring sound in the back of her throat.

She wound her arms around his neck, raked her fingers through the back of his hair, and kissed him. "This might be the biggest mistake I've ever made, but right now I couldn't care less."

"Stop with all the flattery," he teased, caressing her abdomen and then moving his hand up to her breast. "Now tell me, which way to the bathroom?"

"The bathroom?" Her eyes widened.

"A warm bath will help your hip—warm, steamy air, soft filtered light, and I'm betting you have a nice assortment of bath salts and soaps, too."

"I'm more of a 'lights off, under the covers' kind of girl, Logan." She looked down, pursing her lips.

He held her close, nudging her chin up. "I promise there isn't an inch of you I won't have seen by morning, lights or no lights. Besides, there's nothing you need to hide from me. I think you're beautiful, inside and out."

He saw doubt in her eyes, but he would make sure she believed him soon enough. He led her upstairs, curious to see what else he could convince her of before the night was over.

Chapter Twelve

Claire woke with a start and glanced to her left. If she weren't naked, and if the empty side of her bed weren't a tumble of blankets and pillows, she would've thought it'd all been a dream.

Logan must've left before dawn, which was for the best. Strolling into Arcadia House midmorning would've invited questions from Peyton and his parents. Claire couldn't bear that scrutiny. This way, the reckless thing they'd done would remain their secret.

She'd never had secrets before, but now she'd grown weary of people's pity. And pity would be what others would feel for her if they found out about her night with Logan. In no universe would anyone believe she could be more than a passing infatuation for him. Even within his own "fluid" world, she'd be a fluke.

Last night he'd almost made her believe otherwise with tender words and touches, and scorching kisses. Now, with no note or other sign of him, she remembered why she'd been hesitant to follow her heart. Still, she couldn't make herself regret what she'd done. The reality of her long-held fantasy had exceeded her imagination.

A noise from downstairs caused her to bolt upright midyawn. Sliding out of bed to pull on her robe, she then tiptoed across the room.

Did she smell bacon? She cracked open the door. Yes, that was bacon . . . and Logan humming something unfamiliar. She padded down the stairs and wandered to the kitchen, where she found him drinking a cup of coffee in his snug boxer briefs while flipping an omelet.

The sight of his near nakedness—the indents of his six-pack—brought back vivid memories of licking his torso and grabbing hold of his tight behind while he'd—

"Good morning." He smiled lazily.

She stood, frozen. "What are you doing?"

He set his cup down and turned off the stove. After coming over to give her a quick kiss, he pulled out a kitchen stool for her and forced her onto it. "I thought you might be hungry."

She remained dazed by the unexpected sight of him cooking—like she'd awakened in some alternate world. Slowly the reality dawned, and the scrutiny of others would follow. "Thank you, but, I mean, why are you still here?"

He poured her a cup of coffee and slid it across the counter. "Where else would I be?"

"Having breakfast with your family."

"You're not making any sense. Have some caffeine." He cut the omelet in half and then plated her half beside buttered toast. "Eat."

Mindlessly, she obeyed, unprepared for the delightful burst of butter, bacon, and cheese that melted in her mouth. "This is awesome, thanks."

"You're welcome." He kissed her head and sat beside her, which was when she noticed her media scrapbook on the peninsula.

"What's this doing here?" She reached for it, but he stuck out his hand to prevent her from taking it.

"I found it on the bookshelf. The spine piqued my interest." His finger traced along where she'd written "Smoking Guns" in calligraphy, then he opened the binder's cover. "Quite a collection of news clippings, Claire. Now I understand how you're so well informed about gun-violence stats. Morbid, though, don't you think?"

She glowered at him. "You should ask before you snoop into people's private things."

"Sorry." He didn't look terribly sorry, though. "But now that I've seen it, can you tell me about this unhealthy obsession?"

Morbid. Unhealthy. Not the words *she'd* use to describe her interest in the rapid rise of gun violence. As horrible as these incidents were, she needed to dissect them and try to understand why they kept happening. These clippings helped her search for patterns or explanations to better predict when and where such atrocities might occur. They helped her write persuasive letters to politicians about gun control. They gave her some sense, however illusory, that she could exert some kind of control.

Not that it worked. Not yet, anyway. "I don't owe you an explanation."

"Could this hobby be keeping you from getting past your fear?"

"Facts are facts. Even if I didn't collect these reports, I'd still see them in the news. Violence is everywhere and getting worse. Any reasonable person should be wary, considering the statistics." Her appetite fled—a first!

He studied her, his green eyes lit with compassionate determination. "Let's start a new scrapbook. One filled with pictures of places you want to visit. People you admire or want to meet. Anything positive and life affirming."

Instantly, she remembered the Lilac Lane League scrapbook, which was in her old bedroom at her parents' house. It'd been filled with all kinds of hopeful wishes, and look where those got her.

She felt herself tightening into a ball on the kitchen stool. Logan must've noticed, too.

"I'm sorry. I didn't mean to ruin the morning with a lecture. I'm not used to frank conversations with women, so please be patient while I learn the boundaries." He rubbed her back. "Let's change the subject. What's on your agenda today?"

While trying to tamp down her embarrassment at what he'd discovered, she sipped her coffee. "Reality and work."

"It's Sunday, and reality is overrated."

That remark earned him one of her side-eye glances. What must life look like from inside his head? "I got nothing accomplished yesterday."

"Not true." He nipped at her shoulder. "We got a lot accomplished yesterday. Let's not backtrack now."

In the dark, she'd been bold, but sunlight spilled through the window now, and like a hermit crab on the shore, she needed to duck for cover.

"I have to finish a plan for your home. And I need to talk to Mrs. Brewster."

"That can wait until tomorrow."

"I thought you were eager for me to show you sketches?" She pushed the omelet around the plate.

"There are more urgent things I want to see at the moment." His foot hooked on to her stool, and he tugged it closer. He toyed with the robe's lapel and caught his lower lip in his teeth. "Are you wearing anything under that robe?"

Instinctively, she batted his hand away. "Logan, be serious."

"I am. You look enticing in the light coming through the window. How can you expect me to keep my hands to myself?" He ran his hands along her thighs, which sent a shock of heat to her core.

"Please, stop." It killed her, but she pushed them away. Better a little pain today than a mountain of it later.

He raised his brows. "Really?"

"Yes. I painted outside the lines last night, and I don't regret that at all, Logan. But I know me. If this were to go on, those lines will blur and I'll end up hurt. I'm not a fluid kind of girl, and as an only child, I never learned how to share all that well."

He frowned. "I wouldn't see other women while we're together."

She almost laughed. Didn't he hear himself? Maybe that sacrifice meant something to him, but it was a far cry from what she'd need to hear to move forward. While the odds of *any* relationship going the distance were slim for everyone, most people didn't start out rejecting the idea like he did. And honestly, how could she carry on with him when she hadn't resolved her feelings about Peyton—a point she'd conveniently ignored last night?

Fortunately, a knock at the door saved her from that conversation. "Can you run upstairs and get dressed while I answer that? It could be my mom, and she's as fluid as this granite countertop."

He sighed. "Fine."

After stashing her binder back on the shelf, they scurried to the front of the house.

The doorbell rang next, but Claire waited until Logan hit the top of the stairs before opening the door. When she did, she wished she'd been better prepared. "Steffi? What are you doing here so early?"

Claire noticed Logan's shoes by the coatrack too late. Hopefully, Steffi wouldn't see them.

"It's not that early, and I wanted to catch you before you went to church." Steffi strode into the living room like she still lived there, then spun around and extended her left hand to reveal a diamond ring.

"Oh my God!" Claire screeched, grabbing her hand for a closer inspection. The princess-cut stone sparkled almost as much as Steffi's eyes. "When did this happen?"

"Last night. Apparently, Ryan had been planning this with Lucia's staff for a while. Of course, I had no idea when I invited you to join us. Our table had beautiful white lilies, and he did the whole traditional bended-knee thing. People clapped. It was completely corny and wonderful."

Claire hugged Steffi as joyful tears stung her eyes. "I'm so happy for you."

"Thank you." Steffi eased away to stare at her ring again. "These past few months have been a dream. I'm honestly a little nervous that it's all going to disappear."

"It won't. You deserve to be happy." Claire smiled even though she was saddened that she and Steffi both lived in fear that happiness would be stolen from them. Paranoia was one of many invisible scars of surviving a trauma. "I guess it's a good thing Ben and I both canceled last night."

"I've never been so happy that Benny blew me off." She laughed. "And apparently Ryan enlisted Logan to keep you occupied, so it all worked out for everyone."

"It did indeed." Claire kept smiling, although her heart sank. Yesterday hadn't been a spontaneous adventure Logan had planned just for her. He'd been doing a favor for his friend. And she'd gone and slept with him because of it.

Steffi grabbed for Claire's hands. "It goes without saying that I want you to be my maid of honor. Will you?"

"Of course! I'd love to." She hugged her friend.

Steffi eased away again, this time with a slight grimace. "Before you say yes, I have to confess I'd also like Peyton to be in the wedding party."

Claire should've seen that coming, but she was still reeling from the truth behind yesterday's misadventure.

On cue, Logan descended the stairs. "I thought that was your voice, Steffi."

Claire stiffened and watched Steffi's jaw unhinge as if it were happening in slow motion.

Steffi darted a glance between Logan and Claire. "Logan?"

"That's my name." He winked. "Why are you here so early?"

"I could ask the same of you." Steffi's brows rose as her hands gripped her hips.

"Touché." Logan leaned against the newel, casting a glance at her left hand. "Congratulations, by the way. Where's Ryan?"

"At home with Emmy." Steffi frowned without elaborating about the engagement. "What's going on here?"

"Nothing," Claire said at the same time Logan draped an arm around her shoulders and said, "Breakfast. Want some?"

"No thanks. I came to tell Claire my news and ask her to stand up for me, but now my mind is blown. I need to regroup." She kissed Claire's cheek, her gaze unfocused yet concerned. "I'll call you later."

"Steffi," Claire said, about to say that this wasn't how it looked. Except it was exactly how it looked. Heat filled her face. "Congratulations. Please give Ryan all my love."

"Not all of it," Logan interjected playfully.

Steffi shook her head. "I'll let you two get back to whatever you were doing when I interrupted."

"Thanks. Claire and I do have unfinished business." Logan waved and strolled back toward the kitchen, calling, "Bye."

Steffi opened the front door and then said sotto voce, "We *will* talk later."

"I'll call you." Claire closed the door and sighed. She turned and looked toward the rear of the house, then went directly upstairs to shower. She needed privacy to process what she'd learned and figure out how to deal with Logan.

When she emerged from the bathroom, wrapped in only a towel, she discovered him waiting for her in her room, sprawled on her bed.

"You showered too soon. I have plans for us to get all sweaty again." He smiled and beckoned to her, but she backed away.

"That's not happening. And I really don't appreciate how you barged downstairs after I asked you to wait upstairs."

"Hide." He sat up and crossed his arms. "You asked me to hide."

"Well, maybe I'd feel bad about that right now if I hadn't just learned that yesterday's excursion was all about you doing a favor for Ryan instead of you planning something special for me."

"That's not true. Yes, I did Ryan a favor, but I didn't have to take you all the way to Newport to keep you from Lucia's. I *did* plan that trip just for you."

"So last night was for me, too? And this morning, also for me?" Claire headed to her dresser to fish out a pair of sweatpants and a sweater, muttering, "Now Steffi thinks I've been played, and Peyton will have questions, too. Pretty soon the whole town will be talking about this and wondering when you'll be breaking my heart. I'm so sick of being 'Poor Claire.'"

Logan scratched his eyebrow. "I don't know what's more depressing: how little you think of me or how little you think of yourself."

She whirled around on him. "If I'm insecure, it's directly related to what happened with Todd, and we both know who's to blame for that."

"I'm not interested in blame, Claire. It's pointless and, frankly, boring." He stood and finished buttoning his shirt. "We all make mistakes. We all get hurt. We all have to overcome and move on. I know you know this. You told me you were over Todd, but things keep circling around to him. For the life of me, I'll never understand why he's a stumbling block you can't get over."

"Every time you twist my words and defend your sister, you remind me of another reason why this is a mistake."

He shook his head. "Guess I'll take the hint and leave you alone. Just remember, my leaving now has nothing to do with my feelings and everything to do with your attitude. So don't use it as some kind of proof that you were right about me or us all along."

Without another word, he walked out of her room and trotted down the steps. She heard the front door open and close, and a minute later, when she peeked out her bedroom window, his car was gone. She turned back around and, at the sight of her unmade bed, let the tears come.

———

Logan zoomed across the pea-stone driveway to park in the shadow of Arcadia House as his father came through the front door and stooped to get his beloved Sunday *Times*, having yet to embrace digital media. "Where's the fire?"

Logan nodded, uninterested in making small talk with his father when his head felt like it might explode.

His dad narrowed his eyes. "Where've you been all night? Your mother's been concerned."

"I'm thirty-two. Didn't know I needed to check in," he groused as he brushed past his father and made his way toward the stairs.

"It's called being considerate," his father called after him while he closed the front door.

Midstair, Logan stopped and glanced over his shoulder, swallowing a sarcastic remark. He doubted his mom actually had worried about him last night. Moreover, he doubted his father actually believed she had a right to be concerned. But he loved to play doting husband when it suited him, didn't he? All Logan's life, he had watched those two together and still didn't know if they really loved each other or if it was all choreographed for the sake of the family name. "I'll apologize after I get some sleep."

His father shook his head, tucked the paper under his arm, and walked back toward the kitchen without another word.

"Dammit," Logan muttered before continuing his journey to his bedroom, which was situated in the southeast corner of the house.

He shut his door and went directly to his bathroom to brush his teeth and splash cool water on his face. That scrapbook! No wonder Claire hadn't crossed over any boundary line of this small town in years. Even worse was how that fear spilled over into everything else, including her relationships.

His body temperature rose two degrees each time he replayed his argument with Claire.

Sleep should clear his mind. He hadn't gotten much last night. Not that he'd minded. She'd been sweet and warm and willing to experiment. Exactly what he'd hoped for and more.

Every emotion had played out on her face and in those eyes. No wiles or any of the phony things he was used to seeing with other women. Sex with Claire had moved him. He would've enjoyed spending the rest of the day—and several more strung together—that way, but her doubts had dampened all the passion and promise.

He crossed to the window and stared at the Sound. To the left, he could just make out the outline of some of the Thimble Islands. Some of his earliest attempts at photography had been of that view, when he'd crawled out onto the flat roof of the side portico and shot photos on warm summer evenings.

At thirteen, he'd thought those islands looked like an idyllic escape from the stress of Prescott life. Since then, time and travel had taught him there'd never be an escape. Whether professionally or personally, his name and family robbed him of his own identity. Even now, his relationship with his sister stood in his way with Claire. Not that he blamed Peyton.

No. Claire was being pigheaded. Period.

He pulled the blinds closed and then tugged off his pants and shirt and tossed them aside before crawling under the covers, closing his eyes, and vowing not to think about her anymore.

A light knock at the door interrupted his slide into dreamland.

"Logan?" Peyton called.

He sighed. "Come in."

She opened the door. The light in the hallway cast her in shadow. "Can we talk for a minute?"

"What's wrong?" He propped himself up on his elbows.

She crossed the room and sat on the edge of his mattress. "Steffi just called me with her news."

"Yes, I know. Ryan told me earlier."

She smiled. "I'm happy for them."

"Same." He stared at her, wondering what else she wanted. His eyelids grew heavier by the second. "Can we celebrate or whatever later? I'm bushed."

Peyton picked at his comforter. "Where were you yesterday and last night?"

He buried his head in his hands. "First Dad, now you?"

"When you left yesterday, you said you were meeting Claire, but then you never returned." She folded her hands in her lap, avoiding eye contact.

"And?"

She looked at him. "Tell me you didn't do anything stupid."

"That depends on your definition of stupid."

"Oh God." She covered her face with her hands. "You seduced her."

He kept quiet. Seduction sounded more calculating than what had happened. He hadn't set off and planned that whole trip for the sole purpose of getting her into bed. On the other hand, he had thought about having sex with Claire more than once throughout the past couple of weeks.

He shrugged. "It's none of your business, Peyton."

"I asked you not to do that. The last thing Claire needs is to be hurt by another man—or another Prescott."

He jabbed a finger toward her. "Back off, sis. She and I are two consenting adults."

Peyton closed her eyes as if praying for patience. "So now what?"

"What's it to you?" He leaned back into his pillows, hands clasped behind his head.

She slapped his leg. "Dammit, Logan. Did you use her to amuse yourself last night?"

"No. In fact, *she* pushed *me* out the door this morning."

Peyton's eyes went wide. "I find that hard to believe. She's been half in love with you since her family moved onto the street."

"Well, that was before Todd." He shot her a pointed look, then regretted it when she winced at his accusatory tone.

"She's still in love with Todd?"

"No. But he destroyed her self-esteem, and now, because I won't make false promises, she's got her guard up." He was pouting. Pouting never looked good on anyone, but he couldn't help it. Disappointment had him in a tight grip. "I get that she got hurt, but people date and break up all the time. Ryan and Steffi are the exception, not the rule. Just because a relationship doesn't lead to a diamond ring doesn't make it a mistake. But even if she were willing to roll the dice, my loyalty to you is also a problem. Apparently, she can do the forgive part, but not the forget."

"You're upset." Peyton stared at him with open interest. "Do you really like her?"

"Why are you still so surprised? She'd been one of your closest friends for years. Surely you're aware of all of her good qualities."

"Claire's a great person, but you've never really *liked* anyone, and her needs and yours are miles apart." She stretched her arms out to emphasize the point.

He shrugged that off. Yes, they were different people, but emotions didn't run out of gas. They traveled far and wide, crossing all kinds of barriers. "We all have the same needs when it comes to relationships. Claire doesn't care about my money or how I can help her. She sees me for who I am. She makes me believe that maybe I actually do have something more to offer than my last name."

His sister closed her eyes for the second time, this time for even longer. "You want a life of adventure and a way to leave a mark. She wants to nest here in town and head up her daughter's Brownie troop one day. These two things don't exactly fit together."

"Are all women always thinking about marriage? Can't we hang out and see where it leads? Regardless, I think you don't know her as well as you think you do. I think she's yearning for more, but fear"—he thought of how she'd meticulously curated it in that damn scrapbook, and about her parents' suffocating concern—"has sent her down a years-long detour. The real Claire had goals of competing all over the globe. She never planned to live her whole life in this little corner of the world, and dammit, *that* Claire is not dead."

She seemed to weigh that possibility before tipping her head to the side. "And if you're wrong? You've mentioned all these things Claire gives you, but what do you really give her, Logan?"

What indeed. "Apparently she must agree with you, because it's done. So, if that's all, spare me the lecture and let me get some sleep."

"Fine." She rose. "When you wake up, let's take some pictures. I'm feeling stronger today, and I want to capture that."

He managed a smile at that news. "I'm glad *you're* having a good day. Sorry if I spoiled it."

"Don't worry. I'll find a way to make you pay," she teased, but he had a feeling she meant it. If he weren't dead tired, he might've pressed her for details.

Chapter Thirteen

Claire sat at her dining table, surrounded by empty wrappers and a toppled carton of Milk Duds, peeking over her shoulder at that scrapbook less often in the past hour than during the one before that. Most of the time she'd been playing with Logan's living room design on her CAD program.

The sooner she finished his project, the sooner she'd be able to put him behind her. And putting him behind her was now a priority. She'd known better than to let things get this far, yet she'd barreled ahead on impulse. Exactly the kind of thing Peyton would've done. *God! Is that what happened with Todd?*

She slapped her cheeks to clear those thoughts, then refocused on the experimental combinations of furniture layouts meant to create intimate groupings and maximize flow. One involved a traditional U-shaped layout with a sofa and two chairs around a coffee table, the other being four comfortable chairs circling a round ottoman table.

Her stomach growled, so she went to the kitchen to rummage for more snacks. Dishes from breakfast remained in the sink. She suppressed the gnawing ache of how she'd blown everything up before giving it a chance.

After staring inside the refrigerator for a long while, she grabbed two tapioca pudding cups. On her way back to the dining table, the doorbell rang. She clutched the twin cups to her chest and held her breath. *Logan?*

After setting the pudding on the counter, she tried to use the microwave glass as a mirror, which didn't work well. Shrugging, she smoothed her hair back behind her ears and went to the door.

With a deep breath, she opened it and then froze.

"Peyton?" Claire blinked as if looking at a mirage. Peyton stood on her porch, wrapped in a coat and scarf with a wool winter cap pulled down to her ears. Claire couldn't very well let someone with a weakened immune system freeze outside. *Dammit.* "Come in."

"Thank you." Peyton stepped inside and loosened her scarf, but didn't unbutton her coat or remove her hat.

Claire didn't invite her to do so, either. Her heart beat erratically. "Why are you here?"

"Two reasons, actually. The first is about Steffi. I know she asked you to be her maid of honor, and that you know she asked me to be a bridesmaid. I've been thinking about it, and while I'd love to participate, I don't want to ruin the experience for you. I'm sure you'd rather not plan a bachelorette party with me, or other things like that. You and she are partners and have kept in better touch with each other throughout the years. After what I've done . . . well, I'll bow out if it makes it easier for you. I can find other ways to be involved and will be happy in the pews with everyone else."

Claire stared at this stranger masquerading as Peyton. All those weeks she'd dreaded Peyton's return, she'd assumed her old friend would be coming back. The one who'd rarely let other people's hangups prevent her from doing anything. The one who'd craved attention and adulation.

She had no idea how to confront—or trust—this more selfless version. But it made Claire feel small to harbor so much ill will toward her now.

"That's gracious, but if you aren't involved, then it will ruin things for Steffi. It's her day, and her wishes matter most. I won't let our problems interfere with her joy."

"Thank you." She smiled. "I know you aren't doing this for me, but I'm grateful anyway. I don't know what you want to do for a bachelorette party, but if you're busy with work, I'm happy to come up with ideas, make calls, or whatever. Just let me know." Peyton shoved her hands in her coat pockets.

Claire's head spun. "I'm still reeling from the wedding news and need a minute to catch my breath. I'm also in the middle of finishing Logan's design plan, so I can't think about party plans until tomorrow at the earliest."

Peyton held her breath for two seconds before exhaling. "That actually brings me to the other reason I wanted to see you."

Claire tilted her head, praying Logan hadn't said anything, but knowing from the look on Peyton's face that he had. "Which is . . . ?"

"Logan came home late this morning and put himself to bed. He was still sleeping when I left the house." She stared at Claire like she wanted her to confess.

Claire remained silent.

"I know he spent the night here, and then you had an argument. Given the crush you've always had on him, I suspect you have hopes regardless of what you're telling him or yourself." When Claire didn't respond, Peyton added, "I'm concerned."

This pitying look was exactly what Claire had wanted to avoid. "Don't be."

"I can't help it. I don't think his intentions are bad. He's always liked you a lot, Claire, and it seems he's grown more attached to you now. But we both know that when he realizes I'm well enough to survive without him, he'll go right back to his old life."

"One that won't include me." Claire raised one brow.

"Well"—Peyton cleared her throat—"given your preference for staying close to home, it would seem so. And apparently you told him as much. Still, none of us are smart when it comes to our hearts, and I'm worried that you might be in over your head."

Claire closed her eyes and clamped her mouth shut to keep from shouting. She blew out her breath and opened her eyes, controlling her voice as best she could. "Peyton, I don't want to get into an argument, but, honestly, your concern is ironic given how little regard you had for my feelings when it came to Todd."

Peyton nodded but didn't shy away from the accusation. "It's because of Todd that I don't want to see you hurt again."

Claire crossed her arms and tried to remove the scowl from her face. "If Logan were hooking up with Steffi, would you be concerned? Assuming Steffi wasn't with Ryan, of course."

"Probably not, but Steffi's never been as quick to give her heart."

"Well, I'm a grown-up, just like her and you and the rest of the old gang. I'm no different from anyone else who's been hurt in the past, so I'd appreciate it if people would stop treating me special, whether I'm walking on ice or wading into a relationship. For almost sixteen years I've lived with extra scrutiny and pampering. For once, I want to be *normal*." Claire flung her arms out from her sides. "Whatever is or isn't happening with Logan is between him and me, and I will handle the fallout on my own. I don't need kid gloves. Got it?"

Of course, she was being a hypocrite, because if she really meant everything she'd just said, then she needn't have sent Logan packing so soon.

"Loud and clear. I'm sorry I overstepped. I was trying to be a friend." Peyton looked down at the ground. She didn't say it, but Claire heard the unspoken sentiment—that she wanted to be the friend she hadn't been a year ago.

Claire wanted to reject the idea that Peyton actually cared. That she'd come here with good intentions in her ongoing campaign to mend fences. Then a memory of Peyton pranking Beau Miller junior year surged forward. She'd signed him up for a bunch of weird Craigslist stuff after he called Claire gimpy.

Before Peyton reached for the door to leave, Claire asked, "If it weren't for the fact that I've been a homebody, would you still think I'm a bad fit for your brother?"

Peyton stared at Claire, neither smiling nor frowning. "Does my opinion matter to you?"

"I'm not sure." She hugged herself. "You do know Logan better than anyone else."

Peyton flashed a sad smile. "But I don't know you as well anymore."

"True." An ocean of conflicted emotions rolled through the living room like a tidal wave.

"I shouldn't have butted in, especially since there aren't any guarantees when it comes to love . . . or life, for that matter."

Cancer. Whenever Claire thought about what Peyton was facing, she felt not only weak for her attitude about risk but also petty for her inability to be more forgiving. "Logan said the same thing."

Peyton smiled. "Well, we are a lot alike."

That's exactly what scared Claire, but it was also probably why it seemed like she knew Logan better than she otherwise would based solely on the time they'd spent together.

Peyton must've read Claire's mind because she quipped, "Don't hold that against him, though."

Under other circumstances, Claire might've chuckled at her friend's sarcasm. But she *had* been holding it against Logan, even if subconsciously.

"You look a little better than you did the other week." Claire's abrupt change of subject caught Peyton by surprise, judging from the way she quickly opened and closed her mouth.

"I suppose a backhanded compliment is better than none at all." She winked and then sucked her lips inward as if remembering that they were no longer on joking terms. "I am stronger today. More rested. Maybe the sea air is working."

"Well . . ." She wanted to say that she was glad to hear it, but that would sound phony given the resentment she'd clung to for so long. "Steffi and Logan will be happy to hear it."

"Steffi and Logan . . . ," Peyton repeated quietly. "Yes, I think so."

Claire nodded, a hard lump forming in her throat. "Thanks for considering my feelings about the wedding stuff. I'll call you in a couple of days to talk about party ideas, although Steffi's always hated bachelorette parties. Maybe we need to think up some other way to celebrate."

"I'll give it more thought." Peyton tightened her scarf and stepped outside, glancing over her shoulder. "Good luck, Claire."

Claire closed the door but then went to the living room window and watched Peyton drive away. Her empty, quiet house closed in from all sides. She tugged at the collar of her turtleneck in search of oxygen.

No one was there to upset her, but no one was there to comfort her, either. The African violets, though living, were hardly a substitute for a confidante. She was alone, as usual. The difference today was that she knew she didn't have to be if she could only follow Logan's advice and let go . . . of it all.

By four o'clock, she was suffocating. After pulling her hair into a short ponytail, she slipped on shoes, grabbed her keys, and headed to the library. A new book or two would give her the perfect escape hatch.

—ᴡᴡ—

Naomi was at the checkout desk wearing a T-shirt that read "Me? Weird? Always." She looked up when she heard Rosie thumping along the carpet. "Hey, you. Loading up or unloading?"

"Loading up." Claire set down three new novels. Two dukes and one rogue earl—historical-romance nirvana.

Naomi flipped open the first cover and scanned the code. "Guess you already read next month's discussion book?"

"I did." The memoir *Educated* had reminded her, in some ways, of *The Glass Castle*.

"What did you think?" Naomi scanned the second book.

"I can't believe how she triumphed despite all she endured." There'd been moments while reading it that Claire had needed to physically put it down and walk away.

The author had been raised by paranoid Mormon survivalists in Idaho who'd forbidden her to go to school. Despite that and many other crazy things, she eventually became a Brigham Young graduate who earned a PhD from Cambridge. Although the author's tale of transformation was inspiring, Claire also had an unpleasant recognition that her family's PTSD and paranoia resulting from her accident—if taken to extremes—could turn out to be very bad. She saw herself as if standing at the top of a sliding board, and if she kept on her current path, she might slide closer to an extreme place of isolation and fear before she realized what was happening.

"You know I've got a healthy paranoia about our government, but her dad made me look like a poster child for patriotism and pop culture." Naomi scanned Claire's final book, checked her screen, and typed something. She passed the stack across the counter. "These should be a nice change of pace."

"Romantic, escapist, and *happy*." Claire dumped the books into her tote bag.

"If romance is what you crave, you might be better off with a real man instead of those book boyfriends." Naomi set her elbows on the counter and leaned forward.

"Easier said than done."

"I heard you took that job for Logan Prescott." Naomi eyed her. "Pat and her pragmatism got to you, or maybe something more motivated your decision, eh?"

"Just bills. Lots and lots of bills." She knew her blush gave her away, which made her feel doubly foolish.

"I doubt that." With a shrug, Naomi drummed the countertop with her hands. "Want a little advice from an old spinster?"

"Sure."

"You and I, we're not the same kind of people. You're not cut out for the solo gig. You need people, Claire, and you deserve something better than books to keep you up at night. Don't let one bad apple make you run screaming from the orchard. Grab hold and experiment with all kinds of apples until you find one with the perfect bite—or in your case, maybe you'd prefer one covered in caramel."

Claire laughed for the first time all day, although she wondered if Naomi had been hurt deeply in the past. "That does sound tempting. I'll keep it in mind."

"See you later." Naomi waved goodbye and wandered into the admin office behind the circulation desk.

Claire tossed the bag of books on the passenger seat when she got to her car and mulled over Naomi's advice.

Face it, Claire. The only way to get people to stop feeling sorry for her was if she acted bolder and took risks. She had to show people that she could handle life's ups and downs on her own—in business and in her personal life. No one would ever believe her if she didn't believe in herself enough to try.

On her way home, she dialed Steffi but got dumped into her voice mail. "Steffi, give me a buzz. I want to talk to you about making a big pitch."

———

High, thin clouds lent brightness to the late afternoon without creating hot spots. Luck had smiled on Logan, who'd wanted to shoot photos of Peyton on the beach where they'd spent their childhood.

Dressed in jeans, a wool coat, and a black wool bowler cap, his sister looked striking today, and strong. Determined. Maybe even a little pissed at him about the Claire situation. That was okay, though, because anger had put fire in her eyes. A spark of life that had been absent for too long.

She'd been a trouper, taking orders from him about this position or that rocky outcropping, but now she was shivering.

He detached the telephoto lens from his Canon. "Go inside. I'll pack up and follow in a bit."

"I'll make some tea." Her teeth chattered. "Want some?"

"Nah."

"See you inside." She trotted across the shallow beach and up the lawn to the house.

It didn't take long to put his things into the camera bag, but he was in no hurry to go inside. If anything, he welcomed some time alone to think about what to do with Claire. He'd gone to sleep angry and awakened with regrets.

He glanced down the beach a few hundred yards to where a father and his daughter were flying a kite as if it were summer. The contrast of its primary colors against the near-white sky drew the eye. But that wasn't what reached into his chest to squeeze his heart. The bubble of the little girl's laughter carried along the wind from where her dad had crouched to gently support her arms and shoulders.

Logan had no memory of gentle support from his parents, but the scene prompted a foggy memory of Duck, who'd died before Logan's seventh birthday. Logan had been about four, back when many more trees stood along the edge of the property bordering the sea. There'd been a woven hammock strung between two oak trees near the beach, and Duck would let Logan curl up beside him while he read aloud.

The William H. Prescott in Logan's memory was a kind, frail man with a soft voice and a shock of white hair. Photographs of the younger version typically showed his handsome face in a serious state of concentration, but he'd actually laughed easily, sharing the same wry humor as Peyton.

How different might Logan be if Duck had lived longer? Or if his own father had shown him that kind of easygoing attention?

The man who'd written with passion and eloquence—with sharp observations—had carried a deep well of love to draw upon. One can't write fiction that grabs readers' hearts if he has an empty tank.

Maybe that was why Logan hadn't yet found the kind of storytelling success he'd been chasing for a decade. His tank was low on deep love, except for his feelings for Peyton, anyway.

"Logan!" she called from the house behind him, holding his cell phone overhead.

He turned and trotted toward her. "What?"

"Claire's calling." She extended his phone toward him when he reached the back patio, one brow arched. "Please be careful."

He followed her inside as he answered the phone. "Claire."

"Hi."

He cast a glance at Peyton and then strode into the front parlor and closed the double doors. "How are you?"

"I'm fine." She cleared her throat. "Any chance you're free now?"

His heart skipped. "What's up?"

"I completed a few design plans, and I want your opinion before I keep going."

Work, nothing more. His chest hurt. "That was fast."

"I had a breakthrough."

Well, great. He'd put himself to bed because he'd felt shitty; meanwhile, she'd turned their fight into a creative tour de force. "Okay. I'll be over shortly."

He opened the doors to find Peyton sitting on a bench in the entry hall. She stood when he crossed to the stairs. "I'm sorry."

"For what?" He halted, a sick pit opening in his gut.

"Oh . . . Claire didn't . . ."

"Claire didn't what?" He stepped closer, narrowing his eyes.

She sighed, shoulders slumping. "I went to see her while you napped."

"You did what?" He ran one hand over his hair.

"I had to talk to her about being in Steffi's wedding party, and then I brought up your little tryst."

"Tryst?" He pressed his fingers to his temple to keep from throttling her. "Did you actually use that word?"

"No."

"Thank God." He let his hands fall to his sides. "I asked you to butt out."

"If it's any consolation, so did Claire."

"Good." He turned and started up the stairs.

"Logan, she didn't say it, but I saw how much she cares for you written all over her face. She's not like Karina and the others."

"I know that, Peyton." It was precisely why he liked spending time with her. "Now if you'll excuse me, I've got to shower and go."

Chapter Fourteen

Claire couldn't deny that having Logan in her bed last night had been better than any of the tingles she'd gotten from her very best book boyfriends. She stashed her new romance novels in a drawer before taking one last look around her house—newly cleared of empty junk-food wrappers.

Two glasses of pinot noir sat by her laptop, waiting for Logan's arrival without accompanying candles or anything else. Just a hint of her intentions or, rather, an attempt at a new attitude toward their relationship.

Naomi would be proud.

The phone rang. She glanced at the screen, closed her eyes, and let loose a shallow huff. "Mom, this isn't a great time. Can I call you later or tomorrow?"

"Sure. I just wanted to warn you that Nora Williams told me that a burglar tried to break into Janie Jones's house last night. He got away without getting caught, which means he could be on the hunt for a new target. Lock your doors."

"I always do." Claire could practically hear her mom making the sign of the cross. "Please don't worry so much about me."

"Oh, honey, I can't help it," she said on a sigh, but Claire heard the loving smile in her voice, too. "What did you do today?"

"Worked a little. Went to the library."

"Sounds like a wonderful, relaxing day." Her bright voice vibrated genuine happiness. If she knew how miserable Claire had actually been, it would crush her.

"Mom, I'm sorry to rush you, but I'm expecting someone." She stole a glimpse at the door as if it would make Logan appear.

"Who?"

"A client," Claire covered rather than field yet another of her mom's complaints about Logan carting her off to New York. If her mom knew about Newport, she might have a stroke. "I'll swing by tomorrow to see you and Dad. Maybe we can grab dinner."

"Lovely. I'll bake a cheesecake!"

"Make it a chocolate one." If tonight didn't go well, Claire would need that all to herself. "Bye!"

She muted her phone and tossed it onto a bookshelf, then checked herself in the mirror, frowning at the blonde highlights she shouldn't have had done. The fact that she'd thought, even for a moment, that her hair color would magically change her life made her embarrassed.

She started at the bang from the brass knocker outside. Tugging at the miniskirt she'd worn over tights, she then took Rosie in hand. She crossed the room on shaky legs and opened the door. Logan stood in the warm glow of the porch lights with his hands tucked into the pockets of his handsome black wool peacoat.

She let the simple joy of seeing him again fill her. "Thanks for coming."

Logan's green eyes gave no hint of his mood. "Sure."

"Come on in. You can toss your coat on the rack, then join me at the dining table." With her back to him, she closed her eyes and took a deep breath, loosening her grip on Rosie with each step. "I poured some wine."

She handed him a wineglass and then sipped from the other.

"Thanks." He took a full swallow, staring at her over the glass's rim, and waited for her to lead the discussion. When she gestured to his chair and opened her laptop, his eyes dimmed. Apparently, he'd hoped for something more.

"I know we should talk about this morning," she began, her toes curling inside her shoes, "but let's get business out of the way first."

He nodded and set his wineglass on the table, giving her his full attention. This was it—her one chance to dazzle him with her design. Her finger hovered over the "Return" key, paralyzed by a bout of nerves.

"I want to walk you through two potential floor plans and a color scheme I chose." She pressed the key, and her favorite living room image filled the screen.

She studied the design, trying to see it through fresh eyes. The virtual staging depicted navy-blue walls. Two square brown leather LC2 chairs with brass frames flanked an emerald-green tuxedo-style sofa. Beneath an ivory-and-gray coffee table lay a cream-and-navy rug. Embellished throw pillows in the corners of the sofa pulled all the colors of the room together. Mock art and lighting options gave some sense of how the space could look when finished.

When he didn't say anything, she reached for her wine before continuing. "It may seem a bit much at first glance, but give the palette a minute to grow on you. It's very current and handsome." *Like you,* she wanted to add, but didn't. "I'm thinking we play with texture, like mohair, velvet, and tabby, which can be masculine. We could also add texture to one wall with some picture-frame molding, but painted in navy so the pattern doesn't jump out or look too busy."

His gaze roamed the screen.

Sweat dotted her back. He'd asked her to design something just for him, but his silence suggested she'd totally missed the mark. He hated it. Her stomach turned rock hard. "Logan?"

She breathed through the knot tightening in her gut.

He turned to her as a wide smile emerged. "If you would've told me to buy a jewel-toned green sofa, I'd have balked. But seeing all this, it's sophisticated and warm. Spectacular. Exactly the kind of place I'd want to spend my free time."

The praise cascaded over her like warm water. She let loose a whoosh of air as the buzz of his approval breathed new life into her body.

"I'm so relieved. When you were quiet, I got nervous." She laid her hand on his forearm to command his attention. "You know it won't hurt my feelings, though, if you don't like something. You need to be honest with me because it's *your* house, not mine."

"I am being honest. I was just stunned into silence. You're an artist, Claire. This takes such imagination—vision—and an understanding of color and balance, and personality." When he rubbed her shoulder, she felt grateful that her elbow was on the table supporting her—otherwise she might've melted into a puddle. "Thank you for taking the time to get this so right."

She couldn't contain her smile. "You're welcome, but we're not done. There's an alternate floor plan, and I haven't shown you the bedroom yet."

Logan nixed the second floor plan for the living space. His velvet voice curled around her when he said, "Let's see the bedroom."

She pulled up those images, praying her face didn't broadcast the fantasies she'd spun while designing the master suite. The charcoal linen headboard she'd selected looked sharp against pale-gray walls. Two square emerald-green pillows trimmed in navy added a pop of color to the mostly white bed linens. A navy rug with splashes of white lent warmth to the otherwise cool space. Clean, crisp, and soothing. The body-art wall, with its charcoal and gray tones, remained intact.

Logan's lips parted a tad as he studied the image. "I love it."

Her heart filled with satisfaction. "I'm so glad you're happy."

"There's only one problem." His serious tone set her back.

"Oh?" She studied the design, searching for the flaw.

He then flashed an impudent grin. "I might never get out of that bed."

Her chuckle emerged raspy because her throat had gone a bit dry.

"I never appreciated what a good decorator could do until now. The transformation is stunning." He raised his glass. "Well done."

Despite the compliments, coming up with this design wasn't the end of her job. Now she had to locate the right fabrics to mimic what she'd conceived. More important, she'd yet to find the personal touches that would make it distinctly Logan's home. Her mind kept circling around photography and the shore—his passion and his childhood. She just couldn't come up with the right idea. But she would. She had to.

"How long will it take until it looks like this?" he asked.

"It depends on your parameters—stock versus custom order—and so on. Did you want to shop with me, or should I take photos and send them to you?"

"I don't have the patience for shopping. Based on this, I trust your taste implicitly. I'm not picky and don't care about designer labels or custom anything. Whatever is comfortable and works, and the sooner we can do it, the better. I can't wait to call this place home."

She smiled, although that statement fell on her heart like a hammer because his home was nearly one hundred miles away. If she were sly, she'd order handmade furniture from around the world so that it wouldn't be completed for six to nine months.

"I'll get started this week. Steffi will be demolishing Mrs. Brewster's bathroom, too, so suddenly business is looking up for us. If this keeps up, we'll be able to rent a small space in town soon." She drank more of her wine while Logan stared at her in a way that generated combustible heat. But these feelings went so far beyond fleeting passion. A river of gratitude swelled in her heart. "Thank you for hiring me for this job. It's been a lifesaver, in more ways than one."

"Oh?" He leaned closer, widening his feet on the floor, refusing to break eye contact. "In what other ways, Claire?"

She finished her wine before answering him, letting its warm tickle fan through her limbs. "As much as I griped, going to the city and

Rhode Island reminded me of the life I used to take for granted before my injury. I'm not ready to dash off everywhere or throw my scrapbook in the fire, but maybe, in time, I'll get more comfortable traveling beyond these few coastal communities." She shrugged at the meager victory. "At least now I want to try."

His beautiful eyes shimmered. She'd expected a self-satisfied response, not this heartfelt expression. He reached for one of her hands and held it in both of his. "So I helped you?"

"You did." She reached up to touch his cheek with her free hand, then let it fall. "And that's not all. I'm going to pitch your dad for the chance to decorate his new hotels."

"Really?" Logan let go of her hand and sat back, his smile less certain. "I know I suggested that earlier, but I'm not sure you'd like working with him."

"I doubt I'd work directly with him much, but a nonresidential project of that magnitude could do wonders for our bank account and rep. At the very least, we'd definitely have the money to lease the retail space I've been wanting."

"And the travel?"

"First things first. We have to win the contract. If that happens, I'll find a way to force myself to go, just like I did with you. Steffi will be with me." She shrugged. "Can't hurt to submit a bid, anyway."

He tilted his head and folded his arms, appearing to be in conflict with himself. "I thought you didn't want to get more involved with my family because of Peyton."

Claire pictured Peyton, who'd courageously come to face more rejection today. "She and I will never be friends like before, but fate keeps pushing us together—at the upcoming gala, as part of Steffi's bridal party. It's obvious that I have to rebuild some kind of relationship with her. For Steffi's sake, and mine."

Without warning, Logan pulled her onto his lap and laid his cheek against her head. "You have no idea how happy this makes me, for *everyone's* sake, including ours."

Ours. No better word existed in any language. Of course, Logan wasn't implying any long-term promise. He was firmly an "in the moment" guy. For now, she'd give his philosophy a try to savor each second without projecting ahead to maybes and wishes.

She kept her cheek resting on his shoulder, nestling against him, glad for the chance to say some things without having to look in his eyes. "I'm sorry about this morning and for ruining what had otherwise been a memorable night."

He felt so warm and yet solid at the same time. It still astounded her that, after all these years and dreams, she could be sitting on Logan's lap at his invitation.

"Memorable enough to repeat?" He slowly massaged her back and waist, as if waiting for permission to do more. He raised his head, tipping it sideways to catch her eye.

She turned her face until they shared the same breath. "Yes."

He crushed his mouth to hers, gripping her head with one hand while pulling her snugly against him with the other. She could feel him hardening beneath her bottom.

"Let's take the wine upstairs." He nipped at her lower lip. "We're filling the bathtub with bath salts and hot water while you're feeling this adventuresome."

"That's a real thing with you, isn't it." She kept her arms loosely wound around his neck. Her human life raft.

"It is." He kissed her again.

Yet another way he'd push her out of her comfort zone. No more shrouding her scars under blankets and the cover of darkness. Being naked in a tub would fully expose them. He'd see them turn redder the longer they soaked in hot water. Ugly reminders of lifelong limitations and pain.

"Trust me," he urged. "There's nothing you need to hide from me."

She nodded her consent even as she trembled from the thought. Logan rose, keeping her in his arms and carrying her up the stairs to her room.

While Claire undressed and concealed herself with her robe, Logan went to the bathroom. She found him filling the tub with steaming water and lavender bath salts. He'd even stolen a candle from Steffi's old room and lit it on the vanity. Its flickering light bounced off the mirror and reflected little beams of euphoria throughout the room.

Her eyes stung from emotional overload. Here she was—with Logan. And there he was, being romantic and sexy . . . all for her.

Lacking any self-consciousness whatsoever, he dropped his clothes to the ground and stepped into the tub before gesturing for her to join him.

She ogled his sinewy perfection while gripping the knot of her robe. The physical disparity between them was wider than the Gulf of Mexico. Yet she'd set this up, determined to break out of her shell. To try a new way. To prove to herself and others that she didn't need to be coddled or pitied.

Be bold enough to meet him on his terms.

With trembling hands, she untied her robe. It drifted to the ground without a sound, leaving her standing in the middle of the bathroom, naked. She kept her hand by her side instead of using it to shield the scars around her hip—a small but surprisingly proud moment.

He sat and stretched out his legs, his gaze roaming her entire body, lingering a moment on her breasts.

"Come here, beautiful." He reached out one arm.

She stepped into the silky, hot water and laid her back against his chest. Lavender-scented steam calmed her nerves, as did the flickering candlelight.

He handed her one wineglass while keeping hold of his own. Dipping his free hand beneath the surface of the water, he then caressed her abdomen while planting kisses on her neck between sips of wine.

The only sounds in the bathroom were the sloshing water and a low hum in her throat. It felt luxurious and brazen to sit in his lap while he explored her body in the scented, soft water. Anticipation pooled low in her abdomen, making her squirm.

When he emptied his glass, he set it on the floor and she followed suit. In no time, his hands stroked her thighs until his fingers found her center. She arched her back, letting her head fall against his shoulder, and nibbled on his ear while raising her hands overhead to drag through his hair.

Logan.

The leaky faucet marked time with its slow drip. Water spilled over the edge of the tub as their bodies rocked together. Once again she was making love with Logan. "Love." That word threaded through her thoughts and heart like a chain stitch, but she kept it to herself.

Whether the lavender calmed her or she'd truly come to accept the limitations of this relationship, she wasn't sure—nor did she care. Not while inside their steamy, candlelit cocoon. Her full heart was enough for now.

⁓

A few mornings later, Logan waltzed into Arcadia's kitchen, whistling, and grabbed a yogurt from the refrigerator. "Morning, Mom."

From the table where she sat with a notepad, she removed her glasses and twined her arms behind her back for a quick stretch. "Where are you rolling in from, my darling son?"

"Here and there." Claire had asked him to be discreet for now. He peeled back the foil top and tossed it in the trash. "Nothing to report."

One of her perfect brows shot up. "I doubt that. You do have a nice spring in your step, though, so maybe I'll just leave well enough alone."

"Thank you." He glanced around before digging his spoon into the cup. "Where's Peyton?"

"Upstairs."

He debated his plan to help Claire for a millisecond. "Dad?"

"Why?" His mom stared at him, her mouth at half gape.

He spooned another bite, averting her gaze. "I want to talk to him."

"Really?" She put her glasses on and peered at him more closely. "You never want to be in the same room with him if you can avoid it."

"I know." He almost confessed his motive, because an ally would be ideal, but he hadn't cleared it with Claire. "Is he home?"

"Can you tell me why you need to see him? If I have to brace for World War Three, I'd like to know."

"I come in peace, Mom." His mother and he had gone years without sharing secrets, and he saw no reason to confide in her now.

She sipped from her coffee cup, waiting. When he didn't offer more, she conceded. "He's in the office. Please don't rile him up."

"I won't." He tossed the empty container in the trash and crossed to look over her notebook. "Did you finish the seating chart for the gala?"

"Yes, why?"

"Where'd you put me?"

"With Peyton . . ." Her eyes scanned his face as if he were an imposter with his sudden interest in his father and the gala. He might've laughed if he hadn't been working so hard at nonchalance. "And Karina."

Shit. He'd forgotten about Karina. He owed her a call to follow up on her interest in going to interview refugees in Lesbos, Greece, too. "How about our friends, like Ryan, Ben, Steffi . . . Claire?"

"They're at a table together with the Quinns and Mike Lockwood."

"Is it near us?" He strolled to her and glanced over her shoulder to the notebook.

"It can be." She sat back, drumming her fingers on the table. "Is there a reason for this request?"

"You know I'm not a huge fan of this shindig. It'd help to be close to my friends, especially because I'm likely to be leaving for work soon." Karina had mentioned that a court decision on the refugee-migration thing was expected anytime now. If they were going to go, it'd be best to be there when the ruling came down. "I could be gone for several weeks."

"You and your sister are always running far away from home." She made a moue before she reached out and grabbed his hand. Once again, he froze from the unusual contact. The only explanation he could come up with for her recent behavior was that Peyton's illness had made her slightly more aware of the fact that she shouldn't take her kids for granted. "Were we such bad parents that you can't stand to be around us?"

Bad? No. A bit neglectful. A bit standoffish. A bit more concerned with how the family "looked" to others than how it actually functioned.

"I'm not running away from my family." He offered a reassuring squeeze of the hand, having no interest in a heart-to-heart or in making her feel guilty. "I'm doing what I love. Traveling. Seeing other perspectives. Searching for a new story to tell."

She flashed a skeptical smile and dropped his hand. "If you say so."

He leaned forward and kissed the top of her head, the sudden affection making her go still, too. "Talk later."

What was happening? Claire's outlook on family must've infected him.

He wandered out of the kitchen and through the entry to the walnut-paneled office with large windows that offered idyllic views of the Sound—his great-grandfather's personal sanctuary. Duck's old typewriter remained on a bookcase along with signed editions of his work. His Pulitzer Prize certificate hung on the wall in a handsome gilt frame.

Logan wanted to win a Pulitzer for photography more than almost anything else in his life. It'd be validation that he deserved the name he bore, and proof that he hadn't been wasting his time like his dad believed.

His father looked up from behind the desk and paused. "Did you make a wrong turn?"

"Good morning to you, too, Dad." Logan nodded to an empty chair. "May I sit?"

His father's wary expression would be comical if it weren't such a sad statement on their relationship. "Well, don't keep me in suspense. What's wrong?"

"Nothing." Logan cleared his throat. Claire's warning about repeating bad patterns, and her willingness to try new things, might've persuaded him to attempt this fact-finding mission, but he'd have to wade in carefully. "Since I'm here for a while, I thought it'd be nice if we tried to understand each other a little better . . . get along. I know you think I'm a slacker, but I do have goals." He pointed at Duck's award. "That right there is one of mine. My photography might not be as lucrative as your work, but that doesn't make it nonsense. This house is a testament to the value others assign the creative arts."

"You know the odds against *any* creative endeavor breaking through and making money. They don't call them starving artists for nothing, Logan." His chair rocked back as he shifted, its hinge squeaking under his weight. "If it weren't for your trust fund, you'd be living with six people in a walk-up studio."

"I make money. Not huge money, but I can comfortably support myself." He paused. "But if the trust went away, I'd still pursue my art—even if it meant living in squalor. I'm compelled to do it, whether you understand that or not. You don't have to agree with that choice, but you could stop treating me, and my passion, with disdain. Is that so much to ask?"

"You tell me." His dad rose from his desk, crossed to the antique beverage cart, and opened a bottle of bourbon. He poured two tumblers full and handed one to Logan before taking his seat again. "From where I sit, you've shown equal disdain toward me and my business, and taken no more interest in my projects than I have in yours."

"Point taken." Logan sipped the bourbon, sensing he'd be leaving this office with more than he'd bargained for when he'd come in. "Tell me about your vision for these hotels."

"Eager to criticize me?" His dad threw back a healthy swallow and set the glass on a coaster.

"No. I'm being sincere." Logan drew one foot across the opposite knee, settling in for a longer conversation. "Why does this project excite you?"

His dad shrugged with an expression that suggested the answer was obvious. "Because I can take something that's failing and make it a success."

"Like you did with the family fortune after Grandpa practically lost this house." Logan had to admit that had taken courage and tremendous effort.

"I suppose yes, exactly like that." He swiveled in his chair and glanced out the windows at the property he'd saved. From Logan's angle, his dad's partial profile made him look like he'd been carved in marble. Hard. Intense. Indomitable. His dad turned back to face Logan with a soft sigh. "I'm always sorry that I had to sell off so much of this land to do it, but, ultimately, that call saved this house and secured the funds to build something more for our family. Something that didn't require talent and luck to maintain, like publishing and pictures. I didn't inherit a creative gene, but I'm smart, savvy, and not afraid to roll up my sleeves and put in long hours."

At first blush, that speech sounded prideful. But its tone hinted at a bit of envy, too. Despite his protests, perhaps his dad would've liked to follow in *his* grandfather's shoes but couldn't.

Thanks to his dad's choices—sacrifices, even—Logan had had the financial freedom to pursue his passion. Maybe it wasn't disdain, but resentment, that his father felt toward him now.

"Well, you have a talent for turning around failing businesses, Dad. That's a kind of creative thinking."

"I suppose."

"And you must have a vision for this hotel project. What's the secret that suddenly will make them profitable?"

His dad steepled his fingers, staring at Logan as if he didn't trust him. "Why do I feel like there's more to your question than you're sharing?"

"I'm just trying to make a connection with you," he lied. A tiny lie. Yes, he wanted information to share with Claire to help her tailor her pitch, but another part of him did want to prolong the first real adult conversation he could recall having with his father.

"The seller is a third-generation family trust. A classic case of no one being involved in the business." He paused, and Logan suspected his dad bit back a sarcastic quip about how Logan would fit right in with them. "They all collect checks and put their faith in whomever they've hired in each location to manage the property. Big mistake. If anyone had given things a cursory look, they would've seen high rates of employee turnover, a little theft, and the general lack of oversight that led to the hotels going downhill. Dingy decor, mediocre food. None of these things are hard to fix when you hire the right team and manage them well. As for the physical space, I'd like to upgrade them, within reason. Can't go overboard when I need to invest in new employees, new computers and software, and more."

"You'd mentioned they were along the Atlantic, but where specifically?"

"Why?" His dad polished off his drink.

Logan followed suit and finished his, then set the glass on the small table to his left. "Maybe I'll go check out one or two."

"You need a vacation?" Like a boomerang, his father's sarcasm whipped around on him.

Logan sighed.

"Sorry. Old habits." His dad made a wry face. "The chain is called the Seaboard Guest Houses, but I want to change that when we take over. One's up in Blue Hill, Maine. Then Portsmouth, New Hampshire. Up the road in Mystic. Then down in Lewes, Delaware, just north of Bethany Beach. Avalon, New Jersey, and finally Annapolis, Maryland."

"I'll try to take a trip up to Mystic before the transformation so I can enjoy a before-and-after reveal. Good luck."

"Thank you."

Having accomplished what he'd come for, Logan moved to stand, but his father said, "Wait. Your mom tells me you're pushing your sister into some kind of charity project that she's going to regret. I know Darla can . . . exaggerate . . . but what's she talking about?"

That was a nice way of saying that Logan's mom had a tendency to encourage drama. Of course, Logan suspected that half the time she resorted to it because she didn't know how else to get her husband's full attention.

"I'm not forcing Peyton into anything. I've been photographing her at least once a week, sometimes more often, since the night before her first treatment." As soon as he started to think about the work, the fire lit inside. "She's been journaling and I've been keeping other things, like parking stubs, prescription labels, etcetera. We've considered a cool installation at a gallery as a fund-raiser, but now we're more focused on turning it into a memoir. I'd be happy to show you what we've got so far. It's been a positive outlet—I think Peyton's proud of turning something terrifying into something courageous."

His dad rubbed his chin while nodding. "If you can do that for her, then I can't complain."

Not exactly praise, but for them, a lack of criticism equaled huge progress. "Thanks. The only hiccup could be my missing a few weeks of photo shoots if I travel to Greece, but I can't control the timing." He slid another glance at the Pulitzer. "If I find the right refugee story, I could help change lives for the better."

His father's politics were more conservative than his own, so he didn't expect encouragement. "Your mom worries when you take off on dangerous adventures."

"Can't exactly find a great story in these surroundings, can I?"

"Oh, I don't know. Look at the old Sunny von Bülow story. Or your sister's project."

Logan nodded. "Peyton's message could help some people, but the refugee story has the potential to change the world and influence the way people think about bias and politics and immigration."

"I guess that's the biggest difference between us. You want to take pictures and change the world, while I'm content to keep our little world on track."

Peyton had been right when she'd said Logan hadn't appreciated what his father had done well. What he'd provided for them. "Thank you for finding a way to keep this house in our family. I know I don't come home often, but I do love this property and everything it commemorates."

"You're welcome." His dad cleared his throat. "Now, if you don't mind, I need to get back to what I was doing before you showed up."

"Sure." Logan raised himself from the chair, taking his glass with him.

He left the office feeling as if he'd shed ten pounds. When he reached the kitchen, he ran into his mother again.

"You survived without bruises or a black eye. How's your father?" She grinned.

"Also unscathed." Logan set the glass in the sink. "Mom, make an extra seat at our table. I think I'm bringing a date."

"Who?" A smile lit up her face.

"I'll let you know if she says yes." Before he became the subject of an inquisition, he turned on his heel and went in search of his sister.

Chapter Fifteen

Claire signed the last purchase order and handed it to Ellen Westwood, a young decorator at the Design Outlet in Hartford. The massive warehouse space housed hundreds of floor samples, from seating to case goods to lighting and accessories, which were what she'd need if she had any hope of pulling Logan's apartment together in the quick time frame he'd requested.

Luckily, the store kept Sunday-afternoon hours. She'd never been here before, but she had known about it from her days at Ethan Allen. Her new attitude and recent outings with Logan had emboldened her, allowing her to attempt a drive to Hartford today—a first, and a true feat. She'd proven something to herself by coming, and Logan would be pleased, too. The items she'd found had also made the trip worthwhile.

With Ellen's help, she'd ordered two leather chairs—similar to what she'd shown Logan in her virtual plan—that could be delivered immediately. She didn't want them that soon, though. First, Steffi needed to install the trim work on the living room wall and repaint the entire unit.

She'd also selected a round ebony dining table, which perfectly fit the space. The white-and-gray dining chairs she'd bought would complement the other furnishings.

Thankfully, all of those items had been on sale, which enabled her to splurge on a several-thousand-dollar Tibetan carpet for the dining room. Its rampant floral-and-ivy pattern, with bits of gold and blue, was splashed across a black field. "Magnificent" was the only word for the gorgeous woven work of art.

"I'll get back to you this week once I have an estimated delivery date on the Century Del Mar sofa in the green velvet." Ellen collected the papers while handing Claire copies. "We'll hold the rest of these items for you for a few weeks."

"I'll have a better idea of the timing on my end in a few days." Claire needed to speak with Steffi about how soon she could have the unit ready to accept the furniture.

"Perfect." Ellen smiled at Claire, pushing her frameless glasses up onto the bridge of her nose. "I'd love to see pictures when the project is done. Your drawings are fabulous."

"Thank you." Claire stood with her tear sheets, fabric samples, and receipts in hand, and grabbed Rosie. "Have a great evening."

Her shopping-spree high plummeted when she walked outside into an unexpected end-of-March snowfall.

Today's forecast had called for a chance of rain along the coast, but when she'd left home under a pale-gray sky free of storm clouds, she'd figured the weatherman had been wrong. Unfortunately, he was, just not in the way that she'd thought.

A thin sheen of sweat coated her skin once she slid into the driver's seat. She flexed her hands on the steering wheel a few times and licked her lips before turning over the ignition.

You can do this.

Snowflakes melted on the pavement, making the roads slick. Her wipers squeaked against the windshield, each swipe leaving a streaky trail. She performed deep-breathing exercises as she eased onto I-91 southbound.

When she'd driven up to Hartford, the Sunday-morning traffic had been light, as she'd expected. Now, she found herself in the middle of a multilane snake of taillights moving at warp speed. Ski racks and Thules topped half the cars. Obviously, everyone who'd gone to Vermont this weekend for spring skiing had decided to drive home at the same time.

For fifteen minutes, she crept along in the far right lane, wincing with each flashing light and honking horn coming from angry drivers eager to pass her in their rush to wherever they were going. She strained to see through grimy windows littered with the gritty spray kicked up by other tires. Tears streamed down her face, and her fingers ached from their tight grip on the wheel.

Ahead, red taillights lit up one by one like a fall of dominoes. She slammed the brakes, her heart racing. Traffic slowed to a crawl, thanks to a three-car pileup that forced everyone to move over two lanes.

The entire hood of the middle car in that accident had crumpled like an accordion, with steam billowing into the cold air. Its driver appeared to be checking on someone in the passenger seat. The other two cars had sustained moderate damage, and both their drivers stood outside making phone calls. No ambulances or police had arrived on the scene, which meant it had just happened. If she'd left the Design Outlet a few minutes earlier, she might've been hit.

The sickening thought soured her stomach. When her phone rang, she saw Steffi's number on the dashboard.

"Hello?" she choked.

"Hey," Steffi began brightly, but quickly changed her tune. "Are you crying?"

Claire sniffled again, too terrified to think. "Yes."

"What happened? Did Logan do something?" Steffi's anger rang through the line.

"No. I drove to Hartford today, but now there's so much traffic. It's snowing up here, and I just barely missed being in an accident. I'm afraid. I don't think I can make it all the way home."

"Where are you?"

Claire looked ahead to the next green road sign. "Coming up on Meriden."

"Pull off the highway and park somewhere safe. Text me your location and I'll come get you."

Her chin wobbled, but she fought against crying. "I can't leave my car in Meriden, Steffi."

"Ryan will come with me so he can drive our car back while I drive yours."

Claire groaned. "I can't ask you guys to do that."

"You didn't ask. I offered. Just text me and I'll see you in thirty minutes." Steffi hung up without giving Claire a choice.

A wave of relief from being rescued preceded the bigger one that came when she pulled off the highway. She drove into a Red Roof Inn parking lot near the exit, texted Steffi her location, and then let her head fall back against her seat. Periodically, she swept warm tears from her cheeks. Failure had never been something she'd handled well.

Logan wouldn't be too impressed, either. Rosie lay in the passenger seat, taking the place of her mom, who'd be sure to spout a "What were you thinking" lecture.

By the time Steffi and Ryan arrived, the temperature had warmed enough to transform the snow to a steady drizzle. Steffi knocked on her window. "Switch seats."

Claire opened the door and waved at Ryan, whose compassionate expression only heightened her shame. She lumbered around her car and sank onto the passenger seat, picking at her damp skirt and looking anywhere but at her friend.

Before putting the car in reverse, Steffi said, "It's okay, Claire. Everything is just fine."

"It's not okay." Claire pulled a tissue from the glove compartment and blew her nose, then pushed the heels of her palms against her eyes. "I'm nearly thirty-one, and today is the first time I've ever driven alone on a major highway. It wasn't easy, but I was so proud of myself when I got to Hartford." A bitter laugh emerged. "Pitiful, right? Like something every *sixteen*-year-old can do is a flippin' big deal. But it was a huge step for me until you and Ryan had to drag yourself out to rescue me."

"We won't go broadcasting it if that's what you're worried about." Steffi shot her a reassuring smile.

"Thanks, but that's hardly the point. I wanted to do this for myself, and I failed." She frowned, twisting the hem of her sweater in her fingers. Her throat ached from the strain of holding back a sob.

"You didn't fail. You got to Hartford." Steffi stared ahead, giving one sharp nod. "Considering where you started, that's a win."

Claire released a gentle huff. "Perhaps, but we both know most people would roll their eyes."

All this time, she'd been irritated by people treating her like a baby, yet how *could* they see her as anything less than fragile when she'd let fear dictate her choices since the earliest days of her recovery?

Claire's thoughts spun while she stared out the passenger window. Meanwhile, Steffi confidently maneuvered the car along the highway, undaunted by the weather or traffic.

Minutes passed before Steffi asked, "Is there a reason why you decided to do this today?"

Claire stared at her hands, which were knotted on her lap, and thought about Logan. "Logan wants his apartment done as soon as possible. I've known about the Design Outlet's floor samples for years and thought I could pick up a bunch of things right away."

"So Logan's behind this?" Steffi sounded perturbed.

"No. I mean, indirectly, I guess so. Our recent trips to New York and Newport gave me courage."

"Newport?" Steffi's jaw fell open. "When was that?"

"Last Saturday. At the time, I hadn't realized he'd planned the outing to help Ryan carry out his proposal. He took me to see the Breakers. We had a lovely dinner overlooking the sea." Even she heard the lilt in her voice as she recollected the day they'd first made love.

"How is it that *he* can get you to go out of town when Peyton and I never could?" Steffi's voice sounded more hurt than angry.

Claire shrugged, unwilling to admit that lifelong lust proved to be a far more powerful motivator than she would've believed.

"I guess the important point is that you've pushed through some of that fear. That's a good thing, so I won't pout." Steffi slid a quizzical glance Claire's way. "Is Logan also behind your interest in pitching Mr. Prescott about his hotels?"

"He mentioned it a while ago. I was coming off the success of my Newport trip and how well Logan liked my designs when I suggested it to you."

"A big commercial project would be a great credential, but we're not a national company. With me planning a wedding and being a new stepmom, I'm not sure how I'd manage overseeing work in multiple locations." She wrinkled her nose. "And maybe you're not ready to travel as far as you thought, either."

"Gee, you think?" Claire's sarcasm brought the conversation to a halt. Neither said a word as they exited the highway onto the feeder road that led to Sanctuary Sound. The familiar surroundings prompted a relieved sigh. "At least now I won't have to figure out how to approach him at the gala."

"The gala." Steffi tsk-tsked. "Are you going with Logan?"

"No."

"Really?" Her brows shot up. "He'll sleep with you, but he won't take you to his family's fund-raiser?"

Claire turned to Steffi, crushed by her friend's assumption. "He asked, but I said no."

"Why?"

Claire could list several reasons, but the one Steffi would most understand came first. "I didn't want to spend the whole night at a table with Peyton."

Steffi nodded thoughtfully. "It sounds like you might regret that decision now."

Perhaps a little.

"It's not like I won't see him there." Claire shrugged. "I'll be more relaxed eating with all of you."

"Oh, Claire. Is a 'relaxed' time all you want? You've always had a thing for Logan, so why let Peyton or anyone else stand in the way?"

"Because we're not in a relationship. Not a real one, anyway." Although each night they spent together made that harder to remember.

"What's *that* mean?" Steffi wrinkled her nose.

"You know that Logan's only here temporarily. Once he leaves, I'll be a blip in his rearview mirror." She thrust her index finger at Steffi to cut off any sympathetic nonsense. She'd been proud of herself for attempting so-called fluidity. Although her heart and head were not fully aligned, she'd made her bed and would deal with the consequences. "But I can handle that, Steffi. I know what I'm doing. I chose a fling with Logan rather than having none at all. When he leaves, I'll be okay. Better than okay because, at the very least, he got me to take a few risks again."

Steffi stared ahead, but Claire could read her mind. Her friend worried that Claire's taking a risk with her heart would end much like the risk she'd taken today with this drive—in tears.

When they pulled up to Steffi's house, Claire said, "Thank you for wasting an hour of your day off to help me."

"That's what friends are for." Steffi turned off the engine.

Maybe so, but not everyone went to such lengths.

"Just so you know, I bought some great things for Logan's apartment," Claire said, hoping that the productivity of her adventure helped make up for its disastrous end. "Can you get started on the trim and paint soon? And if so, how long will it take to finish that part? I need to schedule deliveries."

"All you want is picture-frame trim on one wall and the whole apartment painted, right?" She tipped her head, looking upward while thinking. "With all the plate glass in that place, it shouldn't take more than a week or so to do the work and painting. I can start in next week, right after the gala. I want to finish the demo and reframing of Mrs. Brewster's bathroom, but Rick can take over tiling and stuff the next week while I run into the city to deal with Logan's place."

Old Mrs. Brewster's master bathroom would be sweet when completed. Claire had been so preoccupied with Logan she hadn't finished helping her pick the final touches.

"I'll tell Logan to clear stuff out before then."

Ryan pulled into the bungalow's driveway, having first stopped to pick up Emmy from his mother's. Those two got out of the car together, then Emmy ran to Claire's car and pressed her nose to the window. "Can we make brownies?"

"Sure," Steffi said, tapping at the spot where Emmy's smashed nose was. "Give me a few minutes with Claire."

Emmy flashed a quick smile at Claire and then ran to meet her dad at the front door. The domestic scene planted an ache in Claire's heart. She'd wanted a happy family for so long, but apparently it was another thing that wasn't meant to be for her.

Claire grabbed Steffi's left hand and studied her engagement ring more closely. "It's so pretty, Stef. I'm sorry I didn't get to ooh and aah over it when you first showed it to me."

Steffi raised a brow. "Well, I think we were all caught a little off guard *that* morning."

"True."

"But even more surprising was the call I got from Peyton this week telling me she got your blessing for her to be in the wedding party."

A slight chill still swept through Claire whenever Peyton's name came up. "I wouldn't be a very good maid of honor if I made any part of your big day about me, would I?"

"But I know I've asked a lot of you, so thank you." She leaned closer to Claire. "Of course, I half wonder if this change of heart is really for Logan. *I* couldn't persuade you to give an inch with Peyton for eighteen months. Logan shows up and"—Steffi snapped her fingers—"you're moving off center."

Claire's shoulders slumped. She hadn't the energy to mount a defense of her feelings for Logan. Luckily, a new box of chocolate-covered pretzels awaited her at home. It'd last five minutes—ten, tops. "Did I drill you when you and Ryan were figuring things out?"

"Not exactly, but you did ask questions, and you did grill me about the whole police-report incident." Steffi gestured a "just saying" kind of motion with her hands and a tilt of her head.

Claire frowned, remembering how much confusion and pain Steffi'd been in back then. "I was *concerned* about you. I wanted you to be well and happy."

"I feel the exact same way about you." She pushed her hair behind her ears and sighed. "Just promise me you aren't expecting Logan to make the kinds of personal changes for you that you've attempted for him this past month. As much as he must like you, he's a charming wanderer who likes his life as it is."

"I've no unrealistic expectations, but thanks for caring." She hugged Steffi, then eased away with a forced smile. "Now go inside and bake brownies while I go home and eat some."

Logan wiped his boots on the welcome mat before knocking on Claire's door. Rain dripped from the edge of the porch roof, its pitter-patter catching his attention because such gentle sounds were rarely noticeable in Manhattan. Senses that had been muted by overstimulation in the city had been reawakening since he'd returned to town.

When her door opened, his evening improved considerably just at the sight of her.

"That was quick," Claire said, stepping back to let him inside.

He'd called from his car after he'd already started toward her house.

"I thought you'd be eager to see these." He held up his laptop after slipping off his boots. "The images came out great, if I say so myself."

"Images?" she asked, looking puzzled.

"The architectural shoots?" He noticed a smear of chocolate at the corner of her mouth. Cupping her jaw, he planted a kiss on that spot and licked it away. Unlike every night this past week, she didn't melt into his arms. At best, she seemed distracted, at worst, disinterested. "What's wrong?"

She shook her head and blinked like she was trying to wake herself up. "Nothing. Can I see the pictures?"

"Of course." He opened his laptop on the coffee table and patted the cushion beside him, brushing off the slight sting of her indifference. "For each location, I narrowed it down to the best dozen images, but then also grouped my three favorites for each location, for what that's worth."

He started the slideshow he'd put together and turned the computer screen toward her. A bright, elegant image of the Duvall bathroom filled the screen.

Claire's lips parted as she flattened her hands on her breastbone. "It's gorgeous! It almost feels like false advertising." She clicked through a few more before sparing him a glance. Her expression—a mix of awe and disbelief—filled him up. "I get so lost in the details of a project that I lose sight of the big picture. Is this *really* what our work looks like to fresh eyes?"

"Pictures don't lie." He caressed her back, immediately soothed by the contact, although *her* attention remained riveted on the screen. Waiting patiently for her to tire of reviewing the photographs proved a true test. "Well? Do you know which you want to use?"

"It's hard to choose, but I think you're right. Less is more. I trust your eye and like the groupings you put together. They'll make the most powerful impact." She smiled broadly before laying her head on his shoulder. "Thank you for doing this for us. I know you might catch some flak because of it."

"The benefits have far exceeded any blowback I might get from some peers," he teased, dipping his head to capture the intriguing view of her ever-changing eyes. "Brace yourself, because this isn't the only favor I've done for you lately."

She raised her head. "I'm almost afraid to ask . . ."

"I got the inside scoop on my dad's hotel plans."

"You spent time with your dad?" She clutched the sofa cushion with both hands.

"And lived to tell the tale." A sad joke, but apt.

"And you did it for me?" Her voice sounded so soft and surprised it actually made his heart hurt. She deserved nice things from him on a regular basis.

"Yes, for you." He rubbed her thigh. "Although, honestly, I got more out of it than I expected. We've called a truce—at least temporarily. We'll see how long it lasts."

She tucked her chin, her eyes sparkling in every shade of blue, chuckling. "I'm speechless."

"Well, I didn't learn much. I know the name of the hotels and the cities they're in—from Maine to Maryland—but it sounds like most of his improvement plans are operational. He wants to 'freshen them up,' but he's not planning to take on structural renovations. At least not until the other things are running better."

She shrugged, a wan smile where he'd hoped to see a brighter—or at least determined—one. "It's probably for the best."

"What?" He turned fully, his knees bumping her thighs. "I thought you were excited to pitch him. That's why I spoke to him."

214

"Thank you, and I was. But some things aren't meant to be." Her words sank beneath his skin, producing a pit in his stomach. She absently twisted one of her earrings and then stood. "I'm thirsty. Do you want something to drink?"

He followed her to the kitchen, where he saw an empty box of chocolate-covered pretzels on the counter. "Hang on. What's really going on? You're not acting like yourself."

An expression he didn't recognize dashed across her face before she opened the refrigerator to grab a pitcher of iced tea.

"The thing is, I am. I'm acting *exactly* like myself." She poured two glasses and handed him one. "It's these past weeks that I *haven't* been myself."

These past weeks that she'd spent with him? He shivered, and not because of the cold drink in his hand. "Is this your way of telling me you regret everything?"

She swallowed the sip she'd started while shaking her head. "I don't regret any of it, but I got ahead of myself thinking I could handle your father's project."

"I'm not following. Is it the competition? 'Cause you're talented enough to compete with any designer."

"Logan, if my history proves anything, it's that I'm not afraid of competition." Her gaze lost focus, and he guessed she was remembering her fierce court presence. She glanced at her feet. "But after today, I have to respect my limits and take things slower."

She limped back to the living room and sank onto the sofa.

"What happened today?" He crouched in front of her, setting his glass on the coffee table so he could rest his hands on her knees.

"It doesn't matter." She sipped more tea, rubbing her hip. He'd noticed it bothered her more often on rainy days.

"It does to me." When he saw the misty sheen in her eyes, he took her glass and set it aside, then clasped her hands. "Don't cry, Claire. Tell me what's happened."

"I don't want to tell you." She wrested her hands free and buried her face in them.

"Why not?" He waited. "Is it Peyton?"

She shook her head, refusing to look at him. "It's all me, and it's more humiliating than when you found my scrapbook."

He'd botched handling his feelings about that fixation. Today he'd do better so she could confide in him.

"Tell me, please. I promise, I won't think less of you."

She splayed her fingers and peeked at him.

"Come on." He pried her hands from her face and kissed her knuckles. "Trust me."

"Fine." She heaved a sigh. "I drove to a design center in Hartford to search for things for your condo. I got up there on my own and bought some great pieces. In fact, the purchase orders are in my bag, and Steffi will be starting to trim out the living room and paint after the gala, so you need to clear out whatever you aren't keeping right away. She'll cover everything else."

"That's great news." He nearly leaped into the air from the fact that she'd driven herself to Hartford. But he didn't want to get sidetracked by discussing that at the moment. "So why are you so upset?"

"Because . . ." She twined her fingers together in her lap and stared at them, tears forming again. "I couldn't make it home. It started snowing when I left, and the traffic was three times as heavy. Cars were honking at me, my wipers made a streaky mess, and there was a big pileup right in front of me. I panicked so bad I thought I was having a heart attack."

"I'm sorry. That sounds awful." He sat beside her and dragged her into a hug. "You should've called me."

When she harrumphed against his chest, he asked, "How'd you finally get home?"

"Steffi and Ryan picked me up in Meriden," she mumbled. "I was mortified. She drove my car back for me."

"This is my fault." He tipped up her chin and kissed her with tenderness that came from the farthest reaches of his heart. "I've been pushing you too hard, too fast."

"Don't." She glowered. "Don't say that like I'm a lapdog with no choice in what happens to me. I thought at least I could count on *you* not to coddle me like everyone else does."

"Sorry." He held up his hands, uncertain of how to comfort her without making her feel worse. "I didn't mean to upset you more."

She punched the seat cushion. "I'm upset with myself for letting things get to this point." Those blue eyes flickered with self-loathing, which bothered him to see. "This weak, scared woman isn't who I ever wanted to be. It isn't who I thought I was or even realized I'd become. Not until you . . ."

His chest took the blow. "Pointed it out . . ."

"You didn't let me finish." She held his gaze. "Not until you challenged me. You pushed me, but I don't regret going to New York or Newport, or painting outside the lines. I'll cherish those memories."

"So you forgive me?"

"There's nothing to forgive." She took his face in her gentle hands. "Your bluntness punched through everything. Got me to take a couple chances. I honestly don't know when—if—I'll try again, but today did feel great when I started out."

He yanked her onto his lap, her petite frame fitting perfectly against his larger one. "If that's true, don't let one small setback stop you. Push harder. Let's ride up to Mystic and check out a prospective Prescott Inn. I'll get us a room." He brushed her hair away and nuzzled her neck. "I'll be your muse."

She let her head fall back and closed her eyes, making a breathy sound of approval before killing his plan. "If I can't get there on my own, I can't take on the project."

"Then you drive. If you get uncomfortable, I'll take over."

She smiled at him. "Thank you, but no."

Her exhausted expression made him ease up. "You don't have to decide today. He's not closing on the projects for several weeks, and he's not making design a priority item."

She craned her neck and kissed him. "Thank you for trying to help, but Steffi also has reservations about trying to manage a project of that scale. For now, we'll stay focused on growing locally."

"Okay." He stroked her jaw and then trailed his fingers down her neck and over her breast. "But do I deserve a reward for my good intentions?"

She smiled, reaching out to unbutton his shirt. "I think I can come up with something to make you happy."

"I'm certain of it." He'd been damn happy all week. Quiet dinners followed by tender nights. The warmth of her body beside his, and the gentle smile that greeted him each morning and had him making up reasons to stick around town longer than planned.

He kissed her deeply. She still tasted like chocolate, which was no shock given her rough day. He started undressing her in the living room.

When she didn't protest, liquid lightning shot through him. She worked quickly to shed his clothes, too, until they fell back onto the sofa in a tangle of arms and legs and hot, wet kisses.

"Claire," he whispered.

They locked gazes as he moved inside her. Breaths mingling, hearts thumping, darkness settling around them until the only thing he could see was the soul in her eyes staring back at his.

His composure slipped until she reached up and joined her lips with his in an intense kiss that simultaneously bent and stopped time.

He rolled over so she could sit astride him. Her hair bounced, her cheeks flushed, and her well-kissed lips turned crimson as she rode the swell of emotion building inside him until it crested and broke apart, leaving him shuddering beneath her.

For a few quiet minutes, he held her. She shivered, so he pulled a throw blanket over her shoulders and then ran his fingers through her damp hair.

"Claire?"

"Hm?" she asked, her head still plastered against his chest.

He kissed her head while stroking her back. "Come with me to the gala."

She traced his collarbone without answering at first. "I thought we were an 'in the moment' thing."

He frowned at the characterization, although he'd been the one to label it so. "Dates, by their nature, are 'in the moment.'"

"A public date—here in our hometown—will imply more to others, who will then have all kinds of opinions."

He stilled his hands. "Are you embarrassed by us?"

She propped her chin on her hands, which were now folded across his chest. "No. But when you leave, people will whisper and feel sorry for my being left behind. I don't need that after what happened with Todd."

Damn Todd and Peyton. Their affair continued to interfere with his life. "Who cares what people say? This is between you and me. Come with me. We can play footsie," he teased. "It'll be fun."

She giggled, nestling her feet between his. "You'll be with your family. You don't need me."

"I prefer you." He slid his hands down her back and squeezed her ass.

Her eyes widened at first, then turned somber. "I've been cordial to Peyton, but sitting with her for hours at your family event . . ."

He stared at the ceiling, thinking about family and friends, past and present, passion and love. Complications and expectations formed sticky webs. But his heart filtered those out in its focus on Claire just like a large aperture blurs a noisy background from a frame's real object.

No one was more surprised by that than he. "It's too bad we didn't meet elsewhere . . . without all the baggage."

"If we'd met elsewhere, you wouldn't have given me a second look. It's our past that linked us."

"So in a way, we owe Peyton for this."

Claire remained quiet.

He squeezed her tightly. "I'll tell you this much. You're one of my few truly fond childhood memories. It's been strange being home now, reconciling the good and bad ones."

"You're being a bit melodramatic, aren't you? My memories of you are of a happy-go-lucky boy with a big imagination. Don't let a few unhappy memories color everything about your past."

"Fair enough. I do have an odd affection for that museum I grew up in, mostly because of Duck. I actually remembered something of him the other day—of how he used to read aloud to me in his hammock by the shore."

"That's sweet." She kissed his chest. "I wish I'd met him."

"He was kind. Driven without trying to prove anything to anyone. He just had things he wanted to say." A messenger of a sort, he thought. "When I was in my dad's office, I stared at his Pulitzer. Wanting one of my own—unlikely as that is—keeps me up nights. I know that fact shouldn't make me feel like a failure, but it does."

"You're not a failure. You're working at what you love. You're a good brother and a good son, despite difficult parents. You're also a good friend."

"With great benefits." He smiled.

"Yes." She laid her head back on his chest. "But think about what you just said about your great-grandfather. He wasn't writing to win a prize. The writing itself was his reward. If you want to emulate him, then focus only on stories that mean something to you, regardless of what they mean to others or to some awards committee."

"Okay, oh wise one." He held her more tightly, if that was possible, because she had a way of shifting his perspective and making him feel better about himself. He wanted to give her that same feeling, but didn't know how.

"Go ahead and tease, but if I could play tennis now, even down the road at the public courts, I would and I'd be overjoyed. I loved it that much. I'm lucky I found something else that I really care about. Something that lets me leave beauty and comfort in other people's lives. Maybe that sounds silly, but it makes me happy."

"It's not silly. It's lovely, Claire. And you do it remarkably well." He turned over so that she was beneath him, then kissed her. "But just to be clear, you do those things just by being you."

Her eyes glittered. "Thank you."

They stared at each other, blanketed by the weight of unspoken sentiment.

"I don't often beg, but, please, come with me to the gala. Take this small risk . . ." He kissed her. "I promise, nothing bad will happen."

Chapter Sixteen

Claire adjusted the strap of the new backless cobalt-blue gown she'd bought for the gala. Her gaze homed in on the pale bit of cleavage visible through the keyhole neckline halter.

Daring. Potentially a mistake. But one that made her feel alive.

Anyone who knew her—which, in this town, would be everyone—might either gawk or laugh at her first-ever attempt at dressing sexy. And they'd know why she'd done it. Logan. She couldn't escape speculation now that she'd agreed to be his date. His *date*! Another thing that sparked all kinds of dangerous hope.

She glanced at the modest black dress hanging in her closet and then smiled at her reflection. Tonight she'd be as glamorous as a woman who couldn't wear high heels could be, and she'd enjoy it. At the very least, this marked another step in her quest to be seen as less helpless and lonely.

After she crossed to her dresser to retrieve the new rhinestone–and–faux sapphire earrings she'd purchased, she fastened them in place and smoothed her hair one last time. Once she stepped back, she took in the full view of herself, trying to pretend she was looking at a stranger. A pretty stranger. Someone who looked like she might even belong with the elegant Logan Prescott.

When she grabbed Rosie, the illusion was shattered.

She hoped Logan wouldn't regret asking her to be his date. Her hip would ache if she tried to dance more than two or three songs. Peyton's presence would keep her hyperaware. People would be whispering all around them. Oh God, the whole evening could turn into a gigantic disaster.

After using a tissue to blot the sweat forming on her hairline, she turned away from the imagined catastrophes and went downstairs to wait for Logan.

When she hit the bottom of the stairwell, her phone rang. "Hi, Mom."

"Dad and I are on our way. Are you sure you don't need a ride?"

"I told you, Logan is bringing me. We'll be there soon."

"I missed our tradition of getting ready together with mimosas. You know I can't do my makeup as well as when you do it, either."

Claire smiled. Her mother's gorgeous eyes didn't need makeup to shine. "I'm sure you look pretty, Mom."

"Thanks, honey. See you soon. Be careful."

"Bye." Claire shook her head, all too aware that they'd never had a conversation that didn't end with some version of "be safe."

The sound of her doorbell caused her to go cold. There'd be no turning back now. She'd face it all—the gossip, the discomfort, and the scrutiny. All to be a princess for a night with the town's very own Prince Charming.

When she opened the door, the sight of Logan in his tux—the one with the snowy-white dinner jacket—made her giddy. He'd paired the jacket with a black kerchief in its breast pocket and a starched tuxedo shirt with black buttons. She refrained from pinching herself, although, honestly, this moment exceeded all of her fantasies.

"Claire, you're stunning." He stepped forward and kissed her cheek. "Don't want to smear the lipstick this early."

"So do you," she babbled before she realized she should've thanked him.

"I knew I'd have to keep up with you." He winked.

"Thank you," she managed, despite the sense she was playing a role in a movie rather than living her real life.

"Shall we go? Mustn't keep Darla waiting . . ." He held out his elbow.

She grabbed her purse and Rosie, took his arm, and headed into the unknown.

Within minutes, they arrived at the Granby House—the stately stone mansion situated near the town green that had been donated to the town decades ago by the Granby family. Its second floor now housed town government offices. The first floor and patio, however, could be rented for private affairs, like weddings or fund-raisers like this annual literacy gala.

A valet attendant opened Claire's door and helped her out of the car before Logan handed over the keys.

"Ready?" Logan asked, taking her by the arm.

"Yes." On Logan's arm, Claire felt more assured. She could do this. She *had* to take another step and show others that she hadn't lost everything when the bullet, or Peyton, had struck. "I hope there will be chocolate."

"Never fear. I come prepared." Logan opened his jacket to reveal a Hershey's almond bar in its inside pocket. "If you need this, give me a signal and I'll help you sneak off to the restroom."

The small yet thoughtful gesture made everything inside flutter. He obviously knew her well and wasn't annoyed by her bad habit. In fact, his grin suggested he even enjoyed her quirk.

All at once, she felt more certain that this night would be okay. Better than okay. It might even be magical. She broke into a smile. "You're awesome."

"Claire, your bar is far too low, but I'm glad you haven't realized that yet." He kissed her hand and led her up the stairs.

Inside, the celebration was underway. No fewer than three hundred people milled around, while thousands of twinkling white lights entwined with gorgeous floral centerpieces sat high on clear stands. Crisp white-and-gold linens draped the tables topped with fine china, crystal, and gold chargers.

She'd attended this event many times in her life. Every other time, she'd watched from the sidelines as other couples danced and laughed. Just as often, she'd stewed with envy of whatever woman Logan had brought with him or flirted with, yet had savored any attention he'd thrown her way.

Tonight *she* would be at the receiving end of most of his attention. All for the admission price of eating at the same table as Peyton and enduring cockeyed glances from the people they both knew.

She stole another glance at Logan, who couldn't look more handsome or make her feel more beautiful. The sacrifice was well worth it.

"How do you like your pain?" he asked.

"What?"

"Pain." He raised a brow. "Do you like it quick, or would you rather delay the inevitable?"

Her scalp prickled with concern. "What are you talking about?"

He huffed a sigh. "Should we go say hello to my family now, or would you rather wait until we must see them at dinner?"

His family—the de facto hosts. People she'd once considered beloved neighbors and friends before a sea of discomfort had separated the past and the present. "Let's say hello now, and then I need to find my parents."

Her mom would be anxiously awaiting confirmation of her safe arrival, no doubt.

"Okay." Logan laid his hand on her bare back as he led her around the outskirts of the main room.

They drew a few stares, but she didn't care. She could hardly think about it because her brain was too busy enjoying the feel of his warm hand on her skin.

Logan craned his neck and located his parents in a corner of the main room, but Claire got lucky because Peyton was not with them.

"Mom, Dad, I made it . . . almost on time." He gave a sharp nod.

Darla didn't look at him as she threw out air-kisses, because she'd fixated on Claire with very round eyes.

"My word, Claire." Darla reached out and hugged her—another discomforting surprise. "This color is *perfect* on you. I'm so glad you're joining us tonight." She then pinched her son's cheek. "I wondered who your mystery woman was. Why were you keeping Claire a secret?"

"To avoid all the questions I see forming in your head," came his smooth reply. He kissed his mother's cheek and then shook his father's hand. "Dad."

"Logan." Mr. Prescott smiled at Claire. "Lovely to see you, Claire. I understand you're renovating Logan's apartment."

She knew from Logan that his father had been there only once. *One* time in almost a decade. He probably didn't even remember what it looked like.

"I am. It's been a great project. You'll have to go visit when it's complete. You won't believe the change."

"Maybe you two will invite us down for dinner one night," Darla interjected, projecting ahead as if Logan and Claire were a real couple.

Claire would be flattered except she suspected Darla's enthusiasm had more to do with what Claire's dating Logan could mean for Peyton than for Logan. Either way she had to remind herself that *that* dinner would never come to pass.

Logan's New York life wouldn't include her, and not only because she doubted she'd feel comfortable leaving her little hamlet anytime soon after her near miss with that multicar pileup on I-91. She hoped her smile didn't falter with that thought. Rather than wallow or make a joke, she nodded, playing along with the pretense.

Mrs. Prescott filled the silence with more chatter. "Peyton always said you could cook up a storm. I used to be jealous of your mom for being such a homemaker. But I got over it." She chuckled. "We all have our strengths and weaknesses."

"Speaking of Peyton, where is she?" Logan asked.

Claire's muscles tensed all at once.

"Around somewhere," his mother replied. "I don't know that she'll stay long. She's still self-conscious about . . ." She vaguely gestured to her chest. "Even with the new wig."

Claire's grip on Rosie strengthened. She knew something about how Peyton felt. It took nothing to recall the earliest days after her surgeries, when her more severe limp had made her feel like Frankenstein. When her angry scars had looked like lumpy lava on her skin. Even now, Rosie reminded everyone in the room of the incident and the damage it had wrought. Empathy caused Claire's nose to tingle, but she kept her tears at bay.

Logan seemed to be searching the room for his sister, his sober expression suggesting his sympathy for her.

"If you'll excuse me, I should find my parents and say hello," Claire said, giving herself a temporary escape from the awkward moment.

"I'll join you." Logan clasped her hand, preventing her getaway, and led her to where her parents were speaking with Steffi's father.

Claire's mom saw them approach, at which point her gaze went straight to Claire's cleavage. Her jaw fell open until she clamped it shut and forced a polite smile. "You bought a new dress?"

Before Claire could answer, her dad wrapped her in a hug. "Claire Bear, look at you. What a beauty!"

"Isn't she?" Logan's hand brushed along her bare back, sending pleasant tingles careening down her spine.

Her mom cleared her throat, failing to erase the apprehension in her eyes when she said, "Logan, you look dashing in that jacket." She brushed her palm across its lapel. "Quite a pair tonight."

"I have the prettiest date in the room, present company excluded." Logan gave her mom a kiss on the cheek and then shook hands with her dad and Mr. Lockwood, but Claire noted a slight tic in his jaw. "Thanks for coming out to support the library's literacy program."

"We look forward to this event all year. So many friends gathered in one place, and so many auction items." Claire's mother gave her dad a pointed look. "There's a beautiful freshwater-pearl necklace that would make a lovely thirty-fifth anniversary gift."

"Thirty-five years. Congratulations." Logan's smile seemed almost impish then. "I'll be sure not to bid up that necklace. However, perhaps you'd have more fun celebrating if you bid on the one-week VRBO in La Jolla."

"Oh no. That's not for us!" Her father laughed.

Mr. Lockwood nodded thoughtfully from the outskirts of the conversation. He'd never been a talker.

Determined not to let Logan pressure her parents, Claire changed the subject. "Mom, have you seen Steffi?"

Her mother's expression faltered again as her eyes darted from Claire to Logan and back. "Yes, she's right over there with Ryan, Ben . . . and Peyton."

Claire turned to spy Steffi and Ryan arm in arm. Ben fiddled with his tie, looking as uncomfortable as Claire felt, while Peyton had tucked herself into a corner of the room, self-consciously playing with her earring, keeping her hand near her face as if it were a shield.

Normally, Peyton would stake out the center of the room, commanding everyone's attention in a daring outfit, with her long golden hair swirling around her shoulders and breasts like a come-on.

Tonight, her demure midnight-blue gown helped her hide in the shadows. Although still beautiful in an ethereal way, none of the sparkle that usually lit Peyton's face or eyes shone tonight. That wig, a gorgeous one—the blonde color looked familiar.

Claire paused, taking another look while asking Logan, "Is that *your* hair?"

"Mm-hmm." His lips curled into a bittersweet smile.

A wave of questions and emotions made her hot. Before Claire could form words, Peyton glanced over her shoulder at them. She froze for a microsecond, then waved.

Logan dipped his head to whisper in Claire's ear. "Can we go say hello?"

"Of course," Claire said, willing her tense legs to move. Despite the level floor, her gait seemed more uneven than usual, her legs heavy, as if climbing stairs. Claire dragged her gaze from Peyton to Ben, while Logan greeted his sister.

Ben smiled at Claire before casting a meaningful look—almost a warning—at Logan.

"Gorgeous dress, Claire. Is it new?" Steffi planted a friendly kiss on her cheek. "What a great color on you."

"You look very pretty," Peyton added quietly.

"Thanks," Claire replied, suppressing the urge to touch the wig made of Logan's silky hair. "So do both of you."

If her words came out stilted, it was because her throat was dry, not because she'd been lying. Not that Peyton knew that.

"I'm sorry to lose my regular dinner date," Ben chimed in, leaning forward to kiss her hello.

"Don't worry. You'll have me back soon enough," she muttered, low enough that only he could hear.

He clenched his jaw and turned to Logan. "I hear you've been helping Claire and my sister with their website. A lucky break for them. Thanks."

"No thanks required." Logan tugged Claire to his side and wound his arm snugly around her waist. "I'm the lucky one."

"As usual." Ben glanced at Claire and back to Logan. "Things always come pretty easily to you. I hope you appreciate it this time."

Claire tapped Rosie before either of the two cavemen threw more shade. She turned to Logan. "Would you mind getting me a drink?"

"Of course. I'll be right back." He looked at the others. "Anyone else?"

Peyton grabbed for his arm like it was an escape ladder thrown into a deep well. "I'll come with you."

As soon as they left, Claire whirled around on Ben. "I don't need a watchdog. Please cut the stink-eye."

"Sorry." He crossed his arms. "I didn't want Logan using his charm to coax you into dealing with Peyton before you're ready."

Shame shot heat through her. "Because there isn't another reason he'd like to spend time with me?"

"That's not what I'm saying—" He looked at Steffi and Ryan for help, but they wisely stayed mum.

"It kind of is what you're saying by jumping to that conclusion, Ben. Thanks for your concern, but don't worry about me. I'm fine. I have no more false illusions about Logan than Melanie does about you."

Ben winced at the mention of his regular booty call. "Sorry. Big-brother mode is hard to turn off."

"Forgiven." She smiled and turned to Steffi. "We should use tonight to drum up business. Everyone who's anyone is here."

"On it." Steffi saluted her with a smile.

Logan and Peyton returned, and he handed her a glass of white wine. "Here you are."

"Thank you." She threw back a full gulp. She'd need several more to help her converse with Peyton for the next three hours. "Let's check out the auction items before the bidding heats up."

"Good idea." He turned to the gang before leading her to the long tables flanking the main room. "We'll see you later."

—⁓—

"Thank you for rescuing me from Ben. I think he wanted to bite my head off," Logan whispered in Claire's ear, glad to be putting some distance between himself and Ben Lockwood. "Tell the truth, did you two ever have a thing?"

"No." She batted at him. "I told you, we're like siblings. We stuck together after you all took off."

Logan cast a glance over his shoulder. Ben was no longer glaring at him. "Well, I'm glad to have you to myself for a few minutes. In fact, can I persuade you to duck into an alcove with me?" He nipped at her shoulder.

She smiled, narrowing her eyes, and squeezed his arm. "I always knew you'd make a perfect rogue earl."

"Is that a yes?" He tugged at her hand.

"Be serious. We're here to raise money, so let's check out the items."

Logan rarely bid on anything because of his family's affiliation with the event and donors. That, plus the fact that his deep pockets would unfairly tip the scales against those with modest bank accounts. He walked beside Claire, occasionally nodding hello to neighbors and acquaintances while she scrutinized each bid sheet.

She paused by the pair of tickets to the final women's round of the US Open. Logan noted the longing in her eyes.

"Do you go often?" he asked.

She shook her head. "I never go."

"Why not?"

She placed her hands on her hips and tipped her head, her expression reading "Duh" loud and clear. "Until last month, I avoided the city."

"Well, now that you've broken that rule, would you like these tickets, or is it too painful to watch what might have been?"

She tipped her head side to side and shrugged. "Ten years ago, when some of the women I'd played with started popping up, it hurt to think, 'That could've been me.' But it wasn't meant to be. Now I watch tennis on TV all the time without getting jealous." She sighed. "The last serious live competition I went to was my own. Anyway, look at the retail value on those tickets. Fifteen hundred dollars is a bit rich for my blood. I need rent money for retail space."

She moved to the next article on the table, inspecting the items in the gift basket.

But Logan remained in front of the tickets. "If you had the money, would you go? Or would you find another excuse to avoid the crowds?"

She paused, glancing over her shoulder at him. "I'd like to think I'd go, but honestly, I don't know. Last time I ventured out on my own was a near disaster—literally and figuratively."

Claire was nothing if not honest, with herself and everyone else. He had to admire that, even if he didn't like the fact that she wouldn't push herself a little harder. "Operative word being 'near.'"

She turned away, dismissing his point, now staring at a gift basket from Connecticut Muffin. Smiling, she bent over and wrote out a bid. "You *know* I have to win *this*."

He snickered as they continued meandering along the tables, looking at the various gifts—jewelry, first-edition signed books, vacation-home rentals, and other items including a 10 percent coupon on Lockwood & McKenna design services for any project over one thousand dollars. Claire also placed a minimum bid for an in-home spa basket and for a color and cut at a local salon.

"Logan!" Karina's familiar voice boomed from behind them. Her tall, shapely frame carried her merlot-colored gown well, its lengthy slit showing off long, toned legs. "Oh, Logan. A sight for sore eyes."

She offered a partial hug, careful to hold her martini away from his jacket, then set her hand on his shoulder while flipping her shiny black hair behind her shoulder. "Cute little shindig. Almost worth the drive up," she teased. "Guess it's the closest thing to a real party you've been to in months, right? But don't worry. We've missed you almost as much as you've missed us."

Ah, the glib repartee commonplace in his circles. Funny how hollow it sounded tonight.

"Karina, let me introduce you to Claire." He reached for Claire, who'd fallen silent, but apparently not before she'd given Karina a once-over and drawn conclusions about her and Logan. Probably not wholly incorrect conclusions, either. "Claire, this is Karina, the journalist I've told you about who I work with on occasion."

"Yes, I remember." Claire smiled, extending her hand. "Nice to meet you, Karina."

Karina shot Logan a curious look and returned Claire's smile. "You too, Claire, although I confess I'm at a slight disadvantage, having not yet heard about you."

If Logan could've stomped on Karina's foot without drawing attention, he might've. "I've known Claire since middle school. She's redecorating my apartment, which is going to be fabulous."

"I can't wait to see it." Karina smiled. "Will it be finished by the time we get back from Lesbos?"

He felt Claire stiffen and assumed it was because he hadn't yet told her about his decision to leave for Lesbos in another week.

"It might even be finished before you leave," Claire tentatively replied.

"So soon?" Karina laughed before knocking back most of her drink. "You must be a miracle worker. Maybe I'll hire you next."

To Claire's credit, she didn't quiz him about when they were taking off. Her smile didn't slip. For all intents and purposes, she looked completely unaffected by his impending plans. That should please him. He'd never liked a clingy woman. Still, he surveyed the heaviness in his chest and knew it didn't feel anything like relief.

"No miracles, sadly. I do try to understand people so that their home reflects something about them." Claire's expression suggested she might've bit back a snarky remark—about what, exactly, he'd never know. Perhaps she thought Karina was the woman with whom he'd painted his bedroom wall. "Of course, compared with what you two do, my job must seem rather ordinary."

233

"Actually, it sounds really nice. Logan and I expose ugly environments in the hope that horrifying others will force change. You create environments designed to make people feel *good*. Must be nice to bring a smile to someone's day." She elbowed Logan, laughing, and polished off her martini. "At the very least, people are happy to see her coming. Us, not so much."

Logan needed to occupy Karina with someone other than Claire, for everyone's sake. He caught Ben eyeing them again and waved him over. "Karina, I want to introduce you to another friend. A good-looking, single one who's here alone, like you."

She narrowed her eyes at him before pasting a smile on her face and turning to greet Ben just as he arrived.

"Ben Lockwood, this is my colleague, Karina Báez. Karina, Ben . . . an old friend."

Karina's smile turned genuine in the face of Ben's rugged good looks. Sandy-colored hair, hazel eyes framed by dark brows and lashes, and a strong, square jaw. All cleaned up he looked sophisticated, unlike when in jeans at the hardware store.

"Nice to meet you, Karina." Ben shook her hand.

"Same." Karina took Logan's hint and, after handing her empty glass to him, threaded her arm through Ben's. "So, Ben, how about we hit up the bartender for another round and you tell me a little about this town."

Logan would feel bad about foisting her on Ben except that Ben didn't look particularly unhappy about having Karina glued to his side. She was quite striking and somewhat of a guy's gal in terms of her interests.

He wound his arm around Claire's waist. "Sorry about that. I forgot she was coming."

"Then you owe her the apology, not me."

"I didn't invite her as a date, Claire. I only meant that I forgot to tell you about our trip to Greece. We recently finalized plans to take off next Tuesday to try to get ahead of an upcoming legal decision about the refugee situation."

Claire's smile thinned. "How long will you be gone?"

"As long as it takes to get the story. Hopefully, no more than a month."

Her brows rose. "I didn't realize . . . that's quite an adventure. Will you be able to communicate with us so we know you're safe?"

"I'm not usually good about checking in. Truthfully, no one's ever asked me to before." A sad truth.

She sighed, resigned. "So it's the 'no news is good news' policy?"

He gently touched her jaw and kissed her in the middle of the party, enjoying the blush that immediately flooded her face. "Thank you for caring so much. It feels nice."

"My caring is nothing new, Logan. We both know that much." Something over his shoulder caught Claire's eye. She squeezed his hand, her voice a little too bright. "Will you excuse me for a minute? I'll meet you at the table."

Before he replied, she turned and disappeared into the crowd just before his sister came to his side.

"Well, she sure can move fast when properly motivated," Peyton said in a self-deprecating tone.

"You look smashing, sis." He put his arm around her and kissed her temple. "This wig is perfect on you, but one day I want to boldly display our short hair together."

"Not until mine starts to look like hair instead of fuzz. I think it might be coming in curly. I heard that could happen."

The event photographer—a middle-aged mother he didn't recognize—stopped them. "I need a photograph of the youngest Prescotts. Do you mind?"

"Sure," Logan said, turning himself and Peyton toward the lens before she had a chance to beg off. He whispered, "Smile."

The photographer took a couple of shots. "Thanks."

After she left, Logan said, "I should've taken photos of you before I left the house . . . for our project."

"We can just use one of hers."

He scowled. "No. All of the photos should be mine. I've got a camera in the trunk of my car, actually. Let's get it and take some shots outside on the side porch while we can take advantage of evening's blue light."

Minutes later, the sounds of the party inside muted as he fell into his own world, seeing the entire scene through new eyes, playing with light and shadow and color to document Peyton's story, while wondering when he would find a story of his own.

Chapter Seventeen

Claire washed her hands and was finger combing her hair when Pat wandered into the ladies' room, looking rather elegant for someone who usually fell on the frumpy side of style. Her pale-blue gown shimmered under the light, and its lace jacket added a feminine touch.

"Claire. You look fantastic." Pat set her hands on Claire's shoulders and spun her so she could admire the new dress. Claire didn't mind her handsy manner, seeing as Pat was almost like an aunt. Pat's eyes twinkled with interest. "Are the rumor mills true? Are you here as Logan Prescott's date?"

Yippee. Gossip had already gripped the old-biddy committee, as she knew it would. They were all here at the party, which meant the news would spread faster than pink eye at a nursery school. No doubt people were already whispering and wondering. Probably doing a lot of head-scratching, too.

Claire nodded, unable to speak past the balled mortification in her throat. *You can take it. You're just having some fun.*

Pat clapped her hands together, her eyes lit up with glee. "Well, now we'll have something fun to talk about at our next meeting. Thank goodness, too, because that book you chose was heavy."

"There's not much to discuss, Pat. Logan and I . . . well, it's not a big deal. I've been working with him these past few weeks, but he leaves for Greece in another week and will be gone for a long time." Admitting that aloud sank her heart deep in her chest, despite having anticipated this inevitable ending. She just hadn't been—wasn't—ready for it to happen this quickly.

Pat frowned. "Oh dear. That's a shame. You two make a handsome pair. I heard Stefanie and Ryan got engaged recently. Maybe their wedding will stir things up again for you and Logan down the road. You never know!"

Claire tamped down the spark of hope those words ignited. Logan and weddings did not go together. "Like I said, don't hold your breath."

"You know me. I always hope for the best. Speaking of that, I understand that you've spoken with Peyton, too. You three girls were such a joy together. I know she hurt you, but I'm proud of you for trying to get past it. She's been through the wringer and could use a fresh start." And then, as if sensing perhaps she'd pushed into dangerous territory, she patted her tummy. "Excuse me, but I must relieve myself."

She wiggled her fingers and ducked into a stall.

Claire bit back a bitter laugh, having completely lost control of her situation. When she left the restroom, she wandered through the crowd with an unfocused gaze to avoid conversation. No matter where she ran, though, she couldn't outrun the truth of Pat's remark. Peyton had suffered a lot this past year, and maybe she did deserve a second chance.

Logan was no longer near the bar with his sister. In fact, Claire didn't see either of them anywhere. Had Peyton gotten sick? Would Logan have left without a word? The main room was crowded with groupings of people and waitstaff passing by with trays of champagne and canapés. The dull roar of conversation overpowered the string quartet's attempt to entertain.

If she stood still for too long, someone else would grab her and drag her off for interrogation. She rose onto her toes, desperately searching for her mother. Instead, she saw Karina coming her way. *Joy of joys.*

"Claire, I need your help." Karina took her by the arm like they were long-lost pals. The arm grabbing must be a thing with her. "You grew up here, right? What's the scoop with Ben Lockwood? He seems nice and handsome, so why is he here alone?"

"Are you suggesting there's something wrong with him because he doesn't have a date?" Claire wasn't about to spill details about her closest friend to a journalist she didn't know.

"At our ages, it's unusual for any handsome catch to be single." Karina leaned in as if they were coconspirators. "I'm thinking this party could end on a brighter note than I'd originally assumed, as long as he's not a closet freak or ax murderer."

"I promise, he's neither of those. He's a wonderful, caring man. He just hasn't found the right woman for a serious commitment yet." Claire didn't know much about what kind of woman Ben wanted for the long haul, but she didn't think it would be one like Karina.

"Perfect. I'm not looking to be anybody's serious anything. Fleeting suits me fine. Is he opposed to that?"

Claire thought of Melanie again, whom she'd yet to bump into this evening. "Is any guy opposed to that?"

"Not that I've ever met." Karina laughed and patted Claire's forearm, which she kept snug to her side. "Funny, I wouldn't have pegged you as a player, but then again, you *are* here with Logan. This is why we shouldn't judge a book by its cover."

Claire's stomach tensed. Did her date with Logan signal that she was up for random flings? Would people whisper about her the way they did about Melanie?

Karina kept babbling, unaware that her long stride challenged Claire and Rosie. "Share some fun childhood stories about Logan that I can torture him with while we're away."

Claire swiped a champagne flute from a passing tray. "Won't you have more important things to focus on in Greece?"

Two gulps polished off the champagne.

"Sure, but humor makes tense conditions bearable. Most of the time, Logan's quick wit gives him the upper hand when we poke at each other. It'd be nice to turn the tables for a change."

Claire deliberately slowed down, hoping to dislodge herself from Karina's clutches. While searching for another waiter, she asked, "How many projects have you two worked on together?"

"This will be our fourth in three years." Karina stopped but didn't release her hold on Claire. "We work together long enough to get sick of each other, then go our separate ways for a while. The cycle works. Keeps the spark alive."

"The spark?" Claire's stomach turned again, this time with the added burn of acid.

"You know," she said, tossing a silky black waterfall of hair over her shoulder. "The creative juice that pulls our work together."

"Oh." The relief in her voice drew Karina's notice and then laughter.

"Oh gosh. You thought I meant something else . . ." She shrugged one shoulder. "Logan and I have had our fun. Sometimes it gets lonely when you're out in the field, working on a depressing story. You need to hold on to something or someone affirming. But it never means anything and always ends."

"Until the next time." Those words escaped before Claire realized what she'd said. A statement, not a question.

Karina paused, as if unsure how honest to be. "You know how it is. You grab what you can when you can, and then you let go when you must. That's what I hope to do tonight with your friend Ben. So tell me the truth. What are my chances?"

"You really have to ask him." Claire felt a stab of sympathy for Melanie and disentangled herself from Karina. She'd met her quota of intimate new details about Logan. "If you'll excuse me, I see my parents over there."

"Oh, sweet. I don't think I've ever been to a party with my parents." Karina smiled and then craned her neck, ostensibly looking for Ben.

Claire didn't know whether to be glad or worried about that. "See you later."

Claire found another glass of champagne before she slipped through the crowd. The bubbly didn't help her to stop picturing Logan and Karina together at the end of an emotionally wrenching day of interviews and photos, under a hot Grecian sun, looking for a place to channel their restless energy and need for comfort.

She shuddered, confirming that, despite her best efforts—her very best—she was *not* anything like Karina or Logan or Melanie. She could not adopt the "grab what you can when you can" philosophy, no matter how much she wanted to extend her little fantasy with Logan.

Facts crowded her thoughts, demanding her attention. He was leaving in a week, something he'd neglected to tell her. He would be away for weeks or longer with a woman with whom he shared an intense friendship with benefits. When he returned from Greece, he'd be living in Manhattan, not at Arcadia House. Unlike her beloved historical romance novels, their rake-and-wallflower story would not end with a happily ever after.

When Logan finally left Sanctuary Sound, he would do so having gotten nearly everything he wanted when he first arrived—a newly decorated house, a thawing of the animosity between Claire and Peyton, and no-strings sex from Claire. Meanwhile, Claire would be left nursing a bruised heart because, despite everything she'd told herself and others, she'd let herself spin tales of "maybes" where he'd been concerned. Silly dreams spun on the fuel of her desire. Useless dreams because, as she'd known in her heart of hearts, she'd be alone again in a sea of happier people, just like now.

Mr. Prescott's voice came over the microphone, pulling her out of the downward mental spiral. "Ladies and gentlemen, thank you all for coming out tonight. I've been told it's time to be seated for dinner. The silent auction will remain open through dessert. We will give a five-minute warning before it closes, then tally the winners. Please have your checkbooks ready. In the meantime, enjoy the meal."

The string quartet broke into Bach's Orchestral Suite no. 3, accompanying people as they scurried around searching out their table assignments. Claire wove through the crowd toward table one, arriving at the same time as Logan and Peyton.

"Claire, *so* sorry." Logan hurried to her side. "We had an impromptu shoot for our project because the light was right and I wanted to capture Peyton the first time she attended a major social event after treatment."

Claire and Peyton held each other's gaze for a moment. Peyton had tried to warn Claire about Logan, and Claire hated that she'd been right. Then again, Peyton knew them both so well—of course she'd been right.

"It's fine. Work comes first." Claire sat in the chair he pulled out for her. Truthfully, she didn't need for him to apologize. He was simply being Logan, and he'd never pretended or promised he would be anyone else. She wouldn't even want him to be, really. His passion for things was what made him exciting. Far be it from her to try to cage him in any way. *And yet* . . . No. She brushed aside ridiculous fantasies and faced her former friend. "Peyton, you look wonderful in that color. I'm sure the photographs will be inspirational."

"Thank you," Peyton replied, a hesitant smile playing on her lips.

Logan sat between Claire and Peyton, which left Karina the seat to Claire's left. Karina slung her arm around Claire's chair and leaned close.

"I'm sorry to report, Ben Lockwood is not interested. I get it, though. I can be overwhelming." She grinned and then snapped open her napkin to set across her lap. "I'm best when paired with another oddball."

If nothing else, this year's dinner conversation would be unusual. Claire did envy Karina's unapologetic self-awareness. That woman would not find herself holding on to false hope.

"Lucky for you, we're all oddballs in our own way." Claire buttered her roll and took a huge bite.

"I knew I liked you straight off." Karina bumped shoulders. "You're no nonsense. I see why Logan enjoys spending time with you."

"Well, thanks . . ." Claire lifted her third glass of champagne and chugged it, drawing a raised brow from Logan. He casually laid his hand on Claire's thigh, clueless about the conflict building inside like the cello's crescendo in the background.

When the Prescotts began peppering Karina with questions about past stories she'd reported, Claire's thoughts turned inward. She picked at her salad, reflecting on women she admired, like Steffi and Pat, even Karina and Peyton. Women who knew themselves and took risks, willing to live with the consequences of potential mistakes.

Unlike them, Claire's recent risk taking hadn't been entirely self-motivated. She'd taken action largely to please Logan, which was probably why she'd never felt wholly comfortable with this no-strings affair. Why she couldn't drive to and from Hartford on her own. Why she backed away from pitching Mr. Prescott for that hotel work.

Whether she ultimately traveled farther than New Haven county, or engaged in a series of meaningless flings, or did any other thing with her life, it should be based on what *she* wanted and who she was, not on how she thought her behavior would affect her relationship with anyone else.

After tonight, she'd regroup. Figure out who she was and who she wanted to become. What life she envisioned, and what goals she'd pursue if she weren't afraid to travel. Perhaps pulling the Lilac Lane League book out of hiding would be the place to start. Revisiting youthful dreams and goals might be a shortcut to her heart-of-hearts wishes. The kind formed before society and life jade you and make you question yourself.

Of course, many of her old dreams had involved Logan. But she was an adult now, which meant she had to learn to distinguish between realistic dreams and fantasies.

Starting now—this very night—she'd make changes. Not for Logan. Not to spite Peyton. Not to prove anything to anyone other than herself.

"Claire," Peyton said, leaning forward to see past Logan. "Logan showed me the drawings you made for his unit. I loved the bold colors and rich accents. It's so him."

"Thanks." She couldn't help smiling at the compliment even though it came from Peyton.

"I'll throw a party once it's finished, and you can all come to sing Claire's praises," Logan announced to the table before kissing her.

"You know I never miss a party," Karina replied.

"Claire, maybe you could offer some advice about how to update older hotels on a budget," Mr. Prescott said.

If more time had passed since Hartford, and if Steffi had been enthusiastic, this opening would excite her. Now it fueled a touch of self-loathing. Not that she'd let anyone see it.

"I'm happy to, although I'm sure whatever designer you hire will do a fabulous job." She forced herself to hold his intimidating gaze.

"I haven't hired a designer yet. I won't bore everyone with business talk, but call me later this week. Maybe I won't need to go out searching for one if I like your ideas." He forked his salad. Darla patted his shoulder in a way that suggested to Claire that she had prompted that offer. That woman knew exactly how to get what she wanted. Claire could take some lessons from her.

She supposed she couldn't blame a mother for wanting to do anything she could to help her children, and Claire had no doubt that one of Darla's goals was to make it harder for Claire to shut Peyton out of her life.

To decline Mr. Prescott's offer right now would be rude. Claire nodded, trying not to let her conflict show on her face. She looked longingly at the table beside them, where Steffi, Ryan, Ben, and their parents were gathered and laughing. What she'd now give for comfortable conversation without subtext and tension.

She swigged more champagne, counting the minutes until others finished their chicken piccata so that dessert could be served. *It'd better be chocolate.* If the portions were tiny, she might steal Logan's, too.

—⁓—

Logan didn't know what had changed this evening, but he noted a shift in Claire's attitude from when they'd first arrived. Had he left her alone too long? Had Karina said something to upset her? Was it Peyton?

"Take a walk with me," he whispered.

"Now?" She polished off his chocolate mousse cake, having already wolfed down her own.

"Is that a problem?"

"Well, I don't want to miss the end of the auction."

"We'll walk by the items you want and make a final bid."

"Okay." She stood, wobbling slightly. He handed her Rosie and took her other arm until he was certain she was steady.

When they got to the auction tables, they wandered to the two she'd most wanted, while he stole a glance at those US Open tickets. The bid was up to twelve seventy-five. After making sure she wasn't looking, he bid sixteen hundred, hoping that would be enough to keep others from outbidding him.

He went to her side. "Let's go outside for a minute. I could use some fresh air, after all that time with my dad." And she'd had a lot to drink, so the chill might sober her up a bit.

"I thought you two formed a truce."

"We did, but it doesn't mean it's easy." He opened the French doors where he'd been photographing Peyton.

"It's chilly out here." She shivered.

He wrapped his arms around her. "Did my family make you uncomfortable?"

"No."

He narrowed his eyes. "Did Karina?"

"No. Why?" Her brows pinched together.

"You drank a lot tonight. I sense something is off now, but I don't know what. Is it because I disappeared for a while?"

"I already told you, no. I can survive thirty minutes on my own, especially here. I've more friends and family in there than you do." Her defensiveness suggested she'd overstated her case, but he still didn't know why.

"Okay." He wanted things to return to how they'd been for the past few weeks, so he kissed her. Unlike every other time, she pursed her lips and pulled away. He released her with a huff. "Claire. What's *wrong*?"

"Nothing." She glanced at the door. "Won't they be announcing the auction winners soon?"

"Yes, but I want to settle this tension first."

She sighed and spun away, walking to the edge of the patio and grabbing hold of a pillar. "I've realized some things tonight, and one of them is that this"—she gestured between them—"has to end."

He hadn't known what to expect, but it wasn't that. "Right now?"

"I wasn't going to say anything until we got home, but I guess there's no point in putting it off. You're leaving for Greece in another week—a fact you failed to mention. Not that it matters, because you'll always be going off on assignments, often with women with whom you have a 'fluid' relationship, like Karina.

"After speaking with her and thinking about things, it struck me. The truth is . . . the truth is that I'm not good at being *fluid*. I've tried it your way, but I disagree that a happy life is one lived only in the moment. I also disagree that goals and expectations make me too rigid to enjoy life. Being loved, having real friends, starting a family . . . these things matter to me. They *do* make me happy.

"You—let's be honest—you've meant so much more to me throughout our lives than I ever meant to you. We came into this thing on unequal footing—something I should be used to by now." She wryly nodded at Rosie. "I have nothing but love for you, Logan. You're exciting and charming and, at heart, a good guy. These past couple of weeks have been like a dream, but it's time to wake up. Our needs are incompatible, so you should stick to women like Karina, and I'll keep searching for someone more like me."

Love. She'd said she loved him. Not exactly in a declarative sense, but that word shimmered between them like the beautiful last bits of glitter before a firework extinguishes. He'd never used that word, not really. Not the way she meant it.

He crossed to her and reached for her hands. "But I don't want Karina, or women like her. I want you."

He'd come to crave her earnestness, and to like himself better with her, where he could drop all pretense and persona.

A wan smile appeared. "I know you care for me, and after all these years, it's been a wonderful surprise. I don't regret what's happened, but I can't pretend to be who I'm not just to hold on to something that we both know has an expiration date. I need something more. Something to build on." She eased her hands out of his grip. "Every day I spend with you only adds to the time it will take me to get over missing you and wishing things were different."

It might have been cold enough outside that Logan could see his breath, but his chest burned. "What did Karina say to you?"

"Nothing I didn't already suspect."

He raised his arms from his sides, irked and more than a little thrown off balance. "I'm not sleeping with Karina."

"Not at the moment. But that's the point. In four weeks, you'll be in Greece, and in *that* moment, we won't be together and you two will . . . you know." She fluttered her hand as if to suggest sex was a forgone conclusion.

"How do you know?" he snapped.

"How do I know what?"

He rolled his hand, mimicking her. "You assume that I'll end up in bed with Karina. You assume I won't miss you or be thinking of you. In fact, I was planning to invite you to meet me in the Mediterranean for a vacation when I'm done working. Maybe Sicily."

Her lips formed a perfect O until she sucked them in for a moment. "That's romantic, but we both know I can't fly to Italy when I couldn't even drive home from Hartford! I'm not proud of that, mind you, but let's be real."

"You love that word, but what's 'being real' even mean, Claire? Reality isn't some fixed thing. It's different for everyone, and changes depending on your perception. If you perceive yourself as unable to fly, then you won't ever fly. If you perceive yourself as unable to experience a relationship as it is instead of as you think it should be, then you won't be able to explore and enjoy it. If you perceive danger everywhere, then you see danger." He went to grab his hair and then remembered he'd cut it off. He balled his hands in fists at his sides. "Don't let your perceptions—your *misconceptions*—affect what's happening here. I'm *not* going to sleep with Karina next month."

She frowned, shaking her head. "It doesn't matter if it's Karina in four weeks or someone else in four months. Logan, you run from your home here, always searching for the next new exciting thing. For this little while, I've been that shiny new thing. But you're an explorer. You've no interest in a picket fence, nursery school, and a quiet life by the sea. And I don't begrudge you what makes you happy. I *want* you to be happy on your journey. I just don't want to go with you."

"Then stay here and build your business, but that doesn't mean we can't enjoy the time we have now and then see what happens when I return from Lesbos." He stroked her arm. "Are you tired of me?"

"No, that's not it."

"Then let this unfold on its own timeline." He shuddered at the thought of being cast out of her warmth.

She hugged herself, turning away and staring down the street toward the town green. For a few seconds, he thought he'd convinced her to reconsider, and his chest filled with helium.

She glanced up at him. "Is there *any* chance in the world that you could see yourself happily committed to me, living here in town, and raising a family?"

He froze—as if all the blood had drained from his body—having never given any thought to such permanence. Not with her or anyone. Not ever.

"See." She thrust her hand toward him, palm up. "Even the idea stops you cold. Letting things unfold when we know it's only going to hurt me is great for you but terrible for me. Though unintentional, that'd be the result."

"I don't know what I want from minute to minute, so how can *you* know what I want or what will be?" He gripped her waist as if the strength of his hands would make her feel what he felt. "You mean something to me, and you know I don't say that lightly. I don't get close to people, but I feel a connection with you, Claire. Something new and different from anything I've had with other women. Please don't push me away so soon."

Her eyes were watery. "You say things like that and it breaks my heart, because I want to believe that there *is* something big enough here to bridge the gap between the different things we want from life."

He pressed his forehead to hers and spoke in hushed but urgent tones. "We won't know if you won't give us more time."

She held his face in her hands. "I'm almost thirty-one. I'd like to have a family. I can't waste time when the odds are so long."

He broke away and took a few steps across the porch, raising his hand in the air. "So what, you're going to hang out here and settle for someone like Ben Lockwood?"

"Settle?" She scowled. "Ben is a fine, fine man, Logan."

"You know what I mean." He'd been pissed at Ben since he'd returned to town. He'd blamed it on Ben's anti-Peyton stance but now had to admit it partly came from jealousy that he'd had such an important place in Claire's life.

"No, actually, I don't. If you're insulting him for building a quiet life near his family, then you might as well insult me and millions and millions of other people."

They stared at each other. His fingers were growing numb from the cold. Goose bumps rose on her arms. The air between them fogged from heavy breaths despite the fact that they were standing still.

He wanted to shake her. Instead, he kissed her.

A deep, possessive kiss, complete with gnashing teeth and plundering tongues. A kiss meant to change her mind . . . or at least make her doubt her hasty decision. His heart beat faster, desperate to hold on to this bond.

She broke the spell when she pulled away. With her cheek pressed to his chest, she begged, "Logan, if you care about me, let me go now."

He touched her hair and shoulders, and then let his arms fall to his side. Inside something broke and sapped the fight out of him. "If that's what you wish."

"Trust me, this is not my *wish*. But my wish would change something essential about you, and I can't want that." She smiled and searched his face as if memorizing it. "Thank you for . . . all of it. I'll catch a ride home with my parents tonight, okay?" She turned to go back inside, then stopped. Without looking back, she said, "I hope you get the story you've been searching for in Lesbos, Logan. And know I'll be praying for your safe return."

She flung open the French door and disappeared inside. It clicked shut behind her, leaving him out in the cold.

Chapter Eighteen

Claire nodded while Mrs. Brewster droned on indecisively about her exhaustive list of pros and cons when comparing the Calacatta gold marble to the jade-green onyx for the countertops in her bathroom. "I just can't decide. What would you do, Claire?"

Standing in the dusty, empty space that Steffi had just demolished, Claire forced herself to focus on the project. And, good God, if *this* decision took so much time, she prayed that Mrs. Brewster didn't begin to second-guess the choices she'd made about drawer pulls and fixtures. "White is classic and timeless, so if you think you might downsize in five or seven years, this will hold up better for potential buyers. But I think you actually like the elegance of the jade tone, so you might be happier every day surrounded by this one."

She held the green square at arm's length. Then she thought of Logan, as she'd done nonstop for the past three days. Not only did the onyx resemble his eyes, but he'd never call it green or even jade—not when it contained cream veins and gold flecks, too.

"They're both so expensive." Mrs. Brewster pressed her hand to her mouth. The light coming through the single large window behind her shone through her thinning hair, which she'd teased into a sort of curly crown. "I don't want to make the wrong decision."

"There is no wrong decision. Both are pretty." Claire tipped her head. "The onyx is slightly more feminine and unique. Some men might not like it, but you don't have to make that compromise."

"Oh, Harold." When Mrs. Brewster sighed, her eyes turned misty even though her husband had passed almost two years ago. "Maybe I should get the white because he would've liked it better."

Love like that—pure and eternal—did exist for some. If Claire kept picking men like Todd and Logan, she'd never experience its power or joy.

Sympathy for Mrs. Brewster's loss smoothed the ruffled feathers of Claire's impatience. The poor woman probably felt alone in the world without her husband of fifty years. "I'm sure Harold would want you to pick whatever made you happiest."

Mrs. Brewster touched Claire's hand with her spindly one and smiled. "You're right. He would. He was always eager to make me happy. Let's go with the green one."

"Perfect." Claire threw the samples back in her bag before Mrs. Brewster had a chance to reconsider. "I'll reserve a slab of this. Once the new floors and cabinetry are installed, they'll come measure and make the template. It'll take a couple of weeks to manufacture the counters. Steffi will give you plywood counters in the interim."

"Oh, I know it'll be a while. Stefanie told me four weeks or more. Hard to believe for this little space, but I know it'll be worth it in the end." She smiled, revealing a tooth smeared with a bit of poppy-red lipstick. "I'm using the hall bathroom anyway."

"I promise, when we're finished, this will be a wonderful little retreat." Claire turned and began walking out of the bathroom and down the stairs. "I'll email you some options for ornamental pieces you might like to place on the vanity or near the soaker tub. You let me know if you like anything."

"I will." Mrs. Brewster led her to the front door. "Thank you, dear. I'm so glad we're doing this. I needed a little project to keep me busy and to have something fun to look forward to."

"Thank you for hiring us. We'll make sure you're happy with the final result." Claire waved, glad for her first whiff of fresh air in thirty minutes. She half thought Mrs. Brewster's overly sweet floral perfume had seeped into her pores now, too. "Speak to you soon."

When Mrs. Brewster closed the door, Claire strode to her car with a sigh, thinking of the mountain of details to sift through to complete Logan's project. She also needed to design new social media ads with the updated website gallery pages. She'd been putting off these tasks for the past three days because any reminder of Logan physically hurt.

While she dug for her keys, her phone rang. "Hello?"

"Claire," came Mr. Prescott's familiar voice. She set her bag aside and gripped the steering wheel. "It's Harrison Prescott."

"How are you, Mr. Prescott?"

"Well, thank you. I'm following up on our brief discussion at the gala. You wouldn't happen to have time now, would you? I find myself with a free hour, thanks to a last-minute cancellation."

"Oh. Well, I . . ." Her heart kicked at her ribs, but then she scowled at herself. She might have given up on pitching him for this project, but who knew what other good might come of this meeting? If she impressed him, he might make introductions to associates with local projects. "Of course."

"Great. Come to Arcadia. We can use my home office."

She gulped. Was Logan at home? Peyton? Closing her eyes, she nodded. "Okay. I'll be there in ten minutes."

She punched off the phone, tipped back her head, and breathed through her nose. A second shot at rummaging through her purse produced her keys. Within the next few minutes, she found herself on the private end of Lilac Lane, her old stomping ground.

She hadn't been to this house in more than two years. Nothing had changed, from what she could see. The elegant curve of its pea-stone driveway led her to the sprawling shingle-style mansion. She could see remnants of the old tree house that had been the Lilac Lane League clubhouse in a large oak tree near the edge of the lawn, although the ladder once nailed to its trunk no longer existed.

The architect and designers who'd built the imposing home, with its tall flagpole set to the side and handsome balustrades around the patios and porches, had created an American dream by the sea. Of course, apparently, it hadn't been a dream life or family for Logan or Peyton, both of whom had taken off as soon as possible.

Every second since she'd ended things with Logan, she'd wondered how and where he was, and with whom was he doing whatever it was that he was doing. At present, she didn't see his car on the property. Relief filled her lungs, then regret immediately deflated them.

You can do this. She exited the car, made her way up the cobblestone stairs to the front door, and rang the doorbell.

Mr. Prescott answered while on the phone, waving her inside with a quick smile. The lemony-clean aroma shot her back to the days when she'd hung out here with her friends. They'd made pitchers of iced tea and baked cookies. They'd had sleepovers often, scribbling in the Lilac Lane League binder, laughing, and falling in love with Colin Firth in *Bridget Jones's Diary.*

But even Colin hadn't made Claire's heart skip like it had whenever Logan had joined them, nor had the handsome Brit made her restless at night the way that knowing Logan was sleeping across the hall had. She knew every crack on Peyton's bedroom ceiling from staring at it for so many sleepless hours.

Bittersweet memories kept coming, reminding her of how much of her life had been shaped here by the Prescott siblings, and yet now they were both out of her life.

She followed Mr. Prescott to his office, where he finally ended his call. This place—

frozen in time with its 1930s walnut writing desk and bookshelves loaded with musty classics—had always been off-limits to all kids.

Claire still remembered the way her heart had beat fast when Peyton had opened the creaky door after midnight the one time she'd sneaked them in here senior year. She vividly recalled the nubby feel of the Aubusson carpet beneath her bare feet, the taste of the bourbon on her finger as they'd each sampled Mr. Prescott's stash.

That night, Peyton had rolled a blank sheet of paper through her great-grandfather's typewriter and let them each take a turn typing on it. Peyton had written, "Never say never." Steffi had written, "I hope my mom can hear my thoughts." Claire had typed, "I'm grateful to be alive." That note remained safely tucked within the Lilac Lane League's binder to this day somewhere in Claire's old room at her parents' house.

Now, being invited into the sanctuary felt a little like going to church. Except here one worshipped from the comfort of a worn leather chair, surrounded by the symbols of the greatness that had brought this house—and family prominence—into being. This strange reverence gave her a better appreciation for Logan's otherwise inexplicable sense of inadequacy.

Mr. Prescott closed the office door and poured himself a drink. "Would you like one?"

"No thank you." She cleared the cobwebs from her throat.

"Then let's get right to it." He crossed to his desk and turned his large desktop screen around to face her. "As you know, I'm buying a chain of small, aging inns along the Atlantic seaboard. Most of my budget must go to upgrading software, hiring and training new personnel, and other operational items. Of course, as you can see, they also all need a face-lift. If I thought it could be supported, I'd completely renovate them. But there's a cap on the room rates tertiary beach-town inns can charge, so it'd be foolhardy to completely upgrade everything. I need less expensive options that will still make a big impact."

Claire scooted her chair closer. She hadn't researched the inns Logan had described because she'd dropped the idea of pitching her services. Now she needed to see what she was up against in order to offer advice. "May I scroll through these for a few minutes?"

"Of course." He gestured with his hands, then sat behind his desk and made himself busy with his phone.

The Portsmouth, New Hampshire, inn's exterior—two stories of neutral clapboard with white trim—looked attractive enough. A fresh coat of paint and some flower boxes and landscaping would perk it up plenty. The square building also included an ample, welcoming wraparound porch and a handsome wood-and-glass front door. The exterior promised something airy and homey inside, which made the sedate mustards and hunter greens, and bold floral wallpaper, all the more depressing. Add to that the old-fashioned rag carpets, heavy mahogany furniture, and antiquated bathrooms and fixtures, and "oppressive" was the only word to describe the emotion it evoked.

"You hate it." His gaze was now fixed on her face, which made her aware of how she'd wrinkled her nose while viewing the images.

She gave a slight shrug. "It's very dated."

"Hopelessly so?" He folded his hands on the desk.

"Nothing's hopeless," she assured him.

"Will I need to replace everything?" When he ran his hand through his hair, he looked like Logan.

She gave herself a mental headshake and refocused. "No. There are quick fixes that won't break the bank yet will give everything a fresh look."

"Such as . . ."

"First and foremost, paint. Strip all the wallpaper and repaint everything in lighter, soothing tones. New England and the mid-Atlantic aren't the Caribbean, so I'd stick to a neutral but sophisticated beach palette, like creams, lilacs, ice blues, and taupes. If you like wallpaper, go for texture—like linen, not bold patterns. People who choose small inns over hotel chains typically want a sense of romance and intimacy. They should feel it the instant they walk through the door, so make sure the mattresses, pillows, and comforters are high quality. Sumptuous linens are a must."

"This sounds good, Claire. What about these old bathrooms? My wife has a fondness for this stuff, but . . ."

The bold green-and-white 1950s tile and fixtures could still work. "Honestly, many people like nostalgia when they're on vacation. You can easily clean up these old sinks and tub showers by getting them reglazed. Even the vivid flooring can be fun if properly cleaned. Green works at the beach, but to help tone it down, I'd repaint the walls—possibly a pale seashell pink or iridescent cream—and perhaps sink a little money into cosmetic upgrades like more-modern faucets and lighting. Glam it up a bit and people will love it.

"The older case goods—dressers and such—won't look as heavy once you have the lighter color scheme with new linens and drapes to distract the eyes. Simplicity—color and texture—works best. You can recover some of the lobby furniture, maybe replace or simply remove other pieces. That's still going to take some money and thought, but it is a lot less than starting from scratch." She sat back.

"And would you recommend that we do all of the inns the same—to create a brand?"

She bobbed her head side to side, thinking. "If you do that, you should be able to negotiate bulk-buy prices for the linens and drapes. But I might add something unique to each inn in the guest rooms. For example, Mystic is known for its aquarium and seaport, while Annapolis is known for its naval academy. Maybe in Annapolis, you work the military naval theme in with throw pillows or pictures, while going with cute octopus-themed and antique-sailboat pillows in Mystic."

"Sounds simple."

"It should be. And lastly, one free way to give any room a totally new look is to reposition the furniture. Surprise guests with an unexpected but comfortable floor plan and it will feel more special than a typical hotel room."

"Those are all great ideas." He leaned forward. "Thank you for sharing them so freely."

"Happy to help." She smiled, pleased to have impressed a man who'd been an intimidating enigma for most of her life. A small but meaningful confidence boost, making this trip worth her initial discomfort.

His expression turned more thoughtful. "I'm surprised you came to help, given how Peyton and Logan have treated you."

"Logan?" She felt her brows pinch together.

"Obviously, he offended you at the gala."

"Mr. Prescott," she said, pausing to swallow. "First of all, I came here as a professional courtesy because you and your wife are always kind to me. I enjoy what I do, so it's my pleasure to think through these kinds of problems. As for Peyton, I'm saddened by what's been lost, and I hope the worst is behind us. But Logan never did anything to hurt me. He's been nothing but honest and respectful."

He swallowed the last of his drink, brows skeptically raised. "I just assumed . . . you left the gala with your parents. He came home mulish as ever and took off for New York the next morning."

Her breath caught in her chest. Logan had left town without saying goodbye—not that she expected it after the way she'd pleaded with him to let her go. But the fact that there was no opportunity for a chance encounter—even though she'd been anxious about what she'd do or say—crushed her. She glanced at the framed Pulitzer. "I'm sure he has a lot of preparations to make before going to Greece."

"I suppose."

She didn't want to discuss Logan or Peyton, so she sat forward, wearing a polite smile. "Well, unless you have other questions for me with regard to your hotels, I should probably make myself scarce."

"I have only one last question."

"Yes?"

He grinned. It was the first time she'd ever noticed he had a shallow dimple on his right cheek. "What's your fee?"

"This one's on the house. Truly." She stood and slung her purse over her shoulder.

He waved her back into her seat. "No, I mean, what would you charge to oversee the updates you described?"

"Oh!" She sank onto the chair, mostly from surprise. "Steffi and I don't really have the workforce to take on a multistate project."

"Couldn't my hotel GMs outsource the local painters and plumbers and such? I'm just talking about having you coordinate the design scheme, the colors, pick the bedding, all that stuff. You'd only have to go see each location at the beginning, and maybe once or twice more to make sure it was all coming together."

"Well . . ." She paused, thinking about the retail space she desperately wanted and about her vow to create a life of her own choosing, not one hampered by her fear or pushed on her by a man. "Send me the floor plans and images from each hotel and let me talk to Steffi. If we think we can manage it, I'll work up an estimate."

"Fine. But don't delay. I do need to start moving on this. The closing is scheduled in six weeks. It'd be great if we could go in quickly with updates and reopen with the new name and look before the summer season gets underway in mid-June."

"When we get to Lesbos, I want to meet with Dr. Passodelis first." Karina folded another pair of shorts and set them next to all the other stuff she'd collected on her dining table, apparently to test what she could cram into her lightweight carry-on. A far cry from the sturdy, sizable equipment cases Logan would be lugging around to keep his camera equipment and editing gear safe.

Logan chugged his IPA, swinging the leg he'd thrown over the arm of her living room chair. They'd finalized last-minute details earlier, but he was lingering at her place to avoid his apartment and Steffi, who was there prepping its walls.

"Who's he?" He didn't recall that name in their research notes.

"That psychologist I mentioned when you showed up—the one who's working with the refugees through Doctors Without Borders. He's helping them unpack all the trauma they've endured—rape, torture, war, and more." Karina then set a bunch of SIM cards, an extra battery charger, and several charging cables on the table.

He finished his third beer, but the buzz he'd been hoping would kill his restlessness hadn't taken hold yet.

"How much torture is happening in the camps?" Unlike Karina, who seemed eager to delve into that pain, he didn't relish the idea of taking close-ups of strangers who'd been raped and tortured. Mining for anguish walked a delicate and uncomfortable line, taking a toll on his soul. He'd prefer to seek out an uplifting, hopeful subject for their story.

"Some, but the more common pattern is torture and war PTSD from the refugees' homeland, then something traumatic happens on the journey to Greece, like an assault or a boat that sinks or something, then they get to camp and the camp guards use tear gas and clubs to beat rioters into submission. The compounding effect of multiple traumas becomes another tragedy refugees must overcome. It's horrible. There has to be a better way to give these unfortunate people a chance at a good life."

Logan stared out the window in Karina's apartment, thinking about trauma. He'd never suffered any, except for an early burst of panic when he'd first learned of Peyton's diagnosis. Deep down, though, he'd always believed she'd beat it. His sister was and remained somewhat invincible so far, thank God.

But Claire knew firsthand about how unexpected trauma could forever change the trajectory of a life.

He'd gone so many years without realizing that in her fervor to heal physically, she'd neglected her psychological and emotional recovery. She'd hidden those wounds like a champ, but year after year, fear had become her closest companion, shutting her off from many facets of life. Now it was one of several things keeping them apart. That and his own reticence about commitment.

"Hello!" Karina snapped her fingers. "Are you paying attention?"

"Sorry." He shook his head to clear away the doldrums. "This is going to be our most grueling investigation. At least after the hurricanes, most people were working *with* each other. Lesbos sounds like a total shit-show."

"We'll stay until we find an angle the other news networks have overlooked."

He'd be looking for that one extraordinary family or person who put an unforgettable face on the problems. Of course, every reporter and photographer who visited would be looking for the same thing. His father's words about the slim chances of ever being that person who rises above the others replayed.

It required more than skill. There was an element of luck to breaking through the noise, like Ryan Kelly's being in the perfect spot to capture that prizewinning, brutal image of the car plowing into the racially charged protests in Charlottesville, Virginia.

What did it say about him that making a name for himself was worth placing himself smack in the middle of a riot, literally putting his life at risk? Claire would never think *any* prize worth a life.

He believed there were things worth dying for—one's country, an uncompromising principle or value, saving the life of another—but an accolade? Could he really have been pursuing his dream for the wrong reasons all along?

Karina batted his foot. "What's the matter with you? You've been mopey all week."

He set the empty bottle on the floor, then stood and walked to the window. From her third-floor walk-up he could see swarms of people on the sidewalk, and streets crowded by cyclists, cars, and delivery vans. He closed his eyes to picture the unpolluted view of the Sound and imagined the echo of the woodpecker's bill drilling the tree outside his bedroom window at Arcadia House. "I'm not mopey."

"Is it Peyton? Was there a setback or something?"

"No. She's doing great. If she weren't, I wouldn't be going with you." He scratched the back of his head. His hair had grown only an inch or so. He supposed it wouldn't be a bad thing to have it short in a hot, dirty place like the refugee camps of Lesbos. He glanced over his shoulder to find Karina scowling at him.

"I've never seen you less enthused to dig for a story than you are right now." Karina crossed her arms. "Is it *Claire*?"

He glanced away at the first sight of her amused expression. "I'm a little tired, that's all. It's been an emotional several months with Peyton, and now I have to switch gears and get back into a working mind-set. I'll be fine by the time we land."

"You'd better be, Logan. You might have a trust fund to fall back on, but my career and rep are all I have."

"Have I ever given less than one thousand percent?" He frowned.

"Not yet . . ." She picked up his empty bottle and carried it to her sink. "But you know the saying. There's a first time for everything."

"Not for me." He turned away from the window.

"Hope you're right, although it seems like it might be your first time for something else."

He narrowed his eyes, failing to follow her logic.

"Claire? You like her . . . like, *like* her." Karina seemed to be tamping down a giggle. "Could she be the woman who finally brings you to heel?"

To *heel*? He shook his head to reject the dog metaphor and then crossed to the door, waving her suggestion away. "I'll see you at the airport tomorrow night."

He could hear her laughter as he closed the door. A thin sheen of sweat coated his forehead, although his discomfort at having his feelings for Claire exposed made little sense. He trotted down the stairs and onto the sidewalk, heading west toward his place. When he arrived, Steffi was still working.

"Didn't expect you to stay so late." He closed his door, forcing a smile despite a dull headache.

She balanced on her ladder, mounting one of the picture-frame moldings to the wall. "Trying to get as much done as possible. No use getting caught in rush-hour traffic, and I'd rather work four long days than come back for a fifth."

"Makes sense." Logan tossed his keys on the counter. Some masochistic part of him wanted to edit those pictures he'd taken of Claire at the Breakers, but first he had to eat something. The apple and three beers he'd had at Karina's wouldn't sustain him for long. "You hungry? I'm ordering takeout."

"Chinese?"

He shrugged. "If you want."

"I'm not starving, but I can always eat a spring roll and pan-fried dumplings." She nailed another section of the molding.

He noted the paint cans, sprayers, brushes, and such collected in one corner. Drop cloths folded into piles. He'd cleared out most of his furniture so they could work while he traveled, but he wasn't looking forward to sleeping on the blow-up mattress tonight. "When will you start painting?"

"I've finished the sanding and caulking, and am almost done with this framing. I should get a coat of primer done by tomorrow afternoon."

"Guess it's a good thing I'm getting out of here tomorrow, so I won't have to sleep with the paint fumes."

"I'm surprised you didn't stay at Arcadia this week." She peered at him as if he might respond to her statement. She could fish all she wanted, but he wasn't biting. Steffi climbed down the ladder and came to the kitchen to get a glass of water. "Are you looking forward to your trip?"

"You say that like I'm going on vacation." He wondered how much Claire had shared with Steffi, and if Steffi agreed with Claire. If he asked about her, Steffi would be all over him, and he didn't want that. Not tonight, anyway. He was leaving for weeks and had no idea what to expect from his trip, let alone worry about what he might want when he returned. "I'm hoping what we do there might make a difference. It'll be draining, no doubt."

"Must be weird to get back into the groove after taking so much time to help Peyton." She patted his shoulder. "You did an awesome thing for your sister. I hope you know how much it meant to her, and how much I admire you for it."

"I didn't do it for praise."

"All the more reason why it deserves some." Steffi gulped down the water.

"Thanks." He pulled out menus from some local Chinese places that delivered.

"You okay? You seem off, like you aren't eager to go. I know Claire's worried about this trip." Steffi held up her hand to stave off questions. "She hasn't said much, and even if she had, I wouldn't tell you anything, but she's distracted, and I know it's because of you."

Logan didn't want to add to Claire's stress, yet hearing about her concern made him happy. She missed him. She still cared. Maybe time apart would make her rethink her hasty decision. "I'll be checking in on Peyton now and then, so she can reassure Claire of my safety while I'm away."

"Why don't you do that yourself?"

"Because she ended it, Steffi." He crossed his arms. "Not me."

Steffi waved him off. "Pfft. That's a technicality."

"A big one, don't you think?"

She rolled her eyes at him. "You and I both know that was a preemptive strike. She nipped it in the bud before saying goodbye would hurt too much."

Maybe, but that still had been her choice, not his. "And now we'll never know what might've happened."

Steffi shook her head. "You're no smarter than I was in college. That's sad, Logan. Especially since I had the excuse of being nineteen at the time."

He leaned against the counter. "Just because you and Ryan found your way back to each other doesn't mean every other couple can or even should make it work. And I'm not the only one with issues here. Claire's got her own to overcome."

"I know. The only reason I'm not pissed at you is because you got her to question what she's been missing out on all these years. I never succeeded, and neither did Peyton. She might not make changes on your preferred time frame or scale, but she's better off for having spent time with you."

Small comfort. "For her sake, I hope so. She deserves a full life."

"So do you, Logan." Her voice echoed in his large, empty apartment.

Chapter Nineteen

"I would've come to your house, Claire." Peyton waved Claire inside Arcadia's entry.

Claire hoped she hid her surprise to see Peyton without the wig or a head scarf. Short, tufted hair dotted her scalp, but she still looked jarringly bald. The ruddiness had begun to fade from Peyton's skin. Her shirt hung flat against her chest. Claire didn't know if Peyton planned to get reconstructive surgery, and wouldn't ask such a personal question. Not with the way things stood between them.

Cancer had lost this round, but its ravages remained, a fact that elicited Claire's empathy despite her lingering disappointment in Peyton.

"It's fine. I need to drop off this information for your father, anyhow, so two birds . . ." After weighing her desire to build a thriving business against her fears, Claire had spoken with Steffi and worked up a bid for the hotel project. If they were hired, the income would enable them to move forward with their retail rental plans as early as this summer. She couldn't pass up an opportunity to get closer to her dream.

But delivering the bid wasn't the only reason she'd wanted to meet with Peyton here. With Logan halfway around the world, Arcadia House was a local place where she could feel his presence.

"I'll put this on my dad's desk." Peyton took the envelope from Claire. "Let's talk at the kitchen table. I made brownies with walnuts."

One of Claire's all-time favorite treats. Peyton knew that, and knew her well enough to know that this meeting would require a chocolate binge. Her gesture made Claire want to smile and cry at the same time. "Thank you."

Peyton headed down the hallway toward her dad's office. Claire meandered to the kitchen, a place where she'd once spent a lot of time. Darla Prescott had always been proud of the home's old-world charm: checkerboard flooring, white cabinets with black pulls and hinges, and butcher-block counters. In the 1990s, they'd installed an island with country cabinetry and a soapstone counter, but Claire thought the kitchen could use additional modern conveniences—like soft-close hinges and new-retro appliances.

A pile of freshly baked, still-warm brownies sat on a plate in the center of the table, its aroma filling the kitchen. Claire couldn't ignore the overture. One of several Peyton had made these past weeks. She told herself to rise above her ego and forgive Peyton in the hope of finally gaining some peace of mind.

Peyton reappeared and poured them each some milk. "I've been thinking about what you said—that Steffi probably wouldn't like a traditional bachelorette party. Since we know her dad and brothers won't think to throw any kind of family event, your wedding shower idea is probably the more practical way to go."

"Practical." Claire sighed, taking a seat while snatching the largest brownie on the plate.

"I didn't mean that as an insult." Peyton's expression stiffened, wary of Claire's reaction.

"I know." The tension between them crackled like static electricity— uncomfortable but not actually painful—despite Claire's vow to set aside their issues so they could plan something special for their friend. "I'm well aware of my own shortcomings."

"Practicality is hardly a fault. It's a better way of life than impulsiveness." A brief smile flickered, then Peyton cast her eyes downward. Her impulsiveness had certainly taken its toll on their friendship.

"Still," Claire replied. "I don't want to throw a boring party for Steffi and Ryan, so please, make free with your ideas."

"Really?" She smiled in that devious way she'd done since adolescence.

Claire's stomach tightened at the mischievous glee in Peyton's eyes. "What do you have in mind?"

"Well, you know how they both love being on the water. What if we rent a private yacht and cruise around the Sound?"

"A yacht?" Claire's palms grew clammy. *Didn't some ferry just burn en route in Florida last winter?* "That sounds . . . expensive."

"Richard Warner, my father's good friend, owns a sixty-some-foot trawler that he keeps at a nearby marina. It's beautiful. My dad said he'd lend it to us as long as we cover the cost of gas and crew for the day. Steffi and Ryan have a relatively small group of friends and family, so everyone would fit. I thought an intimate dinner cruise would be romantic."

Perspiration gathered on every surface of Claire's skin as she struggled to think up reasons to kill the idea. "It would be memorable."

"You look sick." Peyton sighed. "I'm sorry. Logan told me that you'd gone to the city and up to Newport, so I assumed . . . well, it doesn't matter. I'm sure we can come up with something nice to do here in town. We can hold it here on the patio to keep expenses down."

"No, thank you." Claire frowned. "I told you, I want it to be special."

A rivulet of sweat slid down her spine. She reminded herself she'd have a couple of months to prepare for a cruise. In fact, she'd be forced to push herself out of her comfort zone if Mr. Prescott hired her soon.

"So is that a yes to the cruise?"

Claire nodded because her mouth was too pasty to say the word. She bit into the brownie to make her inability to speak less obvious.

Peyton broke into a bright smile and covered Claire's hand with her own, then withdrew it as if she'd been burned.

"Sorry, I . . . well, this is great." Peyton tore off a bit of brownie, popped it in her mouth, and chased it down with a sip of milk. They continued nibbling their brownies during the textbook definition of awkward silence.

"Do you want to make the guest list and hire the caterer, and I'll handle music?" Peyton finally asked. "Logan can be our photographer."

At the mention of his name, Claire shoved the rest of the brownie in her mouth. She'd promised herself she wouldn't ask, but she couldn't help it. His absence this past week had felt more like he'd been gone a full month. After gulping down her milk, Claire asked, "How is he?"

"Logan? Busy. Overwhelmed, I think."

"How so?" She couldn't picture him that way. He always seemed in control of everything to the point of nonchalance.

"He's just outside the Moria refugee camp. Apparently, there are five thousand people jammed in a facility meant for half that number. It's an old military base, but he said it looks like a prison with chain-link fences topped with razor wire. Karina's employer got them a rare pass to get inside for one day. Rats, trash-lined streets, unaccompanied minors, open fires for heat, emotional and physical trauma . . . He sounded appalled, which is saying a lot considering other things he's seen in his travels. He almost sounded hopeless in his description, which is very unlike him."

Claire's heart rate spiked. Those conditions were ripe for violence and riots. "Is it safe?"

"There was no immediate threat when we spoke a couple of days ago. We never hear much from him when he's on assignment. He gets pretty involved in his work, and with the time difference and stuff, it isn't easy to communicate. He'll ping me occasionally so I know he's alive."

Claire swallowed. The Prescotts' cavalier attitude shocked her. *Her* parents couldn't go more than several hours without checking in to make sure she was unharmed and happy. "Did he mention when he'd be home?"

Peyton peered at her, head slightly tilted. "No. But I'm surprised you're so interested, given the way you dumped him at the gala."

"I didn't . . ." Claire blinked. "We shouldn't talk about my relationship with Logan."

"Why not?"

Claire met her gaze. "I still don't trust you."

Peyton's left brow rose. "Despite my past behavior, in this instance you can rest assured that I don't want Logan for myself."

The wry delivery stunned Claire so much she laughed, then covered her mouth. They stared at each other until Claire reached for another brownie and poured herself a second glass of milk.

Peyton tapped her fingers on the table, letting loose with a heavy sigh. "I've apologized in every way I know how, Claire. Will there ever be a day when we might laugh together for real?"

Claire's blood boiled until she thought she might melt right there at the table. It should be enough that she'd consented to work with Peyton on this party for Steffi's sake. But everyone—Steffi, Logan, Peyton—wanted more from her. *"Forgive and forget,"* Logan had once said. How does one forget? She'd never been good at that. "I don't know."

Peyton propped one elbow on the table and rested her cheek in that palm. "Logan thinks I'm one of the reasons you won't let yourself be happy with him. No matter what I do, the ripple effect of my mistake keeps coming back to hurt everyone."

There weren't enough brownies on that plate to get Claire through this conversation.

"You always liked him so much," Peyton continued. "I wouldn't have believed you'd let *anything* stand in the way of making things work."

"Logan loves you more than anyone in the world, Peyton. Even if he wanted a serious relationship—which was never on the table, by the way—it would only work if I could let you all the way back into my life, because you'll always be an integral part of his. A few weeks ago, I couldn't imagine sitting at a table with you." She snorted. "But look at us now . . ."

"There was a time when we both would've thought it a dream for you to end up with my brother." Peyton shook her head with a sigh. "When your name comes up, there's tenderness in his voice. That's rare. It makes me question whether I was wrong to warn you off. I shouldn't have sold him short. Not after everything he sacrificed to help me through the darkest period of my life. He deserved better from me. Besides, it's pretty obvious I don't know anything about what makes love last."

Claire huffed, swallowing the rest of that second brownie and eyeing a third. "Apparently, neither do I."

"Well, at least we have one thing in common, pathetic as it is." Peyton grimaced. Two things, Claire silently amended, because they'd both been fooled by Todd. Peyton sighed. "Who would've ever believed Steffi would be the first of us to get married?"

Claire might've married first had Todd not met Peyton. Then again, after being with Logan, she knew she hadn't belonged with Todd. Not only was he a troll, but also, in retrospect, theirs had been a tepid kind of love. Not one that could sustain them year after year. Not even one that could sustain his meeting Peyton.

"Maybe it's all for the best, though," Peyton continued. "Logan needs someone who can deal with him even when—especially when—he doesn't know what he wants or needs. You like certainty and security. I hope you find that with someone worthy."

Her words echoed what Claire had argued to Logan, but hearing it coming from Peyton made it sound so lame . . . and really, really boring.

Besides, Logan might not know what he needed, but Claire did. Despite his desire to sail the seas and win awards, Logan craved a real home. He didn't yet realize that, and he might never see it, so Claire had yanked her heart safely ashore.

Sitting in Arcadia House, she couldn't help but remember how Logan had spoken of his great-grandfather—the hero who'd inspired his ambition and also the man who'd made him feel treasured right here in this place.

"Peyton, before I go, do you have any old photos of Logan and your great-grandfather lying around? I want to put a personal touch on his condo design."

She shrugged. "We could check some old boxes in the attic. My mom isn't the most sentimental, but she never throws away anything to do with Duck."

Claire dug into the peach pie and ice cream her mom had set in front of her after dinner, because the three brownies she'd scarfed down earlier hadn't quite managed to quell her nerves about the impending cruise or Logan's safety. "This is delicious."

"Well, you've been so busy lately I needed to lure you into hanging out with Dad and me awhile longer." She sat beside Claire and smiled at her husband from across the table.

This scene had repeated weekly throughout most of Claire's life. Love. Family. Familiarity. It reassured her even though she'd started to yearn for more than mere comfort.

"Sounds like you've worked out your business issues on your own." Her dad took off his glasses and rubbed his eyes. "I'm proud of you, Claire Bear."

"Thanks, Dad." She sipped her decaf coffee. It never took much to earn her parents' praise. Poor Logan, on the other hand, never got any from his father. No wonder he was always risking his life to find proof of his worth elsewhere. "Redecorating Logan's apartment got the ball rolling, and then Mrs. Brewster. Did I tell you she sent us a referral? Another nice bathroom-remodeling job. Now, if Mr. Prescott accepts my proposal for those hotels, I'll be able to afford a small retail space in town this year."

"What hotels?" Her mom's brows arched.

This would go over like the Hindenburg, which was probably why she'd never before mentioned the possibility to her parents. "He's buying a chain of old inns along the Atlantic coast and asked for my advice about giving them an interior face-lift. I just submitted a formal proposal for the work today. Six hotels will yield a nice commission and get Lockwood & McKenna some really nice press."

"But . . . won't you have to travel to visit those places in order to do a good job?" Worry lines gathered on her mom's forehead and around her mouth.

Even her father's smile transformed to a concerned frown. "How far will you have to go? You said old . . . are they in run-down neighborhoods?"

Their words stoked her own fear, but she had to fight the cycle. "They're in small beach communities like in Mystic."

Her mom stared into her coffee cup, her face taking on a judgmental expression. "I'm surprised you'd want to work with the Prescotts after everything with Peyton and Logan . . ."

Claire pushed her empty plate away and shoved her seat back an inch or two to make room for her expanding stomach. "Peyton hurt me, and believe me, I haven't forgotten. But she's been through a lot, and maybe we've all suffered enough. Lately, holding on to a grudge seems pointless. It's not making me happier and, in fact, might be keeping me from being happy. She's home for a while, and we have to get along to plan Steffi's bridal shower, so I'm trying to find forgiveness. Today we decided to rent a yacht and plan a sunset cruise for the party."

Her stomach would've lurched again if it hadn't been stuffed full of sugary baked goods.

"On the ocean?" Her mother's fingers clutched her coffee mug so tightly the tips turned white. "What's wrong with the private party room at Lucia's?"

"Steffi and Ryan overcame a lot of heartache and past mistakes to reunite." She didn't elaborate because very few people knew about the sexual assault. "They deserve something special. Something memorable."

"It'll be memorable if someone falls overboard!" Her mom huffed.

"Mom." Claire forced a chuckle to ease the tension, although she still battled her own anxiety. "No one will fall overboard."

"You never know. Things happen." She pointed a finger at Claire. "Drunk people do stupid things."

Her dad was now popping giant red grapes like Claire did M&M's, but remained silent on the subject.

"We're not throwing a frat party." Claire reached for her mom's hand and squeezed. "Please, I'm almost thirty-one, not ten."

Her dad started choking and pounding on his chest, drawing her and her mother's concerned attention.

"Dad, are you okay?" Claire's pulse sped up.

His face turned pale blue, and he raised one hand in the air as the choking stopped and no air went in or out of his chest.

"Oh my God, Tom!" her mom shrieked, although panic seemed to paralyze her, as she sat there, blinking and shaking.

Claire sprang from her seat and circled her dad from behind. Instinctively, she wrapped her arms around him, clasping her fist just beneath his sternum, and attempted the Heimlich. She'd never done that before.

What if she failed? *Oh God, please.*

The first attempt produced nothing but a spike in her own panic. She adjusted her grip and jerked again. Still not hard enough. With all of her strength, she yanked her fists up into his sternum and finally popped the grape loose.

He gasped for air, touching his forehead to his forearms, which rested on the table. Tears of relief slid down Claire's face while she caught her breath and let her own heart settle. When her mom rounded the table to tend to her father, Claire hugged them both.

Thank God. Thank God.

"Let me get you some water," her mom finally said to her dad after kissing his face several times.

While her mom poured a small glass of ice water, Claire pulled her seat closer to her dad and stroked his arm.

"Thank you, honey. You saved my life." His watery eyes set off another round of grateful tears.

"I love you, Daddy." Claire set her cheek on his shoulder.

He patted her head. "I love you, too."

Her mother set the water in front of her dad and collapsed in another chair. Like snow in the moonlight, the sheen on her pale face looked icy. "I don't know what I would've done if Claire hadn't dislodged that stupid grape. I'm getting too old to handle scares like that. You need to be more careful, Tom."

There it was again. The "careful" mantra her family had repeated for the past sixteen years. The one that had cultivated the fear that had become an invisible fence, keeping them all hemmed in.

"My heart." Her mom looked at Claire while patting her chest. "Please reconsider taking a job that requires so much travel. There are drifters in those touristy beach towns."

She studied her parents, her mind churning with its sudden realization. "Dad could've just died right here in this kitchen, a place where, according to you, he should be perfectly safe. Peyton's own body is trying to kill her. Accidents and illnesses don't respect a safety zone. They just happen. Risk is everywhere, every day. And drifters could come into this community as easily as any other."

"I can't keep living my life in a bubble. I want to be normal. To drive on the highway. To go to a crowded place and not drown in my own sweat. Maybe I need therapy. Maybe we all do. I'm not sure, but I *do* know I can't take the guilt of feeling like I'm ruining your life by trying to live mine, Mom."

"I'm not trying to make you feel guilty, but I couldn't bear it if you got hurt again. That was the worst phone call of my life, Claire. You can't understand because you don't have children yet—"

"And I never will if I let fear make my life so small no interesting man will want to be part of it." Claire pressed her hands flat on the table.

Her mom huffed, her eyes brimming with tears. "Is that why Logan left? Is he behind this sudden burst of resentment?"

Claire reached for her mom's hand again. "I don't resent you or Dad. I'm just asking you to hear what I'm saying and support me. We all went through something tragic together. But after all these years, we need a new way to cope before it's too late to enjoy the life we still have."

Her father nodded. "Claire's got a point, Ruth. Maybe we could try family counseling."

"We can't control the monsters out there, and no amount of therapy will change that," her mom replied.

"The truth is that we can't control much of anything, Mom," Claire said. "Only the choices we make."

Chapter Twenty

Logan roamed the narrow streets of Athens's Plaka district, hoping the bustle of excited tourists and shopping would help to subdue memories of the misery he'd seen at the Moria refugee camp. Today he'd perused endless rows of stores and alleys, each strung with bright-colored clothing for sale, all waving like flags along the sidewalk. An excess of distractions—sunlight, the high-pitched drone of passing motorcycles, ancient ruins in plain view—yet none of them quieted the overwhelming questions he had about what would happen to unaccompanied minors, like twelve-year-old Aya Khateb, who were two- and threefold victims of a failing system.

Thank God he hadn't succeeded in convincing Claire to meet him in Italy this week. He'd been out of his mind to think he'd be able to vacation immediately after spending several weeks photographing people trapped in a situation with little human dignity at best, and death or trafficking at worst.

The Council of State's recent ruling might've been lauded by human rights organizations, but the government's swift reactionary imposition of an administrative order to reinstate the containment policy maintained the standstill that had existed for two years. Thousands of refugees imprisoned in hell.

A vibrant sun beat down on the busy streets now, but although temperatures hovered at a mere eighty degrees, Logan felt depleted while forcing himself to pick up a few gifts to take home: olive-oil beauty products and soaps for Peyton and olive-wood salad servers for his parents. Normally, that would be the end of his shopping list, but he'd stumbled upon a beautiful set of lapis lazuli–and–silver *kombolói*, or "worry beads."

Its design resembled a lariat, but the set was actually meant to relieve stress by giving one's hands something to play with. The color of its beads reminded him of Claire's eyes, and kombolói seemed the perfect gift for someone with her constant concerns.

Now he toyed with it as he wandered back to the hotel to grab a shower and a meal.

Claire. Prior to arriving on Lesbos, he'd thought of her often, but then he got swept up in the work, the stories, the pictures, leaving only the wee hours available for missing her. During sleepless nights, he'd stared at the photos he'd snapped of her at the Breakers, wondering if he should send them to her with a note. But what could he say?

Nothing that would comfort her or give her more faith in the world or the goodness of people, although he'd encountered remarkable volunteers who'd come to supply aid to those in need. Even within the camps, many refugees would band together to help each other. But death, illness, and violence went hand in hand in overpopulated, underprepared, sequestered conditions, too.

And the children . . .

Shaking those images loose, he took the hotel stairs two at a time up to his room, eager for a cool shower to wash away his discomfort. Ten minutes later, he turned off the water and stepped out of the shower right before Karina banged on his door.

"Logan . . . are you in there?"

"Hang on." He jogged to the door in his towel, opened it, and then walked to his suitcase to locate shorts and a T-shirt.

"Did it work?" Her gaze lingered on his abdomen, but he felt no stir of interest from it.

He impatiently snagged his underwear, too. "Did what work?"

"Sleeping, shopping, showering? Did any of it make you feel better about what we've learned?" She sank onto his bed and leaned back on her elbows, restlessly fluttering her feet.

"Not really."

"Me neither." She tapped her toes on the floor and sprouted a saucy smile as she pointedly looked at his towel. "There's one *S*-word we haven't tried yet. It's always worked in the past."

That gratifying human connection had been a sort of ritual for them at this juncture of other projects, but it wouldn't help today. After being with Claire, his shallow connection to Karina would be too obvious for him to ignore or enjoy.

They were colleagues and sex buddies, but sex wouldn't fill the space Claire had left in his chest by tunneling in there before pushing him away. In fact, it might make that cavern bigger. The question he couldn't answer yet was why he'd let her go. Each week since the gala, he'd grown more convinced that only she could fill that gap.

"Sorry, but I'm not up to it." He shimmied into his underwear beneath the towel, then tossed it aside and finished dressing.

Karina raised her brows and pushed herself upright. "Didn't see that coming. May I ask why not?"

He supposed he could've been more tactful. Sighing, he defaulted to the world's worst explanation because he hadn't the mental energy to do better. "It's not you. It's me."

She covered her face while chuckling, then waved both hands in the air. "Spare me the platitudes, Logan. We know each other too well for that. I'm not in love with you. I just need to take the edge off."

He chuckled, relieved that he hadn't hurt her feelings. "I'm sure there are plenty of guys who'd happily help you out with that."

"Probably." She stood, holding out one hand. "But I'm not up for strangers at the moment. I'm stuck with you. Let's at least go get a few drinks to celebrate our last day in Greece. I know you wanted to focus on the unaccompanied kids, but we got better information on the long-tail mental-health crisis from our series of interviews with Dr. Passodelis and his patients. Those are the images I want. Do what you want with the others."

He would. Maybe he'd partner with a gallery and an organization that assisted with refugee adoption to put on an exhibition to raise money and awareness. Perhaps that could lead to the rescue of children like young Aya and to the creation of new families.

Gesturing to the door, he said, "Let's go. I saw a café on the corner."

———

Logan swung open his condo door and rolled his luggage and equipment inside, grateful to bring an end to an interminable flight. He would need a good night's sleep in his own bed after a month of practical insomnia, but jet lag would likely wreak havoc with his circadian rhythms for some time.

He tossed his keys on the counter, hit the lights, and went still.

Rich midnight-blue walls enveloped him, glowing in the warmth of soft lighting from new brass fixtures. He walked into the sophisticated yet comfortable living room, noting the handsome wool area rug and two square hammered copper planters in the corners, each now home to some kind of miniature citrus tree.

Floating shelves housed an antique camera, a collection of Duck's first editions, and small pots of ivy. The entire room seemed anchored by the vibrant green sofa, which contained colorful pillows. Only one—a rectangular needlepoint pillow—looked a bit out of place.

He narrowed his gaze, then crossed to lift the pillow off the sofa to read the quote, which he immediately recognized from Duck's work. *"Her love kept him company, even in her absence."* A rush of warmth flooded Logan. He cradled the handmade pillow to his chest, his thumb gently stroking its stitching. Blinking three times, he pinched his nose to quiet the tingling sensation gathering there.

Continuing his tour, he admired his new round dining table and chairs, although he'd need more friends to make good use of them. His gaze bounced around the entire space, taking everything in while he walked toward the bedroom.

It looked strikingly similar to the images Claire'd shown him, so he wasn't surprised until he took a closer look at the set of shadow boxes hung above the headboard. With the needlepoint pillow still tucked under one arm, he crawled across the mattress for a closer inspection of the two enlarged, beautifully matted images.

The first was of him and Duck sitting on the sandy shore near that old hammock; in the second, a family photo he didn't recall, he straddled his father's shoulders and Peyton was in their mother's arms. He had no memory of that kind of family life. They all looked so happy in that photo it almost hurt to see. Family. Connection. Love.

For all the ways he'd criticized Claire for letting fear stop her from trying new things, he'd let fear stop him from grasping on to love.

He squeezed the pillow against his chest as if it could soften the blows of his heartbeat pounding against his ribs. This had all begun as a way to manage a happy ending for his sister, but his manipulations had led to highs and lows—and endings—he'd never imagined.

Still, Claire had thought of everything—mementos, family photographs, plants, and the handmade pillow—in an attempt to infuse his cold apartment with life and love and family. To make it a real home. Yet he saw the illusion for what it was. This apartment would never be a home without love.

His phone pinged with a text from Peyton.

Are you home yet?

Rather than text her, he dialed. "Hey, just walked in."

"I know you must be exhausted, so I won't keep you long. I just wanted to welcome you home. Maybe we can grab lunch in the next day or two. I've been revising the manuscript for our book while you've been away. We should start taking steps toward publication."

The memoir. Another worthy venture, although Aya and the other children in Moria wouldn't fade from his thoughts soon. "I need a couple days to decompress and to edit the last photos I took in Greece. Later this week?"

"Sure." She paused. "Must've been tough to jump back into such a big assignment after so much time off."

He glanced once more at the images of his family. "Let's just say it's good to be home."

"Speaking of home, how do you like your place? I got a peek yesterday when I did the nice-sister thing and stocked your refrigerator with some fresh food."

"You're awesome." He smiled, lowering himself from his knees. He could use a snack, although he was so tired he needed an afternoon nap more. "And I love the place. It's nicer than I deserve."

"Claire was very particular about it. I think she outdid herself."

"Agreed." He slouched against the pillows and headboard, cradling the needlepoint pillow on his lap.

"Have you called and thanked her?"

"I literally just walked in. Plus, we haven't spoken since the gala. I'm not sure what to say." He hesitated, having spent many nights trying to compose a note in his head. "Have you seen her?"

"We met to discuss a bridal shower, and we've spoken twice since then. Things between us are slowly improving. We even shared a laugh, sort of."

"That's big news." A bubble of joy stretched his heart. He'd helped Peyton, as he'd vowed he would. Maybe that was worth this bit of heartache.

"There's more. Dad hired her to revamp his inns. She and Steffi actually went up to Mystic early this morning."

He let his head fall back against the headboard, thinking maybe he'd helped make that possible, too. "No shit."

The time he'd spent in Sanctuary Sound had not been in vain if the two women he loved were better off for it. Loved. There. He'd admitted it, even if not to Claire. "When does she return?"

"I don't know. We still aren't confidantes." Peyton fell silent. "We did talk about you, though."

"Did you?" He sat up straighter.

"She was worried about your safety."

Of course she was. "That's it?"

"Pretty much, but I'm sure you're still very much on her mind, and in her heart."

"Mm." Could there be a thread tying them together that she hadn't yet cut?

When he didn't say more, Peyton said, "Call me tomorrow."

"Sure. Bye." Logan punched off the phone and brushed his palm across the needlepoint pillow in his lap. Closing his eyes, he pictured his last conversation with Claire. Heard her logic. Saw her pleading look. Remembered his inability to tell her what she'd needed to hear—what she deserved to hear.

His own cowardice made his thoughts turn again to the brave refugees who'd overcome hurdles and risked their lives in order to build a better home life for the people they loved. They'd sacrificed and suffered for something he took for granted, which made him wince.

He rolled off the bed and dug his laptop and the kombolói from his bag, then scrolled through the photographs he'd taken of Claire at the Breakers, picking one of his favorites. The one where the corner of her mouth tipped upward, like her eyes, as she caught notice of the billiard room's ceiling mural.

It was so her. Subtle and soft, yet intensely engaged and sincere. Everything he was not, but everything he coveted.

If there was any chance she hadn't yet given up on him, he had to seize it. He opened his email, attached the photo, and typed a note:

> Claire,
>
> I've been staring at this image for weeks, missing you and your delicate beauty, curiosity, and imagination. Look at your awe at that ceiling mural. When I see this picture, I find myself wishing you would spring to life and turn that same gaze on me.
>
> Now I'm back and surrounded by you in this beautiful home you created—yet it feels strangely empty without you.
>
> If any part of you has missed me, please call me. I am changed because of you. I hope you'll let me prove it.
>
> Yours,
> Logan

He hit "Send" and blew out a breath, staring at the screen, hoping . . .

Claire exchanged a silent look with Steffi upon their seeing Peyton get out of her parked car as they pulled up to the curb in front of Claire's house.

"Were you expecting her?" Steffi asked, brows drawn together.

"No." Claire's heart pounded with worry that Peyton had come to share bad news about Logan. A slight tremor whipped through her, but she managed to open the car door when Steffi did the same.

"Why are you here?" Claire blurted, scanning Peyton's face for signs of grief. Her heart settled at the lack of any, but her stomach tightened in anticipation of dealing with Peyton yet again.

"I wanted to talk to you, but you weren't answering my texts." Peyton clasped her hands in front of her body. Dressed in fine gray slacks and a loose-fitting pink spring sweater, she'd also donned the wig made of Logan's hair, all of which made her look more like her old self.

"My phone died and we didn't bring a charger." Claire crossed her arms. "What's the urgency?"

"Logan got home an hour ago." Peyton searched Claire's face now—for what, Claire wasn't sure.

"Is he all right?" Steffi asked.

"He's fine." Peyton looked back to Claire. "Physically, anyway."

"Thank God." A huge weight lifted upon confirming he'd made it home in one piece. "You sound perturbed, though."

"I am. He's not his normal happy self, and I think it's because of you."

"Me?" Claire glowered at the accusation.

"Yes, Claire." Peyton crossed her arms. "Because of you."

"Should I stay and ref?" Steffi darted a glance from Peyton to Claire.

"No," Claire said at the same time Peyton answered, "You can go."

Claire and Peyton stared at each other, a challenge forming in the space between them.

"Please keep it civil." Steffi clasped her hands together in prayer. "I love you both and don't want the truce to end so soon."

Claire closed her eyes and counted to three so she wouldn't argue. She'd made such strides these past several weeks on all fronts. She wouldn't let Peyton derail her, for God's sake.

Before climbing into her car, Steffi flashed an uneasy smile. She started the engine and slowly drove away while watching them as if she expected them to burst into flame.

When the car turned the corner, Claire turned back to Peyton. She'd said Logan was unhappy. "Does he hate the apartment?"

"No, he loves it." She grinned.

Claire flipped one hand over. "Then why are you here? I know we've been working together to plan Steffi's party, but I told you before, I don't want to discuss him with you."

"Let's not have this conversation on the sidewalk, okay? May I come inside for five minutes?" Peyton's calm expression challenged Claire's self-control, even though the last thing she wanted was to invite Peyton inside.

"Fine." Claire led the way into her house, then set Rosie and her bag down by the door and shot Peyton an "out with it" look.

"Here's the thing. I love my brother. His happiness matters to me, and since I think you're an integral part of that for him now, I must get involved." Peyton sank onto a chair with a huff, as if they were old friends—which they were, or had been. "I'd like to think I've learned something from months of pondering my own death, planning a funeral, writing an obituary . . . you know, all the morbid things one thinks about when hit with the big *C*."

With no ready rebuttal to such macabre candor, Claire sat on the sofa and waited. Her living room grew uncommonly warm, but she didn't want to offer Peyton a drink or do anything else that might extend this visit.

"These physical changes"—Peyton gestured to her hair and chest—"have also made me see myself, people, beauty, and love differently. The memoir—one of Logan's great ideas—is definitely adjusting my filter and my priorities."

"This is all . . . interesting, but what's it have to do with me?" Claire scratched at the arm of the sofa, although it was her body that itched.

"You've been where I am—survived something tragic. Until I fought my own battle, I never understood why you've lived scared. Now I get it. For the past several months, I've taken only calculated risks. Afraid of loss. I craved security and stability. But today I've had an epiphany. Timidity only leads to a different kind of suffering—the kind made up of regrets and 'could have beens.'"

Claire's cheeks bloomed with heat. Peyton might not be judging her, but her words were like a pillow pressed over Claire's face.

Peyton leaned forward, elbows on her knees, eyes staring at a distant spot. "I came to town filled with regret and shame, convinced I deserved this illness. I've apologized, tucked my chin all over town, tried to make amends. And while I still feel some of those things, I'm no longer willing to spend whatever time I've got left begging and cowering.

"I've no idea if my surgery and the meds I'm still taking have killed all the cancer and can keep it from spreading, so I need to make the most of my second chance—however long it lasts." She turned her gaze on Claire. "Every single day is a gift, Claire. I came here to remind you of that because I think you're still living scared."

Claire shook her head. "I've been making changes, Peyton, as you know. But regardless of whether you agree, what does any of this have to do with *Logan's* happiness?"

"Last time we talked about him, I suggested your differences were insurmountable. But I hadn't thought through how events and people change us. My cancer changed me. The situation with Todd changed us. And, oddly enough, now I think maybe you changed Logan, too. I hadn't considered that before . . . that maybe *his* needs could change." A sweet, sad little smile flickered. "I see you taking chances again—which is great—but you're not taking the most important risk. The one with your heart. I also know I'm partly to blame for that. That's why I'm here.

"If any part of you regrets walking away from Logan, tell him now. Don't let love slip through your fingers. You'll never forgive yourself if you do—and you'll never forgive me, either. Despite everything, I still hold out hope that, someday, you and I will be friends again. But even if that day never comes, I'll always support your relationship with my brother." Peyton sighed and slouched back into the chair.

Claire could hear the heaviness of her own breath. She stared at Peyton, her body reeling on a sea of emotion whipped up by that speech. A few years ago, this moment might've ended with a hug between the friends. Something in Claire longed to go back in time to when everything had been simpler. But they could only go forward.

"I believe you mean well, so thank you for that. But you're inserting yourself into something you shouldn't." Claire shrugged. "Whatever Logan does or doesn't feel, it's up to him to share it with me, which he hasn't."

"Have you shared yours?" came Peyton's shrewd reply.

Claire stood and crossed to the front door. "I don't want to be rude, but I'm tired and hungry. I heard you out, but this isn't your problem to solve. I think you should go now. Please."

Peyton shook her head as she rose from her seat. Claire opened the front door with a polite smile fixed on her face, preparing to say goodbye, when Peyton surprised her with a fierce hug. She spoke directly in Claire's ear with sad urgency. "Please don't dismiss everything I've said just because you dislike me. Despite everything, I still love you, Claire, and I want to see you happy."

Peyton released Claire and walked out of the house without making eye contact.

For a few seconds, Claire stood there not knowing what to do, unable to make her body move. Eventually, she closed the door. The air seemed hot and heavy, burning her lungs even as she strained to suck it in. Logan was home, in the apartment she'd redesigned. Did he like the personal touches?

She grabbed her bag and went to the kitchen in search of snacks. Unpacking Peyton's visit—and hug—would require chocolate and salt.

Dazedly, she plugged her phone into a charger, then rummaged her cabinets. Twix bars and milk would have to suffice. She poured a small glass and tore into the candy wrapper, then went to see what other messages she'd missed this afternoon. Right now she'd do anything to avoid thinking about Peyton's lecture.

Logan. His name appeared on the screen as if in boldface. She snapped off a gigantic bite of the Twix with her teeth and opened the email, heart thudding with each line of text she read. When she'd finished, she clicked on the attachment, stunned by the portrait of herself captured through his eyes.

He'd sent it almost two hours ago. Was he waiting for a reply even as she sat there rereading the note? A love note. After all the secret love letters she'd written to him and stuffed under her bed as a teen, Logan Prescott had finally sent her one.

She glanced at the clock, then whirled around and went to the bookshelf to retrieve the scrapbook he'd discovered weeks ago. Her heart raced, pumping hope and life through her limbs. She felt so full of them she almost forgot to grab Rosie on her way out the door.

—⁓—

Logan woke with a start. Neither hot nor uncomfortable, he blinked, stretching out against cool sheets. It took a disoriented second to remember he wasn't in Lesbos or Greece but at home, surrounded by the comfort of air-conditioning and potable water. Within the next few seconds, he became aware of a presence—a sound—that didn't belong.

Someone had entered his apartment.

With limbs still heavy from an incomplete nap, he slid out of bed and crept toward the open bedroom door, then froze.

Claire stood at the kitchen island with her back to him. She'd set something on the counter, then turned and noticed him. "Hi."

"Claire." His heart slowed, and he was grateful he had the doorjamb to lean against. After so many weeks away, his greedy eyes scanned her from head to toe as hope boiled over. "Your hair! It's your normal shade."

She ran her hand through it uncertainly. "I decided to just be myself."

"I like it better." He hesitated, somewhat unsure of how to proceed. "You came to Manhattan alone?"

"Apparently miracles happen." A smile flickered, then she held up a key, which she set on the counter. "We still had this from doing the work."

He stepped into the living room, wanting to rush to her, but he'd already pushed Claire enough this spring. He had to let her set the pace. He gestured around the room. "It turned out even better than your drawings. Thank you."

"You're welcome." She stayed frustratingly still at her spot by the island. Her expression seemed conflicted, even as her gaze studied his face. He kept staring, searching for a hint of her intention. "Did I wake you?"

"It's fine. I'm glad to see you." His heart pulsed in his throat. Screw it, he had to say what he felt. "The one thing that was missing from this place is finally here."

Her breath caught and she licked her lips. "I got your email . . . I had to come . . ."

He didn't wait to hear more. He crossed the room in a few quick strides and pulled her into a kiss. The kiss he'd been dreaming about for weeks. One that would tell her everything he hadn't said but should've. Everything he felt and had only recently begun to understand. Everything. Everything. *Everything.*

They broke apart to catch a breath, but she held him tightly, her cheek pressed to his chest. "I missed you, Logan. I thought of you every day. Cursed myself for how I walked away."

"Don't do that. You were brave and honest about your feelings. I was the coward. You'd tried new things for me, but I never once bent for you. Never told you what you deserved to hear. You were right to leave me standing on that patio. If you hadn't, I might not have realized what I'd lost. And, Claire, I don't want to lose you."

He dabbed a tear trailing from her eye.

"Honest, but not brave. I'm getting better, though." She turned away and grabbed the binder she'd brought—the catalog of gun violence. "And to prove it, I thought maybe we could get rid of this and buy a new scrapbook, like you'd suggested. One to fill with new ideas and adventures that we do together."

"I love that plan." He tossed the old binder to the floor, letting its heavy thud reverberate throughout the apartment. He cupped her face for another kiss, then said, "I already bought one thing that can go on the first page."

Holding up a finger, he then went to the kitchen cabinets beside the stove and opened his junk drawer to withdraw an envelope. He waved it overhead before tossing it on the counter and walking back to Claire. "Tickets to the US Open."

"From the auction?" Her mouth opened in surprise.

"Guess I was being optimistic."

"And planning so far ahead—not just in the moment." She smiled widely.

Apparently, his subconscious had been ready to make a commitment long before he could say the words.

"Thank you." She touched his face. "But there's one thing we should discuss before we decide to move forward."

He didn't like the question mark her statement implied. "What's that?"

"On the train down, I kept thinking about how this would work. I like my life and my business in Sanctuary Sound. I like living near my parents and knowing all my neighbors. But I know you'd be stifled there. Trapped."

"You're here now. You came to the city alone. If there weren't so much to say, I'd be speechless. But I can bend, too. What if we split our time? Weekdays in Connecticut, so you can work with Steffi and see your family, and weekends here. When I travel for work, you'd be at home, too."

"You won't get bored in Sanctuary Sound?"

"I've told you many times, Claire—you never bore me." He caressed her face. "Never."

She wrapped her arms around his neck and kissed him so hard he stumbled backward. "How do you like your new bed?"

"It's amazing." He kissed her nose. "Want to test it out?"

She nodded with a smile, so he lifted her off the ground, saying, "Let's go christen our new home."

Epilogue

Ryan, Steffi, and Claire stood near the stern of the yacht's second-story deck, whispering to each other beneath the dusky sky, painted in brilliant shades of orange and magenta, as the boat made its way back toward the marina. Caterers worked quietly on both levels to clear the few tables while guests enjoyed their final glasses of champagne.

Claire's parents sat inside the cabin below with some other guests. Claire didn't recall seeing them outside except before the ship left the marina, but at least they'd come to celebrate.

Peyton appeared beside Claire, tugging her aside before she pulled her silver silk organza wrap around her shoulders. The wind ruffled her short bangs as she leaned in to whisper, "I think they loved this."

"It was a great idea. I'm glad you talked me into it. Thank you." There. She'd done what she'd said she'd never do. She'd thanked Peyton for something. It hadn't been as hard as she would've expected. They'd seen more of each other these past two months, planning for this event, and because of Logan.

"I'm known to have some now and then," she joked. Her old smile flickered, and Claire couldn't help but return it. She did rejoice in seeing Peyton looking healthier. Her skin no longer looked sickly.

Claire knew from Logan that she still suffered from bouts of lethargy and depression, and that her weight wouldn't normalize until after she'd finished the full course of medication. But Peyton put on a brave face in public.

Logan joined them now, having been temporarily detained by Steffi's father, and wrapped his arms around Claire's waist. After planting a quick kiss on her neck, he asked, "Peyton, have you heard back from the two agents who asked for the full manuscript yet?"

"No, but it's only been a few days. I'm sure they have many submissions to read, not to mention work for existing clients." She squeezed his forearm. "Chill."

"Imagine how antsy he'd be if he weren't busy pulling together the installation at KRM Gallery." Claire craned her neck to catch his eye, proud of the show he hoped would raise money and awareness for the unaccompanied minors still stuck in the refugee camps. His images had tugged at Claire's heartstrings, and she was certain the installation would be well received.

He released her and nodded. "Patience isn't really in my DNA."

"No kidding," Claire teased.

More people had filled the deck now, eager to catch the vista and the last rays of sun before darkness closed in.

The clanking of a spoon against a glass hushed all conversation as the crowd turned toward the stern, where Ryan had his arm draped over Steffi's shoulders. He raised his glass and, above the dull roar of the engine, called out, "We want to thank Claire and Peyton for planning this beautiful celebration. We are blessed to have the support of friends and family who wish us well. Who've traveled along the winding road that brought us all back together. We can only hope that each of you find as much happiness as we have."

"Cheers!" cried the crowd before they gulped down their drinks.

Peyton sipped from her glass and smiled, but Claire noted wistfulness in her gaze.

Logan kissed Claire's temple and whispered, "I'm as happy as Ryan and more." Then he turned to Peyton. "Sis, how about you? You've been living here in a sort of limbo."

"I'm not in limbo." She frowned. "I've been busy with all of this, revising the manuscript, and preparing for my reconstruction surgery."

"But are you happy? Are you chasing your dreams?" he asked, referring to her earlier pledge not to waste a single day.

Peyton shrugged. "Everything's changed. I don't look at the future the same way as you. I'm just trying to get from one day to the next. I no longer know what my dream is, so how can I chase it?"

"Maybe I could help." Claire set her glass down on a tray.

"Oh?" Both Peyton and Logan turned curious gazes her way.

"Well, when I lost my way, I dug out our old Lilac Lane League binder. Flipping through those pages put me back in touch with parts of myself that I'd forgotten about. Maybe it'd help you rediscover things about yourself, too. I could drop it off tomorrow."

"Thank you, Claire. I'd love to see it again." Peyton's voice cracked, and her eyes were misty. "Would you two excuse me for a second?"

Before they could answer, she'd ducked down the stairs out of view.

"I think you made her cry . . . happy tears." Logan squeezed Claire. "Thank you."

"You're welcome, but I didn't do it for you. Well, not only for you. It's time—really time—to forgive. Pat was right. In a backward way, Peyton did me a favor by getting Todd to show his true colors. And I'm so happy now, how can I stay bitter?"

"I love you more every single day." Logan kissed her.

She nestled against him. "Good, because I have a request."

"Should I be nervous?" He smiled.

"No. With going in and out of the city and taking the few trips to visit your dad's inns these past two months, I'm feeling bolder. I was thinking, after the gallery opening, maybe we'd finally take our first big trip together, and I know where I want to go."

His grin broadened. "I'm all ears."

"You can't guess?"

He thought for a moment, then remembered their conversation at the bistro. "The Seychelles."

She nodded. The romantic honeymoon spot they'd talked about had drifted through her thoughts many times in recent weeks. They needn't be married to enjoy it, although maybe someday . . .

"Done." He smiled broadly. "And you said the romantic in you had died."

"You revived it."

"I'm glad." He glanced at Ryan and Steffi. "I could never go back to the life I had before you, so don't ever think about leaving me."

"I won't." She kissed him. "Promise."

ACKNOWLEDGMENTS

As always, I have many people to thank for helping me bring this book to all of you, not the least of whom are my family and friends for their continued love, encouragement, and support.

Thanks, also, to my agent, Jill Marsal, as well as to my patient editors, Megan Mulder and Krista Stroever, and the entire Montlake family for believing in me and working so hard on my behalf.

A special thanks to Jane Beiles, a wonderful photographer, who met me for coffee one day and not only taught me some basics about her profession but also gave me great fodder for developing Logan's character. Also, thank you to Jason W. Nascone, MD, for his help in understanding the potential effects of Claire's injury and postsurgical recovery. I owe Laura Sigg, a wonderful friend and fabulous decorator, for helping me come up with the new palette for Logan's apartment, and for teaching me about Claire's career. My sister-in-law, Brooke Simpson Beck, a former USTA Middle States–ranked youth tennis player, provided insight into Claire's tennis competition history. And finally, a big thank-you to Ally Dunlap for sharing her journey with breast cancer so that I could weave Peyton's story throughout this series.

I couldn't produce any of my work without the MTBs, who help me plot and keep my spirits up when doubt grabs hold. I also have a new group of writer friends, my Fiction From The Heart gals, who've brought another dimension of support and encouragement to my life. I'm so grateful!

And I can't leave out the wonderful members of my CTRWA chapter. Year after year, all the CTRWA members provide endless hours of support, feedback, and guidance. I love and thank them for that.

Finally, and most importantly, thank you, readers, for making my work worthwhile. Considering all your options, I'm honored by your choice to spend your time with me.

AN EXCERPT FROM

THE WONDER OF NOW

(The third book in the Sanctuary Sound Series)

Editor's Note: This is an early excerpt and may not reflect the finished book.

Chapter One

Om Namah Shivaya.

"*Let me photograph the treatment,*" *he'd begged.*

Om Namah Shivaya.

"*We'll make art, raise money,*" *he'd promised.*

Om Namah Shivaya.

Dammit, Logan.

Peyton opened one eye and stared across the undulating surface of Long Island Sound, which glittered all the way to the horizon. Six hundred thirty-two attempts at meditation in as many days, and she *still* couldn't master her own mind. Maybe she could blame it on the aftereffects of chemo.

Since childhood, she forced herself to look for silver linings in her darkest moments. By thirty-one, she'd mastered *that* ritual. Last year, she even found two for chemo, like the way she could blame it for all kinds of personal failings. Its other plus? Chemo had been a handy excuse for opting out of her mother's endless list of social and philanthropic invitations. Of course, those benefits didn't outweigh the weight gain, skin discoloration, nausea, mouth ulcers, and hair loss she'd experienced while undergoing treatment for breast cancer. Dwelling for months in a decaying body had forced an existential dread that produced few answers, but she'd never been a quitter.

Peyton curled a jaw-length strand of oddly wavy hair around her finger. Still short, but progress nonetheless.

She uncrossed her legs while taking a deep breath of briny air and then stretched them out, digging her toes into the warm sand, her gaze fixed on the line where sea met sky. These past few months, she'd stared at that distant place for hours, contemplating her life and purpose and other things she'd never before given much thought.

Late afternoon had become her favorite time of day. Lazy hours bookmarked by the high activity of midday and the lonesome stretches of night. These moments of peace and presence were probably the closest she'd ever get to nirvana or zen, or wherever it was one is supposed to arrive at through meditation.

"Peyton!" her brother called from the patio. When she glanced over her shoulder, Logan waved her toward the house. "They're here. Come see!"

A few days after her initial diagnosis two years ago, he'd cornered her with his camera and big idea. He'd always been able to talk her into anything, and she'd relished his schemes until now. If she didn't love him so much, she'd seriously consider lining his shower with shaving cream later.

Logan turned and went back through the French doors without waiting for her. She hugged her legs to her chest, pressing her forehead to her knees. Why bother with meditation? She had no time for serenity. Not with her brother and Mitchell Mathis—PR pain in the butt—constantly coming at her with to-do lists.

Peyton pushed herself up and brushed the sand from her bottom, slipped on her sandals, and strolled up the lawn toward the rambling old mansion. Only recently had she really understood why her great-grandfather built Arcadia House and why he'd come here—away from most of the world—to write. She barely remembered Duck, as Logan had nicknamed him, but his legendary work and name lived on—not just here, but all around the world.

She hadn't even closed the doors when Logan bellowed from the vicinity of their father's office, "Back here."

She found him standing at Duck's old walnut writing desk, surrounded by overstuffed bookshelves imbued with the faintest hint of tobacco, with his hands on either side of a large cardboard box. When she was a child, this room had been off-limits and, consequently, a place she'd snuck into time and again, tempting fate. Funny how, back then, she'd perceived fate and consequence as a game. *Checkmate.*

"Aren't you blown away?" His smile, warmer and more promising than a summer sunrise on the Sound, temporarily settled her. Then he lifted a copy of *A Journey through Shadows* from the open carton.

Her gaze skittered away from the cover image and landed on her Birkenstocks. Before cancer, she wouldn't have been caught dead in such footwear. Lots had changed since her Joie-sandal days. Some for the better and—she wiggled her toes—possibly some for the worse.

"Yes," she replied dryly. Blown away, all right, but not the way he meant it.

Like any little sister who'd ever worshipped her older brother would, she'd agreed to his plan. She'd thought she was dying and had little to lose.

The result? The memoir in his hands. A combination of his pictures—including the austere black-and-white midchemo cover photo she now actively avoided—alongside her most personal fears and naked emotions. The sight of it reminded her that, in a matter of days, people around the world would have access to every nook and cranny of her soul.

And to think, just before her illness, few had thought she still had one.

"Come on." He waved the book in front of her. "Have a look."

She reluctantly accepted the hefty hardcover tome from him and sat in the chair opposite the desk. Duck's framed Pulitzer hung on the paneled wall beside her, mocking the hubris of his great-grandkids' latest undertaking.

In contrast to her desire to hide, soft light filtered through the large open windows behind Logan, setting him aglow. He removed another copy from the box and shook his head in amazement.

"This image was totally the right choice for the cover." His green eyes twinkled, no longer burdened by the alarm they'd reflected when first learning of her illness. "Talk about arresting."

He began leafing through the pages, pausing occasionally to stare at his own work. She couldn't blame him. Every person she knew, including herself, defaulted to self-interest from time to time. It took two minutes for him to notice her utter stillness.

Logan placed his copy back in the box and then pressed his fingertips on the desk, bowing forward a bit—a pose he struck often, putting his lean build and casual elegance on full display. "What's wrong? We should be celebrating, but you look like you want to kill somebody. Me, in fact."

Peyton smoothed the frown lines between her brows with her fingers and then shifted beneath the weight of the book on her thighs. "You know exactly what I'm thinking."

He pushed away from the desk and came to sit in the worn leather chair beside her, running one hand through his hair. His sandy locks would take another few months to grow back to the eight-inch length he'd sported before he'd shorn it off last year in a show of moral support.

"You're anxious about the public response, but early trade reviews have been stellar." He offered a reassuring nod. "You're a fantastic writer."

Travel writer, she thought wryly. *Not* an author. Not like Duck.

She'd never aspired, nor could she ever hope, to live up to her great-grandfather's legacy. Writing witty pieces about hotels, restaurants, and tourist spots around the world had never forced a comparison to his body of work. Venturing into true-author territory would unintentionally invite it, though. Especially after she'd let the publisher talk her into keying off her great-grandfather's most famous book, *A Shadow on Sand*, with her memoir's title. Not that *that* was her biggest concern.

"Thanks, but this isn't fiction. It's my life—my heart—on display for others to judge." She pressed her hand to her stomach and drew a yoga breath. This sick pit in her gut was trepidation, not self-pity.

Her brother shot her a wry look of humor. "A quick scroll through your Insta posts proves you've never been exactly shy."

"I *never* flashed my boobs—or lack thereof—before." Joking kept an onslaught of less-pleasant feelings at bay, but Logan's silence proved her attempt had fallen flat. *No pun intended.* Her carefully cultivated social media presence—one of beauty and privilege and daring—would soon be smashed to bits. Then again, that's probably to be expected after a person receives the kind of news that nobody anticipates or wants.

Everybody dreads bad news. They learn of another's misfortune and, after a quick thanks to God for their own safety, ponder what they would do if handed a worst-case scenario. She'd drawn the short straw and now knew exactly how *she* would respond—with motionlessness caused by the bitter combination of disbelief, panic, and prayer that had pushed through her veins like arctic slush.

Chances were good that the frigid plea would remain her occasional companion until—*if*—she reached the five-year cancer-free milestone. As it stood, her one-year scans were a month away. Cancer cells could be sneaky bitches, traveling, hiding, and replicating like bunnies. Her once playful journal now cataloged every cough, ache, rash, and other symptom so she wouldn't forget to report anything to the doctor.

Peyton knew another truth about bad news. After getting one bit, she could no longer skirt above the fray. No longer feel safe. She expected more bad news at every turn. Consequently, she shivered anytime she projected ahead to those scans.

But she wouldn't burden Logan with her concerns. Not after everything he'd already sacrificed for her.

"I get that this is hard—but you've got courage. Focus on the money we'll be donating to cancer research. And the hope that your story will give other women in your shoes." He reached for her hand and squeezed it. "You're my hero, sis. I've never been prouder of you than while watching you go through treatment and work on this project."

"Thank you." She raised his hand to her cheek and held tight. For most of their lives, he'd been *her* hero, but she deflected from a deeper conversation. "But clearly you need higher standards."

He'd stood by her always, even when she'd made terrible decisions, like when she'd hurt her childhood friend Claire over that idiot Todd. Logan had also moved her into his home and taken months off work to be there, day and night, so that she wouldn't be alone during chemo. And without him she would've been utterly alone after having alienated her friends for the love of a man who'd made off like the Road Runner when she shared her diagnosis.

Logan tugged at her earlobe. "Are you sure I can't take you to JFK tomorrow?"

"No thanks." She hugged the book to her stomach, which fluttered every time she thought of taking off on the weeks-long European promotional tour that seemed to have materialized out of nowhere. "At least a car service gets paid for sitting in hours' worth of traffic. I'm already too indebted to you. Besides, I'll need some downtime before I meet Mitchell and take off for Rome."

She'd looked Mitchell up on LinkedIn and then banged her forehead on her desk a few times. Just her luck to be hitched to a guy who was not only great at his job but also good-looking. Like, *wow*-level handsome, with gobs of gorgeous hair. Ever since she'd lost all hers, she noticed other people's hair before any other feature.

She missed her prechemo hair—a beautifully blonde, long, silky curtain she'd used to flirt or hide or distract. Baldness had been a special kind of hell and, in some ways, made her a stranger to herself. Vanity was another of her flaws; she knew this. But having been born with her father's high cheekbones and blue eyes and her mother's lean figure, she'd been turning heads since puberty.

Her looks had defined her as much as anything else. Now she still carried a few unwanted pounds of postchemo bloat, and her still-too-short, newly wavy hair didn't fit her, somehow. It wasn't terrible, just wrong. And there was no hiding . . . or flirting. But, hey, she was still breathing, and that mattered most.

On the other hand, Mitchell's hair fit *him* perfectly. A rich chestnut mane that had to have a natural wave or cowlick in order to achieve that kind of high flow in his bangs. And those eyes, also brown, with an elongated shape and apparent alertness. She couldn't imagine how they'd affect her in person. His brows were thick like his hair—his lips, full yet firm looking. The serious expression in his profile photo matched her all-business impression of him, which she'd based on what little email communication they'd had to date.

Hallelujah for that, though. The absence of friendly banter was the only thing that made her willing to take this trip with him. At this early point in her recovery, she couldn't cope with, much less encourage, the tingly feelings of desire.

Not that Mitch would be interested in her. Chemo hair aside, even if she were ready to dip her toes back in the dating world, Mitch Mathis would have far better options than someone with her particular scars. After reading her memoir—with her erratic mental state and all the images of her double mastectomy filling its pages—he couldn't possibly find her attractive.

"If I weren't going to Peru next week to photograph Inti Raymi, I'd come with you." Logan sighed.

"It's fine." She stroked the book jacket. "I know this is our collaboration, but it's my story. I'm the one that has to sell it. The only one who can answer reader questions. I'll be fine."

"Still, you know I'd come along for emotional support if I could." He pulled his foot up over his knee.

He would, but she couldn't keep relying on him. He'd already rearranged his life for her and played an important role in helping her begin to mend fences with Claire. She trusted him implicitly, which was why she'd agreed to the crazy project in the first place.

From the beginning, their far-flung venture had seemed more of an impossible dream than anything else, until the arrival of the author copies sealed her fate.

"Spend your free time with your new fiancée." She pushed at his foot. "You're officially fired from this babysitting job."

He smiled again, a content kind of smile, particular to his feelings for Claire. Peyton wouldn't have bet on that opposites-attract relationship, but her brother had fallen hard. Proof that dreams can come true, though, given Claire's long-standing crush on him.

"You'll be back for the engagement party, right?" he asked.

"I wouldn't miss it." These days Peyton was grateful for every breath she drew and every celebration she could share with any of the people she loved, including some of her mom's tedious parties. "I'll be back a week ahead."

He winked. "I'm relieved things with you and Claire are getting better."

Peyton nodded, although her insides still recoiled at the memory of how she'd betrayed her childhood friend. "She still doesn't confide in me, but things are comfortable now rather than merely polite."

"I'm just glad not to be caught in the middle of two women I love anymore." Logan then craned his neck in the direction of their father's crystal carafe of bourbon. "Shall we break into Dad's stash and toast to our success?"

She welcomed a change of subject. "Sure."

"No reason to wait for Mom and Dad, right?" He pushed himself out of the chair and poured the amber liquid two fingers deep into two glasses before handing one tumbler to her.

"Nope." Their mother had not been supportive of the project, having considered it airing "dirty laundry" to the world. Never mind the philanthropic mission or the fact that Peyton and Logan had put in excruciating hours of work. She doubted her mom even had bothered to read the advance copy.

Logan stared at Duck's Pulitzer and then looked back at her while raising his glass. "To keeping the Prescott lit rep alive. Cheers."

The liquid burned its way down her throat. She rarely drank alcohol anymore, so its effect grabbed hold of her quickly, loosening her muscles one by one until her limbs felt soft and heavy and her mood pleasantly fuzzy. Then her phone pinged. She glanced at the text. Mitch.

Checking in. Any last-minute questions or problems?

"My taskmaster." She chuckled, holding up the phone to show her brother.

He patted her shoulder. "I'll let you deal with that. Need to get back to Claire for dinner." He finished his drink and stood. "Can I take a few copies?"

"Of course. They're half yours." She certainly didn't need twenty-four copies of that image staring at her, nor was she in any hurry to distribute them to anyone she knew.

It wasn't a lack of pride that stopped her. She'd worked her ass off on the book. Bled onto those pages. It was good work and she knew it. If she didn't have to promote it, she'd be much happier, though. And the thought of friends and neighbors and strangers picking over her vulnerabilities made her want to vomit. This venture would have to raise a ton of money to make up for what she'd exposed.

Logan smiled and snagged five books. "If you want to meet me for lunch tomorrow before you head down to the airport, shoot me a text." Before breezing out of the office, he kissed her head. "Love you. Good luck."

"Bye." She waited until he left and then set her book on the desk and sighed. Looking at her phone screen, she pictured Mitchell's intense gaze and imagined him tapping his foot impatiently while awaiting her response. That made her smile.

Cancer had changed a lot about her, but apparently it hadn't killed the part that had always enjoyed keeping a man on the edge of his seat. After counting to ten "just because," she replied.

All set here. Not to brag, but I've been known to be a pretty good traveler. No need for hand-holding. :-)

Not that, in another lifetime, she wouldn't enjoy holding his hand.

She caught her lower lip between her teeth while waiting for the little dots to start dancing on the screen. They lit up almost immediately. Confirmation of his workaholic status. She grinned. Would he get the reference to her former career? Might he respond with something clever this time?

Thanks for the reminder. Always enjoy working with a pro. See you tomorrow.

She frowned, doubting he intended any kind of double entendre with that "pro" remark. Just as well. She really could not abide falling in lust with her publicist.

That said, there was no reason not to dig into her old wardrobe and ditch the Birkenstocks for a couple of weeks. Maybe this trip to Europe was exactly what she needed now. A return to her natural habitat.

ABOUT THE AUTHOR

Photo © 2016 Lorah Haskins

National bestselling author Jamie Beck's realistic and heartwarming stories have sold more than two million copies. She's a Booksellers' Best Award and a National Readers' Choice Award finalist; and critics at *Kirkus*, *Publishers Weekly*, and *Booklist* have respectively called her work "smart," "uplifting," and "entertaining." In addition to writing, she enjoys dancing around the kitchen while cooking and hitting the slopes in Vermont and Utah. Above all, she is a grateful wife and mother to a very patient, supportive family.

For fun tips, exclusive content, and a chance to win the monthly birthday reader box, please sign up for her newsletter at jamiebeck.com.

Jamie also loves interacting with everyone on Facebook at www.facebook.com/JamieBeckBooks. For updates, exclusive content and tips, and a chance to win birthday gifts, please subscribe to her newsletter here at https://bit.ly/2QqqV6E.